A LAND
REMEMBERED

Patrick D. Smith

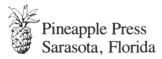

Pineapple Press
Sarasota, Florida

Inquiries should be addressed to:

Pineapple Press, Inc.
P.O. Box 3889
Sarasota, Florida 34230

www.pineapplepress.com

Library of Congress Cataloging-in-Publication Data

Smith, Patrick D., 1927–
        A land remembered.

        1. Title
PS3569.M53785L3 1984 813'.54   84-12098
ISBN 978-0-910923-12-5 (hb: alk. paper)
ISBN 978-1-56164-116-1 (pb: alk. paper)

Hb: 45 44 43 42 41 40 39

Pb: 40 39 38 37 36 35 34

Printed in the United States of America

To the grandchildren –
Dan, Kimberly, Joshua and Matthew –
with love from "Grampy"

1858 St. Mary's

Atlantic Ocean

1864 Olustee

1863

Payne's Prairie
Confederate Cattle

1858 Mc Ivey

1875 Mosquitoes Kill Cows

1892 Railroad

1868 Kissimmee

1875 Ft. Drum (Glenda)

1905 Tampa

1864 Kissimmee River

1867 Drown

Ft. Pierce 1867

Gulf of Mexico

Lake Okeechobee

Trading 18920 Post

Sol's House 1908

1895 Palm Beach

1868 Punta Rassa

Seminole 1875

Sol 1968

1895 Ft. Dallas

Seminole 1968

Sol 1925

1896 Ten Thousand Islands Outlaws

Camps	⚐
Forts	⚑
Battles	✵
Homesteads	◫
Cattle drive	🐂

A Land
Remembered

ONE
MIAMI, FLORIDA
1968

The silver Rolls-Royce glided off Key Biscayne as smoothly as a dolphin cutting the green water of the bay. Solomon MacIvey sat on the back seat, staring intensely at each house they passed, at the spotlessly manicured lawns, as if seeing these things for the first and last time. As they neared the causeway he muttered, "For what this one island is worth today my pappa could have bought the whole damned state back in 1883 when I was born. Folks has gone as crazy as betsybugs."

"That's right, Mister MacIvey," the driver agreed. "They all gone plumb crazy."

When they came to a park bordered by stately royal palms the old man squinted his tired eyes at the entrance sign: "Solomon MacIvey Park." Then he leaned forward, shook the driver's shoulder and said, "You see that, Arthur. Bought that fifteen acres back in oh-nine for forty-seven dollars and fifty cents. Can you imagine it? And some folks thought I'd been skinned for paying that much. Bet not one damned soul who uses the park can say who Solomon MacIvey is or could care less. Probably cuss me as some empire-building bastard who stole everybody blind back in the old days and then gave this park to salve

1

his conscience."

The black driver nodded in agreement as he turned from the Rick-enbacker Causeway and headed up Brickell Avenue. "You sure you want to go through with this, Mister MacIvey?" he asked, knowing what the answer would be but feeling he should ask again for the last time. "I could turn around and go back right now if you'll change your mind."

"I'll not change my mind," MacIvey grunted, "and there'll be no turning back. I don't want to see that big house again. Not ever! Not a single MacIvey died in a fancy place like that, and I'm damned if I'll be the first. We'll go to Punta Rassa as planned, but first I want you to drive up Miami Beach. I want to see it one more time."

"Yes sir, Mister MacIvey. I'll turn across the MacArthur Causeway."

As they crossed the causeway they could see cruise ships making their way into the port, their masts decorated gaily with multi-colored banners. Then the Rolls turned left onto Collins Avenue and moved slowly up South Miami Beach.

The streets here were lined with shabby, rundown apartments and hotels, porches filled with old people sitting in cane-bottom chairs, staring at nothing, some asleep and others perhaps even dead and as yet unnoticed, men and women who had retired from the harsh climate of the North and ended up trapped in the rococo world of South Miami Beach.

"It ain't nothing but a walking cemetery," MacIvey said, staring through heat waves that already drifted up from sultry sidewalks. "Should be turned back to the gulls and terns."

As they continued up Collins Avenue it suddenly changed, as if a boundary line had been drawn across the island, the beach now lined with majestic hotels, one after the other, interspersed with towering condominiums, a concrete and glass canyon blocking the view of the ocean except for those willing to pay to see it from a balcony.

And then they came to the La Florida Hotel, sitting like a stuffed frog, rising boastfully above all of them, thirty stories, with the letters MCI blazened across its top. The old man said, "I hope someday the son-of-a-bitch gets blown down. I should 'a never built it in the first place."

From this point north the avenue was lined with motels and cocktail lounges and fast food emporiums and souvenir stores with their display windows stuffed with junk, some of it authentic Florida souvenirs made in Hong Kong.

MacIvey then said, "That's enough, Arthur. I'd rather try to remember it like it was when I first saw it. Get us off of here at the very next exit."

The driver turned left onto the Julia Tuttle Causeway leading to the mainland. The old man said, "You know who Julia Tuttle was, Arthur?"

"No sir, I sure don't."

"Hell, I do! My mamma visited with her first time we came here in 1895, a few months after the big freeze. She lived in a part of old Fort Dallas. I think Mamma and her had tea together, or maybe it was fruit juice. When the freeze killed everything in Florida except for here, Julia Tuttle sent old man Flagler some orange blossoms up to Palm Beach, just to show him they were still blooming at Fort Dallas. And that's how come he ran his railroad on down to Miami, 'cause the freeze didn't kill the orange trees. Mamma liked her, but she never got to see her again. And I'll bet ole Julia Tuttle would throw a tissy fit if she could see what this causeway leads to now. She'd probably want her name off of it."

They turned left again at the mainland, cruising down Biscayne Boulevard, its northern section jammed with more motels and junk food shops, service stations, massage parlors, porno movies, bars, adult book stores, the sidewalks empty in the early morning sun but teeming at night with prostitutes and junkies and winos and professional muggers. Then they came into the downtown business section of Miami, passing the MacIvey State Bank Building with the letters MCI across the front entrance, then Bayfront Park with more winos and junkies and panhandlers and muggers.

The driver slowed and said, "What you want me to do now, Mister MacIvey, head out Highway Forty-one?"

"Not quite yet," he responded. "Before we leave I want to see one more thing. I want you to drive through the area where they had the riot."

"What?" the driver questioned, not sure he had heard right. "How come you want to do that? I've heard it's not all over yet."

"Dammit, you heard me, Arthur!" the old man snapped. "I want to see! Drive through there!"

"Yes sir, Mister MacIvey," he responded, shaking his head in disagreement but following orders.

He turned left at the next intersection and followed another boulevard, and soon they came to an area of gutted buildings, boarded up store-fronts and burned automobiles not yet removed from the streets. People standing idly along sidewalks stared with hostility as the Rolls ambled by.

"They did a pretty good job of it," MacIvey commented as they moved out of the area. "But this isn't the end of it. You mark my words, Arthur, there'll be more, and the next one will be even worse. You bring this many different kinds of people together it's like throwing wolves and panthers into a pen full of cows. The fur never stops flying."

As they moved slowly through the congested traffic of the lower Tamiami Trail, the old man shook the driver's shoulder again and said, "You know, Arthur, I don't know why some folks was so shocked by the riot. Hell, this whole state was born of violence. You can't go anywhere without stepping on the skull of some man or animal that was killed. The whole damned place is littered with bones."

The driver had heard it all before, but he listened attentively as the old man continued, "What I haven't seen myself I've read about. During these past fourteen years I've holed up in that house alone, I've read enough books to fill up Biscayne Bay. I know about those bloodthirsty Spanish conquistadors who came here with their crosses and killed everything in sight in the name of Christianity. Narvaez cut off the nose of chief Ocita and set greyhounds on the chief's mother. And he stood there and watched as the dogs ate the old woman alive, declaring it a miracle of Christ. They eventually wiped out all the Indians, the Timucuans, Ais, Calusas, Apalachees, Jeagas, Tekestas. Menendez lopped off the heads of two hundred Frenchmen who came here, and he did it just because they were Huguenots. A British general named Moore took a sweep down here from South Carolina two hundred fifty years ago and killed over six thousand cows and seven thousand Indians just for the hell of it. The Seminoles went through it three times, and the third war with them was started because some men in an army survey crew got bored and used ole Billy Bowlegs' pumpkins for target practice. After they shot up his pumpkins they pulled up his beans and squash and chopped down his banana trees, and when he complained to them for what they'd done, they told him if he didn't like it he could stick it. And there it went again. Another war. And there ain't no telling how many men in my pappa's time was bushwhacked or knife-gutted or hung on account of fighting over wild cows. Then later it was over the land itself and the putting up of fences. It went on and on, and it hasn't stopped yet, and most likely never will. You won't find the name of MacIvey in history books, Arthur, but they were right in the thick of it. And I mean the thick! We scattered a few bones too."

"Yes sir, Mister MacIvey. I know what you say is the truth."

By now they had left the city and entered the Everglades with its endless stretches of open sawgrass dotted with distant hammocks of hardwood and palm. The road and both shoulders were littered with the decaying bodies of small animals struck by automobiles. Buzzards flapped out of the way as the car approached, and then returned to the carnage as soon as it passed.

Soon they came to the Miccosukee Indian Reservation bordering the highway, an area lined with air boat rides and tourist villages and craft stores, and after this they entered the Big Cypress Swamp. The road here was stained even worse with the blood and guts of more small animals crushed flat into the steaming asphalt.

The old man studied the passing landscape carefully. "Slow down, Arthur, so I can get my bearings," he cautioned. "It's been a while since I've been here." After another three miles he said, "Turn right at the next dirt trail."

The tires on the Rolls made crunching sounds as it glided slowly along a sandy road heavily lined with palmetto and pond cypress. A mother raccoon with her brood of babies scurried out of the way as they made a sharp turn and came into the edge of a clearing. MacIvey said, "Stop here and wait. It could be we'll have another passenger."

Several chickee huts were spaced at random around the clearing, and beneath one of them an old woman stirred a cooking pot with a wooden spoon. MacIvey approached her and said, "I'm looking for Toby Cypress."

Without speaking she pointed toward a chickee at the far side of the clearing.

MacIvey hesitated for a moment, looking around the Seminole village, remembering the first time he had come here over seventy years ago, seeing that nothing had changed except faces. Then he walked to the chickee and found an old man sitting beside it, his hair solid white, his sun-baked skin as wrinkled as cypress bark. He seemed to be asleep as MacIvey said, "Toby Cypress?"

The old Indian squinted and said, "Yes. I am Toby Cypress. What is it you wish of me?"

"Don't you know who I am?"

Toby Cypress pushed himself up and looked closer, and then he smiled. "Sol MacIvey! It has been many decades now, and age has ravaged both of us, but I would still know you. It is only a MacIvey who is so tall and lanky. Sit here with me and tell me why you have come back to the village after all this time."

MacIvey settled himself to the ground in front of Toby Cypress and said, "You haven't changed so much, Toby. Do you still ride a marsh-tackie like the wind?"

"No, Sol. I have not been on a horse for so long now I don't remember. All I do is sit in the chickee like an old woman. I am growing tired of it."

"We sure used to ride, didn't we?" MacIvey said, remembering fondly. "And we had some good times together, too. I've thought of them often. And I've kept track of you through the years although I haven't been back here. I know you served for a long time as tribal leader and did many good things for your people."

"Yes, this is so. We now have two reservations, but I've never lived there. I would rather stay here in the swamp where I belong. But many of my people live there, and we have cattle once again. But tell me, why have you come back now like a ghost from the past?"

"I'm on my way to Punta Rassa, to live my last days at the cabin Pappa built there. I've left my house in Miami and will never return to it. I would rather see things as they once were."

"There is no more Punta Rassa as you knew it," Toby Cypress said, his eyes reflecting sadness. "It is all gone, Sol, just as Lake Okeechobee as we once knew it is gone, and the custard-apple forest is gone, and the bald cypress trees are gone. You are trying to capture the fog, and no one can do that."

"The cabin is still there, as good as ever, and the land too. I came to ask you to go with me. We can hunt and fish, and plant a garden, and be close like we once were."

Toby Cypress picked up a stick and scratched in the dirt, and then he said, "There is a Seminole legend that says when an old man knows he is going to die, he goes off alone into the woods, searching for the place of his birth. That is what you are doing now, Sol. I will make the same journey very soon. But we must each do it in our own way. I cannot go with you to Punta Rassa."

"I suppose not, Toby, but I just thought I'd ask. But I do want to part with you this last time as friends and as a brother, like it used to be. I'm sorry we broke away in anger those many years ago."

"I am sorry too, and I am no longer angry at you for destroying the land as you did. But Sol, it could have never been different with us. We are brothers only because we had the same father. My mother was Seminole, and yours white, and we were born to live in different worlds. There was no other way. We have each lived our lives as we had to, and now we depart in different ways. But know this, Sol. I have always loved our father, Zech MacIvey, just as my mother loved him. And I have loved you too. I have no hatred in my heart. Believe this now, and we will go in peace."

"That's what I wanted to hear," MacIvey said, his face relieved. "I have no children, Toby, and I am the last of the MacIveys. It ends with me, and that is my biggest regret from the way I messed up my life. But the MacIvey blood runs on in the veins of your sons, and I want you to know I'm proud of this. Pappa would be proud too. And there's another thing I want you to know. All the land I still own that hasn't been turned into concrete, and there is a great deal of it, including the land south of Okeechobee and along the Kissimmee River, I am turning into a preserve where the animals can live again as they once did."

"That is good," Toby Cypress replied, pleased, "but do it soon before there are no more birds in the sky and no more creatures on the land."

"It's already done. And all the money I leave behind will be spent to buy more land for preserves. It's the least I can do now to make up for the bad things I've done in the past. Things I'm not proud of, Toby. And there's a great deal of money to do this, more than you can imagine." He then got up and said, "It's time for me to go now, Toby. We won't see each other again, so I'll say farewell – and happy hunting."

Toby Cypress pushed himself up slowly, then he grasped MacIvey's hand. "Goodbye, Sol. Brother. We are both part of a time that is no more, and it is good that it ends soon for both of us. I hope you capture the fog and find a small part of it again in your last days."

The two old men stood facing each other, Solomon MacIvey gripping the wrinkled brown hands tightly; then he turned and walked away. He did not look back as the Rolls retraced its way down the sandy trail.

Just before noon they came to the southern outskirts of Naples and into a logjam of traffic, cars and trucks moving slowly bumper to bumper, impatient drivers blaring horns and shaking fists at each other in anger. Both sides of the highway were lined solidly with fast food joints and service stations and shopping centers. When they stopped for a traffic light the driver said, "You want to stop now and get something to eat, Mister MacIvey? And it's time for your pill."

"Damn the pill!" MacIvey snapped. "And we'll wait till we get there to eat. All we'd do here is choke to death on carbon monoxide."

The trip became slower and slower until finally they turned from the main highway and followed a two-lane road leading toward the Gulf. It skirted the south bank of the Caloosahatchie River and then turned back inland.

Once again the Rolls glided down a sandy road lined with palmetto, and presently they came to a locked gate. After opening the gate the driver moved the car into a one hundred fifty-acre jungle of cabbage palms and hickory and oaks surrounded by a cyclone fence topped with three strands of barbed wire.

The cabin, located in the center of the forest, was made of cypress boards weathered black but still sturdy and well preserved. The open area around it was freshly mowed. At the edge of the clearing, directly behind the cabin, there was an outhouse and a storage shed.

MacIvey got out of the car and said, "This cabin is older than I am, Arthur, but it's still as good as it was when Pappa built it. They don't make lumber like that no more. And this is one piece of land that'll never feel the bite of a bulldozer blade. I've seen to that."

As soon as everything had been carried inside, MacIvey said, "Fetch us a couple of cans of beans and some beer, Arthur. We'll eat at the table out here."

The driver hesitated, and then he said, "You know you not supposed to drink beer, Mister MacIvey. And you still haven't taken a pill. I put your pill bottle on the stand beside the bed."

"You can just take the damned thing back to Miami with you!" the old man said defiantly. "I'm not taking any more pills! And I'm not having some damned crabby nurse hovering over me all the time, telling me what I can eat and drink and what I can't! Why the hell you think I came up here?"

The driver said gently, trying to calm the old man, "I'm just trying to help, Mister MacIvey. You done had two heart attacks, and you know what the doctor said about the pills."

"I know what he said, and I don't want to hear another damned word about it! Now you go on and fetch us something to eat like I said!"

"Yes sir, Mister MacIvey.'"

The two of them sat at a cypress table facing each other, eating from the cans with spoons. MacIvey took a huge bite, washed it down with beer and said, "That's good, Arthur. Nothing's more fittin' for a man than beans, but the doctor says I can't eat them no more. Causes too much gas. I'll have 'em again for breakfast in the morning. Hell, I've eaten enough beans to bury that doctor and I'm still here. I'll bet I'm the only eighty-five-year-old cracker left with all his own teeth. Wasn't for this bad heart I could go another eighty-five years. But I wouldn't want to, not the way things are now. I've seen too much as it is. My pappa and my grampy would have strokes if they could see what's happened since they left. That road we came over today, Arthur, with the fancy name of Tamiami Trail. Before it was finished back in twenty-eight, it took ten days to cross the Everglades to Miami, and we made the same trip this morning in three hours. But my pappa wouldn't want to see it. He'd rather go by horse and canoe and take the ten days. He'd say, 'Hell, what's the God awful hurry?' " He suddenly changed the subject. "How long you been working for me, Arthur?"

The black man scratched his gray temple and tried to think, counting on his fingers. He finally said, " 'Bout thirty years, Mister MacIvey. Ever since I wandered into your place broker than a haint and you gave me a job tendin' the yard."

"You like to drive that Rolls, don't you?"

"Yessir, I sure do. It beats those clunkers we had back during the war. But they was all we could get then."

"Well, that one is yours now. I've already had the title changed. You can do whatever you want with it."

Surprise flashed into Arthur's face, and then pleasure. "I rightly thank you, Mister MacIvey! I never thought I'd own a car like that. But you didn't have to do it."

"I know I didn't have to!" MacIvey shot back. "A man my age don't have to do anything, including worrying about what he puts in his belly. I did it because I want to. I've also set up a trust fund in your name that will give you all the money you need for the rest of your life. The attorney will tell you about it when you get back to Miami. You can take off that damned chauffeur suit whenever you want to and throw it right into the middle of Biscayne Bay, and you can go down to the social security office and tell them to kiss your butt."

"Lord God, thank you, Mister MacIvey!" Arthur exclaimed, his voice trembling. Then he reached over and grabbed the old man's hand.

"I was worried sick about what I'd do when you left! I don't know what to say, Mister MacIvey!"

"Then don't say nothing. And don't get carried away and slobber on me. I can't stand to see a man slobber. And it's about time you headed back to Miami."

They got up and walked to the car together. MacIvey said, "You can come back in a week and bring more grub. And beer too. The grounds keeper is out here every morning checking on things, so don't worry about me. And don't tell a damn soul where I am. You understand?"

"Yes sir, I understand. I won't tell a soul." He suddenly grabbed MacIvey, hugged the frail body tightly and said, "I thanks you again, Mister MacIvey! God bless you!"

"Damn, Arthur!" the old man roared. "I done told you not to slobber on me! Now git!"

He watched briefly as the Rolls turned around and headed back along the sandy land, then he muttered, "Folks nowadays think a old man can't take care of himself and make it alone. I never knew a MacIvey to need a nursemaid, and I don't either. Hell! I'll throw them pills out for the buzzards to eat."

Then he went inside the cabin and slammed the door.

TWO
La Florida
1863

"Damn!"

The sound of it boomed across the small clearing and seemed to rattle the palmetto trees just beyond. A startled rabbit jumped straight upward and then bounded off into the brush.

"They done it again!"

This second outburst caused a flight of crows to change course abruptly and shriek loudly in protest.

Tobias MacIvey kicked at the dry dirt with his worn brogan shoe. His black-bearded face showed sweat beneath the protection of a wide-brimmed felt hat, and his slim six-foot frame was encased in a pair of badly faded overalls.

Just then Zechariah MacIvey came out of the brush, running as fast as his six-year-old legs would carry him. He scurried through the split-rail fence and shouted, "What's the matter, Pappa? What is it?"

"Them wild hogs done pushed through the fence again and got in the garden. Just look at that! Everything I planted is rooted up, and I ain't got no more seeds. Guess we'll have to eat acorns this winter right alongside the squirrels. From the looks of this mess them hogs ain't been gone from here more than a half hour. Maybe we can at least get some meat out of it. Run fetch my shotgun while I fix the fence and see if I can save anything."

"Yessir, Pappa. I'll run fetch it and be back real soon."

Tobias was on his knees, trying to straighten a collard plant, when the boy returned. He staggered as he half-carried and half-dragged a double barrel ten-gauge shotgun that looked to be as long as the trunk of a cabbage palm. He also had a shell sack around his neck.

Tobias took the shotgun and lifted it to his right shoulder, and then Zech followed as the gaunt man left the garden and followed a trail southward into thick woods. Tobias studied the tracks carefully, and then he said, "Looks to be about six or seven of them. They're heading for the creek to wash down my vegetables. You be careful of snakes. In this heat they'll be laying up under bushes. I wish them hogs would eat snakes like they're supposed to and leave the garden alone."

They moved silently past a thick stand of hickory trees; then the man motioned for the boy to stop. "You be real quiet from here on," he cautioned. "They're just up ahead. We don't want to come on them sudden like and have 'em turn on us. Then you'd really learn how to shinny up a tree in a hurry."

Once again they moved forward slowly, the shotgun now pointing to the ground. Tobias suddenly stopped and lifted the gun to his shoulder. Fifty feet ahead the seven hogs came out of a clump of palmetto and faced him. All were boars, and each had tusks that formed a complete circle. The hogs looked ready to charge when Tobias pulled the trigger, sending forth a tremendous boom followed by a thick cloud of smoke and fire.

For a moment neither man nor boy could see through the smoke, and the sound of animals running frantically overwhelmed the echo of the shotgun. Then the wind whisked the gray cloud away, and before them one boar ran in a close circle, the entire top of its head missing, blood spewing over the ground in a flood. The animal's brains had splattered across the trunk of a tree fifteen feet from where it had been hit. Then the boar fell to the ground, kicked wildly for a moment, and lay still.

Tobias said, "You see where I shot him, Zech. Right in the head. You gut shoot a wild boar, he'll run a hundred yards after he's hit, and tear your leg off with them tusks. Always shoot him in the head so he can't see you and come after you. You best take note of this."

"Yessir, Pappa," the boy said, his voice quivering. The sight of so much blood was making him sick. He forced himself to watch as his father slit the boar's throat to make sure it was dead.

Tobias then ran the knife blade down the hog's stomach, dumping the entrails onto the ground. He said, "There's my collards, right in his belly. He won't eat nothing of ours no more. He's a big one, over two hundred pounds, and he's sure too heavy for me to tote back to the house. You wait here while I go and get one of the oxen. Then we'll drag him back."

The boy sat down reluctantly beside the bloody carcass as the man walked away quickly.

Tobias MacIvey was thirty years old and had been in the Florida scrub for five years. He had come south out of Georgia in 1858. In his horse-drawn wagon there was a sack of corn and a sack of sweet potatoes, a few packets of seeds, a shotgun and a few shells, a frying pan, several pewter dishes and forks, and a cast-iron pot. There were also the tools he would need to clear the land and build a house: two chopping axes, a broadaxe foot adz, crosscut saw, auger bite, a fro and drawing knife.

His wife, Emma, five years younger than he, held the baby as gently as possible as the wagon bounced over an old Indian trail that skirted to the east of the Okefenokee Swamp and then turned due south.

Tobias had owned forty acres of red Georgia clay which he tried to farm and failed. When he sold the cabin and land he had enough money to buy only what was in the wagon.

When they crossed into Florida and reached Fernandina, Tobias traded his horses for a pair of oxen which Zech named Tuck and Buck. Included in the trade was a guinea cow, a strange-looking little Spanish animal with a small body that stood only one foot from the ground. But she had a huge udder and would provide milk for all of them.

The rumble of a coming civil war had already been felt in Georgia when Tobias left the clay hills and headed south to seek a new life in a virtually unknown land. He knew it was just a matter of time. He also thought the war would not affect Florida as it would Georgia, and if he went into the eastern scrub area, he would be left alone for a long time, perhaps forever. There was nothing in the Florida wilderness worth fighting over. And his guess had been right. The war thus far touched only the coastal areas of the state, and because his homestead was so isolated, he knew little of what was happening. Occasionally a stranger would drift by and give him the news. He would also hear of the war when he made trips to a small settlement on the St. Johns River to trade animal hides for supplies.

The first two years in Florida had been a time of near starvation. He cleared a garden and planted his precious seeds, but the poor sandy soil offered little in return. And the wild animals were a constant problem when plants did break through into the sunlight. Deer, turkey, and hogs were plentiful in the woods, but shells were so hard to come by that he could kill only when it was an absolute necessity to survive. Also during the first year, panthers killed the guinea cow and left only a pile of shattered bones.

During this time they lived in a lean-to made of pine limbs and palmetto thatch. There was nothing to ward off the summer mosquitoes and the roaming rattlesnakes and the rain and the biting winter cold. Emma feared for the safety of the baby, and they finally made a crude hammock so that she could at least keep him off the ground.

In the second year, Tobias started building the house, cutting the logs in a nearby hammock and dragging them to the site with the oxen, shaping the logs and lumber by hand, building a wall one torturous foot at a time. The roof was of cypress shingles, and devoting what time he could to produce them, he made twenty-five each day. It took more than five hundred to build the roof. More than a year of sweat and pain went into the rugged structure before it was complete enough for them to move inside. Yet ahead of him was the task of building beds and tables and chairs and completing the mud and stone fireplace.

There were many times when Tobias thought otherwise, but they did survive. He learned many things by trial and error, and passing strangers told him of others. He learned that he could plant a wide-grained rice in rows on sandy ridges and that it would grow without irrigation, depending solely on the natural elements. Some of the seed had been given to him by a family heading south in an oxen caravan. When the first crop came in they whisked off the stalks by hand and then beat them inside a wooden barrel, catching the grains in a cloth sack.

He also found that nothing would grow on pine ridges but many food plants would survive in hammock ground, and after the second year he moved his garden away from the house area and into a nearby hammock.

A man in the St. Johns settlement told him that twenty miles to the west there was a herd of wild cows. They were too wild for anyone to ever catch without dogs and horses, but in one grazing area they had littered the ground with manure. Tobias went there with his wagon and brought back a load of manure for the garden, and each spring he would return for another load of the life-giving fertilizer.

Gradually, he made chairs from sturdy oak and wove cane bottoms onto them, and he fashioned a table from cypress. He trapped enough raccoons to trade their furs for a coal oil lamp so they could have light at night. Brooms were made from sage straw, soap from animal fat and lye; meat was preserved by smoking, and what few vegetables they did harvest were canned or dried for the winter. Emma learned to make flour from cattail roots and they used wild honey as a substitute for sugar. What they all missed most were milk and butter, and there was no substitute for them. He vowed that someday he would own another milk cow, and this time he would protect her better.

The one thing Tobias feared most was the abundance of predators that roamed the land: bears, panthers, and wolves. Nothing was safe from them, and he dared not go into the woods without the shotgun. Darkness was when the predators roamed freely, and he kept the oxen locked inside the small barn each night, even during the hottest part of summer.

Tobias came into the clearing leading the ox with the hog tied behind with a rope. Zech was riding the lumbering animal, kicking his feet into its sides and whooping loudly. The ox paid no heed to the boy as it ambled to the side of the house. Emma came outside at the sound of the commotion.

She was a robust woman dressed in an ankle-length gingham dress and high-topped laced shoes patched with deer hide. Almost as tall as Tobias, she was big-boned and brawny, and her raven-black hair was tied in a bun. Before marrying Tobias she spent her youthful days in cotton fields where her father worked as a sharecropper, and she knew work from the moment she was strong enough to carry a water bucket from well to kitchen. She was the personification of strength, and it affected all those around her.

Emma looked at the hog and said, "He's big, but he sure is scrawny. Not an ounce of fat for lard. I'll have to boil him down good before I can do anything with him, else he'll be tough as shoe leather. Maybe we can grind up some for sausage. Slice off a few thin strips of the loin and I'll fry it for supper."

Emma turned and went back inside the house as Tobias said, "Put ole Tuck back in the barn, son, and I'll start the fire." First, he would scald the hog in the huge black pot, then he would scrape the hide and cut the meat into sections. What they could not eat before it spoiled would be cured in the smokehouse Tobias had built beside the barn. The skin Emma would make into cracklins.

Soon the clearing was filled with smoke as a fire came to life beneath the cast-iron pot. Then the smell of seared flesh permeated the surroundings.

Late that afternoon, they sat down to a meal of fried pork and a pot of boiled poke Emma gathered in the woods behind the barn. There was also a loaf of flat bread made from cattail flour.

Tobias said, "Lord, thank Ye for the vittles. Amen." Then he said, "Ain't much to be thankful for, is it?"

"It's food," Emma said. "But I sure wish we could get some corn-meal. A pone of corn bread would go good with some fresh swamp cabbage."

"What I hanker for is beef," Tobias said, chewing hard on the tough pork. "A roast as big as a saddle blanket. Zech's done growed up without tasting beef, and a boy like him needs beef to make him strong."

"Hog is fine for me, Pappa," Zech said, helping himself to another spoonful of poke greens.

"That's because you ain't had nothing better. If I had knowed it would be so hard here I might have stayed in Georgia. We got to get us a catch dog. If I just had a catch dog, I could round up some wild cows and start a herd. I need a horse too. A horse ain't worth nothing in pulling a wagon through this sandy soil, but you sure can't catch cows without a horse and a dog. And a dog would help keep the varmints away from here at night."

They ate in silence for a moment, and then Emma said, "It will all come in time, Tobias. We're not that bad off. We can make do till times get better for us. The Lord will look over us."

"Well, I don't believe the Lord would like to live all winter on nothing but coon meat and swamp cabbage. I got to have a horse and a dog. And some more powder and shot to make shells. I can trap coons and trade the hides, but I can't trap a 'gator. You got to shoot him. And the man at the trading post told me he would pay a dollar fifty for alligator hides. I bet there's a thousand of them in the creek just waiting to be shot and skinned."

"Maybe we could kill them with an axe," Zech said, becoming excited at the thought of hunting alligators.

"Son, you hit a 'gator on the head with an axe, he'd just grab the handle and eat the whole thing. Then he'd finish up his meal with both your legs. You got to shoot a 'gator to kill him. So for now we'll have to make do with coon hides. Maybe I've got enough of them tacked to the barn to get us some real flour and some cornmeal too. And also a pound of coffee. I done forgot how it tastes. I'll go over to the trading post the end of the week and swap all I have. Tomorrow I'll cut some cypress poles and start building a pen for the cows. Somehow or other I'm going to get me a dog and horse."

THREE

Tobias was at the edge of the swamp just after dawn the next morning, cutting pond cypress to be used as fence rails. As each thin pole was cut he stacked it on a sled tied behind the oxen.

He heard no sound but the thud of the axe, and was unaware that someone was standing behind him. When he turned and faced the two men and the woman, he was startled. His first reaction was to run for his shotgun propped against a tree, but then he noticed that none of the strangers were armed.

The two men stared at him, as if undecided as to what they should do. The woman moved close behind the men. They were Indians, and all of them looked exhausted. The woman was dressed in a tattered deerskin robe, and the men in clothes that were indistinguishable because of a thick covering of dirt.

Tobias said cautiously, "My name is Tobias MacIvey, and I have a homestead nearby. I mean you no harm."

These were the first Seminoles Tobias had seen since coming to Florida although he had heard many tales of the Indian wars. He wondered why they were here now since there were supposed to be no more Indians in this part of the state.

One of the men said, "I am Keith Tiger, and this is Bird Jumper." He made no mention of the woman's name. "We also mean no harm. We need rest and food. Do you have food?"

"There's nothing here," Tobias responded, becoming less uneasy. "We have hog meat back at the house. We can feed you something if you'll go back there with me."

"There is not much time," Keith Tiger said, acting as spokesman for all of them. "They have horses and dogs, and they will be here soon."

"Who?" Tobias asked curiously.

The Indian didn't respond to the question. He said instead, "We do not mean to bring you trouble. We will eat quickly and leave. But we must have food."

Tobias picked up the shotgun and started leading the oxen into the woods. The three Indians followed in silence. They had gone but a short distance when the faint barking of dogs could be heard. Tobias stopped the oxen and said, "What's this all about? Who is it that's coming with those dogs?"

All of the Indians looked frightened. Keith Tiger said, "We killed a calf for food. It had no marking on it, and we thought it to be wild. We were seen by a man on foot, and now riders are coming for us. We have been running since noon yesterday. If they find us with you it might cause you trouble, so we will leave now."

"No," Tobias said firmly. "You will eat first. No one will harm you at my place, I'll see to that. The woods is full of wild cows, and you have as much right to an unmarked calf as anyone."

The Indians followed Tobias reluctantly as the sound of the dogs grew nearer. Just as they entered the clearing the dogs bounded out of the woods and began circling them, growling menacingly.

There were six of them, all curs, part hound and part bulldog. The two oxen bucked away from Tobias and ran for the nearby woods, pulling the loaded sled behind them. Emma and Zech came out the kitchen door, puzzled and frightened by the sight of the circling dogs and Indians.

Tobias shouted, "Go back in the house and bolt the doors! Do it quickly! And don't come back outside no matter what happens!"

They both went back inside and then peeped out a window to watch the strange happening.

Three men on horses came into the clearing at full gallop, and then reined up just short of the dogs. Two jumped from their horses while the third made a loud whistling sound, causing the dogs to back away. All of the men had muskets attached to their saddles, and all carried cowhide whips.

Tobias started backing away from the dogs. He said loudly, "What the hell is going on here? You're invading my private property!"

One of the men said, "They stole a calf and butchered it, so we're going to teach them a lesson about rustling. And besides that, it's against the law for an Indian to be in Florida now. They're all criminals and ought to be in Oklahoma. That's the law."

"You'll do nothing to them here!" Tobias responded. "They told me the calf had no markings, and what's one puny calf to anyone?"

Two of the men suddenly unfurled their whips and started lashing the huddled Indians, making popping sounds as loud as musket fire. Each time the cowhide hit flesh, little plugs of shattered cloth and skin sprayed the air. The Indians doubled up and grunted as the whips slashed back and forth.

Tobias shouted, "Stop, dammit! I say stop!"

The two men idled the whips as the third made the whistling sound again, causing the dogs to rush forward and swarm over the Indians, growling viciously with snapping teeth as they covered the two men and the woman. The Indians tried vainly to beat the dogs away with their arms.

Tobias waited until one dog ran outside the flaying circle and then crouched, ready to spring back into the fray. He aimed quickly and fired, sending forth a cloud of gray smoke. The two unmounted horses broke and ran for the woods, and the startled dogs backed away. One of the dogs was blown in half.

The three men stared in disbelief as the long barrel came their way. One said, "What the hell you mean, fellow? That dog was worth as much as a horse!"

"I told you to stop it!" Tobias said, his voice filled with anger. "I told you, and you wouldn't listen! Now you catch them horses and get the hell away from here, and don't come back!"

"You taking up for them Indians? They're criminals! This ain't the end of this! We'll be back for sure!"

Tobias pointed the shotgun directly in the man's face, the barrel almost touching his nose. "You do, and it'll be the worst mistake you'll ever make! I'll be hiding behind a bush, just waiting, and I'll blow your guts over ten acres of ground! You better leave right now before I do it anyway!"

The three men backed away sullenly. Tobias continued pointing the gun as they disappeared into the woods in the direction of the horses.

Emma and Zech ran outside, and Emma said, "What in the world was that all about, Tobias? Who were those men?"

"Never mind," Tobias answered. "Just go inside and cook up some hog for these people. They're hungry. They ain't et nothing since noon yesterday. And while you're doing that I'll go fetch some swamp cabbage and some poke greens."

As Tobias started towards the woods with an axe, he turned to Zech and said, "You best go find Tuck and Buck and bring them back to the barn. We probably scared the life outen them."

Later that afternoon Tobias and Zech sat on the ground outside the kitchen, watching as the Indians ate ravenously, even cracking the hog bones with their teeth and sucking out the marrow. They did not stop until nothing was left of meat or greens. Zech was fascinated by them and watched each move they made.

Keith Tiger drank the last drop of liquid in the poke bowl and said, "We thank you for this, Tobias MacIvey. We could have gone no further without food. And I know of no other white man who would have risked what you did for an Indian."

"I'm just sorry we don't have more to offer. Them men had no right to do what they did, and if they come back after you I'll make it plenty hot for them." Then he asked curiously, "If it ain't asking too much, how come you folks being here? You're the first Indians I've seen around these parts."

Tiger said, "We have been walking for more than a year now, making our way from Oklahoma, traveling mostly at night. Bird and I were with Billy Bowlegs at the start of the last war, and we went with him to Oklahoma when it ended in 1857. My wife here, Lillie, went also. We stayed there until one year ago but we did not like it, and we are making our way back to join our people who are hiding out in Pay-Hay-Okee, a land far to the south that is yet unknown to the white man. There are still Seminoles hiding in swamps elsewhere, but most are in Pay-Hay-Okee."

"Well, I'm sorry I can't offer food for your journey," Tobias said, "but we just don't have much in the way of vittles. I don't have a dog or a horse and ain't got money to buy them, so I can't round up any cows. We've been having to make do mostly on coon and greens."

"What you need is a marshtackie," Tiger said. "It is a horse left behind by the Spanish soldiers. It is small and runty but very strong and big of heart. It can run all day, and it can take you to places in the swamps where no other horse can go. My people used the marshtackie back in the days before the white men told us we could no longer herd cattle. There are some of them still left in the swamps and woods. Perhaps you can catch one for yourself."

"I don't know how I could do it without a dog to help me. But I'll be on the lookout for one of them. I tried a few times to catch a wild cow with a rope, but ever time I got close enough to throw the rope, that ole cow would just run off a piece and laugh at me."

"There are ways to catch cows without dogs and horses," Tiger said. "Maybe someday we can show you. But we must go now. We have a long journey yet ahead of us."

"Ain't a bit of use in the world to do that," Tobias said. "You can stay the night here and rest, and then go in the morning. If you don't mind sleeping on the floor, you can stay in the kitchen."

"The rest would be good for us," Tiger responded, "but we will sleep in the shed. We are not used to a house."

"You're plumb welcome to do so. And in the morning, we'll scrape up something for you to eat, even if it ain't nothing more than coon stew."

Keith Tiger said, "We thank you again, Tobias MacIvey. We will not forget you for this."

The next morning, just before dawn, Tobias went out to the shed to awaken the Indians to eat coon stew Emma had prepared for them. There was no one there.

FOUR

The wheels creaked loudly as the wagon moved slowly along the old Indian trail that was just wide enough for it to pass. Both sides of the trail were bordered thickly with scrub pine and hickory and giant oaks, whose limbs were entwined with muscadine vines and Spanish moss. Occasionally a palmetto frond blocked the way and Tobias had to duck under it as the wagon passed.

Dawn was just breaking when the wagon left the woods and entered the flat expanse of marsh leading to the west bank of the St. Johns River. Fog lay low over the land, forming a cloud through which Tobias could not see, and he watched the ground ahead of him carefully as he pointed the oxen and wagon in the direction of the settlement.

As the sun rose higher, the fog burned away quickly, exposing huge flights of egrets and herons and wood ibis, winging their way both north and south to favorite feeding grounds.

Tobias could now see a thin spiral of black smoke drifting straight upward from the trading post chimney. This was a good sign, for it meant no rain, and Tobias feared the low-lying river flats when they were muddy or flooded. If the smoke drifted downward, it meant morning rain.

In addition to the trading post, there were three shacks built along the river bank, and all were the homes of mullet fishermen. Tobias guided the oxen to a hitching rail in front of the weathered old building and stopped. The trading post and the shacks were built on pilings ten feet off the ground to protect them from spring floods.

When Tobias climbed the cypress steps and entered, the proprietor, Silas Jenkins, was sitting by a pot-bellied stove. He looked up and said, "Morning, Tobias. It gets a mite chilly on the river in early morning, and a fire feels good." He was a thin man in his fifties, with skin burned black by the Florida sun, his hair solid white and rumpled.

Tobias said, "It's always cooler here than in the scrub. Sometimes I wish I'd settled by the river, but here again we don't have skeeters as bad as you do."

"That's a fact for sure. What can I do for you?"

"I've got twenty coon skins in the wagon I'd like to trade for supplies."

Jenkins shook his head negatively and said, "I got bad news, Tobias. Some Reb soldiers with wagons come in here three weeks ago and took everything I had. Flour, sugar, coffee, cornmeal, bacon, salt. Everything. Paid me just enough to cover my cost. I ain't got one blessed thing left to trade."

This news frightened Tobias. "Lordy, that is bad, Silas. I'm out of everything. I don't know what I'll do."

"It's bad on everyone along the river, including me. I ain't et nothing for three weeks now but mullet. And I won't have nothing else at all to trade unless a boat comes down from Jacksonville, and that ain't likely with them Federal troops taking the city one day and then leaving and coming back the next. They done took it now three times. One of the Reb soldiers told me that the Feds took it again about two months ago, and when they pulled out to go fight up around Savannah, they set fire to the city and burned about seven or eight blocks, including the church and the courthouse."

"How is the war going?" Tobias asked.

"Real bad, they say. The Feds have got every port blockaded, and ain't hardly nothing getting through from Cuba. Even the Reb soldiers ain't got uniforms to wear, much less anything to eat. Women are sewing socks and pants and making bandages from anything they can get their hands on. Them soldiers told me that if it wasn't for the scrawny Florida cattle they wouldn't have no meat at all or no tallow and hides. Even their salt is coming from St. Andrews Bay over on the Gulf. He said they were making coffee from parched meal and sweet potatoes. And it's going to get a lot worse before it gets better."

Tobias felt a deep sinking feeling as Jenkins spoke. "What about powder and shot?" he asked anxiously. "Did they take all that too? There ain't no way I can make it in the scrub without some more powder and shot."

"With that I can help you a mite," Jenkins said, getting up. "I hid some under a plank in the floor. I knowed there would be people around here in deep trouble without it. In even more trouble than the Reb soldiers. They can always surrender if they have to, but there ain't no way a man can surrender to a bear or a panther or a pack of wolves. I'll let you have what I can."

Tobias felt relief as Jenkins removed a box from beneath a loose plank and measured out a sack of lead shot and a sack of black powder. At least he could make more shells for protection and to kill for food when he had to. He said, "I don't know how to thank you, Silas. I'll bring in the skins."

"Just throw them on the porch when you leave. And Tobias, keep a good watch out. Them Feds has got raiding parties out everywhere now. They done hit Palatka and Gainesville, and they're roaming the countryside. What cattle they can't steal, they shoot. They're taking anything that ain't nailed down, and they've burned a lot of homesteads. The Rebs have formed a Cow Cavalry of local men to help fight off the raids and guard the cattle. If they come your way, you best be careful."

"They ain't likely to come into the scrub, unless they get a hankering for coon meat. But I'll keep an eye out, and I rightly thank you for the warning. I'll be back afore long."

"Take care," Jenkins said, sitting again by the stove.

On the way back Tobias decided not to tell Emma and Zech just how severe things were. He would say only that the trading post was temporarily sold out of the things they needed. Maybe a supply boat would get through before winter, and there was no need to cause them unnecessary anxiety.

He was also thinking of the news Jenkins gave him of the Federal raiding parties, the blockades and the burning of Jacksonville. Thus far the war was not real to him. It was something happening elsewhere, but now it was getting closer and becoming very real. The scrub was no longer a sure sanctuary, and he dreaded the thought of what would happen if Federal troops fired the woods. Fire was the most feared killer in scrub land. It could race over the land as quickly as the wind, destroying man and animal before they had any chance of escape.

Before he reached the clearing, he stopped in a low hammock area and allowed the oxen to graze. There was nothing for them to eat on the pine ridge, and since he had no corn or other feed to give them, he had to take them each day to wherever grass could be found.

The sun was setting when he finally unhitched the animals and locked them inside the barn. Layers of red and orange meshed all across the sky and caused the tops of trees to glow a somber yellow. He looked up momentarily as a flight of crows passed over the clearing, cawing loudly, heading for some unknown haven for the night.

When he came into the kitchen with only the small sacks of powder and shot, Emma looked at this and said, "Where are the supplies, Tobias? Do you need help bringing them in?"

Tobias sat at the table and said, "There are none. They were sold out of everything, but a supply boat will come soon from Jacksonville. I'll go back then and get the things we need. I did trade for a small amount of powder and shot."

Emma made no comment as she stirred a pot of poke greens. She dumped them into a bowl, set it on the table and then said, "The Indians ate up the rest of the hog meat, and this is all we have for supper. I'm sorry. Maybe you can trap a coon tonight."

Zech came to the table and sat down, and he and Tobias helped themselves to the greens. Tobias said, "Trapping coons is something that's beginning to worry me. I got nothing left to bait the traps, and ain't no coon or nothing else going to walk into a trap for nothing and then shut the door on himself. Maybe I can build some bird traps. I could bait them with grass seeds or berries or something. They's plenty of birds in the woods just waiting to be et."

Emma joined them, and for several minutes they ate in silence. Then she said, "Did Mister Jenkins say anything about the war? Did he have news?"

"Not too much. He said the Feds took Jacksonville about two months ago, but they're gone now, up to Savannah. He also said there are Federal raiding parties up to the north of us, but they won't come here. The Rebs have formed a Cow Cavalry of local men to keep the raiders away from the herds."

Emma looked up anxiously. "What if they come for you, Tobias? What if they make you join this Cow Cavalry?"

"They don't even know we're here," Tobias responded, noticing her sudden fear. "I don't think they'll ever come into the scrub."

Emma had never complained about her isolated and lonely existence. Sometimes she ached for female companionship, for just someone to talk to, for a church social or a quilting bee. But she kept these yearnings to herself. Tobias and Zech would never know. But the fear of being left alone in the scrub without Tobias was overwhelming.

Tobias watched her closely, and then he said assuringly, "They'll never come here, Emma. There's nothing to fear."

"I hope so. It would be hard for me and Zech to be out here alone."

Changing the subject, Tobias said, "Since I have powder and shot, I can make shells tonight. Maybe tomorrow morning I can kill a deer. I know a place on the other side of the creek where there's a patch of wild rye grass, and the deer are feeding there. The last time I took the oxen there to graze, I seen deer tracks everywhere."

"Can I go with you, Pappa?" Zech asked quickly. He had never been further from the clearing than the south hammock or the east bank of the creek where they killed the boar.

"Yes, you can go. It's about time you learned something about the woods over there."

Zech became even more excited. "Can I shoot the gun, Pappa? Will you teach me how to shoot it?"

Tobias laughed. "We better not do that just yet. You fire that big ole cannon, it would probably knock you slam from here to the St. Johns. You ain't growed up enough for that yet."

FIVE

Tobias waited until dawn for them to leave the clearing and enter the woods. The pine ridges and bottom lands were filled with rattlesnakes. He knew he could probably avoid them, and instantly hear their warning, but Zech could be hit before he knew what was happening. And this would be even more likely in the dark.

Mist seeped through the woods like smoke, and the ground was damp with a thin covering of dew. Squirrels barked constantly as they scurried from their nests and bounded off through tree limbs, jumping from tree to tree, starting a daily circus which would continue until they went back to the nests in mid-morning to rest. Then it would begin once more in late afternoon.

Zech became more and more excited as they penetrated the thick woods and went past the spot where Tobias shot the hog. They soon entered bottom land, and here there were thick canebrakes and huckleberry bushes and rotted logs and clumps of palmetto and Spanish bayonet.

They turned south and followed the east bank of the shallow creek. Its water was crystal clear, and green moss on the bottom waved gently with the slow-moving current. Bass could be seen darting in and out of the foliage, chasing small perch and minnows.

They suddenly heard a series of harsh, loud screams come from somewhere above them. It sounded like quarrelsome old men fussing at each other. Tobias put his hand on Zech's shoulder and cautioned him to be very quiet.

A flock of ten birds lit in an oak tree just ahead of them. Zech's eyes widened in wonderment as he stared at them. They were a foot long and six inches tall, with long pointed tails and yellow heads that became rich orange around their bills.

Zech whispered, "What are they, Pappa? I've never seen birds like that." He was afraid they would fly away too soon, and he felt that he could stare at them forever.

"They're Carolina parakeets. I come on them down here ever once in a while, but not often. They stay mostly along bottom land. They used to be in swamps up in Georgia in the summer, but they're gone now. Folks killed them for the meat and the tail feathers. The cold kills them too, and that's why they'd always fly south in winter. If it ever comes a hard enough freeze down here and stays that way long enough, it will probably wipe them out if they ain't all been shot and et by then."

"I wouldn't kill them," Zech said, his eyes still wide. "They're too purty to kill. I'd rather shoot a ugly ole crow and let the parakeets alone just to look at."

"Some folks don't care," Tobias said. "When I was about your age I followed some men on a hunt, and they come on some of these birds in a swamp. They shot one, and when it fell to the ground, the others flew off into the trees. In a few seconds one of them came back to the dead one, and then they all started coming back, one by one. They are the only birds I have known to do this. They kept coming back to the dead till the men just sat there and killed every one of them. Maybe they were coming back to grieve over the dead. I don't rightly know. But when them men found out that if you kill one Carolina, then the others will keep coming back to the dead, they hunted them and shot every one in the county. Wiped them out clean. Let's let the birds be and move on now and see can we find us a deer."

As they started forward, the birds flew away, again screaming loudly. Zech wondered if he would see them again. He stared after them until the sound could no longer be heard.

Tobias said, "We best cross the creek here. The meadow is just over yonder."

They waded through the cool water and skirted the south end of a canebrake. Just past this there were more dense woods; then the trees thinned out along the edge of the meadow.

As they approached the opening, they got down on hands and knees and crawled. The clearing was covered by a slightly swaying carpet of deep green rye, but it was empty. No deer were to be seen.

Tobias eased out into the meadow cautiously, searching each path that led back into the woods. Then he stopped and dropped to his knees. There was a pile of manure on the ground, and when he touched it, it was warm. He said, "We must of just missed them. They ain't been gone two minutes. Maybe they heard us coming and took off. Let's ease back to the edge of the woods and wait. They might come back if we'll be real quiet."

They hid behind a bush and waited. Crows flew by and cawed, and squirrels barked in the trees above them, but no deer came. Tobias was just about ready to give up when he heard a sound in the woods across the meadow. It was a thrashing sound, not like a deer, more like a bear or a pack of bears.

The sound grew louder, and then the bushes shook as the animal suddenly broke through them and ambled into the clearing. Tobias exclaimed, "God 'a mighty, Zech, it's a Andalusian bull!"

Zech was too fascinated to say anything. And he was also frightened. The bull was a bluish roan in color, with huge horns that came upward out of its head and then turned outward, spanning three feet each.

Tobias had seen wild cattle in the woods before, but they had been the smaller, runty yellowhammers, some not much larger than deer. He knew there were also Andalusians, but this was the first time one had come this close to the homestead. They usually stayed on open prairies where they could band together to fight off predators. One lone bull this size would stand no chance if attacked in thick woods by a band of wolves.

As the bull started grazing, Tobias eased up the shotgun and cocked one hammer. He was awed by the bull's majesty and sleek strength, knowing that this animal and its kind had survived in the wilderness over the centuries since it was brought here by the Spanish, overcoming tremendous odds. He hated to kill it, but he knew he was seeing enough beef on the hoof to keep his family alive for a long time to come. He hesitated for a moment more, and then he aimed and fired.

At first the bull just stood there, and then it bellowed loudly and fell on its left side. It was dead instantly, its heart having caught the full load of shot. Blood rushed from a huge hole in its side and from its mouth. Its eyes rolled upward and then inward, as if trying to see inside its own body and determine what had happened.

Tobias trembled as he walked across the meadow to the downed animal. A hugh spot of the green grass was now stained red. He put his foot on the bull's back and shoved, to see if there was any life left. His brogan pushed only dead weight. Then he turned to Zech and said, "There ain't no way we can get this critter out of here by ourselves. You think you know the way back to the house?"

"I know, Pappa. What you want me to do?"

"Go and get both Tuck and Buck and bring them back here. And bring an axe. I can cut some poles and make a sled, and we can haul it out of here on that. While you're gone I'll go on and gut it. Can you do this, Zech? If you ain't sure, I can go back with you. I just don't want the buzzards to get at all this meat."

"I can do it, Pappa. Don't you worry none at all. I'll be back before you know it." He turned and ran quickly into the woods.

It was dark when Tobias hung the last section of meat in the smoke-house and stoked the fire. Every ounce of the bull would be used. The tail was skinned and chopped into sections for stew, and the leg bones and ribs would go into soup. The brains would be scooped out and fried, and the hooves boiled into jelly. Tobias would take the hide and the horns to the settlement. He thought he would get at least two dollars in trade for the hide.

Emma was taking a roast from the pot and putting it on the table when Tobias came into the kitchen. He said, "Thank the Lord for all blessings and for making that bull come out of the woods just when he did. Now we can keep old man hunger away for a while longer."

Emma smiled and said, "In the morning I'll boil the heart and liver for breakfast. It will be good for Zech. Beef liver makes a boy grow strong."

Tobias sniffed deeply. "Lordy, Lordy, that meat smells good. I don't know if my belly can still handle a beef roast. It's so used to coon and poke. But I'm sure willing to try."

They all sat at the table and relished the meal in silence. Afterwards, Emma cleaned the plates and then they sat on the stoop outside the kitchen. Tobias patted his stomach and said, "I wish I had a pipe and some tobacco. A man needs a smoke after a meal like that."

Zech groaned, "I et too much, and I'm kind of tired after all we done today. Is it all right if I go on to bed now?"

"We're all tired," Tobias replied, "and we'll all go on to bed. I'll have to get up around midnight and see to the fire in the smokehouse."

As soon as they were inside, Zech climbed the ladder to the loft where he slept. Almost instantly they could hear the sound of snoring.

Emma sat on the edge of the moss-stuffed bed and removed the string tying her hair. When she did this, a black mass sprang to life and swirled down over her shoulders, covering the top of her cotton nightgown.

Tobias watched her, and then he crossed the room and said, "You're a right good-looking woman, Emma. Every time I see you do your hair like that it hits me just as hard as it did the first night I seen it. Makes me want to stomp around in it."

Emma blushed, just as she always blushed when he paid her an intimate compliment. It was her only feminine pleasure out here in the scrub.

Tobias sat down beside her and put his hand on hers. "Zech needs a companion out here, Emma, and I know you would like to have another baby. But it just ain't the right time now. Things is too hard for us, and I can't hardly feed what we got, much less another one. It will be better soon. Someday there'll be a whole flock of MacIveys. You'll see."

"I know," she said, turning to him. "It will get better for us someday. And there's time yet. We're young, and there's time. And I know you're doing the best you can. I'm right proud of you, Tobias."

He took off his overalls, blew out the lamp, and lay down beside her. Then he pulled her close to him, feeling the firm flesh and absorbing her strength. He thought that of the two of them, she was probably the stronger. A man could live alone in the woods if he had to and never miss anything, but this was not the natural way of a woman. She needed women things in a way a man cannot understand. He knew he had never known another woman with the courage of Emma. Someday he would do better by her. Someday.

He continued holding her until she drifted into sleep. Then he turned on his back and stared upward into the darkness of the cypress roof. His thoughts moved from Silas Jenkins' warning about the Federal raiders to the wonderment in Zech's eyes on seeing the Carolinas. He thought that perhaps the war would come to an end quickly if men would do like the parakeets: kill one, then let the others come to it, one by one, and be destroyed easily, like shooting bottles off a fence. No battles, no raiders, no blockades – just kill one and wait for the others. But he knew this would never be; men aren't Carolina parakeets, and they don't die so easily.

Although he tried to make Emma believe it, he was not so sure that the raiders or the Cow Cavalry recruiters would never come into the scrub. It was possible they would come, and he knew this. He wondered what would happen if such a thing did come to pass, but there was no need to alarm Emma without cause. If it came he would do what he must do. This time he would not run away from it. He did not run before because he was afraid of fighting or dying. It was not that at all. He simply could make no sense of a war pitting countrymen against each other, and he wanted no part of it if he could avoid it.

From far in the distance he heard the lone cry of a wolf. Then it was answered with another cry, and then another, a mournful, menacing sound. He wished he had a dog, or better still, a pack of them. If he had at least one, it would help keep the varmints away. And maybe with it, he could catch a cow.

SIX

Summer passed slowly into early fall as Tobias finally finished building the fence where he hoped to someday pen his wild cattle. One row of corn in the garden had been made to grow again, and there was a patch of collards. But there were no beans or potatoes. The hogs had taken care of that. They had eaten as little as possible of the beef and were saving it for the coming winter months when things would be even more lean than they were now.

He also made another trip to the trading post on the banks of the St. Johns. No supply boat came south out of Jacksonville, and there would be no flour or cornmeal or sugar or salt and no oil to light the lamp. Jenkins gave him the last few ounces of the hoarded powder and shot, and each precious shell would have to be used wisely.

Tobias was out by the shed, chopping fire wood, when he heard the sound of a rider coming through the woods. He put down the axe and picked up the shotgun, which he always kept nearby.

The man was riding a tall black stallion. He wore a huge brown hat and boots that came up to his knees. His face was completely covered by a red beard. A pistol was strapped to his side, and there was a rifle in his saddle holster. He rode directly to Tobias and dismounted.

"Howdy," Tobias said cautiously, holding the shotgun with his right hand on the hammer, relieved that the rider was not wearing an army uniform.

"Howdy," the man responded, "Name's Henry Addler."

"Tobias MacIvey."

"You can put down that blunderbuss. You don't need it with me."

Tobias leaned the shotgun against the shed wall. "It pays to be cautious these days," he said.

"That it do."

The man looked around for a moment, and then he said, "Some place you got here, but it's sure isolated. I ain't seen nothing for two days but woods. How long you been here?"

"Going on six years. Came down out of Georgia in fifty-eight. Built the house myself and cleared the garden."

"Don't see how you folks make it out here in the scrub."

"It ain't easy. Times has been hard."

"You ever herded cattle?" Addler asked.

"All I ever done is farmed."

"Don't matter. You'll learn fast."

This statement puzzled Tobias. He said, "What you mean by that?"

"I'm a state marshal, commissioned by the Governor, and I'm rounding up drovers to move a herd up to Georgia. Most ever able bodied man who's not in the army is riding patrol with the Cow Cavalry. You the first one I found who ain't, so I'm recruiting you as a drover. I got the authority to do so."

Tobias felt a deep sinking feeling. He said, "How do I know you're what you say you are? You got proof?"

The man pulled a piece of paper from his pocket and handed it to Tobias. "Read this. It's my commission from the Governor.

Tobias took the paper, glanced at it briefly and handed it back. "I can't read. I'll just have to take your word for it. But I got a wife and a boy out here. It would be hard on them if I left them alone."

"Ever man's got a wife and boy sommers. It's hard on all of us. This war ain't no church social. If we don't get them cows to the army, our soldiers won't have nothin' to eat. And if they don't eat, they can't fight. It's as simple as that."

"Just what is it I'm supposed to do?"

"The herd is up north of here, on the Alachua savanna. We got to move them to Trader Hill on the St. Marys River. From there an army squad will take them over the state line and up to Atlanta."

"How long will it take?"

"I can't rightly say. We'll have to let them walk at their own pace, and graze along the way, else time we get them there they wouldn't be

nothing but hide and bones, not even fittin' for soup. I'd say we'll cover
eight or nine miles a day at best. You ought to be back home in a few
weeks."

"Damn!" Tobias muttered.

"You got a horse?" Addler asked.

"No. I only got oxen."

"They's horses up at the savanna. And you don't need to bring along
that cannon. That's the biggest shotgun I ever seen. You try to take that
thing on a horse, there wouldn't be no room for the saddle."

"It hits what you aim at."

"I'll wait here while you go tell your woman, but get a move on.
Them cows should 'a been in Georgia two weeks ago."

Tobias turned and walked slowly to the house, feeling as if the weight
of an ox had suddenly been dropped on his shoulders. Emma was
standing outside the kitchen door, watching. She too had heard the
approach of the rider. She could tell by the expression on Tobias' face
that it was something serious.

Before Tobias could speak she said, "You've got to go, haven't you?"

"Yes. He's a state marshal. I got to help move a herd of cattle up to
the Georgia border. It's for the army. Soon as we get them there I'm
done with it and can come on back home. It ought not take too long."

"We'll make do all right," she said, trying hard to conceal the fear
that would cause Tobias additional worry. "We got meat, and there's
greens enough. We'll make do fine."

Zech was standing nearby, listening. He didn't understand what was
happening, only that his father must go away. He said, "I'll take care
of the garden, Pappa. And I can chop wood too."

Tobias put his hand on the boy's shoulder. "You ain't hardly big enough
to pick up a axe, much less chop logs. But do the best you can by your
mamma, and give her all the help you can. You hear?"

"I hear, Pappa."

Tobias then turned to Emma. "The shotgun is loaded, and there's
more shells in the kitchen cabinet. I should have taught you how to
shoot it, but I didn't think this time would come. Use it if you have
too. And don't let no strangers come in the house."

"I know how to point a gun," she responded. "Just don't you worry.
We'll be fine."

"There's one thing you'll have to do, Zech," Tobias then said. "Take
ole Tuck and Buck down to the hammock ever morning and let them

graze awhile. And don't ever leave them outside the barn at night. Not ever! And be sure the barn door is locked."

"I'll do it, Pappa. I can look after them."

Tobias took Emma's hand and pulled her to him. He held her close for a moment, and then he said, "I'm sorry. He's a state marshal, and I've got to go. I'll be back just as soon as I can."

With that he turned and walked away quickly, following the mounted rider into the woods.

Emma stood on the stoop and watched him disappear. Then she looked around the empty clearing and at the wood shed. She said to Zech, "I best cut some more firewood. Tobias didn't get to finish the chopping."

By the time they reached the Alachua savanna three days later, Addler had recruited five more men to act as drovers. All of them were older than Tobias, and one had a left arm missing. Another wore a patch over his right eye.

Most of the trip had been through dense pine woods and swampy river bottoms, and they passed several large lakes. The land around one was planted thickly with orange trees.

They gradually left the pine land and came into a forest of tall magnolias, live oaks, and cabbage palms. Then suddenly they stepped onto a slight bluff overlooking the edge of the savanna. Tobias could not believe what his eyes were seeing. The plain was as flat as a table top and stretched away to the horizon. There were no trees to break its vastness or to judge distances, and its size and openness were awesome and mindboggling.

"That's the biggest pasture I ever seen," Tobias said to Addler. "It looks like what I always thought Africa would be."

"You won't find no elephants here," Addler responded, "but at times they's been as many as thirty thousand cows grazing out there at one time, and they was just a drop in the bucket. And you couldn't count the wild horses. They say a long time ago there was buffalo from here clear up past Tallahassee, but they all been killed now, or run off sommers. Our herd is up to the northeast. We'll have to cut across the plain."

As they descended into the basin, the ground was spongy to their feet. There were great flocks of birds everywhere, ducks and coots and bitterns and plovers and rails. Hawks and eagles circled overhead, and tall sandhill cranes danced out of the way as the men made their way through the marsh. There were also vast herds of deer, and frightened bobcats scurried out of grass clumps at the sound of approaching feet and hooves. The entire area teemed with life, and Tobias wished that Zech could see it.

After an hour they came to the edge of a wooded area bordering the east rim. Here a small creek suddenly formed a wide sinkhole and vanished underground. Alligators lounged around the edges, seemingly asleep, their jaws open and their eyes staring blankly. Herons waded in the shallows of the creek, pecking at minnows and frogs.

A half mile further they came to the herd, six hundred head, all with huge horns like the one Tobias killed on the rye grass meadow. Several men were riding around them, and off to one side, there were additional horses tied to a rail.

One of the men came to Addler and said, "They're all yours now. Me and my crew's got to go down to the Caloosahatchie and try to pop another herd out of the swamps. We'll see you back here in a few weeks. And good luck."

As the men rode off, Addler's crew followed him to where the horses were tied. He opened a box and handed each drover a rawhide whip. Then he took one himself and swished it back and forth, making it pop. He said, "After you learn to use this thing, you can pop off a rattler's head at twenty feet. And there ain't no cow alive you can't turn with it. So best you learn how to use it real fast."

Tobias and three of the other men selected horses and mounted. All of the horses had McClellan military saddles without horns. Addler then motioned them into a circle and said, "We'll move 'em along an old military road as far as we can and try to keep 'em out of the woods. If one goes off into the woods, go after him right away. And don't try to push them. Just let 'em walk along as slow as they want, and eat. Last time we pushed a herd too fast the cows lost a hundred and fifty pounds apiece time we got to Georgia. An extra hundred and fifty pounds per cow will feed a lot of men. So let 'em go slow. And just remember one thing. These are wild swamp cows. They didn't come out of somebody's barn. They ain't used to being drove, and they spook easy. If one goes, they all go. They can take off like thunder and stomp a man and a horse as flat as a pancake before you know what's happening. So be careful."

Addler then furled the whip and said, "O.K., that's it. Let's go to Georgia. They's a lot of hungry soldiers waiting on us."

The first week of the drive was uneventful, the cows setting their own pace and moving slowly. For four days they followed an old military trail that had been built by soldiers during the first Seminole war, then they turned north and entered areas of pine flats and open plains.

It had been so long since Tobias rode a horse steadily that every muscle in his body ached. At night the men took turns riding guard around the herd, and they also took turns cooking meals of salt bacon and beans. Gradually Tobias became proficient with the whip, and he could pop a burr off a pine limb high above him.

On the first evening of the second week they came to a corral close by an abandoned farm house. The fence was twelve rails high, and the gate still intact. They drove the herd into the pen for the night.

It was at midnight when the first cry of a wolf broke the stillness. Almost instantly it was answered, and then it was repeated again and again, now coming from all sides of the corral.

Tobias had just been awakened to go on guard duty and was sitting by the fire, putting on his brogans. Addler was lying close by, and he jumped up quickly. He said to Tobias, "Good God a'mighty, that's all we need! Them cows will tear up the countryside. Ride out and tell all the men to come in real fast."

By the time the drovers were back to the fire the howls had increased in tempo and seemed to come from everywhere. Addler said urgently, "There ain't no way we can fight off them damned wolves in the dark. Each of you take a axe and build a fire ever twenty yards around the corral. Fire is the only way we can keep 'em back. And do it in a hurry before them cows spook and come out of there."

Soon the darkness was broken by the glare of glowing fires. The cows were lowing now, and their sound made the wolves howl even harder. Tobias was on the south side of the corral when he heard the crashing of timber. Suddenly the rails flew into the air like shattered twigs, and a bellowing flood came directly at him. He jumped his horse away quickly, barely avoiding the avalanche of horns that rushed by.

Cursing men and popping whips could be heard everywhere, and Addler's voice screamed above all of it, "Go after them! Go after them!

Turn 'em before they go plumb down to Tampa!"

Tobias wheeled his horse and rushed off into the darkness, blindly following the sound of thudding hooves. He raced full speed, not knowing if at any instant he would crash into a tree or go under a limb and be knocked senseless. He was the first to reach the lead bull, and he rode just ahead of the thunder, popping his whip rapidly, praying that his horse would not hit a hole and go down.

Finally three more men came up beside him, and after a wild three-mile ride, they slowed the herd and then stopped it. Far behind them they could see the dim glow of the fires.

Addler came up to them and said, "Ain't no use to even try to move 'em back to the pen. It's so black out here I can't even see my saddle. I don't think they'll run again, and them wolves won't follow us down here after all that commotion. Some of them probably got stomped to a bloody pulp in the ruckus."

Two of the men stayed mounted while the others slept, and at daybreak they were all out rounding up strays. The herd was intact, with not a single cow lost. As they sat by a fire eating salt bacon, Addler said wearily, "Well, we got through that one real lucky. Now if we just don't get bushwhacked by Federal raiders or one of them damned bands of Reb deserters, I think we'll make it to Georgia."

"Reb deserters?" Tobias questioned, surprised.

"Hell, yes," Addler said, chewing on the tough meat. "They give us more trouble on drives than the Federals. Them bastards will hide behind bushes and shoot you down like dogs. Then they steal the cows, eat some and drive the rest to Fernandina and sell 'em to the Federals. They're worse than wolves or rattlers."

Tobias did not understand this but accepted it. He had surmised that their only danger of losing the herd would come from Federal raiders.

It was on the fifth night after Tobias left that Emma was awakened by the sound of the oxen kicking the barn wall. Zech heard it too, and they both went to a window and looked out apprehensively. Zech said, "What is it, Mamma? The oxen are trying to tear down the barn."

"I don't know, but something is sure frightening them."

A full moon bathed the clearing with light, revealing the barn and the shed and the woods beyond. From behind the barn there suddenly appeared a black form, and then another. Then came the sound of growling.

"Bears!" Emma said. "They're trying to get in the barn. Oh Lord, Tobias! I don't know what to do!"

"Pappa always said fire," Zech said. "He said they're afraid of fire."

"We can't go out there, Zech. There's nothing we can do but hope they don't break into the house. I best get the shotgun ready in case we need it."

Zech grabbed his mother's arm and said, "We got to do something, Mamma! Pappa put me in charge of Tuck and Buck! We got to do something!"

His insistence calmed her. She said, "We'll light two pine torches and go outside. But if they come after us, run back in the house as fast as you can. Do you understand me, Zech? Don't try anything foolish!"

Emma lit the torches and handed one to Zech; then they went into the yard just outside the kitchen. The bears were circling the barn and scratching at the door, causing the oxen to shriek like screech owls and kick the walls violently. One bear turned and ran directly at them. When Zech thrust his torch forward, the bear stopped and reared, looming over both of them. Emma and Zech started backing toward the stoop.

Emma said, "They're not afraid of the fire, Zech. We'll never drive them away. We best go back in the house."

"They're hungry, Mamma, and they're after something to eat," Zech said. "Maybe if we open the smokehouse they'll smell the meat and go after it and leave the barn alone."

"Maybe so, and maybe not," Emma replied doubtfully. "But I guess it's worth a try. You stay here and I'll go open the smokehouse door."

Zech watched as his mother made her way slowly to the smokehouse, undetected thus far. The bears were still clawing at the barn, and the sound of kicking hooves became louder. She unlatched the door and propped it open with a stick, and then she started backing toward the stoop.

Emma was halfway across the yard when both of the bears rushed over and circled her, blocking her escape route. She whirled around and around, terrified, pushing her torch at them. Fear gripped Zech as he watched; then he threw down his torch, ran inside and returned dragging the shotgun.

The bears circled and growled as Zech tried vainly to lift the heavy gun and point it. Then he went to the side of the house and picked up a piece of firewood. He sat on the ground, propped the long barrel on top of the split wood, and took aim at the nearest bear. When he pulled the trigger, the shotgun flew out of his hands and he was knocked backward, tumbling over and over in the dirt.

The load of shot hit the bear with such force that it knocked him into the wall of the woodshed ten feet away. The tremendous boom caused the other bear to scurry off into the edge of the woods. Emma dropped her torch and ran for the house, knowing that the retreat was only temporary.

Zech was stunned senseless for a moment, and then he pushed himself up and crawled to the shotgun. He picked it up as Emma shouted frantically, "Go in the house, Zech! Go in the house!"

They both rushed inside and looked out a window as the other bear came back and invaded the smokehouse, growling as it slashed into chunks of meat. For more than an hour the fierce sounds broke the stillness of the night, and then the bear ran into the woods and did not return.

When she felt sure the bear was gone for good, Emma lit more torches and they went outside cautiously, watching the edge of the woods for any sign of activity. Zech noticed now that his shoulder hurt badly. He unlocked the barn door, went inside and patted the oxen, saying gently, "Don't you worry none. It's all over. They ain't going to hurt you. Pappa put me in charge, and I'll see to it."

Emma was by the woodshed, holding the torch over the lifeless form. Zech came back out, locked the barn door and went over to his mother. The bear was covered with blood and its eyes were wide open, staring at them, its mouth peeled back in a snarl.

Emma shuddered, and then she said, "I don't want to look any more. I'll have nightmares all night as it is. Let's go back inside and bolt the doors. I wish that thing would just get up and go away. We'll have to do something with it in the morning."

As they started toward the house Zech said, "Pappa put me in charge of the oxen. That bear better not come back here no more. He better not!"

Emma put her arm around him. She thought that perhaps he had missed his childhood, that he had been forced to grow up too soon. She said gently, "I love you, Zech. And Tobias will be real proud of you. Real proud."

The drive went unmolested after the encounter with the wolves, and on the fourteenth day they reached the banks of the St. Marys where Confederate soldiers waited to take over the herd and cross the river into Georgia.

Tobias stood on a bluff and watched as the lead bull plunged into the water and started swimming. A crowd of some sixty people had gathered there to watch the crossing.

Cow followed cow until soon there was a long line of struggling animals churning the river. Soldiers swam their horses to the right and left, forcing back any cow that tried to break away.

Two bulls in the rear of the line managed to swim away and drift downstream. They were caught in a current and sucked under briefly; then they resurfaced, only to go under again. Finally they floated on their sides and bobbed shoreward.

In an instant the spectators were in the water, pulling the bulls ashore and up the bank. Men and women unsheathed knives and swarmed over the carcasses like ants, and in a matter of minutes there was no trace left of meat, hides, hooves or horns.

Tobias watched the spectacle as the shoving crowd splattered each other with blood, running away with chunks of dripping meat on their shoulders, entrails wound around their arms. He muttered, "Lordy, them folks must be hungry. They done picked them bulls cleaner than buzzards. And I thought we had it bad."

He then turned away from the sight of it and walked over to where Addler as standing with the other drovers. Addler said to them, "Any man who wants to can ride back with me to the savanna, but some of you might want to take a more direct route home. It's up to you."

"I'll turn straight south," Tobias said. "Ain't no use in me going back that far north. Can I take the horse?"

"No way!" Addler said firmly, surprised that Tobias had even asked. "You ought to know better than that. We got to have them horses for the next drive."

"Without a horse, how am I supposed to get all the way from here back to my place?"

"Same way you got from your place to the savanna. Walk. You know I can't give you a horse. But you got some pay coming. Every man gets a dollar a day for the drive."

This surprised Tobias, for he had not expected pay. As he took the coins he said, "I sure thank you for this, Mister Addler. It's the first cash money I've had in a long time. But can I at least keep the whip? I would be a great help to me in the scrub."

"Yes, you can have the whip. We can replace it but not a horse."

Tobias put the money in his pocket. "I'm glad we made it with the cattle," he said. "But Mister Addler, please don't come after me again. I fear for the safety of my wife and boy."

"Maybe I will and maybe I won't," Addler said. "I try to spread the job around as best I can. So maybe I won't. I know how you feel about your family so far out in the woods. But let me tell you one thing for sure, MacIvey. If soldiers come to recruit you into the army, tell them you're a drover just home between trips. If they think you're one of my men they'll leave you alone. We need drovers right now a lot worse than we need soldiers."

"I'll do that," Tobias said gratefully. "And I thank you for telling me. It's best I start now. I've got a long walk ahead of me."

Addler watched him for a moment, and then he called after him, "Good luck, MacIvey! And be careful! Maybe I won't see you no more!"

It took Tobias eight days to make his way down the west bank of the St. Johns to the trading post and then through the woods to his homestead. Along the way he scrounged whatever he could find to eat. One night he slipped into a barnyard and stole a chicken, gripping its throat tightly so it would not cackle and give him away. This lasted for two days. He also caught frogs along the river bank and cooked their legs on sticks.

When finally he walked into the clearing he was even more gaunt than he had always been. No one was in sight as he came around the side of the house to the kitchen door.

The moment she saw him Emma rushed to him and said, "Tobias! I'm so glad you're home! I'm so glad!"

Zech heard her and came running from the direction of the barn, shouting, "I killed a bear, Pappa! They tried to get Tuck and Buck and we wouldn't let 'em! I killed one, Pappa!"

"You killed a bear?" Tobias questioned.

"I shot him, Pappa! Blowed him clear across the yard and into the woodshed. That old gun knocked me all the way back to the stoop. It got a real kick, ain't it?"

"I guess it has." He then looked at Emma. "What's Zech talking about?"

"They came one night, Tobias, two of them, trying to get in the barn. They was in a real frenzy, and we didn't know what to do. We tried to run them off with torches, but they wouldn't go away. I finally opened the smokehouse so they would leave the barn and go after the meat. They hemmed me up, and Zech shot one of them. Hadn't been for Zech I don't know what would have happened to me."

"Good Lord!" Tobias exclaimed. "They could have kilt you as easy as nothing. But it's good you opened the smokehouse. All the meat in the world ain't worth one of you getting hurt or kilt. You're a good boy, Zech! You done real good. I couldn't have handled it better myself."

"Where'd you get the whip, Pappa?" Zech asked. "Can I see it?"

Tobias handed it to him. "They gave it to me after the drive. It's what you use to herd cattle. And it will kill, too, if you want it to. It's rawhide."

"Did you fight a battle, Pappa?" Zech then asked, unfurling the whip.

"Yes. We had a real ruckus one night."

"With soldiers?"

"No. With wolves. We had as bad a time with them as you did with the bears."

"Can I try the whip, Pappa?"

"Yes. You can try all you want. But be careful. That thing can strip the hide off a bull at twenty feet. It ain't no plaything. Drovers kill rattlers with them."

Zech slashed the whip back and forth as Tobias and Emma went into the kitchen and sat at the table. Emma said, "I'm really glad you're back, Tobias. It was a bad night when the bears came. But Zech did you proud. If he was afraid he never showed it. The next morning he tried to skin out the bear by himself, but he just couldn't cut through the hide. I helped him, and we got out some meat. One of the bears shredded everything in the smokehouse, and there was nothing left that was fit to eat."

"It don't matter none at all, Emma. I'll get more meat somehow before winter sets in. I'm just glad you were done no harm. I don't want to go away again and leave you here by yourself."

"Was the drive bad?"

"Not too much. It was rough at first, me sitting in a saddle all day and not used it to. I could hardly squat down at night to take a meal. At the end of the drive Mister Addler gave me fourteen dollars, a dollar a day in pay. It ought to be a big help to us if Jenkins ever gets in more supplies. I come by there yesterday and he still didn't have anything."

"We'll make do somehow, We always have."

Tobias told Emma about the drowned bulls and how the people swarmed over them. He said, "It must be real bad up in Georgia now. Real bad. Folks is likely starving. And it's going to get worse. Sometimes I wish we'd never stopped here but kept going south, as far away from the war as we could go. I hope they don't come after me again."

"Did the man say he would?"

"No. He wouldn't say for sure. He said he'd try not to, but he's got a job to do, and he has to do it any way he can. I'll just have to wait and see."

Emma then said, "Are you hungry? I clear forgot to ask."

"I'm about to starve. I didn't have much along the way."

"You sit right here and rest while I go pick some collards. I'll make you a big pot of greens. And I'll fry the bear meat that's left in the smokehouse. It won't take me but a few minutes."

As he sat alone at the table he could hear the whip popping. He got up and looked outside, watching as Zech cracked it almost as well as Addler could.

SEVEN

A sharp February wind stung his face as Tobias stood beneath the bare hickory tree, watching the squirrel come closer. The leaves were gone now, as were the patches of wild poke, and only the palmetto and the cabbage palm looked the same as it did in summer.

The squirrel flicked its tail nervously; then it came further down the limb. When the whip cracked, it knocked the small animal senseless. As soon as it hit the ground Tobias grabbed it and broke its neck. Then he put it in the hunting sack with the others.

Zech had also become expert with the whip and had killed several rabbits with it. It was the only thing keeping meat on the table.

Tobias folded the whip and started back along the path to the clearing. His feet made crunching sounds as he walked over thick beds of brown leaves. He thought that tomorrow he would go down to the creek bottom and gather cattail roots which Emma would roast and then pound into flour.

When he reached the garden he paused for a moment and looked at the bare ground. He said to himself, "Next spring I'll make the fence stronger and add a few rails. There's bound to be a way to keep the critters out."

When he came around the side of the barn he noticed the horse immediately. No rider was in sight, and he thought that perhaps Addler had returned for him. He had really been expecting it but hoped it would not happen.

Then a man in a uniform came from the kitchen, followed by Emma and Zech. The uniform was Confederate gray. The soldier was the same age as Tobias, and he too wore a black beard.

Tobias approached the house with dread, remembering what Addler told him to say if an army recruiter came. He said, "Howdy." Then he threw the sack of squirrels onto the stoop floor.

The soldier returned the greeting, and then he said, "I'm Captain Graham. We need your help."

"I can't go in the army," Tobias said quickly. "I'm a drover."

"Who do you work for?"

"Addler. Henry Addler. We run from the Alachua savanna over to the St. Marys. I'm just home between drives."

"I'm not here to recruit you in the army, so it don't matter if you're a drover or not."

"If you don't want me to soldier, what is it you want me to do?" Tobias asked, puzzled.

"Cut logs for fortifications. The Federals have sent thirty-five troop ships out of Hilton Head. They'll land at the mouth of the St. Johns. Then they'll try to cut the state in two and stop the supply lines. If they do that, there won't be no more cows heading north for you to drive, and there won't be nothing more for our men to eat. We've got to stop them or it'll be all over. We've got two thousand troops ready now and three thousand more on the way. We're making our stand at Olustee, a few miles east of Lake City. And we're in bad need of log cutters."

"And what if I don't want to go?" Tobias asked.

"Mister, there's a war on if you don't know it. This whole state is under martial law. If you refuse, I got the right to shoot you right here on the spot, and I will too. So you ain't got no choice. And I'm not going to stand here and argue. Them Federal troops could have already landed by now. Are you ready to go?"

"You done said I got no choice. Do I need to take along my shotgun? And I ain't got a horse."

"You don't need to take nothing but yourself. If it gets down to where you have to shoot, we'll give you a gun. And I've got log wagons just up north of here. You can ride from there."

Tobias turned to Emma. "Maybe I'll be back real soon. A battle sure couldn't take as much time as a cattle drive." Then he said to Zech, "You clean them squirrels there for your mamma. And take the whip and kill something ever day for the two of you to eat."

"They's rabbits on that patch of winter rye where I take Tuck and Buck ever morning, Pappa. I'll kill one ever time I go there."

Tobias embraced Emma briefly. Then once again he followed a mounted rider across the clearing and into the woods.

Tobias passed down the line and was handed a tin cup of thin beef stew and a piece of black bread. Then he sat on a log and started eating.

A man beside him said, "A soldier told me that them Federal troops has raided Baldwin and Gainesville and took everything they could get their hands on. Cows, horses, mules, corn. Whatever. They're even taking ever nigger they can find. And they're on their way here now. It could happen tomorrow."

"I wish it would and be done with," Tobias responded, chewing the tough bread. "I been here over two weeks and I'm ready to go back home and see to my wife and boy."

"I know what you mean. I don't ever want to cut down another tree. We must of chopped two thousand logs by now."

"I guess. And maybe more. They ought to have built a barricade from here to Tallahassee. If we're done with it I wish they'd let us go."

The logging camp was three miles south of the battle site, in a thick forest of hickory, pine, and oak. Logs were carried from here to the fortifications on huge oxen-drawn wagons.

Tobias finished the stew and said, "Did the soldier you talked to say how many troops the Federals have?"

"Maybe five and a half thousand."

"It's about even then. I guess the Rebs has a good chance to win. But I wish they'd get on with it. I need to go back to the scrub."

It was just past noon the next day when the men finished loading a wagon and started north across an area of open meadow. Tobias stopped the oxen and said, "Look yonder, over to the west. What the hell are them soldiers doing?"

A line of horses were pulling cannons at a fast trot and were followed by cavalry and foot soldiers.

"Don't know. But it looks like ever man at the fortifications is high-tailing it down here. Maybe they decided to shuck out and not fight."

"Don't seem likely," Tobias said. Then he looked to the east and exclaimed, "Yonder! Over Yonder! There's the reason!"

Three long columns of Federal troops were marching toward them, and the columns were flanked on both sides by cavalry.

Tobias then said, "Good God allmighty! They're going to have the battle down here and not up there where they built all them barracades! And we're going to be caught right in the middle of it!"

"I guess they couldn't direct the Federals where to fight," the man next to Tobias said. "But I tell you one thing for sure. We better be to hell and gone from here when they start firing them cannons at each other."

"The woods!" Tobis said urgently. "Run back to the woods! It's our only chance!"

One of the men cut the oxen loose from the wagon and they all ran back toward the line of trees. They were halfway there when Confederate cannons belched fire and smoke. This was returned instantly from the east. Shells dropped and exploded fifty yards north of the fleeing men.

When Tobias reached the woods he ran right over a stump and fell hard to the ground. Then he crawled into a clump of bushes and watched as the tempo of cannon fire increased. The cannons continued to thunder for more than an hour before men in both armies rushed forward toward each other.

At one point the advancing soldiers overran each other and formed one big mass of slashing swords and firing guns. It was impossible to tell one army from the other except for the color of uniforms. As he watched the battle intensify, Tobias wondered what would have happened if they were all dressed in overalls as he was.

The plain was now engulfed with a low-hanging cloud of smoke, making it difficult to see what was happening. Once a troop of Confederate cavalry rushed through the woods and jumped their horses right over the brush where Tobias was hiding. He was not sure if they saw him or not, or of what they would do if they did. He knew there was no way for them to know that their own log cutters were hiding in these woods.

The battle raged back and forth for four hours, and then the Federal troops turned and retreated rapidly back to the east. Confederates swooped after them, rushing over a plain now littered with bodies, lifeless men in both blue and gray.

Tobias did not come out of the woods even after the battle had passed.

He spent the night beneath the brush, and at first dawn he walked to the edge of the woods and looked out, seeing that the dead had not yet been removed. Then a troop of soldiers came from the north, picking up bodies and putting them into wagons. When one wagon came close Tobias ran to it and said, "Is it all done now? I'm one of the log cutters, and if it's over I need to go home."

"We whupped the hell outen them," one soldier said. "Them Feds is back in Jacksonville by now. But it was a bloody one for both sides. We got to get these men up before the buzzards come after them."

"I guess it's done then," Tobias said.

"This battle is done, but it ain't over by a long shot," the soldier said. "There's more Feds where them come from, and we'll see them again. But I don't think nobody could give a damn less what you do now, fellow."

Tobias turned and went back into the woods. He could see no sign of any of the other loggers, so he headed south alone. He had walked just over a mile when he cut around a canebrake and found the horse. It was tied to a bush, and the rider was lying on the ground, wearing a blood-soaked blue uniform.

He was a boy of no more than eighteen. Lead balls had caught him in the neck and chest, and Tobias wondered how he could have ridden this far from the battle before falling.

Tobias removed a pistol and scabbard from the soldier's side, and then he unfastened the ammunition belt and put it in one saddlebag. There was also a rifle strapped to the saddle. He said, "I might as well take all of this, fellow, but I want you to understand I ain't stealing from the dead. It ain't no use to you any more, and it will be a godsend for me out in the scrub. I won't bury you, 'cause they'll find you sooner or later and send you back home. And I know you'd rather be with your folks than here in these woods."

He then searched the other saddlebag and found a knife and several tins of beef. He opened one can and ate ravenously, washing it down with water from the soldier's canteen. Then he mounted the horse and rode south.

When Tobias rode into the clearing he could not believe what he was seeing. Then the realization of it caused his hands to tremble. The house was no longer there, nor the barn, nor the smokehouse. Where they once stood, there were now piles of ashes. Only the woodshed remained.

He moved the horse forward slowly, dreading what he might find in the ashes. Then he heard movement behind the shed. Slowly and cautiously, Emma emerged from a bush, and then Zech peeked from behind the shed.

"Tobias!" Emma shouted, rushing to him. "We didn't know it was you. We only heard a horse coming. We thought one of them had come back."

Tobias jumped from the horse. "What has happened here, Emma? What is all this?"

"They came a week ago, fifteen of them. When they left the next morning they set fire to all but the shed."

Zech said excitedly, "They killed Tuck, Pappa! They cooked him and et him right here in the yard! And they took Buck with them when they left!"

"Damned Federal bastards!" Tobias exploded angrily.

"They weren't Federals," Emma said quickly. "They were Confederate deserters, Tobias. Some of them still had on pieces of their uniforms. They must have known about the battle and all the men being gone up there, 'cause they weren't in no hurry at all."

"Our own people did this to us?" Tobias questioned, finding it hard to believe. "Rebs?"

"Yes, Tobias. They were the meanest looking men I've ever seen."

"Did they do harm to you?" Tobias then asked.

"They did us no harm, but I begged them not to burn the house, and they did it anyway."

"Damn them! They didn't have to do this. They could have just took what they wanted and left. Did you save anything?"

"Not much," Emma replied. "They left soon as they set the fires, and me and Zech ran in and got what we could. But the house went up too fast. We got an axe, a saw, the frying pan and a few blankets. But we didn't get any clothes. It just went up too fast."

"They took the shotgun, Pappa," Zech said, "But I still got the whip. Where'd you get the horse?"

"Off a dead soldier. A Federal."

Tobias walked over and looked at the scorched ground where the house had been. He kicked the ashes and said, "Ain't no man ever gonna do this to me again! Not ever! I'll kill the first one who tries!

And I'll kill a thousand more if I have to! So help me God I will!"

"We could live in the shed while you build another house," Emma said, frightened by the bitterness in his voice. "It's better than what we had when we first came here."

"No! We'll go south. This time we'll go to a place where nobody can find us till the war is over. That's what I should have done in the first place."

"They didn't burn the wagon, Pappa," Zech said. "It's behind the shed."

"I don't know if this cavalry horse can pull it or not," Tobias said. "He's trained to run, not pull. But we'll try. There's tinned beef and hardtack in the saddlebag. Soon as we eat a bite we'll leave. This time we'll go to a place where they can't find us, just like the Indians done."

At first Tobias headed directly south, leading the horse and wagon through thick woods, sometimes having to backtrack when he came to swampy bottoms and then follow higher ridges of dry ground.

On the second day he came into the lower scrub, an area he had never before explored. Here there were rolling sand hills thickly covered with titi, runty scrub oak, and impenetrable clumps of Spanish bayonet. The dead trunks of pines pointed upward forlornly, some peppered with woodpecker holes, the limbless trees giving evidence of some great fire that had once rushed over the land, destroying all in its path.

Every small oak had bear marks on its trunk, deep slashes made by claws, and buzzards circled overhead constantly. Occasionally Tobias came too close to the bayonet plants and jumped back in pain as they cut into his flesh.

Emma held the reins as Tobias took the axe and tried to cut a path for them to pass. Even in the cold he was sweating, and damp splotches covered his overalls. Again and again the wagon wheels sank down into the sand and stuck, and when this happened, they all pushed as the horse strained and neighed loudly, bucking and straining again, trying vainly to move the wagon forward.

"It ain't no use," Tobias finally said, putting the axe back into the wagon. "This is the most hellish place I've ever seen. There ain't no way we can get through it with the wagon. We'll have to turn and go back, then take the trail down to the St. Johns and follow the river south. There ought to be open land along the river."

Tobias unhitched the panting horse and tied it to a bush, then the three of them pulled the wagon from the sand and turned it.

EIGHT
Kissimmee River
1866

The runty black cow snorted and tossed its head from side to side, as if daring the horse and rider to come after it. Tobias eyed it cautiously, trying to maneuver the horse to one side. Then the cow snorted again, wheeled, and darted off into a thick stand of trees, its wide horns making clanking sounds as they struck vines.

Tobias kicked the horse into full pursuit. He dodged low-hanging limbs and then felt his body crash into the side of a tree, causing him to depart the saddle, flip over backward, and hit the ground with a thud.

"Damn you!" he shouted as the horse disappeared into the brush.

Zech was off to one side, watching. He ran to his father and said, "He done it again, didn't he, Pappa?"

"Cussed army horse don't know how to do nothing but run in a straight line!" Tobias said, getting up and brushing dirt from his overalls. He ain't worth spit in a swamp. We'll never catch them cows till we get a horse that knows how to run around trees instead of into them. Even a mule would know better than that."

"I'll go fetch him back," Zech said. "You wait here, Pappa. He's just right down yonder."

Tobias hobbled over to a tree and sat down, and in a few minutes

Zech returned with the horse. He said, "We going to try some more, Pappa? They's two more cows in the brush. I seen them."

"We best go on back now. I've got chores to do at the house."

"Can I ride the horse now?"

"You can have that blasted critter. Just be sure he don't walk head-on into a tree and knock your brains out. I feel like my tail is broke."

Zech scrambled onto the saddle and they went along a path that wound beneath huge oaks. Soon they came to a small plot of ground that was fenced with split cypress rails. Inside the pen there was one cow with the letters MCI burned into its side.

Tobias looked at the cow and said, "It ain't much, but it's a start. We ought to have a dozen by now. We'll try again tomorrow."

"Maybe we ought to build us a trap," Zech said, bouncing up and down in the saddle as if the horse were in full gallop. "We could catch 'em like you trap coons."

"That'd be some trap. A wild cow ain't a coon, and you know that. What we need is a horse with sense and some dogs."

The small cabin was in a clearing on the east bank of the Kissimmee River. It was built of cypress logs fastened together with pegs, and the roof was palmetto fronds. It contained two rooms, one a kitchen and eating area and the other a sleeping room. Tobias and Emma occupied the small private room and Zech slept on a pallet in the kitchen.

It took Tobias six months to find the place. They followed the west bank of the St Johns, stopping for days at a time to let the tired horse rest and gather strength, taking what food they could from the woods and the water. Nights were spent beneath the thin protection of bushy cabbage palm tops or the outspread limbs of water oaks.

When they reached the source of the St. Johns in a lake that seemed to mesh into an impenetrable swamp, they camped there for a month, fishing with crude hooks Tobias made from thorn bushes, and killing coons and rabbits with the whip. Then they turned inland and wandered again, finally coming to a dense hammock along the bank of the Kissimmee.

Tobias knew at once that this isolated place was what he was looking for. There were no other homesteads nearby, and the nearest trading post was at Fort Capron, fifty miles to the east.

Since arriving at the hammock, Tobias had been to the trading post only once, and it was then he learned the war was over, that the south had lost. He had gone there to buy salt, and he also paid a blacksmith two dollars of the fourteen dollars he earned on the cattle drive to make a branding iron. His pen stood empty for almost a year after that. There was nothing to brand, and for practice he burned the letters MCI into every log on the side of the house. And then one day he caught the lone cow. After herding it into the pen, he held it on the ground while Zech pressed the hot iron to its side. Tobias then stood for an hour just looking at the burned MCI that proclaimed the cow to be his own.

While scouting the surrounding countryside, he came upon an abandoned village where Seminoles once lived. The chickees were rotten and had fallen into decayed heaps, but there were also the remains of a garden that still contained corn, squash, beans and pumpkins, and a small plot of sugar cane. From this he started his own garden, and he hoped it would thrive in the black river bottom soil.

His next project was to build a small barn for the horse and add several rails to the cow pen fence. These woods too were filled with predators. Each night he tied the horse to a post just outside the cabin door. It was no good for chasing cows in a swamp, but it was his only means of pulling the wagon to the trading post or elsewhere.

Spring had just passed into early summer, and the woods were alive with the sounds of chattering birds and rambling animals. Squirrels barked and great blue herons squawked loudly as they glided along the nearby river. A red fox flicked its bushy tail and ran across the path as Tobias and Zech entered the clearing. Zech stayed on the horse, racing it back and forth between the cabin and the edge of the woods.

Emma was at a table in the kitchen area, chopping coon meat into small pieces and putting them into the frying pan. When Tobias entered she put down the knife and said, "Do you know when you might make another trip to the trading post?"

"I guess I ought to go pretty soon. I've got a whole passel of coon skins. Maybe they've got in some flour. A batch of biscuits would sure go good. Seems I ain't et one for ten years."

She hesitated for a moment, and then she said, "Do you have enough in trade for a Dutch oven? It's hard to make good stew or bake anything in this frying pan. I could fix better meals with an oven, and I sure miss the one we lost in the fire."

Her question brought immediate guilt to Tobias. He should have thought of this himself without being asked. Emma never complained about anything and never asked for things he knew she missed. It had been ten years since she had a new dress, and her shoes were the ones she wore when they left Georgia. And now she asked only for a cooking tool.

"I'm sure I have enough for that. I should have got one on the last trip. There's a lot of things I should have done for you that I ain't, Emma. And I know it. Someday I'll make it up to you."

"There's nothing I need that can't wait."

"I've about got the poles cut to add to the cow pen fence and the garden. I'll finish it this afternoon, and at sunup tomorrow I'll go to the trading post. There'll be enough skins for the oven."

He went back outside and down to the garden, studying the plants that had broken through the rich soil, hoping that wild hogs would not raid him constantly as they had in the scrub. He also thought of the hardships his family had endured during those years in the scrub and on the trip here. Zech was eight years old now and had never tasted an apple or eaten a piece of sugar candy. There had been no jackknife to play with and no kite to fly and no whistle to blow. He felt a sudden urgency to do something for both Emma and Zech, to somehow better their lives. If he did not hurry, the void would become too big for him to ever fill.

Just then Zech came riding by at full gallop, his slim body seemingly glued to the saddle. He reined up, made the horse rear on its hind legs, and shouted, "I bet you I could ride him in the swamp, Pappa! I bet you I could!" Then he raced away to the far side of the clearing.

Tobias watched after him, noticing that boy and horse seemed to be one and the same. He thought of that night in the scrub when a man-child picked up a shotgun weighing as much as he and killed a bear without fear or hesitation. He said, "I'll just bet you could, Zech. I bet you really could."

NINE

Ten miles down the river Tobias left the woods and turned east. Here he entered a prairie dotted with palmetto and broken occasionally by cypress stands and clumps of cabbage palms.

There was an early morning haze over the land, adding to the majesty of its vastness. Flights of egrets and herons glided gracefully over the brown grass and then landed in cypress stands, turning the trees into solid masses of white and gray.

Mile after mile the wagon creaked forward, and it seemed to Tobias that the prairie was endless. Here there was no circular border of thick forests like on the Alachua savanna, but like the savanna, he could see herds of deer moving across the land, and also wild cattle. Once he came within a hundred yards of a small herd, and when he stopped to look, the cows jerked their heads up quickly, standing alert as they stared at him for a moment, then wheeled and bounded away. For a half mile they thundered over the ground; then they stopped and ignored him, and continued to graze.

At noon he stopped at a cypress stand and ate the fried coon Emma had prepared for him, washing it down with water from the canteen that had come with the horse. To stretch his legs he walked over to the stand. The little island of pond cypress was so thick he found it difficult to enter. As he made his way toward the center, he thought that in this one stand alone there were enough cypress poles to fence the entire prairie.

He was startled when he heard the sound just ahead of him, a combination grunting-growl. He stepped cautiously around a tree and came face to face with a wild boar. Man and animal looked at each other for a moment, both equally surprised by the other's sudden presence, then Tobias slowly backed away, leaving the boar sole claim to its prairie home. He hoped it would stay there and not come his way.

It was late afternoon when Tobias reached the trading post. The cypress shack was on the west side of an inlet to the north of Fort Pierce. He hitched the horse and stood for several minutes gazing out across the water, thinking that someday he would bring Emma and Zech here to walk the beach and gather shells, or just sit on the sand and watch the gulls and pelicans at play.

The proprietor of the trading post, Elias Thompson, was a short fat man in his fifties, with a bald head and tomato-red face. When Tobias entered he said, "Howdy. I seen you coming a good while ago. That wagon's a load for one hoss to pull. What you need is a buckboard. It ain't as heavy, and it rides better on the prairie. Oxen is what you ought to have to pull that farm wagon."

"I had oxen once," Tobias said. "But all I got now is the horse. It'll have to do."

"What can I do for you?" Thompson then asked.

"I've got coon skins to trade. A lot of them."

"You got any cash money? I mean silver or gold coins, not Confederate paper. That stuff ain't worth shucks but some folks still tries to pass it off on me."

"I got a little. And it's coins."

"Well, them coon skins ain't worth much. And besides that, I got hardly no supplies at all. Things is scarce everwhere now. Fellow come through here the other day told me it's so bad up in Georgia and Alabama that folks is eating pine cones and sassafras roots. Folks is in real bad shape on account of the war done tore up everthing. Only goods I can get comes on a schooner out of Baltimore, and it sure ain't much. What is it you got in mind?"

"Mainly I want a Dutch oven, and a little wheat flour if you got it. And I could use some salt."

"I got no flour at all, and I ain't seen a Dutch oven in five years. It all went into cannon balls. But I got some salt."

"I wouldn't give my cash money for salt," Tobias said. "Will you take the skins in trade?"

"Yeah, I'll take 'em. Next time the schooner comes I'll send 'em north. Folks up there has still got the money to buy stuff like that. The schooner captain told me what they really want now is polecat hides. Bring as much as two dollars each. Now ain't that something? Polecat hides. I reckon the women up there fancy a coat with white stripes. Next time you come in, bring me some if you can figure out a way to relieve a skunk of his hide without getting the worst end of it."

"I'll think on it," Tobias said. "But I don't relish the idea of trapping skunks. I got sprayed once and had to stay out in the barn for a week."

"Where you live?" Thompson asked.

"On the east side of the Kissimmee, a full day's travel from here."

"I hear tell them little steamboats is going to start running the river again, down to Lake Okeechobee. I bet you could sell them boatmen some alligator hides. 'Gator hides bring from a buck fifty to three dollars now, depending on the size. And the tail meat is as good as beef. You could probably sell fresh deer meat too. Nowdays it's easy to sell anything a man can eat if you can find somebody with cash."

"I've never seen a boat on the river since I've lived there. But if they come again I'll know it. My place is right off the bank."

Tobias went outside, brought in the skins and put them on the counter. Thompson examined them briefly and said, "Them's real good hides. I can let you have ten pounds of salt in trade."

"Done," Tobias said, disappointed about the other things but glad to at least get salt out of the long trip.

When Thompson came back with the salt he said, "You got a gun?"

"I've got a rifle and a pistol, both of them military."

"You want some shells? That's one thing they got plenty of up north, leftover ammunition. I bought three whole cases off the schooner. I can let you have a couple of boxes for a dollar cash."

"Are they forty-fours?"

"That's right."

"I'll take them," Tobias then said, surprised by the offer. "But I want four boxes. Here's two dollars cash."

Tobias put the shells and the salt into a cloth sack. "Next time the supply boat comes, ask about a Dutch oven. I want one real bad, and I'll pay cash if I have to."

"I'll do that."

Thompson followed Tobias to the wagon and said "You going to travel out there at night?"

"Nope. I'll go a ways before it gets too dark and make camp. Then I'll move on at sunup."

"You best be real careful," Thompson warned, a seriousness in his voice. "Since the war there's been a lot of drifters in these parts. There's a lot of men scouting around now, looking for something to eat. And maybe for somebody to kill too. One day last month about fifteen come by here in one pack, riding horses, and they was the meanest-looking bunch I ever seen. Looked as if they'd as soon kill a man as look at him. They plumb scared the hell outen me, and my boots shook till they finally rode off. You best watch out for yourself. A man ought not be out on the prairie alone."

"I'll keep a sharp eye," Tobias said. "And I rightly thank you for the warning."

As the wagon creaked away, Thompson shouted, "What you need is a buckboard! You decide to trade off that wagon let me know and I'll see can I find one!"

Tobias waved back to him.

The last rays of sundown were vanishing rapidly when Tobias stopped at a small hammock and unhitched the horse. Then he gathered palm fronds, placed them on the wagon floor and covered them with a blanket Because of snakes, he would sleep in the wagon rather than on the ground.

He started a fire and then sat by it, eating the last small scrap of coon meat. Shadows from the fire flickered through tree limbs and vanished upward, like dancers performing a mystic ritual. From somewhere across the prairie came the lonesome cry of a whip-poor-will.

Tobias had heard no sound of footsteps, but when he glanced to the far reaches of the fire's light, he saw two men and a woman standing there, looking at him. He jumped backward quickly and grabbed the rifle, remembering Thompson's warning.

One of the men said, "We did not mean to frighten you. We saw your fire and came to it. We mean no harm."

As they came closer Tobias recognized them as Indians. He stared at them intensely, trying to bring forth something long since forgotten. There was a familiarity about them, something in their faces that tugged at his memory.

Then it came to him. He said, "I know you. I don't remember the names, but you came to my place in the scrub when the men were chasing you for killing a calf."

"We remember you well," one of the men said. "You are Tobias MacIvey. We have never forgotten what you did for us, and all of our people know of this. But we never expected to find you here. Do you not still live where you did?"

"No. Some men burned the place while I was away and we left after that. We live now in a hammock on the east bank of the Kissimmee, about a day's journey from here."

"I know the place you speak of. My people once had a village not far from there. I know it well."

"I found your place and took seed from the garden," Tobias said, putting down the rifle. "I'm sorry, but I have no food to offer you now."

"We have food. We will prepare it here if we can share your fire."

"You are welcome," Tobias said. "And you can stay the night if you wish. It would be better for all of us to be together. I've been told there are many strangers wandering the countryside."

One of the men went into the darkness and returned pulling a sled made of two poles covered with deer hide. Several bundles were on the sled. He said, "I do not blame you for not remembering our names. That was a long time ago, and it was also a very bad day when we met. I am Keith Tiger, and this is Bird Jumper. And she is my wife, Lillie."

"I won't forget again." Tobias promised.

The men sat with Tobias by the fire as the woman took a pot from the sled and filled it from a deer hide pouch. Then she poured water into the pot and set it on the fire.

"It is sofkee," Keith Tiger said, noticing Tobias' curiosity as he watched Lillie. "We make it by soaking crushed corn in wood ash lye. Then we boil it with water. It is a favorite of our people. When it is done you will eat with us."

Tobias appreciated the offer since the small portion of coon left him still hungry. He said, "When you left the scrub you said you were going to a land far in the south to join your people there. Why are you here now?"

"We are on our way to Fort Capron for bullets. The man who owns the trading post at Fort Dallas will not sell guns or bullets to an Indian, and we have heard that the man here will. We need them badly to kill game, and we are on the way to trade for them."

"I had coon skins," Tobias said, "and all I could get for them was salt. For everything else he wanted cash. What do you have to trade?"

"Flour."

"Flour?" Tobias questioned, his interest aroused immediately. "You've got flour?"

"Yes," Keith Tiger responded, amused by Tobias' reaction. "Koonti flour. It is as good as the white man's flour. We like it better. It is made from the root of the sago palm, and it is free for the taking."

"I've never heard of it, but I reckon I've eaten a ton of cattail flour."

"This is better. We will tell you how to gather it and how to prepare it. In hard times, koonti will nourish you and keep you alive. It saved my people from hunger many times during the wars."

"I'd be right pleased to know all about it," Tobias said. "And the man at the trading post did say he can sell anything a man can eat. You ought to make a good trade."

Keith Tiger motioned toward the sled; then the woman went to it and removed one of the bundles. As she handed it to Tobias, Tiger said, "Take some of the koonti with you. We have enough to share. Tell your woman to use it as she would the white man's flour."

"I really appreciate this," Tobias said, accepting the bundle. "I'll have my wife make biscuits as soon as I get back home. And I have something to share too, just in case things go wrong at the trading post." He removed two boxes of the shells from his saddlebag and handed them to Tiger. "I've got more, and I don't need to shoot as much game as you do to feed a whole village."

The Indian's eyes flashed pleasure and gratitude. "This is truly a great gift to my people," he said. "We will use them wisely, and we do thank you."

"I'm just glad I had them to share."

Tiger then said, "I see you have a horse now. I remember you did not have one in the scrub."

"I took him off a dead soldier during the war. He's fair at pulling the wagon, but he ain't no good at all in the woods and swamps. He's too big, and he runs in a straight line. Ever time I've chased a cow with him I've nigh on got my neck broke."

"You remember I told you once before that what you need is a marshtackie. A marshtackie can take you through the swamp and the thickest of woods as swiftly as a deer. It is the best cow horse there is."

"Well, I sure ain't had no luck with that fellow. So far I've got only one cow."

"Where do you keep your cow?" Tiger asked.

"In a pen close by the house in the hammock."

"That is not good. You could not do this at all with a herd, even a small one. In the summer you must let them wander the range freely, grazing wherever they find grass. You must follow the herd and not keep them penned. When my people had cattle they would let them range as far as a hundred miles and more in a summer. In the winter, turn them loose in the woods and swamps and they will survive. And in the spring, round them up and put your mark on the new ones. If you keep them penned they will die. The marsh grass in flood areas along the rivers has salt, and without this your cattle will become sick. The best salt grass is along the St. Johns."

"You mean if I want to own cattle I'll have to leave the house and follow them wherever they go?"

"This is true. There were times when my people had herds that stretched as far as the eye could see, and we followed them everywhere. Those who wandered with the herds were called Ishmaelites by the white soldiers. I do not know what the word means, but I think it is something bad. They did not say this of those who stayed in the villages and farmed, only those who wandered the land. But if you do not wish to follow the herd, it is best that you stay home and grow pumpkins."

"Ishmaelites," Tobias said, as if weighing the word. "Maybe I will do as you say. I wouldn't like to be just a pumpkin grower."

"If you catch a cow in the swamp, put your mark on it and let it go. Then catch another and mark it. You can return for them later. If you keep them in a pen all the time they will die."

By now the pot in the fire was bubbling, and the mixture had formed a thick gruel. Lillie removed it from the fire, then she handed a huge wooden spoon to Keith Tiger. He passed it to Tobias and said, "You must eat first. It is the custom of our people."

Tobias dipped the spoon into the pot, put it to his mouth and chewed. "It's good," he said, swallowing and then smiling. "It's really good. I hope we have corn this fall. I'll tell Emma about this."

He passed the spoon back to Keith Tiger, and after he dipped it into the pot, he passed it to Bird Jumper. They would all eat from a communal spoon and pot. When Bird Jumper ate, he passed it back to Tobias.

Lillie would wait until the men finished before eating.

Later that night, after two hours of talking, Tobias yawned and said, "I guess I better turn in now. It's been a long day, and I need to hit the trail by sunup tomorrow."

Keith Tiger said, "We must start early too. We have been traveling mostly at night. It is best that no one sees us. But I am glad we came to your fire. If we had not recognized you, we would have remained in the darkness." He then handed the sofkee spoon to Tobias. "Take this as a gift to your woman. Perhaps she can make use of it. We have many more of them at the village. And if you ever have need of my people, go to the far shore of the great lake Okeechobee. From there, walk south. You will not see us, but we will know you are there."

Tobias took the spoon and put it into his saddlebag. He said, "I thank you for this. It will make Emma proud, and I know she'll have use of it. I'm glad you stopped here for the night, and I wish you much luck with the trading."

"We'll have more food together before we depart at sunup," Tiger said.

Tobias then climbed into the wagon and lay down on the palmetto bed, thinking for a long time of the strange word Ishmaelite.

TEN

The morning after Tobias arrived home from the trading post he left the house early and strode briskly through the woods toward the cow pen. Zech had to trot to keep up with him. He said excitedly, "Where we going in such a hurry, Pappa? What we going to do?"

Tobias felt good, his stomach full of koonti biscuits. His lanky legs covered three feet per step. When he reached the pen he gazed for a moment at the cow, then he opened the gate and propped a stick against it to keep it open.

"What you doing, Pappa?" Zech asked anxiously, completely puzzled by his father's actions. "You going to turn him loose after all that ruckus we had catching him?"

"If I don't he'll die."

"How come? He looks fine to me."

"Look there at the ground," Tobias said, pointing. "Not a blade of grass left, and we sure don't have any hay or corn to feed him. He's got our mark. I'll turn him loose now so's he can eat, then we'll catch him again later. Go back to the house and fetch the horse and the branding iron. We'll catch another one this morning and mark him right there in the woods."

Zech turned and ran toward the clearing, still not understanding what had come over his father.

The cow too seemed puzzled. It stood still, eyeing the man and the open gate. Then it shook its horns and backed into the far side of the pen.

Tobias went inside and circled the cow. When it still did not move he said loudly, "Shu! Shu cow! Git!"

The cow backed further against the fence and snorted.

Tobias said, "Damn you, critter! As much as you fought getting in here, now you won't go out!"

Then he started jumping up and down, flailing his arms wildly, shouting, "Git! Git! I said git!"

The cow watched Tobias for a moment more, then it rushed forward, bounded out the gate and into the woods, bellowing loudly.

Just then Zech came back, riding the horse at full gallop. He reined up, got off and said, "I got the iron, Pappa. But if you're going to turn them loose, how come we got to catch another one?"

"Just do it, Zech," Tobias said. "Let's go down by the hickory flat and see what's there."

When they reached the grove of hickory trees Tobias mounted the horse. They remained very still, listening. After a few minutes Zech whispered, "I hear one, Pappa. He's over to the right in the brush."

"I'll go after him," Tobias said. "If I can get up to him I'll jump off and grab him by the horns. Then you run in and help me."

Tobias moved the horse toward the sound, and when he came around the side of a clump of huckleberry bushes, a runty black bull was standing there. It immediately turned and ran.

When Tobias kicked it in the flanks, the horse bounded forward quickly. For fifty yards horse and rider rushed after the bull, then the bull made a sudden turn to the left. The horse crashed headlong into a thick growth of muscadine vines and became entangled. It kicked and bucked, trying to break free, then it threw Tobias right over its head and into the vines, entangling him even worse.

Zech ran up and said, "Gimme your hand, Pappa! I'll pull you out!"

The horse continued to buck as Zech pulled and strained, and finally Tobias popped free. They broke the vines from around the horse's legs and backed it out of the entanglement. Tobias then shouted, "Idiot! Fool! You could have turned with the bull!"

Zech said, "It ain't all his fault, Pappa. I was watching. You didn't try to turn him quick enough. You got to give him better directions so he'll know what to do."

"Maybe so, but this ain't going to work. I tell you what, Zech. You get on the horse, and I'll climb up in a tree. Try to turn the bull under the tree and I'll drop down on top of him and catch him. It just might work."

Zech got on the horse and rode off into the brush as Tobias climbed the nearest tree. As soon as he found the bull, Zech circled slowly to the right and came up behind it. Then he charged, herding the bull back the way it had come.

Tobias sat on the limb, watching. The bull was coming straight to him, with Zech in hot pursuit. Just as the bull reached the tree, Tobias turned loose, dropped down and landed solidly on the bull's back. He grabbed the horns with both hands and locked his long legs round its stomach.

The bull continued running full speed for twenty yards, then bull and rider crashed to the ground. The breath was knocked from him, but Tobias managed to shout, "Get the fire going, Zech! Hurry! Get the iron hot! I don't think I can hold him for long!"

Before Zech could even start gathering sticks for a fire, the bull jumped up, bucked around and around, and started running again. Tobias tightened his legs and hung on. The bull changed directions twice, and then it ran under a low-hanging limb that caught Tobias in the chest. He let go the horns and grabbed the limb, and for a moment both bull and rider left the ground and hung suspended in midair; then Tobias' legs turned loose and he flipped backward, hitting the ground upside down as the bull dropped down and bounded away.

Zech shouted, "You done good, Pappa! You was really riding him till he run under that limb!"

Tobias got up and examined himself to see if anything was broken. He said, "I wasn't trying to ride him! I was trying to throw him! What we need is a rope. When I get one on the ground you can tie his legs, then he can't get up afore we put the mark on. Next time we'll bring rope."

Zech was awed by his father's performance. He said again, "You done real good, Pappa. You had that bull going some before he knocked you off. Hadn't been for that limb you could have rode him slam back to the house. We going to try it again?"

"Maybe tomorrow. I'm a mite sore just now. But there's got to be a way if we can figure it out."

It was early morning a month later when Zech ran into the clearing, shouting, "Come quick, Pappa! Hurry! Down to the cow pen!"

Tobias rushed outside and followed the fleeing boy, having to run full stride to catch up with him. When they reached the pen Zech shouted, "Look there, Pappa! Look!"

Inside the pen there was a small black stallion, its sleek body glistening with muscles. On its back was mounted a McClellan saddle. Tied to the outside of the fence there were two dogs, both tall, gray and shaggy, looking almost exactly like wolves.

Zech jumped up and down with excitement. "Where'd they come from, Pappa? Who brought them here?"

"Can't say," Tobias said, "but that horse didn't put himself in there. That's for sure. But I think I know. He's a marshtackie."

Zech ran into the pen and leaped onto the saddle. He whirled the horse around and around, shouting, "Look here, Pappa! He can turn quicker than a rabbit!" Then he kicked it in the side, bounded the fence in one leap and made a wide circle through the woods.

When he came back to the pen, Zech jumped off and said, "He flies like a bird, Pappa. We'll get cows now. Ain't no cow can outrun him, even in the swamp. He needs a name. What we going to call him?"

Tobias thought for a moment, and then he said, "Ishmael. We'll call him Ishmael. That's a good name for a horse."

"What about the dogs?" Zech then asked. "What we going to name them? A dog's got to have a name when you call him."

"We'll name one after ole Tuck. And the other Nip. Nip and Tuck. How's that?"

"That's fine. That's real fine." Zech then went over and patted one of the dogs on the head, causing its tail to wag vigorously. He said, "You're Nip. And you're Tuck. I'll bet you can keep them wild hogs out of the garden."

"I expect they will," Tobias said. "They look like they could take on a bear. But I swear they could pass for wolves."

"They ain't, Pappa. They's good dogs. I can tell."

"We best go on back to the house now and tell your mamma about this. You scared the life out of her when you come running into the clearing, shouting like you was. She don't know what the ruckus was about. We best go tell her so she won't worry."

Zech untied the dogs, jumped back on the horse and bounded away. The dogs took after him, barking loudly. Tobias said, "If that sight don't put Emma up a tree, nothing will."

When Tobias reached the clearing Emma was outside, looking at the horse. The dogs were circling her, their tails wagging. She said, "What is all this, Tobias? Has someone lost their horse and dogs?"

"Well, it looks like Christmas done finally come for us. Let's go inside and talk about it."

Zech galloped away as they went into the cabin and sat at the table. Tobias said, "The Indians brung them. It couldn't be nodody else.

"Why? Why would they do this? They owe us nothing."

"They think they do. For what we did for them in the scrub. And it could be they just wanted to do it. Whatever the reason, it's a blessing. I could have never bought that horse and them dogs, not in a hundred years. There ain't that many coons in the swamp."

"Are they wild, the horse and the dogs?"

"Don't seem to be. They're probably trained real good. Keith Tiger told me his people had great herds of cattle before the soldiers took them away, and the horse they used was the marshtackie. They've probably been keeping some of them horses and dogs all this time, hoping that someday they would have cattle again and be able to use them. But that ain't likely to happen, at least not anytime soon. I guess they wanted somebody to put the horse and the dogs to use again."

"First the flour, and now this," Emma said. "I wish they would have come to the house. We could have given them something to eat and thanked them."

"I would have liked to see them too. Maybe they just didn't want to make a big deal out of it. It could be the Indian way."

"I still wish we could have thanked them. I know this means a lot to you and Zech."

"Emma," Tobias said, putting his hand on hers, "it means more than you know. At least we got a chance now. Before this we didn't have no chance at all. We were just fooling ourselves, me and Zech, and I knowed it. I just didn't have the heart to tell him. But now we got a chance."

ELEVEN

The two dogs ran straight to the bull, as if they knew beforehand exactly where they would find it. Nip rushed in and grabbed it by the nose, and Tuck sank his teeth into its left rear leg.

Zech was riding just behind them, the small horse darting effortlessly around trees and jumping over vines. Tobias followed on the other horse.

When the bull tried to break free, Nip sank his teeth in deeper, causing a trickle of blood to stain the tip of his nose. Then the bull stood motionless, its eyes wild and staring downward at the dog.

Tobias jumped from his horse and grabbed the bull by its horns, putting all his strength into a twisting motion that finally sent the bull sprawling on its side. As Zech tied its legs together, the dogs turned loose and backed away.

Tobias started a fire, and when the flames were burning brightly he put the branding iron into the center. He said, "It seems to me we're still doing this wrong, running around all over the woods and making a fire ever time we put on a mark. We ought to build a pen down here and wait till we get five or six cows in a bunch, then brand them all at one time."

"It do make sense," Zech replied. "And I bet you that Nip and Tuck could bring in cows by themselves, without no help at all from us. I already seen them do it. They can make a cow go any way they want to. All we'd have to do is show them the pen and say git 'em.

"We'll start a pen tomorrow. Fact is, we'll build two, and put them about a mile apart. That ought to be even better."

"I can bring them in by myself too, Pappa. The other day Ishmael made a cow walk a straight line right through the brush. Seemed he knowed ever move that cow was going to make, and then he made it first. I think he's part cow himself. He sure knows what a cow is going to do."

When the iron glowed red, Tobias took it from the fire and pressed it to the bull's side. Smoke boiled upward from burning hair as the iron seared the letters MCI into the bull's hide. He kicked twice and tried to get up; then Tobias released the ropes. The bull struggled to its feet and ran off into the woods.

The dogs watched attentively, awaiting a signal for them to hunt again; then Tobias patted one on the head and said, "Go git 'em, dogs! Git 'em!" They immediately streaked away into the brush.

Zech said, "Them dogs is a sight, ain't they, Pappa?"

"They surely are. I don't know how we ever got along without them. They keep this up they's going to be MacIvey cows all over the place. You best put out that fire now. And do it real good. Seems like a fool idea to be running around building fires all over the swamp."

The sound of yelping came from a half mile away and Zech said, "They done struck another one already."

"Sure sounds like it. They don't even give us a chance to rest. Let's ride on over and see to it."

This time they did not race the horses, knowing that the dogs would hold the cow, even to sundown if necessary. When they reached the spot, the dogs were running around and around a thick clump of palmetto, barking and growling at the same time.

Tobias watched for a moment, and then he said, "That sure ain't no cow they've got in there this time. Don't go in yet. It could be a bear in them bushes."

The dogs continued circling and growling, and Tobias took the rifle from the saddle holster. He said, "Whatever it is, it sure don't want to come out. Must be something besides a bear else the horses would have done smelled him by now and put on a show. Ain't no horses nowheres going to stand still for a bear, not even Ishmael."

For five minutes the dogs continued circling the palmetto, then Tobias said, "We're going to have to flush it out, whatever it is. Get a big stick and throw in there. I'll keep the gun aimed."

Zech dismounted and picked up a hickory limb. Tobias said to him,

"Don't go any closer. Throw it from as far back as you can."

Zech whirled around and around; then he released the limb. It arched upward and crashed down right into the center of the palmetto clump.

Nothing happened for a moment more, and then they heard a rustling sound, as if something were crawling. Then a black head peeked through a frond.

The Negro crawled forward slowly, watching the dogs, his eyes pure terror. He glanced upward and saw the rifle pointing at him, and then he said, "Don't shoot me, mister. And call off them critters. I don't mean no harm." His voice trembled as he spoke.

Tobias and Zech were both so surprised they did nothing but stare. Finally Tobias said, "Get the dogs away from him, Zech. Make them hush up."

Zech called the dogs to him and held them as Tobias dismounted, the rifle still in his hand. He said, "Fellow, what the hell you doing hiding in there? I could have shot in there blind and killed you."

"The dogs," the Negro said, his voice still shaky. "They got to me before I could go up a tree, and there wad'n no where else for me to go. I thought they was wolves."

"They do favor a mite," Tobias said. "But they won't hurt you now. You can come out of there. We don't aim to do you any harm."

When the Negro stood up he was even taller than Tobias, at least six and a half feet, and his forearm was as large as Tobias' thigh. He was dressed in a tattered blue shirt and had on a pair of pants that seemed to have been made from a feed sack. He appeared to be about the same age as Tobias, and he was the blackest Negro Tobias had ever seen. When he spoke, his white teeth gleamed like elephant ivory.

He said, "You ain't got a little scrap of food, has you? I ain't et since day befo' yesterday."

"Don't have nothing here," Tobias said, "but there's vittles back at the house. We'll be glad to feed you. Where'd you come from, anyway?"

"Just to the south of Tallahassee."

"Tallahassee?" Tobias repeated. "You mean you walked slam down here from Tallahassee?"

"Sho' did. I been driftin' now for nigh on a year. I been shot at and stomped and chased by dogs, but this the first time I been treed by wolves."

"They ain't wolves," Zech said, listening curiously. "They's dogs."

"Well, you could 'a fooled me. I would have swore fo' God they was wolves."

Tobias said, "I'm Tobias MacIvey, and this is my boy, Zech. Who be you?"

"Skillit."

"Your name's Skillit?"

"That's all I ever been knowed as. Skillit."

"Well, Skillit, I sure would like to hear what you've got to say for yourself. But I know you're about to starve, so let's go to the house and see to your belly first. We'll talk later."

"That would sho' be fine. But just don't let them wolves get to me."

"They ain't wolves," Zech said again. "They's dogs. Their names are Nip and Tuck. And they can catch any cow you ever seen."

"I just bet they can," Skillit said. "And any nigger too."

Tobias watched the Negro as he wolfed down the bowl of stewed squash and then chomped a fried coon leg, bone and all. Emma watched too, thinking that he was about the hungriest man she had ever seen. She said, "Would you like more squash? That's the last piece of coon meat till I cook some more."

"I sho' would, missus. I'd be right proud to et another bowl. You be's a fine cook, a fine one."

Tobias said, "Soon as I get a smokehouse built I aim to shoot a cow. Fresh meat wouldn't keep no time at all in this heat. We'll have beef soon as I'm done with the smokehouse."

"I ain't never et a smoked cow," Skillit said, stuffing his mouth with squash. "Only hog. And not much of that. Sow belly mostly."

"It's right good," Tobias said. "I smoked one once before when we lived up in the scrub."

Zech said, "You ride a horse? I bet you ain't never seen a horse like Ishmael. He's a marshtackie."

"I've rid plenty of them," Skillit said. "And mules too. When I was a boy I used to ride a goat. Turn your back on him, he'd knock you over a fence."

Zech was fascinated by the black man. He said, "You been a slave?"

"Zech!" Emma snapped. "Why you ask him a question like that?"

"It's all right, missus. I been that too. I was born on a plantation in Georgia. My daddy and my grandaddy was slaves. When I was four years old I was sold to a man at Tallahassee and went to the farm there.

I guess I'd still be a slave had'n been for the war."

"What happened to you after the war?" Tobias asked.

"When the war ended they said all us niggers was free, and we could do whatever we wanted. Some folks went up North, and some stayed where they was. I claimed me a little piece of land and built me a cabin on it, and then I started to farm. Had a fine garden. Wad'n long after that that some men come to the house one night. Said they didn't want no nigger buildin' a house or runnin' a farm. They was all dressed in white sheets and had hoods over their faces. I told them I was supposed to be free and I didn't see how a garden could hurt nobody. They rawhided me good, whupped me like I ain't never been whupped befo'; then they tromped down my garden with their horses, and set fire to the cabin. Ever since then I been driftin' south, sleepin' wherever I could, and stealin' chickens when I could find one. I guess someday I got to find me a place and stop."

"They whup you with a whip?" Zech asked.

"They sho' did."

"We got a whip that kills rabbits and squirrels and coons and rattlers too. You want to see it?"

"Zech!" Emma said again. "He don't want to see no whip. Hush up now, and let Skillit talk. We want to hear."

"That's about the end of it," Skillit said. "I guess I should 'a turned north 'stead of south. They don't seem to be nothin' down here but woods and swamps. You the first white folks ever give me a meal."

"Where will you go from here?" Tobias asked.

"Don't know. Don't even know where I'm at now."

"So far as I know there ain't nothing in the far south but swamp and Indians," Tobias said. "I've never met a white man who's been there. It was Indians from down there who gave us the marshtackie and dogs. They was Seminoles."

"How come they do that?" Skillit asked.

"We done them a favor once. I got a idea, Skillit. Why don't you stay on here for a while? You would be a big help to me and Zech. We couldn't pay you nothing, 'cause we ain't got nothing. But we could build you a little cabin to stay in. The garden ought to come in soon, and if you help me with the smokehouse, we'll kill us a cow."

"You mean you'd let me stay here?" Skillit asked, not sure he was hearing what Tobias said.

"What do you say, Emma?" Tobias asked.

"It's fine with me. He would be a big help to you and Zech. And it's just as easy to cook for four as three. It won't be no bother at all."

"Will you stay?" Tobias asked.

"I sho' will!" Skillit said, grinning and flashing the ivory teeth. "I's awful tired of driftin'. I'm beholdin' to you, Mistuh Tobias! And to you, Missus Emma! I never knowed them wolves was doin' me such a favor by putting me in them bushes."

"They ain't wolves," Zech said. "They's dogs." Then he turned to Tobias and said, "Can Skillit ride your horse, Pappa? I found a eagle nest down by the river, and I want to show it to him. It's got babies in it. Can he, Pappa?"

"He can ride whenever he wants."

Zech jumped up and said, "Come on, Skillit! But you better watch that ole big horse. He ain't no marshtackie. He runs straight, and if you don't watch him he'll knock you off on a tree."

When he reached the door Skillit turned and said, "Soon's we're back we'll start on that smokehouse, Mistuh Tobias. It won't take us no time at all to build one. No time at all."

Zech grabbed his arm and pulled him out the door, saying, "Come on, Skillit! Come on!"

Tobias and Emma were both smiling.

TWELVE

A thin spiral of smoke drifted upward as Tobias put on more wood and placed the branding iron on the fire. Zech and Skillit stood just outside the gate, waiting for the iron to get hot.

Inside the pen, six cows milled about, poking their huge horns at the rails, trying to find a weak spot in the fence. Nip and Tuck were lying under a huckleberry bush, panting from the heat.

Tobias said, "It's ready now. Zech, you do the tying when Skillit gets one on the ground."

"Don't need no rope," Skillit said. "That just take up more time. You just stand back out of the way, Mistuh Zech. Let me handle it."

Skillit was shirtless, and his black skin glistened with sweat. Summer was boring in now with its full fury, and it seemed that even the water of the river was warm.

When Tobias came over to the pen Skillit went inside and grabbed a cow by the horns. In one quick motion he had it on the ground and was on top of it. Muscles became taut in his arms and back as the bull struggled uselessly. Tobias pushed the branding iron to flesh, then Skillit released it and grabbed another one. In an instant the cow was on the ground and the iron made its mark again.

Tobias said, "Lordy, Skillit, with you here we can brand as many cows in a half hour as it used to take me and Zech a week. You're the strongest man I ever seen."

"It ain't nothin' workin' these little ole runty cows. I could down a mule if'n I had to."

As soon as the branding was finished, the cows were turned loose. Tobias said, "That's about enough for today. It's too hot to do this. Let's go on back and finish your cabin."

Skillit picked up his shirt and said, "Mister Tobias, what you gone ever do with all these cows? You can't et all of them, not even with someone around with a belly like mine."

Tobias scratched his head. "You know, I ain't never thought of that. Me and Zech stayed so busy trying to catch one and put on a mark, I never put no mind to what I'd do if we did catch it. I been told that come spring we ought to round them up and let them graze as a herd on the prairie. They sure don't seem to gain no weight in these woods. After that I guess we ought to sell them sommers. They ain't worth a red cent to us roaming the woods. But I don't rightly know where to take them for the selling."

"Place where I stayed had a lot of cattle. During the war they all went to the soldiers, but they sho' ain't no Confederate army around no more to buy 'em."

"Next time I go to the trading post I'll ask Elias Thompson. He ought to know. But they sure don't put nothing in your pocket like this. We need to get us some cash money."

"What's that?" Skillit asked, grinning. "In all my life I ain't never had even a single coin of my own. I guess you done noticed these cracker sack britches ain't got no pockets."

"You will," Tobias said. "We'll just keep on marking like we got good sense. It ain't costing us nothing to brand them."

They were about halfway to the clearing when a shrill tooting sound came from the direction of the river. Zech stopped his horse and said, "What's that, Pappa? I ain't never heard no bull holler like that."

"I'd say it's a steam whistle," Tobias said. "I ain't heard a sound like that since we left Georgia."

"I've heard it before," Skillit said. "Trains up to Tallahassee made that sound when they wanted to run cows off the tracks."

"Well, there ain't no train out there coming through the woods," Tobias said, "so it must be on the river. Elias Thompson told me he heard the boats was going to run the river again down to Okeechobee. That must be one of them. He said they might want to buy stuff or trade. Let's go and see."

The whistle blew again just as they reached the river, then the boat came into view. It was a stern-wheeler, forty feet long, with black smoke boiling from its one stack. The deck was crowded with crates, and a sign across the wheelhouse said MARY BELLE.

Tobias jumped up and down, waving his arms and shouting as the boat came abreast of them. Then the stern-wheel was reversed, sending bubbling brown water rushing beneath the boat and into the bank. The boat stopped slowly, backed up, and turned into the bank.

A man came out to the rail and shouted, "What is it? You want passage down to Okeechobee?"

"No," Tobias answered. "You want to buy something, or trade?"

"What you got?"

"What you want?"

"Damn, fellow!" the man shouted. "You stop us for a fool question like that? You got something to sell, say it!"

Tobias said, "We got beef."

"What kind?"

"Cows."

The man shook his head, exasperated. "All beef is cows! Are you talking about them wild swamp critters?"

"We catch 'em in the swamp."

"Hell no! I don't want none of the scrawny yellowhammers! They don't even make good soup. You got deer?"

"We could."

"Pay you three cents a pound, dressed. But it's got to be fresh killed. If it ain't, you can just feed it to the buzzards. We'll be back by here three days from now."

"How about 'gator hides?" Tobias asked.

"Two bucks each if they're big enough."

"Coons?"

"Twenty five cents a hide."

"That the best you can do?"

"Damn!"

Just then the whistle shrieked loudly, causing both horses to buck. The man shouted, "We ain't got all day, you idiot! You got something to sell, be back here in three days!" Then the boat pulled away from the bank and continued downstream.

"Seemed to be a mite riled up, didn't he?" Tobias said.

"I guess," Skillit said, trying to calm the horse.

"They must be a hundred 'gators in that big pond down by the hickory flat," Tobias said. "We get 'em all, that's more money than I ever seen."

"Could be," Skillit said. "But a 'gator don't part with his hide easy. Don't count yo' money yet."

Zech said, "Pappa, why don't me and Skillit ride back to the woods and see if we can find deer signs? We'll be back to the clearing real soon."

"While you do that I'll go on to the house and tell Emma. That whistle probably scared her real good."

Tobias watched as Skillit mounted the horse. He said, "You know, Skillit, it's a good thing we got that big ole army horse. You get on one of them marshtackies your feet would drag the ground."

"That's the God's truth," Skillit said. "That little hoss ain't made fo' a big nigger like me. I'd as soon ride that goat I had when I was a boy."

"We find a deer trail you want us to put Nip and Tuck on it?" Zech asked.

"Nope. You heard the man say it has to be fresh killed. I ain't wasting a bullet on buzzard bait. We'll go after a 'gator first."

They set out for the pond early the next morning, Tobias and Zech on the horses and Skillit following, carrying an axe, a six-foot cypress pole, and a length of rope. Just past the hickory flat they tied the horses to a bush and walked the remaining distance. Nip and Tuck had been left behind at the house for fear they would strike the scent of a cow and go after it alone.

The bank of the pond was covered thickly with button bush and pickerel weed, but on the south side a mud flat formed an open area that ran forty feet out into the water. A fallen cypress limb to the left of the flat was covered solidly with turtles, and at the sound of approaching footsteps, they rolled over sideways and splashed into the water.

Six alligators were lying on the flat, motionless, their jaws cocked open. They paid no heed as the two men and a boy came to within thirty feet of them and stopped. If they were even aware of the intruders, they did not show it.

Skillit said, "How we going to go about this, Mistuh Tobias? I ain't never even tried to kill a 'gator."

"Me neither. But it appears they're sleeping. That ought to make it easy."

For a few moments they just looked, and then Tobias said, "We'll try the one nearest to us. Ease in there, Skillit, and bash him on the head with that pole. Then me and Zech will come in and help pull him out."

"Are you sho' about this?" Skillit asked. "What if he don't bash? He got a mighty hard lookin' head to me."

"That pole could knock down a bull. Just give him a good one."

Skillit eased forward, and when he stepped out onto the flat, his feet sank down into the mud. He took two more steps forward, each time making a sucking sound with his shoes; then suddenly the alligators started hissing.

Skillit looked back and said, "What I do now? Them things is givin' me a warnin', like a rattlesnake."

"They ain't even looking at you," Tobias said. "That hissing don't mean nothing. They can't bite you with their heads turned away from you."

As Skillit took another step forward, the hissing grew louder. The alligators were sideways to him, still motionless. He pulled one foot from the muck and leaped forward as best he could, lifting the pole above his head. Before he could start the downswing, the nearest alligator whirled around quickly and charged, its massive jaws snapping wildly. The pole came down and hit the alligator on top of its head, then it bounced away, ricocheting off the fallen cypress tree and landing in the water ten feet beyond.

Skillit fell backward into the mud and rolled over. He struggled free just as the alligator's jaws snapped to within a foot of his face. Then he scrambled up the bank and ran back to Tobias and Zech.

"I told you!" he exclaimed excitedly. "I done told you them things don't part with their hides easy! What we gone do now?"

Three of the alligators pushed off into the water and swam away. One of the remaining ones was still hissing, and the other two became silent again.

"I guess I'll just have to shoot one," Tobias said. "He can't bounce off a bullet like he did that pole." He took the rifle from its holster and came closer to the flat. "I best hit him halfway up from his tail, around where the heart ought to be. If I hit him in the snout it probably wouldn't do nothing but make him mad."

Tobias aimed carefully and fired. The alligator jumped two feet sideways and lay still as the other two scrambled into the water.

"Let's just stay back a minute and see if he moves," Tobias said.

They continued to watch, and then Tobias said, "He's dead for sure. Let's go in and get him, Skillit. Zech, you stay up here out of the way."

As they started across the flat Tobias said, "I'll get the tail and you get his head. The way he's lying, we'll have to pull him out sideways."

Skillit had just reached the head when Tobias grabbed the tail and jerked it. The huge tail lashed out like a whip, striking Tobias in the side. He landed six feet out in the water and went under. The 'gator then whirled around, jaws snapping, and caught the bottom of Skillit's pants in its teeth. Skillit kicked frantically, trying to break free, shouting, "Oh Lordy! Oh Lordy!"

Tobias came up spitting water, and then he managed to shout, "Get the gun, Zech! Shoot him! In the head, Zech! Shoot!"

Zech scrambled for the rifle as Skillit's pants were jerked off, making flapping sounds as the 'gator swished its head from side to side, popping the cloth in the air.

Zech aimed quickly and fired, and was knocked flat on his back. The alligator pumped blood from a hole directly between the eyes. He bucked up and down for a moment and then became still.

Tobias and Skillit scrambled up the bank simultaneously. Skillit said, "That son of a bitch done tore up my britches, Mistuh Tobias! What I gone do? That the only pair I got!"

"Emma can patch 'em," Tobias said, still spitting water. "Don't worry about it. You all right, Zech?"

"I'm O.K., Pappa. It just knocked the breath out of me."

"You ready to try again?" Tobias said to Skillit. "We done come too far to quit now. Let's get him out and see can we skin out the hide. And we can get your pants out of his mouth."

"I guess," Skillit said without enthusiasm. "But I tell you the truth, Mistuh Tobias, this ain't worth no two dollars. I'd as soon skin out eight coons or shoot a buck. I don't want no more truck with them 'gators."

"Might be best we stick with coons," Tobias said. "I'm a bit shook up myself. Tomorrow morning we'll let them 'gators be and try to kill us a deer and a few coons."

THIRTEEN
Spring
1867

The holding pen was built just past the edge of the woods, at the point where forest ends and prairie begins. Inside there were one hundred forty-eight cows, all with the MCI brand.

Zech put his hand on the gate latch and shouted, "You ready, Pappa?"

"Let 'em go!"

Zech threw open the gate and one cow ambled out slowly, then a few others followed and milled about. Others stayed inside, swishing their tails and bobbing their horns.

Tobias shouted, "Don't get in front of them, nobody! And don't push! Just let 'em eat and we'll follow!"

Tobias and Zech then mounted their horses, standing ready to rush after strays. Skillit was on the wagon seat with Emma beside him, and Nip and Tuck were off to the right, looking bewildered, waiting for something to happen.

The horse pulling the wagon was tall and black, with rib and hip bones showing beneath its hide. Tobias had been at the Fort Capron trading post when a man from St. Louis came through with a string of thirty ex-army horses. He purchased one for twenty dollars, knowing the old nag wasn't worth it but hoping he could fatten it on prairie grass and bring back some of its strength. He had to have something to pull the wagon on their first summer grazing drive and this was the best he could do.

They worked steadily for months selling hides and deer meat to the river boat, and after purchasing the horse, Tobias had enough left for a three-gallon cast iron cooking pot, two cowhide whips, salt and flour, and a used tarpaulin for the wagon. There still was no Dutch oven.

Zech had visions of following a thundering herd across the prairie, cracking his whip constantly, riding wildly as he forced escaping cows back into the herd; but by now a noon sun was directly overhead and the cows were still within a hundred yards of the pen, grazing contentedly. The wagon stood ready, but the wheels had not turned even one spoke.

Tobias rode up to Skillit and said, "Kinda slow, ain't it?"

"Sho' is. But this pore old hoss is glad of it. I'm gone turn him loose now and let him eat. If them cows decides to move, I'll hitch him up again."

Tobias said, "It's best we keep heading south. Over to the east, along the coast, there's too much palmetto and rattlers. Them snakes was thick as skeeters last time I was over there."

Emma adjusted her bonnet and said, "There ought to be some shade out here sommers. The sun is really coming down on me just sitting here like this. There's not even a breeze like back in the hammock."

"You get too tired go in the wagon and rest. The tarp will keep the sun off."

"I tried that, and it's hotter than an oven in there. I wish the cows would do something so we could move about some."

The afternoon drifted by slowly, and by sundown they had moved less than two miles. Skillit pulled the wagon to the edge of a cypress stand, unhitched the horse and started a fire. Then he cut thin poles, gathered palm fronds and built a lean-to where he and Zech would sleep. Tobias and Emma would share the wagon.

Emma made a stew of smoked beef and onions, and she baked sweet potatoes in the edge of the coals. There was still no coffee, but she boiled hot tea from sassafras roots and sweetened it with cane syrup.

They ate from tin plates and then sat by the fire, deciding who would stand first watch. Someone would circle the herd all night, changing guard every four hours.

It was decided that Zech would go first when there was less chance of danger. Skillit said to him, "Mistuh Zech, when you come in tonight, be real careful befo' you lie down to sleep. And in the mornin', look real good befo' you make a sudden move. I knowed a man who slept one night on the prairie, and the next mornin' he grabbed a boot and slapped it on without lookin' first. They was a rattler in the bottom of it. His leg swelled up big as a tree trunk, and he like to have died. You be real careful. Them snakes sho' love to crawl in and sleep with people."

"Lordy, Skillit," Emma exclaimed, her eyes widening, "can they climb wagon wheels too?"

"I've seen 'em go up a tree easy as nothin'. You best look in yo shoes too."

Emma shuddered, "I'll sleep with them on!"

Tobias said, "Skillit, you're going to spook Emma before we even get started. Let's worry about keeping the cows in a bunch and forget the snakes. If one comes in the wagon I'll know what to do."

"Yes sir, Mistuh Tobias," Skillit said, grinning, "just like you knows how to hit a 'gator on the head with a cypress pole."

Tobias laughed, and then he said, "Before anybody goes on watch we ought to work out a signal. If there's trouble, and you need help, crack your whip three times real fast. Three cracks and we'll come to you quick as we can. And if the cows break and run for any reason, get out of the way. I've seen what they can do when they stampede. You understand me, Zech?"

"Yes, Pappa. I'll get out of the way. But if they run off in the dark, how we going to ever find them?"

"We will. They can't hide on the prairie. Just don't do something foolish. It ain't worth it."

Nothing happened during Zech's watch, and at ten o'clock he rode in and was relieved by Skillit. An hour later the cry of a wolf came from about a mile away. It was answered immediately by Nip and Tuck, and before the sound could spook the cows, the dogs raced around them, nipping legs, forcing them to remain in a circle. Then they stopped and sat alert, waiting anxiously for the cry to come again so they could go after it; but it was heard no more.

A full moon bathed the prairie when Tobias rode out to the herd. Cabbage palms stood like silent sentinels in the distance, and cypress stands were dark silhouettes on a sea of yellow. The quiet land seemed awesome, too vast for any man to ever conquer. Animals could survive its hazards, but Tobias wondered if he could.

He also wondered if he were being foolish, taking the advice of an Indian he really hardly knew, leaving the relative safety of his hidden hammock and following cattle into the unknown. But the cows did not grow in the swamp, and even the boatmen didn't want them. Out here there was grass to fatten them and ready them for market, and they would be worth something someday. He did not want to go on forever skinning coons and killing deer and growing just enough vegetables to survive. And this was apparently the only way out of the trap.

But what worried him most was Emma. He did not know what hardships lay ahead for her, things he and Zech and Skillit could overcome easily but would be an ordeal for her. Drifting a prairie was not exactly a woman's way of life. But she had to come along, for leaving her alone in the hammock was unthinkable. There was safety in numbers, safety from predators and from the bands of men Thompson said were roaming the countryside. He hoped that this wandering life would be uneventful, but one thing he knew: she would not complain, and no matter what came their way, she would have the strength to face it.

They followed the herd southward for a month, sometimes moving several miles in a day, other times not moving at all. The cows grew larger each day, and even their hides took on a sleek luster. Tobias swore he could actually see them put on weight with each mouthful of grass they swallowed. Even the old nag horse seemed to thrive on the rich prairie and grow stronger.

Several times they passed within sight of wild herds, some of them five times larger than the one they tended. But they did not go after them. Tobias thought it would be too much for the three of them to handle. It would take more men and more horses to capture and brand cows in such large numbers, and his mind was already searching for a way to hire drovers to join his little band.

One night when they were eating supper Zech said, "Pappa, who owns all this land out here?"

Tobias wondered why a boy Zech's age would even ask such a question. He said, "The Lord."

"You reckon He would give us some of it?"

"You've got it now. You can roam it wherever you please. The Lord put it here for everybody."

"But what if somebody else comes here besides us with a herd? How could we keep the cows apart?"

"It's big enough for everyone. There ain't enough cows and people in the whole world to fill it up."

Zech then said, "Skillit told me that the place where he was a slave was owned by a man. He owned all the land and nobody else couldn't come on it. If we owned the land we could put a fence around it, like the pen we built, and then we wouldn't have to follow the cows. We could just turn 'em loose 'cause they couldn't get out."

"That's foolish boy talk," Tobias said. "Nobody will ever fence this land. There's too much of it. This right here ain't a drop in the bucket. There ain't no man ever even seen all of it. The Lord put it here for everyone to use."

Emma was listening. She said, "Somebody might own it someday, Tobias. All the land in Georgia is owned. You know that."

"A man would have to be a fool to buy something he can use for nothing," Tobias replied. "This ain't Georgia. There they farm the land, here they don't. This land ain't worth nothing except to graze cows. The whole place is wilderness. Georgia ain't."

Tobias then changed the subject. "Speaking of cows, it's about time I found out what to do with the ones we got. I figure we're probably out to the west of Fort Pierce by now. In the morning I'm going to ride over to the east and find it. Somebody there will know about the market."

"Will you be gone long?" Emma asked.

"Not more than a day and a night. It couldn't be far to the coast. But I got to find out where we can sell the cows."

"If you find lard, buy some. We don't have any more, and I can't make biscuits without it."

There were orange groves on the outskirts, and a dirt road ran past them and into the village of Fort Pierce. There was no activity on the sultry streets as Tobias walked the horse slowly, going past a dock where a coastal schooner was being loaded, then coming to a barnlike building with a sign: GENERAL MERCHANDISE. After tying his horse to a rail, he went inside.

The store was deserted except for a man sitting beside the counter, swatting flies with a matted palm fan. He said to Tobias, "Flies gets bad this time of year. Skeeters too. Sometimes I wish they'd go after each other."

"You got lard?" Tobias asked.

"How much you want?"

"A bucket."

The man went behind the counter and brought out a one-gallon can. "Twenty-five cents. Be anything else?"

"You got a Dutch-oven?"

"Nope. But I got some frying pans."

"I got a frying pan." Tobias sniffed the air. "Is that coffee I smell?"

"Sure is. Just ground a fresh batch. It came in on the schooner yesterday."

"How much is it?"

"Dollar for a five-pound bag."

"I'll take it. And a coffee pot too if you got one."

The man went to a shelf and returned with a tin coffee pot. "Dollar-fifty for both."

As Tobias was counting out the money, he said, "What they do with them oranges I seen coming here?"

"Ship 'em up north on the schooner. And some goes up the inland waterway to Jacksonville on them little boats."

"How much they sell for?"

"Bringing five cents a hundred-pound weight right now. Man can make a good living with oranges. In a good season you can clear up to three dollars a tree. And they're going to be worth more than that. It's a smart move to plant a grove."

"I just might do that."

The man put all of Tobias' purchases into a brown paper sack. "Anything else now?"

"Just some information. You know anything about selling cattle?"

"Right smart. A man in my business has to keep up with things. What you want to know?"

"Where to sell them."

"You got a herd?"

"Yes. Out on the prairie west of here."

"Well, there ain't no market for cows in Fort Pierce except a few at a time to the butcher shop. If you sell them out there on the prairie you'll get about four dollars a head tops. Best place to sell now is over on the west coast. The Cuba trade is getting real good again. You take them over there to a shipping point you'll get a least twelve dollars a head, maybe more."

"Where over there?"

"Best place is Punta Rassa. And they're shipping out of Tampa too."

"Where's Punta Rassa?"

"Down south of Fort Myers."

"Where's Fort Myers?"

The man gave Tobias a penetrating look. "I tell you what you ought to do, fellow. You got a herd, point it straight west. When you come to a big body of water, that will be the Gulf of Mexico. You can turn right or left. If you turn right, sooner or later you'll come to Tampa, unless you go past it and end up in Pensacola. If you turn left, you'll come to Fort Myers or Punta Rassa. If you miss both of them, you're headed for Key West. But it's a long swim down there."

Tobias picked up the sack and said, "I thank you for the information." Then he walked out.

During the ride back to join the herd his mind was calculating figures. Four dollars a head for one hundred forty-eight cows was more money than he had ever seen or hoped to see. With that he could buy Emma a wood stove instead of a Dutch oven. And many other things too. But twelve dollars a head boggled his imagination and was beyond comprehension. And all that additional money just to drive the cattle over to a place called Punta Rassa, a thing he and Zech and Skillit could do easily. He could see visions of someday soon hiring drovers and moving herds ten times as large as his present one, masses of cows all cutting a trail to Punta Rassa.

When he found the herd it was late afternoon and they had already made camp for the night. Emma was by a fire cooking supper, and Zech and Skillit were out with the cows.

Tobias tied the horse to a wagon wheel as Emma said, "Did you get the information you wanted?"

"Sure did. And the lard too." He took the can from the sack and handed it to her.

"That's good. I'll make biscuits for supper. I know Zech and Skillit are hungry."

"There's more too," Tobias said teasingly. "Turn your head and close your eyes."

When he put the sack beneath her nose she sniffed and then cried, "Coffee! You got coffee!"

"And a pot to make it in."

"I'll go now and fill it with water," she said eagerly. "Then you can sit and watch as it boils. I bet the smell will bring Skillit in. Zech won't know what it is."

As soon as the pot was bubbling Tobias poured a tin cup of the steaming liquid and sipped slowly. "Coffee and biscuits at the same time," he moaned. "It's been a long time, Emma."

Zech and Skillit rode in and tied their horses, and Skillit said immediately, "Do I smell what I think I smell?"

"What you think you smell?" Tobias asked.

"Coffee?"

"Sure is. And it's ready now. Pour out a cup."

Skillit picked up the pot and said, "A voice been tellin' me all day something good was goin' to happen to ole Skillit. And now it's come to pass. Praise the Lord!"

Emma turned from the cooking pot and said, "What did you find out about the cattle, Tobias? With all the excitement about the coffee I forgot to ask."

"How would you like to see a place called Punta Rassa?"

"Where's that?" Zech asked.

"Over on the west coast, clear across the state. They're buying cows there now for Cuba, at twelve dollars a head. As soon as our cows hit about five hundred pounds each we're heading west. I figure it ought not to be more than three weeks, maybe less."

"Punta Rassa," Emma repeated. "That's a pretty name. Does it mean anything?"

"It means twelve dollars a cow, and we got a hundred and forty-eight of them. I can't even figure that high."

"I'll go out there and make them ole cows eat faster," Zech said. "I want to go now. How far is it, Pappa?"

"Don't know. But it's over there. All we got to do is head west."

FOURTEEN

It was mid-afternoon in the middle of the next week when the sky in the east turned solid black. Clouds boiled like smoke and inched upward, blocking out more and more blue; and an increasing wind rattled the fronds of cabbage palms and shook the palmetto clumps.

Streaks of lightning flashed downward and then turned horizontal, forming fingers that ran crazily for a moment and disappeared into the earth. The boom of thunder broke the stillness of the prairie and caused great flights of egrets to rise upward and move away to the west.

Tobias rode up to the wagon and said to Skillit, "Must be a storm coming from out over the ocean. Looks to be a good one. This thunder keeps up, the cows is liable to run in four directions all at the same time."

"You want me to unhitch from the wagon and ride herd with you and Zech?"

"You best do that till we see what this storm is going to do. We might need your help. Are you all right, Emma?"

"I'm fine. I'll stay with the wagon till it blows past. Then we can make camp and have supper."

Soon the sky overhead was black too, and the winds increased to a steady howl, bending the prairie grass flat against the ground and filling the air with dead fronds from palm trees. Skillit rode up to Tobias and said, "Just look at that, Mistuh Tobias. I ain't never seen anything like it, and I sho' don't like the looks of it."

Droves of small animals – foxes, rabbits, raccoons – were running together, enemies no longer, moving rapidly westward; and deer bounded across the land, leaping bushes as they rushed past the smaller animals and disappeared.

They rode around and around the herd, trying to hold in the frightened cattle, and even the horses became skittish and whinnied nervously. Nip and Tuck worked full speed as they went after cow after cow that broke free and tried to run away.

The first pelts of wind-driven rain stung like bees as they slashed into Tobias' face. All light was vanishing rapidly, giving the prairie the yellowish look of late sundown.

Tobias turned one cow with his whip as Skillit galloped up to him and said, "What we goin' to do, Mistuh Tobias? We can't hold the cows no longer. There just ain't no way we can do it."

"We got to try," Tobias said. "They'll be ready to start to Punta Rassa by next week. If they run now as scared as they are, they'll be scattered all over hell and back come morning. Tell Zech to go and see to Emma. Me and you and the dogs will try."

As Skillit rode off, the rain came in a blinding sheet, obscuring cows, hammocks and sky. Tobias rode back in the direction of the wagon, groping slowly, feeling the wind knock the horse sideways and cause it to stumble.

When he finally found the wagon, both Skillit and Zech were there. The dogs were tied to a wheel and were huddled beneath the wagon floor, whimpering. The tarpaulin top popped constantly, sounding louder than cracking whips.

Skillit came close to Tobias and said, "This marsh is the lowest land we been on since we started the drive. There ain't no place for the water to run off. If it keeps on rainin' like this the whole place goin' turn to a lake."

"I know," Tobias agreed. "But we can't turn back now. It's too late. It's ten miles back to higher ground, and we'd never make it."

Skillit pointed south and said, "Yesterday afternoon when I scouted ahead I seen a Indian mound, right over yonder. We go there, we be out of the water. It's only a mile. We can look for the cows tomorrow."

"Hitch Ishmael to the wagon too and we'll make a run for it. You take my horse and lead the way. I'll throw the dogs in there with Emma and Zech."

Both horses strained to their limit as the wagon inched slowly across the soggy ground. Wind gusts hitting the tarp almost turned the wagon over before they took it off; then all protection for Emma and Zech was gone.

The mound loomed above them just before they became engulfed in total darkness. A few minutes more and it would have blended black into black and become impossible to find. They tried to drive the wagon up the slope but the horses slipped and fell backward. Finally they unhitched them and led them upward to the flat top.

The mound was fifty feet across and covered with dwarf cypress. They tied the horses and dogs and then huddled together, linking their arms and bracing themselves against the runty trees. By now the rain was not rain but solid water, tons of wind-driven water that felt like a river rushing over them. It poured into their eyes and noses, almost suffocating them, causing them to gasp for breath and hold their hands against their faces in hope of relief.

The storm raged unabated for eight hours; three hours before dawn it returned from solid water to a torrential downpour. When a faint light finally broke the darkness, the rain still came down with such force as to limit vision to less than fifty yards.

Tobias felt around him and touched flesh; then he said, "Emma. Are you all right, Emma? Zech? Skillit? Is everybody here?" He opened his eyes but his sight was blurred by the night of pounding water.

Emma said feebly, "I'm not sure. I've never been so soaked. I feel like my skin is washed off."

"I'm fine, Pappa," Zech said. "But I need to check on Ishmael. I hope he ain't floated off."

Skillit stirred and said, "I knows now how it feels to be a ole catfish. That storm must a went right up the coast. If we'd been in the center of it, it would of blowed us off here like leaves."

"It was bad enough," Tobias said, pushing himself to his feet. He walked to the edge of the mound and looked downward, seeing solid water. Only the tip of the wagon seat was visible.

In another hour the rain slackened to a drizzle, and they all looked out over a vast lake stretching as far as they could see. The water had come eight feet up the side of the mound.

Emma said, "The wagon, Tobias. Everything in it is gone. It's all ruined. The salt and the flour and the coffee and the lard. Everything."

"The cows too," Tobias said. "Ain't no way they could have got out of that alive. They done all ended up as buzzard meat."

"Maybe the Lord didn't mean for us to own them," Emma said, brushing her eyes. "Maybe He means for them to be wild and free, like the deer and the birds."

"This ain't the Lord's doing," Tobias said. "It was only a storm. We'll start again, but I'm damned if I'll spend another year popping cows out of swamps one at a time. This time we'll find a better way to do it."

"The horses is O.K., Pappa," Zech said. "And the dogs too. But they seem to be powerful hungry."

"We're all going to be hungry before we get out of this. Our bellies has rumbled before and we got through it, and we'll do it again. Soon as the water goes down we'll start out of here. It's going to take more than a storm to keep me from Punta Rassa. And that's the God's truth, so help me. We're going to see Punta Rassa."

Tobias then turned to Skillit and said, "Are you still with us, Skillit? You want to try again, or have you had enough by now?"

"I ain't goin' nowhere but with you, Mistuh Tobias. This is the onliest family I ever had, and ain't no storm goin' take it away from me. I'm ready whenever you are."

FIFTEEN
Spring
1868

Tobias stood by the corral gate, listening to the popping of whips far in the distance. Then came a faint sound like the drone of bees, and he felt a trembling in the ground. He watched intensely as the tiny black specks grew larger and formed a small herd of cows thundering straight toward him. When he could see their horns point upward he opened the gate and moved off hurriedly to the side of the corral.

Zech turned at the last possible moment and just missed crashing headlong into the rails; then Ishmael started bucking and kicking, as if to show the cows who had won the race. Nip and Tuck ran around in circles, and then they plopped to the ground, panting.

Tobias came back and closed the gate. Zech and Skillit calmed their horses and dismounted. Skillit said, "Mistuh Zech, you don't quit runnin' that little hoss flat-out like that, you gone go right over a cow's back one of these days."

"He wasn't wide open," Zech said. "I let him go, he'd be a mile out in front of the cows. He just likes to run in real close and bite their hind legs, like Nip and Tuck."

Tobias was busy counting. He said, "This sure beats one-on-one in the swamp. Must be over thirty in that bunch. It pains me just to think about how we used to spend a whole day trying to catch one cow, and then most likely he'd get away. We got all we can handle now. Soon's this bunch is marked we'll round up the whole herd and pen them for a final count. Then we'll get started."

"How long you figure it take us to drive all them cows to Punta Rassa?" Skillit asked.

"Don't rightly know, but we'll do it like we done with the herd we lost, go real slow and let 'em graze on the way. Time we get there, they ought to be fattened up and in good shape."

"Well, I sho' hope we make it there this time. I get a little something to spend, I needs a new pair of britches real bad. These I got about to fall apart. They done got patches on patches, and they ain't nothing more Missus Emma can do for them. And they's something else I need to see about too."

"What's that?" Tobias asked, mildly curious.

"Best not say," Skillit replied, grinning. "They might not have none, so it best I wait and see."

"What I want is a pair of boots," Tobias said. "We sell the cows, everbody gets boots. And a Dutch oven for Emma. Or maybe one of them spank-new wood cook stoves. She ain't never had one of them. What you want, Zech?"

Zech thought for a moment, and then he said, "A sack of apples for me and Ishmael. You reckon they got apples over there, Pappa?"

"I reckon. But is that all you want?"

"Well, maybe a brush too. Then I could brush Ishmael down and make him look real shiny. He's never had a chance to look his best, and I know it would feel good to him."

"We'll do it!" Tobias said, slapping Zech on the shoulder. "We'll get it all. Britches, boots, oven, apples and brushes. And maybe whatever else it is that Skillit's got in mind. But right now we best stop spending money we ain't got and get on with the branding. And we got a few calves with this bunch. We need to get them back to the right mammy so's they can suck."

"Let's get them cows marked and them calves mammied-up!" Skillit shouted enthusiastically. "These old britches might not hold up 'till we gets to Punta Rassa. Then I'd be in a worse fix than what the ole 'gator done to me. I'd have to stay hid in the woods and miss all the fun. And I sho' wouldn't like that."

When they reached the homestead later that afternoon, Zech and
Skillit took a bundle of raccoon hides down to the river to hail one of
the boats. Another stern-wheeler had been put into service, the *Osceola*,
and they had sold the boatmen enough venison and hides to purchase
supplies for the trip to Punta Rassa.

Emmas was at the cooking pot when Tobias came inside and sat at
the table. He said to her, "You figure we got enough of everything to
make the trip? We done branded the last bunch, so we'll be ready to
leave soon."

"We can make do. You'll have to shoot meat along the way. It's
getting too hot to carry along much meat, even if it's smoked. How
long have the supplies got to last?"

"A few weeks. That time I helped drive the cows for the Confederates
we went a far piece in two weeks, and this ought not be much further."

Emma put down the spoon and sat at the table. "That's what worries
me, Tobias. When you went on that drive you were with men who had
been there before. They knew where they were going and how long it
would take. Now you don't. And there were a lot more men. Zech's
not a man, Tobias. I know he tries to act like one instead of a boy. But
he is a boy. It's really just you and Skillit."

Tobias remained silent for a moment, and then he said, "You're right,
Emma, and I know it. It worries me too. We got over seven hundred
cows, and that's more than we herded for the army with seven men.
Lord, what would the three of us do if we run into something like that
pack of wolves? But I don't know what else to do. We just got to sell
the cows. It's our only chance."

"Why don't you find some help? There must be a lot of men somewhere who need work. Didn't Mister Thompson tell you there's men
everywhere who are hungry and looking for anything to do? You could
try to get help up at Kissimmee. That's the closest place."

"He did say that. But I ain't got no money to pay drovers, and nobody
works for free."

"Pay them at the end of the drive. That would make them want to
get the herd there as much as you. If we lose the herd with just the
three of you, we end up with nothing again. Seems to me that paying
a few wages is better than risking nothing at all."

Tobias smiled. "You know, Emma, you got a heap more sense than me. This family would fall apart without you. It just might work. I can promise to pay them when I sell the cattle, and feed them along the way. If a man's hungry enough he'll go for it. It's worth a try."

Emmas was pleased that he agreed. "I just fear for the three of you trying it alone. Zech would kill himself for you if need be, but he's still just a boy."

"I'll go to Kissimmee at daybreak tomorrow. I ain't never been there but I can find it. All I got to do is follow the river. And soon as I come back with some help we'll be on our way." He took her hands in his and said, "You're the only MacIvey with brains, Emma. Except Zech. Just you and Zech. Me, I'm a dumb ole coot and I know it. I'm as dumb as that army horse, running in a straight line full speed ahead without looking where I'm going. It could get me busted wide open, and all of you too."

"That ain't so, Tobias," she said gently. "Hadn't been for you we'd still be up in Georgia, probably starved by now. Wouldn't many men strike out like you did. And like you always say, we're going to make it. Somehow. Now you just go on and look for them drovers."

Tobias followed the river hammocks until he came to Lake Kissimmee. Here he skirted the east shore and then headed through a marsh area, soon coming to two more lakes. Late in the afternoon he met a family traveling south by ox cart, and they told him it was just a few more miles into the village. He decided to make camp for the night and continue at daybreak.

The next morning he ate a sparse breakfast of smoked beef and a biscuit, saving most of his food for the drovers on the return trip. Then after a short ride he approached Kissimmee along a dirt road deeply embedded by cows' hooves.

The main street extended for two blocks and was lined with unpainted clapboard buildings containing two general stores, a small cafe, a blacksmith shop, and three saloons. Wooden benches bordered the sidewalk in front of each store, and vacant lots separating the buildings were overgrown with weeds.

Tobias first rode all the way through town and into the residential section containing a half dozen frame houses with small front porches and drawn window shades. A dog ran from one yard and barked as he passed, and in another, chickens pecked at the bare ground. This was the most houses he had seen in years, and he observed carefully the details of each, comparing them with his own homemade cabin.

When he came back into the business section, loud curses were coming from one of the saloons. He watched curiously as a lone rider rode up to a window cut into the side of the building, was handed a filled glass in exchange for a coin, drank it in one gulp and sauntered off, never dismounting his horse.

Just then a man crashed through the swinging doors and landed flat on his back in the street. He got up painfully, brushed dirt from his pants, then walked down to one of the stores and sat on a bench.

Tobias rode by slowly, studying the man out of the corner of his eye. He was around thirty, six feet tall and thin as a cypress pole, with a bushy black beard. On top of his head was a huge black felt hat covered with dust. He stared dejectedly at the ground and paid no heed as the horse passed.

At the next store Tobias dismounted, tied his horse to a rail and walked back to the man. He hesitated for a moment, not knowing how to make the approach, and then he said bluntly, "You looking for work?"

The man glanced up. "Doing what?"

"Brush popping."

"What's that?"

"Working cows. Herding."

"What do it pay?"

"Fifty cents a day plus keep. But I can't pay till I sell the cows. You got a horse?"

"Piece of one. I rode him in the army."

"Which army?"

"Reb. Do I smell like a friggin' Federal?"

"Nope. More like a skunk. When's the last time you went down to a creek and washed?"

"Don't rightly remember. Must 'a been sometime back in '65."

Tobias shifted his feet and said, "You want the job or not? I got a herd to move to Punta Rassa and I ain't got time to stand here jawing with you."

"One thing for sure. I ain't had a dollar on me in over three years. And I've et so many possums I feel like I could hang by my tail from a tree limb. When do I start?"

"I'm riding out of here just as soon as I can. I'm Tobias MacIvey. What's your name?"

"Frog."

"Frog? Frog what?"

"Just Frog. That's all the name I need. I got a buddy down the street. Can he go too?"

"Yes. I need two drovers. What's his name?"

"Bonzo."

"Lordy me," Tobias said, shaking his head. "Frog and Bonzo. This going to be some cattle crew. Go and tell him we'll leave from right here in a half hour. And both of you better be on time."

"Could I have fifty cents in advance?" Frog asked.

"What for?"

"I done been throwed out of ever saloon betwix here and Tallahassee, and I'd like to just one time have a drink and pay cash for it. That way I wouldn't end up flat on my back in the street."

"Hell no!" Tobias replied harshly. "I ain't paying my hard-earned money to put whiskey in your gut! Now you go on and fetch your buddy back here!"

"It was just a thought," Frog said, turning and walking away.

Tobias went into the store and said to the clerk, "You got cheese?"

"How much you want?"

"Two one-pound blocks. And wrap them separate."

The clerk cut two chunks from a hoop, wrapped them and handed them to Tobias. "Now what else?"

"Can you make a sign?"

"What kind of a sign?"

"A small one. About three feet long."

"Sure. We got stencils."

"How long will it take and how much will it cost?"

"Seventy-five cents, counting the board. It won't take but a couple of minutes, but you'll have to be careful with it till the paint dries. What you want it to say?"

"MacIvey Cattle Company."

"How you spell that name?"

"M-a-c-I-v-e-y."

The clerk said, "Why don't you just write it all down for me on this piece of paper and I'll copy it."

"If I could write it all down, I'd make the sign myself," Tobias said impatiently. "I can count cows and money but I ain't no good at writing. And besides, that's what I'm paying you for."

"Very well. It won't take but a minute."

As the clerk went to the back of the store Tobias said, "Punch two holes in the top of the board so's I can tie it to the side of a wagon."

While waiting he walked around the store, looking at the sparsely stocked shelves, thinking that goods here were not much more plentiful than at Fort Capron. But the emphasis here seemed to be on things needed by cattlemen.

On one counter he found a basket of pink ribbons, and when the clerk came back, he said, "How much are these?"

"Five cents each. Purty, ain't they? We got them in about a month ago but don't have much call for ribbons. Mostly men in these parts."

"I'll take one. You got a Dutch oven?"

"That I don't have."

"How much I owe?"

"All together it comes to a dollar twenty-five."

Tobias paid the bill and picked up the sign carefully so as not to smear it. He said, "Much obliged," and started out.

The clerk called after him, "Don't touch the paint for an hour. It ought to be dry by then."

Frog and Bonzo were standing in the street, holding their horses, when Tobias came from the store. He did a double take when he saw Bonzo, then he said, "You two look like twin brothers. You must be cut from the same mold."

"We ain't," Frog said. "It just appears that way. I ain't no kin to this varmint."

Tobias scratched his head. "I thought I looked like a cattail stalk, but you two are worse than me. You look like you need worming. When's the last time you et?"

"Can't say for sure," Frog said, "but right now I could eat a cut off a saddle."

"Here, take this," Tobias said, handing each of them a package. "I bought it for you." He watched as they opened the cheese and ate eagerly, then he said, "My wife's a good cook. Her name's Emma. She can make a polecat taste like ham. She'll put some meat on them bones. I got smoked beef and biscuits in the saddlebag. We'll have that for supper."

"How long it going to take to get where we're going?" Bonzo asked, stuffing his mouth.

"We'll be there in the morning. Best we take it easy on the way.

Them horses you got looks like they'd faint dead away if you put them in a trot. Bones stick out worse than on you. What they need is some good prairie grass. Let's mount up and go soon as I finish tying this sign to my saddle. You can eat on the way."

Tobias secured the board; then they mounted and rode down the dirt street. He wondered what Emma, Zech, and Skillit would do when they saw Frog and Bonzo come riding out of the woods. He felt sure that Nip and Tuck would put them up a tree.

Frog said, "Mister MacIvey, don't you worry none about these horses. They old and skinny but they tough. And me and Bonzo might look like rotten bean poles, but we're like these old nags. We knows how to hang in there. And we thank you for the cheese. You the first one who just up and give us something besides a hard time."

"Just hope you enjoyed it," Tobias said. "It might stop up your innards but it'll fill your belly for a while. We got some riding to do afore dark and the next meal."

They had ridden but three miles out of town when two men on horses came at them from both sides of the trail. Both were drunk, and each held a rifle.

One of the men said, "Just hold up there a minute, fellows. I ain't never seen nothing like the three of you. Looks like three scarecrows in a pumpkin patch. What you think we ought to do, Con?"

The other man said, "Make 'em buck dance. They'd look like skeletons on a string. You fellows know how to dance?"

Tobias looked at the rifle pointing at him and said, "I've never done much of it, but I guess I could if I had to." He could see they were drunk and wanted to humor them, hoping they would soon tire of this and ride away.

"O.K., fellows, get down off them horses and let's see what you can do."

The three dismounted and started shuffling their feet up and down, bucking around in circles. Little puffs of dust came from the ground as sweat beaded on their foreheads. One man finally said, "You can take a rest now. That ain't bad. I've seen a heap worse. You fellows could make a good living dancing in the saloons. Or maybe a circus." Both men then fell into fits of laughter.

Frog said, "That got me kind of hot. Would you fellows care to join us in some refreshments? I got a bottle in my saddlebag."

"I could sure use a snort," one man said. "That's right neighborly of you."

Frog reached in the saddlebag and pulled out an army pistol with a two-foot barrel. He pointed it upward and said, "Just put them rifles back in the holsters and come on down off there."

One man stared at the size of the pistol, and then he said, "Ah, come on, fellow. We were just funning. We didn't mean nothing by it."

"If you ain't off them horses in two seconds I'm going to blow your brains slam back to Kissimmee!"

As the men dismounted Tobias said, "Let it go, Frog. They're just drunk. It ain't worth trouble. Let's ride on away from here. We got a herd to move."

"Ain't no trouble," Frog said. "Maybe I can sober 'em up a bit. I've seen bastards like them all my life. They wasn't funning. They meant it. Next thing they'd do is ride off with everything we got, including the horses."

One man said, "What you going to do?"

"Well, first thing, take off them boots. Then all your clothes. Soon's that's done, we'll see."

Tobias watched curiously as the men removed their boots and clothes, wondering what Frog would do next.

Frog then said, "Now put the boots back on. A man needs his boots." When this was done he said, "You fellows ever seen a frog jump?"

"Yeah, we seen it."

"What I want is for you to get down on all fours, then hop like a frog from here to that tree over yonder and back. You think you can do it?"

Both men started hopping, and then Frog said, "Now ain't that a sight? Two buck naked grown men jumping around like frogs. Maybe we ought to take 'em back to Kissimmee so's everybody can see. They must be tetched, don't you think, Bonzo?"

"They's tetched for sure. And I ain't never seen such shiny butts in all my life. Looks like two big buckets of lard."

When the men came back to the horses, Frog said, "Tell you what I'm going to do, fellows. I'm going to take your horses five miles down the trail and tie them to a bush. The guns will be in the holsters. I ain't got no use for them. But I shore like the clothes. I'll just take them along with me."

"Ah hell, fellow!" one of the men snapped. "Ain't you done enough? How we going to get back into town like this?"

"That's your problem. Why don't you buckdance into town? Whatever you do will be fine with me, so we'll just ride on now and leave you to your pleasure. It was real nice making your acquaintance."

Frog mounted and took the two horses in tow. As they rode away Tobias said, "You left them in a bad fix, didn't you?"

"I ain't really going to keep their clothes. I'll leave them with the horses. But it'll sure give them something to study on for a while. I don't think they'll want to see no more buck dancing again any time soon."

Tobias grinned as he pictured again the naked men hopping over the ground. He also thought that perhaps his hiring of Frog and Bonzo wasn't too bad a choice after all.

As Tobias and the two men rode into the clearing, Emma and Zech came from the house. Tobias stopped his horse and said uncertainly, "Emma, this is Frog and Bonzo, my new drovers."

"Howdy, ma'am," they said in unison, removing their hats.

"This is my son, Zech."

"Howdy, Zech. Pleased to meet you."

They all dismounted as Emma and Zech continued to stare at the gaunt strangers. Tobias watched their reaction closely. Zech said, "What kind of horses is them?"

"Just horses," Frog responded.

"They's worse than the one Pappa bought at Fort Capron. Looks like they needs some grass."

Emma said, "Are you men hungry? I fixed a big pot of stew in case Tobias brought somebody back with him."

"They's always hungry," Tobias said. "Last night they ate everything but my saddlebag. From now on you best make stew in a wash tub instead of the cooking pot. Where's Skillit?"

"In his cabin," Zech said. "He's putting in some shelves. I'll go and get him."

Before Zech could move, Skillit came from the cabin. Frog took one look and exclaimed, "Gawd-a-mighty! Where'd you get him? That's the biggest nigger I ever seen."

"His name's Skillit," Tobias said. "He's my right-hand man. You and Bonzo can bunk in with him tonight."

"I ain't sleeping with no nigger," Bonzo said.

Tobias' eyes flashed anger. "If you ain't, then you can sleep in the woods with the snakes! And if you don't like his being here, you can get on them flea-bit nags and leave right now! You understand me?"

"Ain't no need to get riled up," Frog said quickly. "It's just that we ain't never bunked in with a nigger."

Tobias said, "Well, they's a lot of things I never done that when I finally done it, I found out it wasn't so bad after all. It might turn out to be the same with you."

"Pleased to meet you, Skillit," Frog said pleasantly, remembering what Emma said about stew. "I'm Frog, and this here is Bonzo. He didn't mean no harm by what he said. It's just that he ain't too bright. We'll all get along fine."

"Sho we will," Skillit said, towering over both of them. "You ever seen a man pick up a grown bull and hold him off the ground by his tail?"

"Can't say as I have," Frog said, again eyeing Skillit's huge body.

"Now that we got all this settled we can have some vittles," Tobias said. "And you ought to know that Skillit takes his meals at the table with us. You got any objections?"

"No, sir, we got no objections," Frog said.

Just then Nip and Tuck came running from the woods, yapping loudly. They bounded across the clearing and came straight for the two men.

Frog and Bonzo reached Skillit's cabin just ahead of the dogs and scrambled to the roof. The dogs then ran around and around the cabin and tried to climb the wall.

"I knew it!" Tobias shouted. "I just knew they'd do it! Call 'em off, Zech!"

Zech whistled, and the dogs came to him. Frog and Bonzo peeked over the edge of the roof, and Frog said "Where'd you get them damned wolves?"

"They ain't wolves," Zech said. "They's dogs. Their names are Nip and Tuck. They ain't going to hurt you. They just didn't know who you are."

"You better make an introduction afore I come down off of here," Frog said. "They done scared the livin' hell outen me."

Skillit was watching it all, grinning.

"They won't do it again," Tobias said. "Soon as they know you're part of the crew they'll like you."

Frog and Bonzo climbed down from the roof reluctantly, Frog muttering, "Damned giant nigger and a pack of wolves. . ." Then they all went into the house and took tin plates from a shelf.

Just before they went to bed that night, Tobias and Emma sat at the table alone, talking. Emma said, "Where'd you find those two, Tobias?"

"On the street in Kissimmee. But don't let their looks fool you. They're tough. I've done seen it. They'll be a big help to us."

"I'm not worried about that. It's the supplies. I've never seen men eat like them. They keep it up we'll have to kill and cook every cow we got before we reach Punta Rassa."

Tobias smiled. "It's just that they're empty right now and have been that way for a long time. They're bound to fill up soon."

"I hope so. I don't know how I could keep a cook fire going all day every day during the drive."

Tobias then took the ribbon from his pocket and held it behind him. "I bought a little something for you in Kissimmee. It ain't much, but I thought you'd like it."

When he handed it to her she said, "It's real purty, Tobias. Real purty. And I thank you. But I won't wear it myself. I'll put it away. Pink is for a baby girl. I'll save it."

Tobias felt his face flush. He reached out and touched her, and then he said, "You'll use it someday, Emma. Now that I got some help, things are going to change for us."

SIXTEEN

The line of cattle stretched out over a quarter mile, moving slowly, the men and dogs flanking the sides, the wagon in the rear. Frog told Tobias he had never been to Punta Rassa but knew of men who had, and that they should go south to Fort Basinger where there was a ferry to take the wagon across the Kissimmee River. From that point on it was unknown territory.

When they reached the fort, Tobias was charged two dollars to load the wagon on a small wooden barge that was pulled across the river by ropes. The cattle, horses and men swam, and it reminded Tobias of the time he stood on the bank of the St. Marys and watched the cows cross the water in a long black line of bobbing horns. Only this time none were lost, and there was no crowd of hungry spectators watching, hoping for a drowned cow to wash ashore.

They were two days past the river when a rider came across the plain and to the wagon. Tobias saw him speak briefly to Emma, then he rode back to meet him. The man said, "Name's Sam Lowry. Are you MacIvey?" He had seen the MacIvey Cattle Company sign on the side of the wagon.

"Tobias MacIvey."

"Where you headed?"

"Punta Rassa."

The man shifted in his saddle. "You want to buy some cows?"

"What you mean?" Tobias responded, not expecting such a question.

"I got a little spread couple of miles north of here. I seen you coming.

I farm mostly, but I got sixty-five cows. Ain't no way I can get them to market by myself, so I'll sell them to you for three dollars each. You can put 'em in with your herd."

Tobias calculated in his mind what they were said to be worth in Punta Rassa. If the market was as Thompson indicated, there would be a profit of nine dollars per cow. He said, "I don't have that much money on me. Tell you what I'll do, though. I'll take them and pay you on the way back."

"Well, I don't know about that. I wanted cash. How do I know you'll come back by here and pay me?"

"You've got the word of Tobias MacIvey," Tobias said firmly. "I've never broken my word to no man, and I'm not going to do it for sixty-five cows. When we come back I'll pay you."

"For sure they ain't doing me any good just chewing grass. You've got the look of an honest man, and your missus has too. I'll take a chance with you and do it. You want to sign some kind of a paper?"

"Don't need no paper 'less you want it. You got my word. And next time we come through with a herd I'll pay you cash for whatever you got. I'll make a stop ever time at your place."

"Sounds good enough. But we ought to at least shake on it."

Tobias clasped the man's hand. "It's did."

Frog and Bonzo rode to the homestead with Lowry and drove his cows back to the herd. This pushed the number past eight hundred.

That night after supper, Tobias was sitting in the wagon with Emma, waiting his turn for second watch. She said, "Next time we make a drive, we better bring a whole barrel of flour, or maybe a wagon load. Frog and Bonzo ate twelve biscuits each. They eat more than Skillit, and look how big he is."

"Don't seem right for a man to eat that much and stay thin as a snake. But look at me. I ain't much better. Maybe some men don't get fat no matter what they eat."

"Zech's going to be the same way. He keeps getting taller all the time but he don't have no meat on his bones. Seems I'm the only one who puts on flesh."

"You're just right," Tobias smiled, patting her shoulder. "Don't no man want to sleep with a snake. I'll take you over any skinny woman I ever seen."

"Oh, Tobias, be serious!" she said, smiling too.

Tobias then said, "You know, Emma, I been thinking about the cows we got from Lowry. They must be men scattered all over the place with small herds and no way to get them to market. We get enough cash money, I could ride ahead of the drive and buy cows for three dollars each. What we got here now ain't nothing to what we could have. We could end a drive with thousands of cows and not even have to go to the trouble of catching them."

"That's true," Emma agreed. "But when you just give your word for payment, like you did today, what will you do if we lose this herd like we did once before. How will you pay anyone?"

"That ain't likely. We're bound to get through with some of them. We got the men to do it. But if we make Punta Rassa with only sixty-five cows they belong to Lowry. I gave my word."

"Yes, you did. And I know by now how a MacIvey thinks." She took his hand and pressed it against her bosom. "If I were Lowry I would trust you."

Tobias smiled again. "It's worth thinking on, buying cows along the way. But don't do what you're doing with my hand, Emma. You're getting my furnace heated up, and I got to go on watch in a few minutes."

"Tobias!" Emma giggled, snatching his hand away. "I swan, sometimes I don't know what to make of you. We lie together in a bed in the house and you go sound asleep snoring. Then we get out here in the wilderness and you go to acting foolish like you did ten years ago."

"Like I told you, Emma, you ain't no snake. Man got a fine fleshy woman like you he can't tell the difference between a bed and a wagon floor."

"Tobias!" she said again. "You stop that!" Then she took his hand and pressed it again. "You go on now and stand your watch like you're supposed to. If I'm asleep when you get back you can wake me."

"I will," Tobias said, getting down from the wagon. "Lordy, Emma, I surely will."

For three days they moved over a marsh flat just to the south of a dense swamp. The grass here was rich and bountiful, and Tobias thought it would be a good place to bring cows for summer grazing.

It was just before midnight on the third day when Tobias was awakened by the sound of a whip cracking three times, a signal of danger. He dressed hurriedly, jumped from the wagon and saddled his horse.

Skillit and Zech heard it too and were already mounted. Frog and Bonzo were with the herd.

The cracking came again, and Skillit said, "Whatever it is, they must figure they need help bad. They keep poppin' them whips, they'll spook the cows for sure."

There was a full moon flooding the marsh, and the herd was easily visible a quarter mile away. As they rode forward, they could hear bellowing and the dull thump of hooves striking the ground.

Zech said, "You want me to go back and untie the dogs, Pappa?"

"Not yet. Let's see what the trouble is first."

They rode to the right of the herd and found Frog. He said, "I'm sure glad you got here this quick. We couldn't hold the cows in much longer without help."

"What's happening?" Tobias asked, puzzled. "I don't see anything to stir them up."

"You will. Look over yonder to the edge of the swamp."

Tobias shifted in his saddle and looked to the north; then he said, "Oh Lord! Wolves! A whole passel of 'em, just like I seen on the Confederate cattle drive."

Dark forms darted everywhere in the moonlight, running forward, turning back to the woods, coming forward again, each time getting closer to the herd.

"I don't know how to handle something like this," Frog said. "You'll have to tell me what you want me to do."

"Even if they don't attack, they'll stampede the herd," Tobias said. "We got to keep 'em back. Frog, you and Bonzo keep circling the herd. Zech, you and Skillit go back to the wagon and turn the dogs loose. Then bring all the firewood we got back here. Me and Skillit will use torches, and Zech, you go to the herd and help out there. If the cows break, get out of the way and let 'em go. We'll round them up in the morning. Just don't get in the way. And hurry now!"

Tobias' horse danced nervously as he waited for Zech and Skillit to return. When one wolf rushed forward, he unfurled his whip and charged it, slashing at the darting form again and again, feeling cowhide touch flesh as the wolf howled in pain and turned back. The horse bucked and kicked, terrorized by the wolf-smell, almost throwing him from the saddle.

Nip and Tuck streaked through the yellow grass, barking and snarling, two gray forms moving so fast that Tobias lost track of them. They rushed right through the wolves; then they came back and positioned themselves halfway between the woods and the herd, apparently fearless of what stalked in front of them.

Skillit rode up with a burlap sack full of pine knots. He said, "I didn't mean to be so long, but I built a fire by the wagon. Missus Emma is all fretted up and I didn't want to leave her in the dark."

"That's good," Tobias said, dismounting. "You done right. Tie the horses to a bush while I light the torches. We best stay on foot with the fire. We can move around better this way."

Tobias and Skillit then ran constantly, moving with the wolves, thrusting fire forward when a dark form came close, smelling singed hair and running again. The sound of whips blended with bellowing as the cows charged in one direction and were turned back, then stomped their hooves and charged again, crashing into each other.

One wolf broke into the outside circle of the herd and a shrill, almost human scream overwhelmed all other sound as a calf hit the ground and struggled frantically to get away. Nip and Tuck were on the wolf's back instantly, snarling, teeth snapping, hair flying, biting chunks from the wolf and jumping back, then rushing in again to send the wolf sprawling across the ground.

Some of the cows broke away from the battle site and ran, and no amount of men or whips could stop them. Tobias glanced at them briefly as they thundered away and disappeared in the direction of the swamp.

A death cry came from the wolf as the dogs ripped its throat open. It stumbled back toward the woods, leaving a trail of hot blood, falling and then scrambling forward, howling again as its life rapidly poured out onto the ground. The mournful sound seemed to frighten the other wolves. For a few minutes they moved back and forth among themselves, bewildered and undecided; then they ran swiftly to the edge of the woods and disappeared.

Tobias and Skillit put out their torches, mounted and rode to the herd. Frog came to them and said, "About thirty broke out, Mister MacIvey. We couldn't stop them. It was when that wolf got in there."

"I know. I seen it. We're just lucky it wasn't more than that. We'll find them in the morning. All of us need to stay out here the rest of the night in case the wolves come back. Where's Zech?"

"Over to the right," Frog said. "He had that little hoss going like a jackrabbit. And I sure wouldn't want him to turn that whip on me the way he was using it on them wolves."

"Go and tell him to stay with his mamma till the rest of us come in. She's probably up in the top of a tree by now. Tell him to hurry on in to the wagon."

Once more during the night, the cattle tried to break but were turned back, and when daylight came, they started grazing as peacefully as if nothing had happened.

Tobias noticed one calf with a cut across its side but it was not a serious injury. He figured it was the one the wolf knocked down. Skillit came up to him and said, "How many of us you want to keep staying here?"

"Tell everybody to go back to the wagon. The cows are calm now, and we all need some food and rest."

Emma had biscuits and beef waiting when they rode in. She also dipped into their meager supply of coffee, and the aroma made the men jump from their horses and grab tin cups from the wagon.

Frog took a deep drink and said, "Zech, I ain't going to say nothing more but good about them dogs of yours. When that wolf got in there, if it hadn't been for the dogs them cows would 'a been scattered over Georgia by now. They really done a job on that wolf."

Both Nip and Tuck's faces were covered with caked blood. Zech patted one of them and said, "They's good dogs, and they ain't scared of nothing."

Emma passed around a plate of hot biscuits. "I thought everybody was getting killed," she said. "I've never heard so many different sounds at one time."

"It was a ruckus all right," Tobias said. "I just hope it don't happen again. Maybe we've seen the last of them."

Zech said, "Pappa, if the wolves come back, why don't we just shoot them?"

"That'd scare the cows as bad as the wolves." He yawned, and then he said, "Frog, you and Bonzo stay here and get some sleep. You're probably shucked out since you haven't been to bed all night. Me and Zech and Skillit will look for the cows that ran off."

"We'll stay, but I'll keep one eye open. If anything happens we'll go out to the herd real fast."

As soon as the coffee was gone, Tobias, Zech and Skillit mounted up and rode to the north side of the herd. Tobias said, "The last time I seen them they were heading straight for the swamp, about a quarter mile west of the wolves. Let's go down that way and see if we can pick up their tracks."

The ground close to the line of cypress trees was soft, and they easily found the trail of hoof prints. When they entered the woods, they could see ferns that had been stomped flat by the cows. Tobias said, "I hope they didn't go far. If they did, we'll never get them out of there."

Bald cypress trees towered over a hundred feet into the sky and were surrounded by thick clumps of knees, and the ground was covered solidly with lush ferns and beds of velvet moss. There was an eerie quietness about the place, no barking of squirrels and no flapping of wings.

The ground took a sudden downward slant that led into a cup-shaped slough, and here the hoof marks went down a foot into black muck. Tobias stopped his horse and said, "Lord have mercy! Just look at that!"

Forty yards ahead of them, cow horns were sticking out of the ground, nothing but horns, and not even the bare tip of a head could be seen.

"They done buried themselves alive in that sinkhole," Skillit said, his eyes wide. "Even the buzzards can't get at 'em. They ain't nothing left but worm bait."

Zech started backing Ishmael. "I don't want to look, Pappa. Let's leave. I don't want to see it."

"I don't either. That ain't a fit way for even an animal to die. I don't want to see this place again."

For another week they stayed on open prairie, skirting just to the south of the line of trees that marked swamp land. Then one day the trees appeared on the horizon ahead of them as well as to the north; and as they moved forward, a wall of tall cypress blocked their view to the south.

For two more days they moved westward, letting the cows graze and set their own pace, and each day the corridor between the north and south trees became narrower, and the wall ahead of them loomed closer.

Tobias rode from the wagon and over to Skillit on the herd's right flank. "I don't like the looks of this," he said. "Seems like we're heading into some kind of a dead-end canyon, right into a swamp. I hope there's a way through it. If there ain't, we've got three or four days of backtracking to do."

"Don't look good. And we sho' ought not push 'em into a swamp after what we seen back at the other one."

By late afternoon, the wall in front of them was only a half mile away, and the north and south corridor had narrowed to less than a mile. Heat coming from the ground was stifling, and the air was so thin the horses puffed as they walked.

Tobias told the men to stop the herd and circle them until they were settled, then come back to the wagon for supper. He hoped there were no bears or wolves here, for if the herd spooked for any reason, there was nowhere for them to run and seek safety.

Emma cooked the last of the smoked beef and also baked sweet potatoes. As the men ate silently, she said to Tobias, "Tomorrow you've got to either shoot a deer or kill one of the cows. There's no meat left, and the flour is almost gone too. We'll have to make koonti to get us through."

"I'll see to it as soon as I can," Tobias said. "What worries me more than vittles is this fix we're in. In the morning I'll scout ahead and see if there's a way out of here without turning back."

"This place spooks me," Frog said. "I got a feeling somebody is watching us. I don't know how to explain it, but something ain't right. Times like this it pays to be a dumbo like Bonzo."

Bonzo either didn't hear the remark or ignored it. He stuffed a burned potato peeling into his mouth and chomped, paying no heed to the conversation.

"I got the same feeling," Skillit said. "Black man say someone walkin' on yo' grave. It strong enough to make my flesh crawl."

"You men!" Emma exclaimed, dipping herself a plate of stew. "You're seeing ghosts everywhere. All you're doing is remembering the wolves, and we may never seen those wolves again. And when it comes down to the truth, all you really worry about is your stomachs, whether or not some woman can fill them up."

"There's fact in that," Frog said. "The only thing that counts in life is a woman's cooking pot. Is yours empty now, Miz Emma?"

"Almost," Emma said, taking his plate. "There's a little left. But you just proved what I said."

Zech was listening, but he seldom broke into a conversation when adults were talking; but now he spoke up. "Ishmael feels it too, Pappa. I can put my hand on his neck and feel him tremble. He knowed the wolves were coming before we seen them, before the cows got riled up. He sees things nobody else can see, and he has a way of letting me know. He ain't happy here, Pappa. He says we ought not be here. He's a Indian pony, and he has a way of knowing things we don't know."

Everyone became silent for a moment, wondering if this were truth or fantasy coming from a small boy who talked as if he really believed it; then Tobias said, "Ishmael is a horse, Zech, and that's all. He's just a horse like all the others. It's time we stopped this gibberish and go on watch. Me and you will go first. That way, if Ishmael has something special to say, maybe I can hear it too."

"You don't have to believe it," Zech said. "I was just trying to tell you Ishmael ain't happy here. I can tell when he is and when he ain't."

Tobias got up from the fire. "Let's go, before you get me too spooked to ride watch. Tomorrow morning we'll leave this place one way or another."

There was no moon during the first of the watch, and it was impossible to distinguish cows from trees. Tobias and Zech rode only by sound, hearing the swish of a tail or the thump of a hoof, circling what they hoped was the herd. The fire back at the wagon was their only beacon, and without it, they would have had no sense of direction at all.

Tobias sat still in the saddle for a moment, staring blindly into the darkness, thinking what a catastrophe it would be if danger struck the herd in such a sea of ink. If the cows ran, there would be no way of knowing which direction they took; and with sw·.mp on three sides of them, they would have to hunt for the cows one at a time, just as he and Zech had once hunted them in the swamp beyond the hammock.

He moved the horse forward again, feeling his way, not wanting to bump into a cow and frighten it; then he stopped and listened, hearing a faint tinkling sound, like bells. The sound went away, and then it came again, this time closer. The next time he heard it, it seemed to be moving back into the swamp.

Zech rode up to him, moving swiftly, the small horse surefooted in the darkness. "Did you hear something, Pappa?" he asked, holding the reins tight to stop the horse's dancing.

"I thought I did. But it could have been the wind in the trees. Did you?"

"It sounded like bells. I heard it two or three times, and then it went away."

"That's what I heard too, something tinkling. It's for sure nobody's belled a milk cow and turned it loose out here. It must have been something in the trees. Whatever it was, I haven't heard it again."

Just before the watch ended, the moon came from behind a cloud bank, casting a yellow glow over the herd and the trees. Although he had felt no movement, Tobias discovered that the cows were a quarter mile closer to the edge of the swamp. He wanted to move them back again but did not do so for fear of spooking them.

When he got back to the wagon after being relieved, Emma stirred and said, "Well, did you see any buggers out there tonight?" She said it in jest, not really expecting an answer.

"No. But I swear 'fore God, Emma, I heard bells. Zech heard it too, and I told him it was just the wind in the trees. But it wasn't. It was bells."

"Bells?"

"It was a tinkling sound at first. It came close to the herd once, and then it went away. Neither one of us didn't hear it no more."

"Why would anyone be out here in the wilderness with bells?"

"I don't know. But come sunup I aim to find out."

Tobias left before breakfast the next morning. Zech wanted to come with him, but he said no, he would do this alone. If there was a way through the swamp he would find it and come back as soon as possible.

He approached the line of cypress trees reluctantly, walking the horse slowly, looking back at the grazing herd and at the wagon beyond. It seemed to him that all this land they had moved over for three days was a funnel, directing them to this one impassable spot. His instinct was to turn back now, to backtrack the herd and leave this place as hurriedly as possible, but he walked the horse straight into the woods.

The land looked the same as where the cows buried themselves: towering bald cypress, thick clumps of lush ferns, fallen rotten limbs covered with moss, palmetto clumps and cocoplum bushes. There were also pools of stagnant water covered with slime, cut in places by moccasin trails.

Tobias followed a small ridge of higher ground, moving gingerly, remembering what happened to the cows that ran into the sinkhole muck. He already knew there was no way to move cattle through here but he did not turn back. He was a mile into the swamp when he heard it, the bells, the one thing he had come looking for – not a passage for the herd but for the strange sound that had come out of the night.

It was off to the right, no more than a hundred yards distant, tinkling, moving and then stopping, then moving again. He sat in the saddle mesmerized, not thinking of the herd or of Emma or Zech or anything but the bells, somehow knowing that if he sat still it would come to him.

The horse whinnied and backed away a few steps as the sound grew louder; then it came past the last clump of palmetto and stood before him.

The man was beyond age, so old that his skin was cracked like alligator hide. He was almost seven feet tall, and his hair was tied on top of his head with bands of reeds, making him seem even taller. He wore only a girdle of silver-colored balls and small brass bells, and around his neck there were six strings of shells. His wrists were covered with bracelets of fish teeth, and his entire body was stained red.

Tobias stared, unbelieving at first and then believing, but feeling no fear. He knew this was not an apparition or a hallucination but a man, a flesh and blood man beneath all those strange trappings. There was a calmness about him that dissipated fear, making Tobias calm too, an overwhelming calmness that flooded his body and caused him to slump forward in the saddle.

For several moments no word was spoken, and then the old man said, "I am a Timucuan, the last of my people. I am the keeper of the graves. Soon I will join the others. We came here a long time ago to hide from the Spanish solders. I am the only one left, and I have lived beyond my time."

Tobias said, "We didn't know. We are lost and trying to find a passage for the herd."

"Do not bring your cows in here," the old man cautioned. "In here there is only death. If you come in here you will never return. Go back the way you came. This swamp is a burial ground for all who enter. My people have known this to be true."

"Is there no other way? We're trying to reach the sea to the west. If we turn back it means three or four days of traveling."

"It is best that you travel those days. Only death awaits you if you enter. Do not go into the south swamp either. Go all the way back and around the swamp. It is the only way."

Without speaking further, the old man turned and walked away. Tobias wondered if he had really seen this or not, but as he listened to the bells fading into the distance, he knew.

Zech rode to him swiftly as soon as he emerged from the woods. He asked anxiously, "Did you find it, Pappa?"

"Find what?" Tobias responded absently.

"A way to get through."

"There is no way to get through. We'll have to turn the herd and go back. It's the only way."

"The bells, Pappa? Did you find the bells?

"It was the wind. Only the wind. Ride on ahead and tell the men to move the cows out of here right away. Hurry now!"

Tobias sat still for several minutes, thinking of the old man who had been in there alone for such a long time; then he put his horse into a trot and headed for the herd.

For two days they turned back eastward, following the south line of trees, seeing the funnel gradually widen until the swamp on the north lay on the far horizon.

Tobias was strangely silent, even at night around the supper fire. They killed one cow and dressed it, and the fresh beef satisfied all but Tobias, who seemed to be preoccupied with something besides food. He could not dismiss the strange Indian from his mind, and he wanted to get away as quickly as possible and never return.

At dawn on the third morning he rode into the edge of the swamp alone. The trees were not so thick here, and for a half mile the ground was solid. From this point forward there was water, and the trees became even thinner. He stared at what seemed to be an opening on the far side; then he turned and went back to the wagon.

Everyone was at the breakfast fire except Bonzo, who was with the herd. Tobias took a strip of fried beef, ate a few bites and threw the rest to Nip. He said, "I think the swamp is narrow here. There's water, but it don't look too bad. If we can push through here it will save us a couple more days of backtracking. Then we'll be away from this place."

"There's really no hurry, is there?" Emma asked. "The cows seem to be doing fine on the grass."

"I want to try it anyway. We'll cut out six cows. Me and Zech and Skillit will take them in there. If we make it with no trouble, Zech can wait on the other side while we come back and push the rest of the herd through."

"You want the dogs to come with us?" Zech asked.

"Maybe they ought to. They could be a big help in there, and the water don't look too deep for them."

"Are you sure about this?" Skillit asked doubtfully, hoping Tobias would change his mind. "Don't seem to me it make no difference we get to Punta Rassa one day or another, just so we get there."

"It's worth a try. If we can't make it, we'll turn around, come back and head east again."

"You the boss," Skillit said resignedly, getting up and mounting his horse.

They cut six cows from the herd and entered the woods, and when they reached the point where water met solid ground, the cows hesitated and tried to turn back. Nip and Tuck bit at their rear legs, forcing them forward, and soon they were wading through a foot of water.

"So far it's not too deep for the wagon," Tobias said. "If it don't get no worse than this we can make it easy."

Ishmael started to buck, and the splashing water caused herons to flap out of a cypress tree and squawk loudly. Tobias said, "Calm him down, Zech, afore he scares the cows and makes them run."

Zech steadied the horse, and they moved forward again, churning up black mud as they rippled the calm surface. Skillit said, "I don't like this, Mistuh Tobias. Something don't seem right about this place."

"We'll go a bit further. If it gets deeper, we'll turn back."

The dogs were now having to jump to stay above the water level, and they were useless in herding the cows. Suddenly the lead cow plunged downward, went under and came up bellowing; then it seemed that dynamite was being set off beneath the surface. Violence came from everywhere, all at once without warning, tails slashing and jaws popping. One cow was snatched under instantly; then it came up fighting to break free, its head firmly locked in an alligator's mouth. It bellowed and went under again as blood bubbled to the surface and spread out in a widening circle.

"'Gators!" Tobias shouted, clinging to the saddle as his horse reared up. "Turn back! Turn back!"

Nip was already swimming toward high ground, but Tuck went straight ahead, heading for the panic-stricken cows. Zech kicked Ishmael in the flanks and plunged after the dog, the water now almost over the saddle.

Tobias watched, frozen with fear; then he managed to shout frantically, "No, Zech! No!"

The small horse swam right into the death orgy, staining its hide with blood; then Zech grabbed the dog and pulled it onto the saddle and turned back. Water exploded all around him as Ishmael churned desperately, gradually moving away.

Skillit had already snatched Nip up and was galloping through the water. Tobias continued to watch, unable to move, as the black surface turned solid red; and it was only after Zech rushed by him that he wheeled his horse and followed.

When they reached the edge of the woods, they stopped and put the dogs down. Tobias said weakly, "You could 'a got killed back there, Zech. You shouldn't ought to have done it. A dog ain't worth the chance you took."

"I wasn't going to let no 'gator eat Tuck, Pappa. I knew Ishmael could do it. I could feel it."

"Lord, what I could have caused," Tobias sighed, putting his hand on Zech's shoulder.

"It wasn't your fault," Skillit said quickly, concerned by the stricken look on Tobias' face. "Wasn't no way to know that place is a 'gator den."

"I knew. I knew before we went in there. He warned me, and I didn't pay heed. He told me there is only death in there, and I went anyway."

"You ain't making sense, Mistuh Tobias," Skillit said. "Who warned you?"

"Back there. In the swamp. He said not to enter, to go around."

"You want to go to the wagon and take a rest? Maybe we ought to stop here for a day or two."

"No! Get the herd started. We'll go east as far as we have to and go around the rest of this swamp. I should 'a listened."

"We'll move on then," Skillit said, still looking at Tobias strangely. "But don't blame yo'self for anything. At least we know not to come this way again. It was worth something. Best we lose a few cows than a whole herd."

"Next time we'll know," Tobias agreed. Then he watched the two dogs as they streaked through the grass toward the herd, Zech and Ishmael close behind them.

When they rounded the tip of the swamp and turned westward again, they came into open prairie land. The herd moved lazily, grazing in one spot until it was cleaned, then drifting on.

Tobias gradually dismissed the Timucuan from his mind, and all of the men seemed to regain confidence after the experience of being boxed into the dead-end swamp. Tobias also made mental notes of the route they should take the next time.

One morning they approached a lake with a dense hardwood hammock on the east side. Tobias was riding right flank, and he saw the rider come from the woods and head in his direction. He left the herd and met him halfway.

This man said directly, "I got a few cows to sell. Are you interested?" He was an older man, around sixty, with solid white hair and a beard to match.

Tobias responded, "Well, yes and no. I don't have money to pay cash. I picked up sixty-five head from a man named Lowry back at the Kissimmee for three dollars a head and promised to pay him on my way back. I could do the same for you. How many you got?"

"A hundred and ten. And I ain't got no help to move them. What's your name?"

"Tobias MacIvey."

"Windell Lykes."

"Pleased to meet you."

Both men looked at each other as if sizing each other up, and then Lykes said, "How do I know you'll come back and pay me?"

"Same way as Lowry. You got my word, and I've never broken it to no man. So far we've lost near on forty cows and Lowry will get paid for every one of his. What we lose is mine. And like I told Lowry, next trip through I'll take whatever you got and pay cash."

The man scratched his head for a moment, pondering a decision. "You coming straight back here after the drive?"

"Straight back. I live over on the east bank of the Kissimmee."

"Well, O.K., it's a deal. Where you taking the herd? Tampa?"

"Nope. Punta Rassa. I've been told the price is better there."

"You're too far north for Punta Rassa. You need to cut south."

"You been there?"

"Several times, but not driving a herd. Is this your first trip there?"

"For a fact, and we done got lost on several occasions. Maybe you could give us directions."

"Well, best thing you can do is go due south till you hit the Caloosahatchie. It's the first river you'll come to. It goes into Punta Rassa, but you'll have to cross the river to get there. It's on the south bank, right at the Gulf. There's a ferry about four miles north of there that can take your wagon across, but you'll have to swim the cows."

"Is there 'gators in the river?"

"Mister, there ain't no water in Florida without 'gators, less you got a tub of it in your house. And one's liable to get in there too if you leave the door open. But I ain't heard of nobody losing cows to 'gators on the Caloosahatchie. It's pretty deep water, and 'gators lay up mostly in shallows."

"Just thought I'd ask."

Tobias unfurled his whip and cracked it two times; then he saw Skillit and Zech ride away from the wagon and come toward him. He said, "They'll go with you and bring in your cows."

"Don't you want to count them first and sign a paper?"

"If you say you've got a hundred and ten, that's good enough for me. You get paid for a hundred and ten. And I don't need a paper if you don't."

"Fair enough. I hope we get to do business again."

Tobias turned his horse; then he looked back and said, "Thanks rightly for the directions. I was beginning to believe there ain't no such place as Punta Rassa. I'll see you again soon, and we'll take good care of your cows."

Four days later they reached the Caloosahatchie and then followed its bank until they found the ferry. It was late afternoon when the last cow staggered from the river, but they made the crossing without incident.

Tobias could not believe they were within four miles of their destination. Although this close, Punta Rassa still seemed to him to be as distant as Babylon, and just as unreachable.

He also had a strong premonition that something bad would happen yet, a storm, a flood, wolves, alligators, something. Or Thompson's information about the Cuban market would be in error, and there would be no buyers on hand who wanted the cattle. The long path to this point had been too lined with disappointment, disaster and grief for him to feel premature joy.

They moved the herd a mile down the river and then circled them for the night. Tobias would ride on alone the next morning and seek a buyer, then return and share the news with everyone, good or bad.

At supper that night everyone seemed strangely subdued, as if they too did not yet believe. Tobias had surmised that Frog and Bonzo would try to get advance pay and ride off to the village, leaving the rest of them alone to protect the herd; but they made no mention of this. Even Zech showed no boyish enthusiasm of reaching trail's end, and he spent an hour after dark quietly rubbing Ishmael's neck and talking to him.

Tobias noticed all of this, thinking that perhaps they were all tired beyond realization and it was just now hitting them, like hunters who pursue the prey through the woods relentlessly for an entire day, and after the kill is finally made, fall down exhausted. Whatever the reason, it was the quietest night the camp spent.

They still posted the same guard as they had in the wilderness, and an hour before midnight Tobias was still awake, awaiting his turn. He sat on the wagon seat as Emma aroused from a fitful sleep and came to him. She sensed at supper he was restless, anxious for the night to pass and the dawn to come, that he would not lie down and rest either before his watch or when it ended.

She sat beside him silently, watching a full moon come over cypress trees lining the banks of the river. Spanish moss swayed from limbs like blobs of cotton and absorbed the moonbeams, changing the dull gray beards to glowing yellow. The cattle were visible in the distance, quiet now, standing deathly still, resembling not flesh and blood creatures hounded by predators but miniature statues on a kitchen shelf. The herd was all together now for the last time, a mass rather than individual fragments, and she thought of all those days and weeks and months Tobias and Zech and Skillit struggled to assemble what stood on this small plot of ground and would soon be no more. They had survived only to come to an end, and the cycle would begin anew when they returned to the homestead.

She finally said, "Don't be too disappointed if this doesn't turn out right, Tobias. It's not the end of everything."

For a moment he made no answer, and then he said, "I was going to say the same thing to you, and ask you not to be disappointed. You beat me to it."

"I would be disappointed only for you and Zech. You've worked too hard to fail now. I know what it means to you."

"I'm not sure I know myself what it means," he said, putting his hand on hers. "All those times me and Zech chased some scrawny cow through the woods and didn't catch it, it wasn't the money. I want the money now for you and Zech. For me, I guess I just been trying to prove something to myself. All my life when I tried to do something worth anything I never made it, not here or back in Georgia. It was the same with my daddy, and he finally gave up and quit trying. When he did, it killed my mamma, just as sure as those 'gators killed the cows back in the swamp. And it was just as awful to see. Then it got Daddy too. We almost made it in the scrub, me and you and Zech; then somebody comes along and burns it all for no reason. Ever time I try, it seems somebody burns it or floods it or kills it. Maybe this time the Lord won't throw a roadblock in front of me. But if He does, I'll just stumble over it and try again. I'm not ready to give up yet, and I ain't going to quit no matter what happens tomorrow morning."

She leaned over and put her head on his shoulder. "I've known that all along, Tobias. And whatever happens, we'll work it out together. That's the way I want it to be."

"Emma. . ." he said hesitantly, unsure of his words; then he started again, "Emma,. . . I'm not always a gentle man, and I know it. I guess it's because of the things I seen growing up. I want to be, but I don't know how. You could have done better than me, a fine woman like you, and I always knowed that too. I ain't much to look at, but someday I'm going to make you proud, and Zech too. I'm not going to quit trying till I do."

She reached up and kissed him. "You're the most gentle man I've ever known. I'm proud now, and Zech is too."

He suddenly jumped from the wagon. "There you go again," he said, smiling, "doing the same thing you done to me that night out on the prairie when I had to go on watch. I've got to relieve Skillit now. You best get some sleep. We've got a big day ahead of us tomorrow."

SEVENTEEN

Tobias passed several large holding pens and then turned down a rutted road leading to the waterfront. There were two stores, one containing a cafe and a post office, the other general merchandise. Between them was a saloon, and behind this a livery stable, feed store and blacksmith shop were housed together in a barnlike structure. Across from one store a two-story clapboard house offered rooms for rent. The whole area reeked of cow manure, and Tobias wondered how the people who lived and worked here could stand the constant odor.

At the end of the street a dock ran one hundred feet out into the bay, and adjacent to the dock there was a cattle shute. A small shack on pilings was at the left of the dock, and at the end, a sidewheel steamer belched smoke from its two stacks. Two more steamers lay at anchor further out in the bay.

The village had a desolate look, almost forbidding, peppered with fierce-looking Spanish bayonet and clumps of salt-burned palmetto. Sea grapes covered large sand dunes to the right and left of the dock. Tobias had pictured it differently, the name Punta Rassa conjuring visions of something exotic, things he had never seen before. But except for the cattle dock and the more numerous buildings, it was no different from Kissimmee. He was more than mildly disappointed.

Several men were sitting on the porch of one store, and Tobias rode up to them and dismounted. Two one-gallon jugs of Cuban rum were on the floor in front of them. He said, "I'm looking for a cattle buyer.

You know where I can find one?"

"Down yonder," one of the men said, pointing. "The shack on the dock. You want to see Cap'n Hendry."

Tobias tied the horse to a hitching post and walked to the dock. He knocked on the closed door and a voice came to him, "It ain't locked. Come on in."

There were three men inside, two sitting on tall stools at shelves containing ledgers, the other in a rocking chair with his feet propped on a desk. The man in the rocker was dressed in black leather boots, brown canvas pants and a blue chambray shirt. He wore a large straw hat with turkey feathers on one side.

Tobias said, "Name's Tobias MacIvey. I was told I could find a cattle buyer here."

"You come to the right place," the man said, getting up from the rocker. He was a tall, slim man of about fifty. "I'm Sam Hendry. Where's your herd?"

"Three miles up the river."

"How many you got?"

"Can't say for sure. We lost some on the drive, and ate a couple. I figure it to be around eight hundred and fifty, maybe a few more than that."

"They in good shape?"

"Real good. We moved slow coming here and let 'em eat all they wanted. They ought to go over five hundred pounds each."

"That's the kind we need," Hendry said, showing interest. "Some men run them yellowhammers down here hell bent for leather, like they was rabbits instead of cows, and time they get here they're not much more than skin and bones. Then we have to fatten them ourselves. If yours are in good shape like you say, we'll pay sixteen dollars a head. If not, twelve is tops."

Tobias felt a faintness flush through him, causing his throat to turn dry. Even after hearing it, he still could not believe that the cows were actually worth cash money. To him they were still just stubborn critters they had popped out of swamps and chased across prairies. He finally managed to croak, "Sounds fair to me. When you want to see them?"

"Drive the herd on down here and put them in one of the holding pens. We'll take a look and make a head count. We pay in Spanish gold doubloons worth fifteen dollars each, five hundred and twenty-five dollars to a sack. You better go to the store and buy a trunk to carry it in, unless you've got a big wooden box with you."

"Yes sir, Mister Hendry, I'll do that. And I'll go back right now and move the herd."

"Captain Hendry," the man corrected. "If I'm not here when you get done with it, I'll be in my office in back of the general store."

Tobias had an overwhelming urge to run, but he walked casually up the street to his horse. He moved slowly until out of sight of the men. Then he let out a whoop that could be heard back at the dock and put the old horse in a gallop.

When he reached the wagon he was breathless. He jumped from the panting horse and said in gasps, "We done it! We done it! Sixteen dollars a head! Spanish gold!"

Skillit's eyes widened. "Ho-ly shit!" he exclaimed loudly; then he turned quickly to Emma and said, "Lordy, Missus Emma, I'm sorry! I didn't mean to say that. It just come out."

"I almost said it myself," Emma replied. Then she turned to Tobias. "Calm yourself down a bit, and then tell us what happened."

"Captain Hendry. He's the buyer. He said if they're in good shape, he'll pay sixteen dollars each. If not, twelve is tops. You know how much money that is, Emma?"

"Not really. I'm not sure I can count that high."

"It's a bunch. I'm going to buy a steamer trunk down at the store just to haul it back to the hammock. But right now we got to move the herd. He said bring them to a holding pen so he can look and make a head count. Ride on out there, Skillit, and tell everybody to start moving the cows. I'll come on later with Emma. I'm going to tie the dogs in some bushes and leave 'em a pan of water. They follow us into town, somebody is liable to take them for wolves and shoot them."

Skillit leaped on his horse and said, "We'll have them cows down there in no time at all, Mistuh Tobias."

"No!" Tobias exclaimed. "Walk 'em slow. Real slow. They need to keep ever pound they got. Just take it easy."

Tobias sat in a chair in front of the desk, watching Hendry make figures with a pencil. He scratched for a moment more, then he looked up and said, "Well, MacIvey, you've got eight hundred and sixty-five head, all in good shape, so the price is sixteen. That comes to thirteen thousand, eight hundred and forty dollars. You want to count all of the money?"

"No sir, Captain Hendry, that ain't necessary," Tobias replied, over-whelmed by the figures. "I trust you to do the right thing. But if you got one of them gold coins on you right now, I'd sure like to keep it separate. It's the first I ever earned."

Hendry took a doubloon from his pocket and handed it to Tobias. "You want the rest of the money now?"

"I'll buy a trunk first and then come back with the wagon. But I'd like to have eight more coins now. We all need boots, and I want to treat everbody to a meal in the cafe. My boy's never been in a cafe."

"You've got them."

While Hendry counted out the coins Tobias said, "Captain Hendry, I ain't never had this much money in all my life, and never thought I would. Will somebody here try to take it from me?"

"I figured that would cross your mind, especially since this is your first time in with a herd. Won't nobody here pay any more attention to that gold than they would biscuits. I've seen men come in with six thousand head, then dump all those sacks of doubloons on the store porch and go in the saloon, just leaving it set there. If somebody took it, they couldn't put it on a horse. If they used a wagon, you could catch them in less than a mile. You've got nothing to worry about here in Punta Rassa. Of course I wouldn't go back out in the wilderness and flaunt it around. Somebody out there would take the challenge for sure."

Tobias then accepted the coins. "I thank you for the advice. We'll be back in about an hour for the rest of the money."

He went outside and up the street to where the horses and the wagon were tied in front of the cafe. Zech was prancing Ishmael, and the others were sitting on the edge of the porch. Tobias said, "It'll be a while before we pick up the money. Let's go in the cafe and get something to eat."

It was an hour before noon and there were no other customers in the building. They all took chairs at a table covered with a red checkered oil cloth. The waiter, a short, fat man wearing a dirty apron, came to them and said, "What'll it be, folks?"

Tobias said, "What you got?"

"Well, today we're serving country-fried steak, pork chops, fried snapper, and fried chicken. Take your choice."

"What else goes with it?"

"Rice and gravy, black-eyed peas, turnips, corn bread and biscuits."

"Sounds good," Tobias said. "We'll take six fried chicken dinners, but cook us a whole chicken each. And all the rest of that stuff plus a gallon of hot coffee. You got eggs too?"

"Yeah, we got eggs," the waiter said, eyeing Tobias curiously.

"Fry us three dozen on a side platter. Zech's never eaten a egg, or chicken either. What kind of pie you got?"

"Apple."

"We'll take six."

The waiter looked at the scratch pad. "Now let me get this straight. Six fried chicken dinners, a whole chicken each. Three dozen eggs, six apple pies and a gallon of coffee. You sure that's all you want?"

"That ought to do for a start. If it don't, we'll let you know."

The waiter then pointed to Skillit. "When the food's done, he'll have to eat out back. We don't serve niggers in the dining room."

"What'd you say?" Tobias asked quickly.

"There's a table on the stoop outside the kitchen. He can eat there. We don't serve niggers in here."

"Excuse me a minute," Tobias said, getting up. "I left something in my saddlebag. I'll be right back."

Emma said, "Tobias, don't you. . ."

"I said I'd be right back!" he snapped.

Frog also got up. "I need to check my saddlebag too. I'll go with Mister MacIvey."

They both returned carrying military pistols. Tobias sat down and placed his pistol on the table. Skillit said to him, "Mistuh Tobias, this ain't worth trouble. I'd as soon go out to the stoop. It don't make no difference to me. The chicken will taste just as good out there as in here."

"Sit still," Tobias said. "Ain't no member of the MacIvey clan going to eat on a back porch, not here or anywhere. If one of us gets kicked out, we all go. And that's a fact."

The waiter came back from the kitchen and announced, "Mister Lassiter is the cook and the owner. He says he ain't going to. . ."

Tobias and Frog cocked the pistols, and then Tobias said, "You go and tell mister whoever-he-is that he's about to serve his first nigger in here. If he don't, we'll all leave. And if we do, you're going to have some real bad trouble with the roof next time it rains."

"Very well," he said distastefully, eyeing the pistols. In a moment he returned. "Mister Lassiter says he can bend the rule this time, but he don't understand why anyone would make such a fuss over a nigger. He says don't shoot no damn holes in the roof, and he hopes you enjoy the chicken."

"We will," Tobias said, "if it ever gets here."

Frog uncocked the pistol. "He just learned that some things you do for the first time ain't nearly so bad as you thought it'd be. Ain't that right, Mister MacIvey?"

Tobias smiled. "If you say so, Frog. And I tell you what I'm gonna do. After I pay you and Bonzo the wages I promised, I'm gonna give each one of you a hundred dollar bonus. How would that suit you?"

"Just fine," Frog answered, surprised and pleased. "That much money will probably burn a hole in my pockets, but it's real fine. We thank you, don't we, Bonzo." He kicked Bonzo under the table.

"That's real fine," Bonzo echoed quickly. "We didn't expect that much. We're obliged to you."

"You said that real good, Bonzo," Frog said. "I'm right proud of you."

Just then the waiter started bringing steaming platters and bowls to the table. Zech helped himself to a chicken breast and two fried eggs. He gulped them down and said, "That's real good, Pappa, a heap better than coon. How come we don't get us some chickens? I'd take care of them."

"We will someday. But it might be hard to keep them in the hammock. Foxes and panthers eat chickens, and wolves do too. It's like inviting them to supper. And coons steal eggs. We'd have to watch over them real careful."

"Nip and Tuck would help me do that. It's real good, Pappa. The best I've ever et."

"Wait till you get to the apple pie," Emma said, smiling. "You'll like that too. I know how to make pies but it's hard to do in a frying pan. If we ever get another Dutch oven or a cook stove I'll bake you a pie every day. And cookies too."

Frog and Bonzo heard none of it. Their plates were piled with bones, and the side dishes were empty. Tobias said, "I'll order more rice and peas and turnips and another pone of corn bread. Maybe we'll need more chicken too afore we're done."

Skillit smacked his lips. "Mistuh Tobias, this worth all them floods and wolves and 'gators too. You keep the vittles comin', we might be here for a week."

"We can't stay that long," Tobias said, "cause I got to go to the store and buy a trunk. I told Captain Hendry we'd be back for the money in a hour or so. But we might eat ever chicken in Punta Rassa before we head back to the hammock." He then took the gold doubloon from his pocket and handed it to Zech. "This's the first coin Captain Hendry gave me. I want you to have it, Zech, and keep it. If you don't ever spend it, you'll never be flat-out broke like I always been."

Zech turned the coin over in his hand, looking at the engravings. "It's real purty, Pappa. But if you don't mind, I'd rather spend it and buy some apples for Ishmael. I promised him."

"I'll buy the apples. You keep the coin. I don't want you to spend it, now or ever."

Zech put the doubloon in his pocket. "I'll keep it, Pappa. I promise. When we get back to the hammock I'll put it away. Can I have some more chicken now, and some more biscuits and gravy too?"

"Eat all you want," Emma said, piling his plate. "Maybe it will put meat on those bones. You're beginning to look just like your daddy."

"Speaking of bones," Tobias said, "save all them chicken bones for Nip and Tuck. And I'll have the waiter sack up a whole fried chicken for each of them. They've earned it too, much as anyone. We'll feed 'em good this afternoon."

The waiter came from the kitchen with another platter. "Mister Lassiter sent you some snapper. He cooks real good fish, and he thought you might like some. Way you folks eats, he wants all of you to come back ever time you brings in a herd." He put the platter down, motioned at Skillit and said sheepishly, "Mister Lassiter says him too."

"We'll just do that," Tobias said. "You got a good cafe. Tell Mister Lassiter this is right neighborly of him, right neighborly."

The four men placed the steamer trunk in the wagon. Tobias opened one sack and counted out coins to Frog and Bonzo. Skillit watched and said nothing as no money was offered to him.

Frog put the doubloons in his pocket and shook his pants leg to make them jingle. "Just wanted to make sure I ain't dreaming," he said. "Me and Bonzo's got a little chore to do, Mister MacIvey. Where you want us to meet after you get done in the store?"

"Right here, I guess. Then we'll go back out of town and make camp. We all got some talking to do."

Emma, Zech and Skillit followed Tobias into the building. A clerk came to them immediately and said, "Yes, sir, what can I do for you today?"

Tobias said, "Well, we want a bunch of things. Boots for everyone, and dresses for my wife, Emma. That'll do for a start."

"I'm sorry, sir. We don't carry ladies' apparel. There's just no call for it here. For that you'll have to go up to Fort Myers. But we do have boots."

"Aw hell!" Tobias said, disappointed. "You ought to get in some stuff for women. If you ain't got dresses, I guess you best see to Skillit first. He needs the most."

"Which one is Skillit?"

"Him," Tobias said, pointing. "This here's my boy, Zech."

The clerk studied Skillit carefully, and then he said, "He's really a whopper. What you got in mind?"

"Everything. Boots, socks, britches, shirt, underwear, the whole works. And a felt hat too."

Skillit beamed. "You mean I get all that, Mistuh Tobias? I was only expectin' britches."

"That and anything else you want."

The clerk said, "As I said, he's awful big. I hope we have his size in everything. I'll do my best. Why don't you folks just look around while I take care of him."

Skillit followed the clerk as Tobias said to Emma, "I'm sorry. Real sorry. I wanted to get you some dresses."

"Doesn't matter," Emma said, trying to ease his disappointment. "Maybe they've got a pair of boy's boots that will fit me. That would do me fine on trail drives. And I don't need new dresses in the hammock."

"Maybe they've got something else you want. Look around and see."

The three of them wandered around the aisles until Skillit and the clerk returned from the back of the store. Skillit was dressed in brown leather boots, blue denim pants, blue chambray shirt, and wide-brimmed black hat. The pants came four inches up the boots.

Emma said, "My, my, Skillit, you sure look nice."

Skillit grinned broadly. "Don't hardly know myself in all this. It's the first sto-bought stuff I ever owned. And it don't matter none about the britches being short. I can tuck 'em in the boots and never know the difference." Then he looked to Tobias. "Can I have this too? It's only ten cents." In his hand he held a red bandanna.

"Sure you can. Put it on and let's see how it looks."

Skillit put the bandanna around his neck and tied it in front. "Always did want one of these things," he said. "Foreman on the plantation at Tallahassee wore one."

"It looks real nice with the blue," Emma said.

"Now let's get the other boots," Tobias said. "Skillit's done put us all to shame."

Skillit grinned again; then he went over to a mirror hanging on one wall.

"Don't forget the apples, Pappa," Zech said anxiously.

"Don't you worry about that. I won't forget. We'll get a whole sackful before we leave. And you need britches too, and a hat if he's got one your size."

"I'd like a hat too," Emma said. "It might not look right on a woman but it would sure keep the sun off me out on the prairie."

After everyone had been outfitted Tobias motioned for the clerk to follow him to the back of the store. He whispered, "You by any chance got a cook stove?"

"Just so happens I have," the clerk answered, whispering also but not knowing why. "Follow me."

They went into a storeroom. The clerk said, "We've had this thing for over a year and nobody's bought it. It's a mite fancy for folks here. Came down by ship from New Orleans. You want it, you can have it for cost plus the shipping charge."

Sitting in one corner was a dust-covered cast-iron stove. The left bottom section was an oven and the right side was the fire box. The flat surface on top of this contained four round cooking plates. Two warmer ovens formed a top over the entire stove, and the door of each oven was decorated with golden angels playing harps. All four legs were shaped like clusters of grapes and were also painted gold. A unicorn was engraved across the main oven door and was charging a cringing devil on the fire box door. Both were gold painted and outlined in blue.

Tobias gulped, not believing he had finally found such an item. He said, "It's the purtiest thing I ever seen. How much is it?"

"I can let you have it for thirty-six dollars plus the twelve dollar shipping cost."

"Sold!" Tobias said quickly. "I'll pay you for it now, but I don't want to pick it up till in the morning. Can you have somebody clean the dust off it?"

"Surely," the clerk said, breathing a sigh of relief. "You've made a wise decision, Mister MacIvey. This should make your missus real proud. It's a mighty fine stove."

"When you total up the bill, don't say nothing about it in front of Emma. I want it to be a surprise. And when we get back up there, sack up a dozen apples for Zech."

"Be glad to. And they're on the house. You've been a good customer and we hope you'll come back every time you're in Punta Rassa."

"Thanks. I appreciate it. That's right nice of you."

Emma selected two baking pans and a long kitchen knife, and when everything was paid for they all went back out to the wagon. Everyone, including Emma and Zech, wore a new wide-brimmed black felt hat.

Zech took an apple from the sack and put it in front of Ishmael's nose. The horse sniffed, then he grabbed the apple with his teeth and chomped vigorously. After swallowing, he jerked his head up and down, whinnying loudly.

Zech said, "Good, ain't it." Then he put another apple into Ishmael's mouth.

The horse ate six. Zech put the rest in the wagon and leaped onto the saddle. He streaked down to the dock at full gallop, turned abruptly, then raced back to the store and made the horse rear up, kicking its front legs high into the air, as if fighting.

Captain Hendry was standing on the store porch, watching. He came to Tobias and said, "That your boy?"

"Sure is. His name's Zechariah, but we call him Zech."

"How old is he?"

"Going on eleven."

Hendry leaned against the wagon. "He rides that horse like a tick on a hound's back. He must have been born in a saddle."

"He does right well," Tobias said, pleased by the compliment.

'Where'd you get that little horse? He's right swift.'

"Indians gave him to us. His name's Ishmael."

"Ishmael? That's a queer name for a horse. You want to race him?"

"Do what?" Tobias said, surprised.

"Race him. That's my one weakness, a good horse race. I've got a Tennessee bay I'd like to put against him. Just to make it interesting, I'll bet the deed to a hundred and fifty acres just up the river. You can put up seven of those doubloons I paid you. That's good odds, about the same as seven cows against a hundred and fifty acres of land. What say? Is it a bet?"

Tobias was still too surprised by the challenge to answer. He scratched his head, trying to think clearly, and then he finally said, "Well, I don't know, Captain Hendry. I've never done nothing like that. Let's see what your horse looks like."

Hendry turned to a man sitting on the porch and said, "Go to the stable and tell Willie to saddle Thunder and bring him out here."

"Yessir, Cap'n Hendry. Right away."

Tobias said, "While he's getting the horse I'll speak to my family. I still ain't sure this is the right thing to do."

"Don't do it if you don't want to," Hendry replied. "I never push a man into anything. It's up to you."

Tobias went back to the wagon and said hesitantly, "I don't exactly know how to explain this, but Captain Hendry wants to race a horse against Ishmael. The bet is seven doubloons against a hundred and fifty acres of land just up the river. I said I'd talk it over before I give an answer."

"Let's do it, Pappa!" Zech said eagerly. "Can't no horse outrun Ishmael."

"Maybe yes, and maybe no," Tobias said. "You ain't never been in a horse race. It's a heap different from running down cows."

"What kind of horse he got?" Skillit asked.

"A Tennessee bay, name of Thunder. He's having it brought out here now."

"How long is the race?" Skillit then asked.

"He ain't made no mention of that yet."

Just then a man came around the side of the store, leading a red stallion twice the size of Ishmael. Skillit said, "Lawd-a-mercy, Mistuh Tobias, look at that! You could set a cow on top of him."

Tobias stared, and then he said, "Ain't no way! We can't race Ishmael against a elephant like that. He wouldn't have a chance."

"Yes he would, Pappa!" Zech insisted. "Size don't mean nothing. Ishmael ain't afraid of him. I can feel it."

Skillit said in a low voice, not wanting anyone standing nearby to hear, "Mistuh Tobias, I seen men up in Tallahassee race horses just like that one. They go like the wind for a mile, then they tucker out. Zech can ride Ishmael flat out for five miles on the prairie. I seen it.

When he turn three miles, Ishmael just gettin' warmed up. Tell Cap'n Hendry it's a three-mile race or nothin'. Zech make that big hoss look like a fool."

"You really think so?"

"I done seen what that little hoss can do. He got more heart than any critter I ever knowed."

Emma was listening but remained silent. Tobias turned to her and said, "What you think, Emma? It's gambling, and maybe it's wrong. But it's no more than seven cows against the land, and the 'gators ate more of them than that on the way here. And I know Zech would enjoy the race."

"We been gambling just to get here," Emma replied. "Go on and do it if you want to. I don't think the Lord will frown on us for a horse race. Not if we look on it as fun for Zech and don't make a habit of it."

"Thanks, Mamma!" Zech smiled. "I knew you'd let me do it!"

"All right, all right!" Tobias exclaimed, wanting Zech to calm himself. "We'll do it, but just this once. And don't fret none if you take a whuppin' from that bay."

Hendry called over to him, "What about it, MacIvey? Is it a race or not?"

Tobias went over to the porch and said, "How far you want to race, Captain Hendry?"

"Well, it's usually a mile, but I don't care. Whatever you say is fine with me."

"Three miles," Tobias said.

"Three miles it is," Hendry agreed. "It's about a mile and a half to the last holding pen outside town. The race will be to there and back."

One of the nearest spectators shouted, "Hoss race! Hoss race!" As soon as he said it, men poured from the saloon and seemingly out of trees, forming a chattering crowd in front of the store.

One man waved his arms and shouted, "I'll take Thunder and give odds three to one! Who wants to bet on the little hoss?" There were no takers. "All right then, five to one!"

Frog and Bonzo came from the saloon and toward the store. Frog said to a man at the edge of the crowd, "What's happening? How come all the commotion?"

"Ole Cap'n Hendry's done got hisself another sucker. It's a race between his bay and that marshtackie. Odds is five to one."

"You mean Ishmael?" Frog questioned.

"Don't know nothing about no Ishmael. It's the black hoss that boy is riding. You reckon them folks is really dumb enough to race that little fart against Thunder?"

"Maybe so. How long is the race?"

"Three miles."

"Did you say three miles?" Frog asked, his mind clicking.

"Three miles is what I said. Ole Thunder'll be back here before that runt gets started."

"Who's taking bets?"

"Man right over there. With the red shirt and straw hat."

Frog waved his hand and shouted, "I got two hundred dollars on the black! Five to one and you got a bet!" He said to Bonzo, "Gimme that bonus money quick. We done got us a sucker bet. Ishmael'll put dust in that big hoss's mouth afore they turn the two-mile mark."

Several men snickered as Frog put the doubloons into a wooden betting box.

The man who brought the bay from the stable sprang onto the saddle; then he and Zech lined the horses up in the middle of the street. Hendry shouted, "When I fire my pistol, let 'em go!"

Ishmael danced nervously as they waited, and when the boom came, the bay lunged forward and pulled away rapidly. Before they reached the end of the street he was forty yards ahead.

Zech watched the big horse move away. He patted Ishmael's neck and said, "Not now, Ishmael. Let him go. Just trail him, like we do a cow. You can bite his legs later."

When they reached the holding pen marking the halfway point, the bay turned in a tight circle, never breaking stride. Zech wheeled Ishmael quickly, cutting the distance between them to thirty yards. Then the bay increased the gap back to forty.

Zech waited for several moments more, and then he said, "Now, Ishmael! Bite him now!"

Ishmael sprang forward as if until this point he had not been running at all. He stretched his neck out like a heron in flight, and his hooves barely touched the ground as he streaked across the rutted sand. In five seconds he was abreast the bay and moving ahead; and when they reached the finish line, he was fifty yards in front of Thunder.

All but the man who had taken the bets cheered wildly, and even he showed respect for the little horse and its boy rider.

Hendry came to Tobias immediately and handed him a paper. "It's all yours," he said. "I'll have one of my men ride out in the morning and show you the land lines."

Tobias accepted the deed reluctantly. "I hate to take your land over a horse race, Captain Hendry. It don't seem right."

"Nonsense!" Hendry replied. "You won fair and square, and it's yours now. And besides that, it's nothing to me. I won that deed myself in a poker game."

"Well, I don't exactly know what we'll do with land in Punta Rassa. I guest I'll give it to Zech. He's the one who won it, not me."

Zech stopped Ishmael just short of the dock, then he trotted him back to the wagon. "I told you he could do it, Pappa!" he said excitedly. "He ain't even got his wind up. Ishmael could run from here to the hammock and back if he wanted to."

"Not that far, Zech, But he sure did a job on that three-mile stretch."

Hendry ran his hand across Ishmael's neck; then he said to Zech, "That's some horse, son. He's not even sweating. You want to sell him? I'll give you three hundred dollars for him."

"No sir!" Zech said quickly. "Ishmael is my friend. I'd never sell my friend for no kind of money."

"I figured you'd say that, and I don't blame you. I just thought I'd make an offer. He's the first horse to dust Thunder like that. Tell you what I want you to do. Go in the store and get a whole bushel of apples for you and him, and tell the clerk to put it on my bill. He'll do it, 'cause I own the store. You and that little horse earned it."

Zech jumped from the saddle and said, "Thanks, Captain Hendry! Thanks a lot! Ishmael never ate a apple before we come here, and me either. We both like it, and Ishmael thanks you too."

"Some boy you got there," Hendry said, watching Zech run into the store. "He'll make a mark someday."

"Thank you kindly," Tobias and Emma both said at the same time. Then they laughed. "I've never seen such a good loser as you," Tobias then said.

Hendry laughed too. "What the hell, it's all in fun. Keeps the blood flowing, and there's not much else to do in Punta Rassa. It's been a real pleasure knowing you folks."

"Same here," Tobias said.

Frog came to the wagon carrying the box of money. He said, "Just got four years' pay for nothing. Me and Bonzo'll ride out and find you a little later this afternoon. We need to spend some of these coins and find out how it feels to pay cash for a change."

"We'll be along the river where we first camped," Tobias said. "We got to get on out there now and feed the dogs. You and Bonzo don't be too late. We still got some talking to do."

After they reached the campsite and built a fire, Emma started supper while Zech fed the dogs. Tobias was alone at the wagon with Skillit. He said to him, "I wanted to wait till we got back out here to tell you this. Those sacks of gold in the trunk are worth five hundred and twenty-five dollars each. One sack is yours."

"Say whut?" Skillit asked, his eyes suddenly bulging.

"One sack is yours. You've earned it."

"Aw Mistuh Tobias, you don't need to do that," Skillit said, still shocked. "You and yo folks needs that money more than I do. These clothes you bought me is enough. If I could have just two or three coins for my own I'd be satisfied. You done enough for me already."

"Nope. Without you, me and Zech could never have rounded up all them cows. And from now on, ever time we sell a herd your share will be a dollar for each cow."

"Lawd, Lawd, Mistuh Tobias, I don't know what to say. I ain't never had even a dollar of my own, much less five hundred. What I gone do with all that money?"

"Save it and let it build up. You'll find a use for it someday."

"Can I open a sack and just look?" Skillit asked. "Then I'll put it back in the trunk with the rest."

"Help yourself."

Skillit climbed into the wagon, opened the trunk and removed one of the canvas bags. He untied the top and ran his hands as far as he could push them into the coins. Then he scooped out a handful and let them drop back into the sack one by one, mesmerized by the clinking sound as metal bounced against metal. He said, "It sho' is purty. I never thought all them ole yellowhammers we chased and marked would turn into this."

"Me either," Tobias responded, amused by the look on Skillit's face. "And I'm not sure I believe it yet. But that ain't nails in them sacks. It's gold."

"Can I put two or three in my pocket, just to hear 'em jingle?"

"Take all you want. It's yours. Just cut a nick in the sack so you'll know which one it is."

Skillit took a knife from his pocket and cut the sack, then he put three coins in his pocket and put the sack back in the trunk. He climbed out of the wagon and said, "I never thought somethin' like this would ever happen to me. I's worked all my life like a mule and never got a penny fo' it, and I gave up hopin' a long time ago. When you found me hid in them bushes I hadn't had nothin' to et for a week but roots and berries. Now I got a belly full of fried chicken, a new pair of britches and boots, and a sack full of gold. Lawd God, Mistuh Tobias, you's the best white folks they's ever been!"

"You've earned ever bit of it," Tobias said. "But we got to go back and try it again. We don't want to quit on this."

Frog and Bonzo came riding into the camp, each with a gallon jug sloshing in the saddlebag. They dismounted, then Frog pulled out the jug and said, "Cuban rum. Either one of you want a snort?"

"I don't drink that rotgut," Tobias said. "I seen my daddy die of that stuff time he was thirty years old, and I aim to live longer than he did."

Frog turned up the jug and let the brown liquid gurgle down his throat; then he hacked twice and said, "I been drinking it for over thirty years now, since I was old enough to pull the stopper from a jug, and I ain't dead yet. And at fifty cents a gallon, I got money on me now to empty enough jugs to line a prairie."

"If you do, your innards will be pickled for sure. But suit yourself. If you want to turn all your money into stale piss, that's your business. Me, I got other uses for mine."

Frog put the jug on the wagon floor. "You know, I never thought about it like that, but you're right. I guess all I'm doing is running my money right through my gut and on the ground. Ever time I take a leak I'm squirtin' out gold. But I'll just go on and enjoy this jug before I think about quittin'."

Tobias said, "What I want to talk to you about is what you aim to do now. If you want to stay on with us you're welcome to do so."

"Well, I don't know, Mister MacIvey," Frog said hesitantly. "Me and Bonzo is kind of drifters, and I have to stay with him. He ain't got much to say, and nothing much to think with, so I have to look out for him. But you and Missus Emma has been real good to us, and I'd like to know what you got in mind."

"If you want to join us permanent, I'll raise the pay to a dollar a day, and it'll be all the time, not just on a drive. And for ever cow you and Bonzo round up and put in the herd, you'll get a dollar a cow when we sell 'em. You'll do the branding and cutting, and we'll keep a tab. Captain Hendry told me we ought to start cutting the balls off them bulls and turn 'em into steers. He said it makes 'em grow faster."

"Let me see if I got this straight," Frog said, scratching his head. "If me and Bonzo was to round up a hundred wild cows and put 'em in the herd, we'd get a hundred-dollar bonus to split. And if we got a thousand, it would be a thousand-dollar bonus. Is that what you're sayin'?"

"That's right. A dollar a cow. Plus a regular salary and all you can eat."

"We just quit driftin' for a while," Frog said, grinning. "You got a deal, Mister MacIvey. Hell, we'll pop ever cow out of ever swamp and prairie in Florida. Next time we come to Punta Rassa we'll have a herd that stretches ten miles."

"It ain't that easy," Tobias cautioned. "Don't count your money before you get it. This time you just helped drive the cows, not round them up. We lost a whole herd one time to a storm. And we still got to run through wolves and 'gators. But we'll sure try."

Frog then said, "Where's Zech?"

"He was over there a few minutes ago cramming chicken down them dog's throats. You need to see him?"

"I got a ten-pound bag of sugar for Ishmael. That little hoss done made me more money than I ever seen in a lifetime. How come you all didn't bet on the race?"

'We did. Won a hundred and fifty acres. We might be camped right now on land Zech owns. One of Captain Hendry's men is going to show me the land lines in the morning."

"Well I'm damned!" Frog exclaimed. "Wasn't no way that big hoss could outrun Ishmael for three miles, and I wondered why you didn't take advantage of it. I guess I done joined up with the right outfit for sure. I'll go and find Zech. I want to feed Ishmael myself."

"Apples and sugar," Tobias said. "Don't spoil that horse. He won a race, but he's still got to work for his keep."

Frog turned to leave. "Just one thing, Mister MacIvey. Me and Bonzo wants to ride up to Fort Myers and see what it's like. Would it be O.K. with you? We'll catch up with you in a few days."

"That's fine with me. We got to stop going back and pay Lykes and Lowry for their cows. And we're just going to mosey along anyway, shoot a deer or two and eat, and camp when we want to. We ain't in no hurry, and it'll probably be two weeks or more before we get back to the hammock. But if you miss us on the trail, are you sure you can find my place?"

"We'll find it. And we'll scout out a better trail than we had coming down here. I don't ever want to get boxed in again like we did in that 'gator swamp."

"I had the same thing in mind," Tobias said, "Are you and Bonzo staying for supper? Emma brought some chickens back from the store and she's making stew."

Frog sniffed the air and said eagerly. "We'll stay. We can head out for Fort Myers later."

Bonzo followed Frog, and Tobias said to Skillit, "Well, it seems we still got us a cattle company. I'm glad they're staying."

"Me too," Skillit said. "Them two looks like scarecrows, but they sho' got guts beneath all them bones. And if it hadn't been for you, Mistuh Tobias, I'd a joined them in a snort of that rum. It's like hoss racin', it ain't too bad if you don't do it too often."

"Don't let me stop you. It's ever man to his own liking. And by the way, what happened with the chore you wanted to do in Punta Rassa? You never told me what it was."

Skillit was surprised that Tobias remembered. "I asked around in town this mornin' and they ain't no colored folk in Punta Rassa. I'll take care of it some other time."

Tobias sensed that Skillit didn't want to dicuss whatever it was he wanted to do. "Well, whenever. If it's something you need time off for, take all you want."

"It can wait, but not too much longer. I'll see to it later."

"Watch it now! Be careful! Don't scratch it!"

Tobias, Skillit, the clerk and one other man lifted the stove to the wagon floor and pushed it as far as possible from the edge.

Tobias said, "It'll have to ride there. Don't shove it against the trunk. It's a good thing we don't have any Georgia mountains to cross."

"Where you want me to put the stovepipe?" the clerk asked.

"Right behind the stove, where it can't roll out."

"We go across a wet marsh, we'll have to hitch another hoss to the wagon," Skillit said. "That thing's a heap heavier than it looks."

"We just might have to do that," Tobias said. "It do weigh a right smart."

Tobias thanked the clerk and the man for their help before he climbed to the seat and started down the street. The extra weight caused the wagon wheels to cut a three-inch rut in the sand.

They moved slowly out of town and past the holding pens, then along the road bordering the river. Tobias cursed the pace, wanting to trot the horse, hurry to the camp and see Emma's reaction.

When they reached the camp Emma came to the wagon and stared open-mouthed. She finally said, "What on earth, Tobias? Where'd you get the stove?"

"At the store. I bought it yesterday as a surprise for you. You like it?"

"Lordy yes! It's the purtiest one I've ever seen." She climbed into the wagon and started opening doors and looking inside.

Zech rode up on Ishmael, gazed for a moment and then said, "What kind of a horse is that on the stove, Pappa? It's got a horn on its head."

"Don't know. But it's sure fancy, ain't it?"

Emma said, "I can hardly wait to try it out. Can I cook on it on the way back?"

"If me and Skillit and Zech can get it off the wagon. We don't want to set the wagon afire. We can sure do it when Frog and Bonzo joins us. I think I'll put in some of the pipe and see how it looks."

Tobias climbed into the wagon and put three lengths of stovepipe into the stove. Then he got out, backed away and studied carefully. "Looks fine. Just like the stack on them steamboats in Punta Rassa. I'll leave it there till we have to go under a tree."

"I ain't never seen a horse like that," Zech said again, still puzzled. "You want us to load the rest of the stuff now?"

"Yes," Tobias answered. "We need to go on and get across the river."

As soon as the wagon was loaded they moved up the road to the ferry. The ferry tender looked curiously at the "MacIvey Cattle Company" sign on the wagon, at the four new black felt hats, the wolf-dogs and miniature horse, the lanky, bearded man and the giant Negro. He said, "That's a mighty fancy stove you folks got there. When I first seen you coming I thought it was a calliope."

Tobias drove the wagon onto the barge as Zech and Skillit plunged their horses into the river and swam. When the ferry reached the other side the tender said, "Where you folks headed?"

"Over to the Kissimmee," Tobias replied. Then he whipped the horse and moved up the bank.

The ferry tender shouted, "Good luck, folks!" Then he continued staring until they turned past a clump of palmetto and passed from view. As he started back across the river he muttered, "Shoot! I thought for sure it was a circus coming."

EIGHTEEN
Spring
1875

"Hell fire!" Tobias roared. "They done it again!"

He kicked the stump of an orange tree and said, "Cussed cows! Damned stupid critters!"

He was inside a three-acre plot surrounded by a split rail fence. A half dozen cows were standing in a group, swishing their tails and looking at him. Rows of small orange trees had been eaten to the ground and looked like dead sticks protruding from the sandy soil.

Tobias jerked one tree from the ground and threw it at the cows, causing them to wheel quickly and trot off to the far side of the fence. They turned, faced him again and shook their horns menacingly.

"Cuss you!" he shouted as he left the plot and walked hurriedly back into the hammock.

The house was three rooms larger now: one a kitchen built especially for the stove, another a bedroom for Zech, and a storeroom containing two steamer trunks. The palmetto thatch was replaced with cypress shingles, and there was a porch across the front of the house. A cabin had been built for Frog and Bonzo, and Skillit had added an additional room to his cabin. There was also a barn down by the garden area.

Tobias stomped into the house and said, "The cows has et my orange tree again! That's the third time I've planted them, and them damned critters has done it ever time!"

Emma continued chopping onions as she said, "Why don't you keep the cows away from them."

"Man who sells them to me says if I don't put cows in there to do the fertilizing, the trees won't grow. And that makes sense."

"Then buy taller trees."

"Taller trees," Tobias repeated. "How come I didn't think of that? If the trees is taller than the cows, then the cows can't eat them. That's what I'll do! Buy taller trees! I'll send Skillit for another wagon load."

Emma smiled as Tobias walked out briskly.

Tobias had made four more drives into Punta Rassa, each one larger than the one before. He now had regular buying points along the trail, and his last herd numbered over three thousand. Predators still stalked them, and many nights they kept fires burning to turn away wolves, but there had been no major disasters.

The old army horse died and was replaced by a tall black mare, and Tobias also purchased a buckboard and another horse to pull it. He bought two oxen which were used to pull the supply wagon during trail drives and when they followed grazing herds in summer months.

Other than this and the purchase of orange trees, the money from the sale of cows had been stockpiled, and now one steamer trunk was filled with sacks of gold doubloons and another started. Frog and Bonzo were the only ones interested in the coins as something to spend, and for two weeks after each drive they disappeared. To the others, the doubloons were just something to pile into a trunk and exchange for supplies when needed. The MacIvey clan's lifestyle changed none at all.

Zech had grown along with the homestead and was now as tall as his father and ten pounds heavier. But unlike Tobias, his hair turned a sandy brown. The most visible change in Tobias was the white specks that invaded his black beard.

Tobias found Skillit down at the barn, mending a harness strap. He said straightaway, "I want you to take the wagon and get me some more orange trees. Same place as last, out west of Fort Pierce."

Skillit noticed the agitation in Tobias' voice and manner. He said,

"Them cows done et yo trees again, ain't they?"

Tobias ignored the question. "This time get taller trees. I don't want nothing less than six feet or more. Stand by each one of them, and if one's shorter than you, don't buy it. Get all you can cram on the wagon. Emma will give you the money."

"All right, Mistuh Tobias. I'll start right away. But would it be O.K. if I stay for a day or two? I got a chore to do while I'm down there."

"What kind of a chore?" Tobias asked, still agitated. "You been saying now for over five years you got a chore to do ever time you leave the hammock, and you ain't done it yet. If you got something you want to do, why the hell don't you go on and do it 'stead of just talking about it?"

"It ain't never worked out yet," Skillit replied. "Maybe this time it will."

"Must be some chore," Tobias muttered. "Take what time you have to, but don't be gone too long. Soon as they get in with this last bunch of cows, we got to move the herd to grazing ground. Ain't enough grass left here for a billygoat to eat."

"Sho' ain't," Skillit agreed. "We don't get some rain soon, the whole place gone look like a frost hit it. I ain't never seen it be this dry for so long this time of year."

Zech popped the whip just over the cow's head, turning it sharp right and into the pen. He leaped from the saddle and closed the gate, then he called for the dogs to leave the cows and come to him.

Frog wheeled his horse and said, "That's the last of this bunch. We can start back tomorrow."

The corral held sixty cows. They had spent idle winter months building small pens ten miles apart along the areas of the spring roundup, using them to brand and cut the cattle as they caught them and also contain them at night or while they hunted others.

Zech rode over to a nearby cypress stand and tied Ishmael; then he gave each dog a strip of dried beef. It was late afternoon, and long flights of herons and egrets drifted eastward. The sky in the west was cloudless and streaked with red and orange, marking the time when day creatures retreated and night dwellers emerged. Zech watched with amusement as a mother raccoon ambled by with her brood, chattering a loud protest of his presence.

Frog and Bonzo rode to the stand and dismounted. Frog stretched and groaned, and then he said, "Ain't nothing but a fool makes his living rubbing his butt against a saddle all day. Sometimes mine feels like it's busted. What you got left in the way of grub?"

Zech said, "Nothing but a couple of strips of dried beef and a few biscuits, and they're as hard as hickernuts."

"Don't even have that," Bonzo said. "Just one scrap of meat that looks like it ought to be buried."

"You want me to kill a rabbit?" Zech asked. "If you do, I best see to it now before it gets too dark."

"What I miss most out here is Miz Emma's vittles," Frog said. "I ain't got nothing left. We ought to have brought more supplies or turned back two days ago. We could have come back and got them cows some other time."

"Pappa said we're not coming back after this," Zech said. "We're heading out for grazing. And besides that, none of these cows is marked yet. You and Bonzo'll get credit for all of them."

"Maybe so," Frog said, "but that don't help my belly none. I'd a soon have a big bowl of Miz Emma's hot stew just now as the sixty dollars over yonder in the pen."

"We could go on and cut some of the bulls and roast their balls," Bonzo said. "That tastes better to me than jerky, and it'd be hot too."

"Dammit, Bonzo, shuddup!" Frog snapped. "You trying to make me throw up? I ain't hankerin' for no bull nuts. And I done et enough rabbit that my ears is beginning to grow." He scratched his head in thought, and then he said, "I got a good idea. We couldn't be over a hour's ride from Fort Drum, maybe less. We could go over there and get some fresh grub and be back here not long after dark."

"What about the cows?" Zech asked. "We can't go off and leave them unguarded."

"Hell, they ain't going nowhere inside that pen. And I ain't seen a wolf sign in three days. We could leave the dogs tied to the fence to watch after them."

"That'd be like using Nip and Tuck for fishbait," Zech said, shaking his head in disagreement. "Some bears or other varmints come in here, the dogs wouldn't have a chance tied to a rail. We'd have to take them with us."

"Ain't nothing going to happen to the cows," Frog insisted. "We can build a fire on both sides of the corral. That would keep off anything that comes around till we get back."

"You two go on and I'll stay," Zech said. "I'm not all that hungry anyway. I can make do on what I got."

"We ain't about to leave you out here by yourself. If something happened to you while we're gone, your pappa would raise more hell than you ever seen. Either you go or nobody goes."

"You think I can't handle things by myself?" Zech asked angrily.

"It ain't that, and you know it. And there's no use in getting riled up. Your pappa wouldn't want nobody left alone at night on the prairie, not you or me or Bonzo. We going to go or not? If we ain't, then you might as well shoot that damned rabbit."

"Well, if your belly's in that bad a shape, I guess I'll go," Zech said reluctantly. "But I don't like it. I've seen what can happen to a cow at night, and you have too."

"Ain't nothing going to happen," Frog repeated.

As soon as the fires were glowing they rode eastward, cantering the horses as the dogs followed, moving at a steady pace across the palmetto prairie. The sunset reflected light ahead of them, a dim glow rapidly fading into the tops of cabbage palms; and cypress stands stood out like darkened castles looming upward from the flat land.

Just as the last sunbeam died they spotted a bonfire a mile to the north. Trading posts in the wilderness often put out such beacons at night, guiding unfamiliar travelers to a spot they could never find in darkness.

The horses panted slightly when the trio rode in and stopped in front of the store. Soft coal oil light spilled out from the two front windows and the open door, and several men sat on the building's porch, chewing and spitting silently.

Zech followed Frog and Bonzo inside, still doubtful about the journey and wishing he had remained behind. He wanted them to make their purchases quickly and head back to the corral.

Frog said to a man wearing a white apron, "You got cheese?"

"Enough to stop up a horse. How much you want?"

"Three pounds. And six cans of beans. You got bread and tinned sausage?"

"My wife bakes bread ever day, and we got sausages."

"Three each."

The man put the order into a brown sack and said, "Be anything else?"

"Them men out front just chewing their cuds like cows, or is that tobacco?" Frog asked.

"Tobacco."

"Then throw in a twist."

"That'll be two fifty," the man said, putting into the sack a link of twisted tobacco that looked like smoked sausage. He took the money and made change from a small wooden box. "You men just passing through?"

"Naw," Frog responded. "We got some cows penned out on the prairie west of here. We ran out of grub."

"If you ain't in a hurry, they's going to be a hoedown here soon as the folks come in out of the woods. You're welcome to stay."

Frog's face brightened. "You hear that, fellows? They're having a frolic here in a little while. You want to stay?"

"I do," Bonzo said quickly.

"What's a frolic?" Zech asked, annoyed that something might change their plans to leave immediately.

"Fiddles and dancin'," Frog responded. "Ain't you ever been to one?"

"If I had, I wouldn't ask what it is. We need to go now. We ain't got time for such stuff."

"If you ain't never held a girl and stomped to the fiddles, boy, you're old enough now to learn what it's like. It's more fun to kiss a girl than a cow, and a girl's a heap softer to lie on than that hard prairie ground. You might make out tonight if you'd just give it a shot."

Zech felt a hot blush sweep across his face. He said harshly, "We need to go on now and see to the cows! We ain't got time to fool with no girls!"

"Cows ain't everthing, Zech. Just take it easy. We'll stay for a short spell and leave. You might enjoy it if you'd try."

They went outside, sat at the edge of the porch and started eating. People drifted in out of the darkness, on horses and in ox-drawn wagons, and soon a milling crowd filled the clearing.

Several men threw more logs on the fire, bringing the front of the store into focus; then three men with fiddles mounted the porch and played briskly. Another shouted cadence as men grabbed women, starting the first round of a square dance.

Zech watched sullenly as Frog and Bonzo joined the line of dancers, kicking their boots into the soft dirt, swaying, linking arms, then swinging down the line as they changed partners again and again.

He was unaware of the girl's presence until he looked up, and he wondered how long she had been standing there. She had flaming red hair that flowed past her shoulders, pale green eyes, and white skin not burned brown by prairie sun. A blue cotton dress came down to her shoes, and she wore a matching ribbon around her slim waist.

She said, "It's better on a wooden floor where you can hear the shoes tapping. The men are going to build a meeting hall soon so we can have the frolics inside. You look like you're not enjoying it. Don't you feel good?"

"Well, I. . . I. . ." Zech stammered, unable to form a coherent answer.

"I've never seen you here before. My daddy owns the store, and I usually know everybody who comes to the frolic. My name's Glenda Turner. What's yours?"

"Zech," he managed to say. "Zech MacIvey. We came in for food. We've got cows penned out on the prairie."

"You live nearby?"

"Up on the Kissimmee, about a day's ride from here. We're in the cattle business and we're finishing the spring roundup."

She waited for him to ask, and when he remained silent, she said, "You want to dance the next one with me?"

Zech felt like he had swallowed a pine burr that lodged in his throat. He forced out the words, "I don't know how. I've never been to a frolic before."

"That's too bad. Would you like some punch? I helped my mother make it and I know it's good. The bowl is on the table at the end of the porch."

"That would be fine."

Zech was still sitting, and when he got up to follow her, she came only to the top of his shoulder.

When they reached the table she filled a cup with red liquid and handed it to him. He downed it in one gulp and said, "That's real good. I've never tasted anything like it."

"It's sugar that makes it sweet. But it's better if you just sip."

His face turned crimson as he said, "I'm sorry I drank it so fast. Next time I won't."

"Here, let me get you another."

As she refilled the cup she brushed against him. Zech immediately smelled a scent he had never before known, lilac water. He breathed deeply, drawing the fragrance into his lungs, feeling a strange sensation pulse through his veins, making him giddy.

"How old are you?" she asked for the second time with no answer.

He shook his head, feeling as if he had jumped a ten-rail fence. "I'm sorry. I didn't hear you at first. I'm seventeen, going on eighteen."

"I'm fourteen, but my mother says I look older. Do you think I look older than fourteen?"

"I don't know. I've never been around girls. Only my mamma. But you look fine to me."

"Thank you. I've never been around boys very much either. There's not many young people in Fort Drum."

The music stopped between dances, and Zech noticed Frog and Bonzo out by a wagon with several sweating men, drinking from gallon jugs. He started to go to them and insist they leave, but said instead, "You want to see my dogs? They look like wolves. They're on the other side of the store."

"I'd like to. I've never seen a wolf, or a dog that looked like one."

They walked past the crowd of people and found the dogs sitting in the shadows, waiting patiently as Zech told them to do. He said, "This one is Nip, and that one Tuck. They're the best cow dogs that's ever been."

"Aren't you afraid of them?" she asked. "They're so big."

"They's good dogs. They won't hurt you. Touch one."

She put her hand on Nip's head, causing his tail to wag vigorously.

"See. I told you. He likes you. You want to see my horse too? His name is Ishmael, and he's a marshtackie. The Seminoles gave him to us."

They went to the rail where Ishmael was tied. Zech said, "He's little, but he runs like the wind. I won a race with him in Punta Rassa. Outran a big Tennessee bay twice his size." Then on an impulse he said, "You want to ride? We'll just go a short piece and come back."

"If you'll help me in the saddle. I can't get up there in this long dress."

Zech picked her up gently and placed her sideways in the saddle; then he put his foot in the stirrup and mounted Ishmael behind her. He reached around her slim body and took the rein, moving the horse slowly away from the building.

The smell of her came to him even stronger as their bodies brushed

together constantly with the rhythm of the horse. Her closeness overwhelmed him, making him forget the cows and Frog and Bonzo and
the frolic and even where he was. His arms tightened around her with
each step, and he trotted Ishmael for a half mile before he realized
how far he had gone. Then he turned and headed back toward the light
in the distance.

When they came back to the store and the people and the screaming
fiddle, he was jolted back to reality. He jumped from the horse, lifted
her down and said, "I've got to find Frog and Bonzo and go now.
There's bears and wolves out on the prairie, and the cows might be in
danger. I didn't mean to take you so far."

"I enjoyed it," she said, touching his hands that still gripped her
waist. "Will you be coming back soon?"

He jerked his hands away, not realizing he was still holding her. "I
don't know. We're taking the cows grazing soon as we get back to the
hammock, and after that we'll go to Punta Rassa to sell them. If I don't
come back this summer I will in the fall."

"If you do, I'll teach you to dance. Will you promise me you'll try?"

"I promise. And I'll be back as soon as I can."

Frog and Bonzo were still at the wagon, drinking, and Glenda watched
as Zech turned quickly and walked straight to them. He said, "We best
go. We've been here long enough. We've got to see to the cows?"

"Seems you been seeing to something all evening," Frog said, taking
another drink. "That little red-headed gal you been herding around is
the best-looking heifer I've ever seen. You did right well for the first
time at a frolic."

"I wasn't doing anything," Zech said defensively. "I was just showing
her the dogs and Ishmael."

"Way she was looking at you, you could as well showed her a rattler
and she wouldn't have knowed the difference. But don't make no apology
because she latched on to you and stayed with you, Zech. Ever woman
I danced with told me I smell like a polecat, and wouldn't dance no
more. And I guess I do. Maybe it's best we go on now and head back
to the corral. We done all the damage we can do here tonight. Next
time I'll wash up some first."

They mounted and rode westward, putting the horses into a canter
again, crossing a plain now flooded with soft moonlight. It seemed to
Zech that the cabbage palms and palmetto had turned to lilacs. The
scent clung to him and the saddle, coming from everywhere, making

the ride last only moments before they approached the corral.

Even before they reached the pen, Zech sensed something was wrong. Apprehension drove away the smell and the thought of Glenda, and he put Ishmael into a fast gallop. He stopped just short of the rails and stared disbelieving into an empty corral.

Frog rode up beside him and said, "Now how the hell did they do that? I checked that gate myself and it was shut tight. They must have pushed it open and took off."

"I told you we shouldn't have gone off and left them alone," Zech said, guilt in his voice. "I told you! We should have stayed here and watched after them."

"They're sommers close by," Frog said assuringly. "Cows don't run at night 'less they're afraid. If something had been after them they'd have busted down the fence, not just opened the gate and walked out. There's not a single rail even pushed sideways. We'll find 'em in the morning."

"I hope so," Zech said doubtfully. "I've never lost a bunch of cows like this, for no reason at all. We best start looking for them at first sunup. If we don't find them, I'll have a hard time explaining it to Pappa."

Frog looked down from his horse and said, "It's for sure nothing spooked them. The tracks is too close together for them to be running. They walked away from here calm as raccoons."

"We must not have locked the gate good," Zech said.

"Maybe so. But I could have sworn it was shut tight. I checked it right before we left."

"I'll put Nip and Tuck on the trail. They can sniff 'em out a lot quicker than we can follow the tracks."

Zech dismounted and whistled for the dogs. When they came to him he pushed their noses to the ground and said, "Go and find them! Go!"

They didn't bolt forward instantly and race away. Instead, they moved slowly and carefully at first, sniffing constantly, going off to the right and left to determine if any cow had wandered off alone.

The trail led south for four miles, then it turned west into an area of dense palmetto. Frog signaled for Zech and Bonzo to stop, and then he said, "You think this is really worth it, Zech? If them cows scatters out in this palmetto thicket, we'll have to pop them out one at a time.

We can round up a new bunch quicker than this."

Zech knew what Frog said was true, but he was thinking of Tobias and the trust he placed in him to handle the roundup. He said, "Let's go just a bit further. The tracks is still all together. If we don't find them soon, we'll turn back and head for the hammock."

They followed the tracks for a half mile more, going deeper into thick scrub; then they came to a trail that ran straight into a narrow, dry slough bordered on both sides by Spanish bayonet and thick clumps of palmetto.

Zech was just about to call the dogs and turn back when it came, a shattering boom, ear splitting, coming from somewhere on the right just ahead of them. Tuck's head flew off and rolled forward, blood gushing from the stump and spilling out in a flood. Rifle bullets peppered the ground around Nip. He braked quickly, tumbling over and over; then he scrambled to his feet and retreated, running for the nearest cover. Then he fell again.

Ishmael jumped sideways instinctively, somehow knowing what he must do even before Zech realized what was happening. He staggered and then righted himself, almost throwing Zech from the saddle, then he bolted into a clump of palmetto.

Zech left the saddle and fell to the ground, stunned momentarily, before he heard someone close by shouting, "Bushwhackers! Bushwhackers! Stay hid! Stay hid!"

The popping sounds continued as Zech lay still. A limb above him shattered, sending a fine spray of palmetto fiber into his eyes. He brushed it away and pushed himself to a sitting position.

Then for the first time he realized what he had seen, Tuck's head departing its body, the instantly lifeless form tumbling over and over through its own blood; then Nip falling also, scrambling and falling again, not knowing if he had escaped death or not.

Fear gripped Zech, and then it turned to instant rage, uncontrollable rage. He snapped a frond from the palmetto and beat the ground with it, shouting, "Bastards! Bastards! Sons-of-bitches!"

The firing stopped as suddenly as it began. The voice of Frog came again, "Stay put! Don't come out yet!"

Zech ignored the warning. He jumped to his feet and staggered forward blindly, trying to see through tears that fogged his eyes. He walked into the open slough and to the body. He fell to his knees and touched the shaggy fur. Tuck's eyes were open, staring, seemingly puzzled as to what happened to him so swiftly. Zech reached out, grabbed the head and placed it back to the body.

Shouting came again, "Zech! Get the hell outen there! They might not be gone yet!"

He went to the sound and located Frog's horse; then he ripped the pistol from the saddlebag and started running, screaming again, "Bastards! Bastards!"

Frog tackled him from behind and struggled to hold him, the two of them tumbling over and over like wildcats fighting. The pistol went off, spewing smoke into their eyes; then Frog shouted, "Don't be a fool, Zech! Anybody who'd do this for some scrawny yellowhammers would as soon shoot you as a buzzard! Let go the gun!"

Zech loosened his grip and lay still. He looked up, rubbing his eyes, seeing that it was Frog on top of him. He said, "What about Nip? Did they kill him too?"

"I don't know. Last time I seen him he was making for the bushes over to the left of us. Let's go and see."

The two of them got up, crossed the slough and entered the palmetto. They found Nip twenty feet inside the brush. He was lying on his side, whimpering, trying to lift his head but unable to do so. When he saw Zech he wagged his tail feebly.

Zech dropped down and touched him. "He's shot, but I can make him well. We'll take him back to the hammock."

"No, Zech. His guts is blowed apart. He's hurtin' real bad. You'll have to finish him."

Zech looked at the bloodied stomach, the gaping hole, realizing what must be done. "I can't do it, Frog. You'll have to." Then he walked away quickly. He cringed when the pistol fired, tears forming again in his eyes.

Bonzo was standing by his horse, his left arm hanging limp and blood-stained. When Zech saw this he went to him and said, "Are you hit bad, Bonzo?"

"Naw, ain't nothing but a flesh wound. The bullet went clear through. I'll be O.K. soon as I tie a cloth to it. The bastard who cracked down on me ain't too good a shot."

Frog came from the palmetto and joined them. "Let's get the hell out of here before them crazy fools decide to come back," he said.

"Not before I bury Nip and Tuck," Zech said. "I ain't going to leave them here for buzzard bait."

"Aw come on, Zech, How the hell you going to bury them dogs without a shovel?"

"With my hands if I have to. I'll not leave till it's done."

"I'll help then," Frog said, knowing he could not get Zech away otherwise. "I'll get some sticks to dig with."

They scraped a hole in the ground, using both hands and hickory, and put the dogs in a common grave. Zech covered them by himself, patting the dirt firmly, hoping some panther or wolf would not come along, find them and dig them up. He said, "I ain't never been able to read the Book. If I could, I'd say words, but I don't know how. I hope the Lord blesses them."

As they mounted the horses to leave, Zech said, "I ain't never going nowhere again without a gun. And if I ever find the bastards who done this, I'll blow their heads slam off, just like they done to Tuck."

"We don't even know who it was," Frog said. "And chances are we'll never know. There's varmints like them everwhere."

"I'll know. If I ever come on them, I'll know. Just like Ishmael knowed the wolves were coming. Someday I'll find them."

Zech looked back briefly at the grave; then he put Ishmael into a fast trot.

"Don't try to blame all this on yourself, Zech," Tobias said. "It ain't your fault. And it don't matter none at all about the cows. We got plenty more. I'm just glad all of you got out of it alive."

"But I know it's my fault, Pappa," Zech insisted. "I killed Nip and Tuck just as sure as if I pulled the trigger myself. If I hadn't gone to the store and stayed for the frolic, none of this would have happened. They'd be alive."

"Them men was backshooters, Zech!" Tobias said harshly. "Don't you understand that? Staying for the frolic might have saved your life."

"Maybe so. But I won't leave a herd unguarded again. And when we get to Punta Rassa you've got to get me a gun."

"I'll do that. You ought to carry one anyway. But don't go around shooting every man you think might have killed the dogs."

Frog said, "Mister MacIvey, what kind of a gun could blow a dog's head slam off, like it done Tuck's? I ain't never seen nothing like that before."

"In all my lifetime I've never seen but one that could do it. It was stole from me when we lived in the scrub. It's a ten-gauge breechloader with two forty-inch barrels. It was made by a gunsmith just for my daddy, and it's the only thing he left me besides grief. There may be others like it but I ain't seen one. It has my mark on the stock. Some of them varmints who bushwhacked you could be the same ones who burned my house."

"I'm glad they turned a rifle on Bonzo 'stead of that thing," Frog said. "If they had, he'd be scattered all over the prairie."

"I killed a bear with it once," Zech said, "and it like to have broke my shoulder. If I ever see that old gun again, I'll know it even without the mark."

Frog said, "I been trying to figure out what's missing around here. Where's Skillit?"

"I sent him after some orange trees five days ago and he ain't come back yet. I've done dug all the holes while he's been gone. Maybe he ended up in Georgia 'stead of Fort Pierce. I don't think nobody would bushwhack a wagon full of orange trees."

Bonzo sat on the stoop while Emma put a fresh dressing on the wound. When she finished she said, "You'll be as good as new in a couple of days. Go on now and join that man talk while I fix supper."

"Thanks, Miz Emma," Bonzo said. "I appreciate your doing this for me."

"You're welcome. And I'll see to your stomach next. It's probably in worse shape than your arm."

Tobias said, "Frog, you and Bonzo take the horses down to the barn. They probably need some rest after you run 'em like you did."

"I'll go and help," Zech said.

"No. You stay here. I want to talk to you."

Zech and Tobias sat on the edge of the stoop while the horses were led away. Tobias said, "Son, I know you're hurtin' now, hurtin' real bad. I've felt the pain myself, and I know how it is. But don't grieve too long for Nip and Tuck. Let it go soon. What you just seen and been through will come again and again. This whole wilderness is built on such as that, and it's going to get worse before it gets better, if it ever does. You've got to learn to take the bad as well as the good, no matter what comes along. Don't go on hurtin' too long."

"Pappa, I don't think I'll ever forget seeing what I seen. Not ever."

"Yes you will. There ain't no pain that don't fade away. We'll get other dogs, and you'll like them too, and a time will come when they take the place of Nip and Tuck. The new dogs will be the ones close to you, and the ones you remember, not the old ones. That's the way it is. Something you like and lose will be replaced, and it'll go on and on, over and over again."

"Would you forget Mamma if she left us?"

Tobias did not expect such a response. He said, "That's different. I'm not talking about people. I'm talking about critters. But there's men who can replace a woman, and a year later hardly remember her name or anything about her. Only the one with them at the time matters. But no, Zech, I would not forget your mamma. Or replace her either."

"That's what I thought you'd say. And I feel the same about Nip and Tuck. I don't think I'll ever want any more dogs."

Tobias put his arm on Zech's shoulder. "We don't talk much like this, and maybe we ought to do it more often. I guess we've both been too busy chasing cows. What I said I've said badly. I ain't good with words, and you know that. All I'm trying to tell you is to be strong. Don't ever let nothing get you down. Don't be afraid or ashamed to love, or to grieve when the thing you love is gone. Just don't let it throw you, no matter how much it hurts. If you make it in this wilderness, you got to be strong. Do you understand me?"

"Yes, Pappa, I understand. And I'm sorry I cried for the dogs."

"Don't be. Don't ever be sorry for something like that. There ain't nothing wrong with a man crying. I done it for a week when my mamma died. But when you get done with it, start over again, and don't ever look back. Now go on down to the barn and see to Ishmael. He probably won't let Frog or Bonzo touch him."

"I'll see to him, Pappa. I'll feed him and water him and brush him down too. I ran him pretty hard coming back to the hammock."

Tobias watched him run away, seeing him as a boy again but knowing that such a time was gone forever. He said. "You'll see to it proper, Zech. You always have."

After supper Tobias went to the barn to pen the oxen for the night, leaving Emma and Zech alone in the house. Zech was at the table, still brooding about the dogs in spite of what his father said.

Emma sat beside him, wanting to distract him from such thoughts. She said, "Did you have a good time at the frolic?"

"I guess. But I didn't dance. I don't know how."

"Did you meet someone?"

"Yes ma'am."

"Was she pretty?"

"The prettiest thing I ever seen," Zech responded, knowing he could talk to his mother more frankly about something like this than he could his father. "She had hair as red as a sunset, and she smelled like flowers."

"I smelled like flowers once, but not anymore."

"You smell just fine, Mamma," he said, touching her hand, "and you always have."

"Not like flowers anymore. That's for young girls. Did you like her?"

"She rode with me on Ishmael. Her name is Glenda. Glenda Turner. Her daddy owns the store at Fort Drum."

"But did you like her?" she asked again.

"I never been that close to a girl before. I guess I did. She made me dizzy, like I was spinning around and around. She said if I come back she'll teach me to dance."

Emma put her hand on his. "Zech, if you like her, don't stay away too long. Flowers has a way of being plucked by someone, and there's not many nice ones out here in the wilderness. They don't stay in bloom forever."

"Maybe I can go back there after the drive. If I can find the time, I'll go."

"You best make the time. Cows won't ever smell good like flowers. Someday you'll know that."

Zech remembered Frog saying to him, "Cows ain't everything." He said, "Thanks, Mamma. I won't forget what you've told me. I'll go back to Fort Drum first chance I get."

Everyone was in the house at noon the next day, just finishing dinner, when the wagon creaked into the clearing. It looked like a mobile grove, with orange trees crammed into every inch of available space. Skillit stopped just beside the stoop and shouted, "I's back, everbody! I's back! Come and see what I got!"

Tobias expected only trees, and he was surprised like everyone else at the sight of a girl on the wagon seat, perched there like a frightened owl, her eyes wide and blinking.

Skillit said, "This here's Pearlie Mae. Preacher done married us, proper and legal." His face was split by a grin, with only teeth showing.

"So that's what your chore has been!" Tobias exclaimed, still staring. "If you wanted a wife, Skillit, why the hell didn't you just say so?"

"I's over forty years old now, Mistuh Tobias, and if I don't start me a family now, I'll soon be too old to even try. Pearlie Mae be a big help to Missus Emma. She knows how to cook and wash and sew and do most everything. You don't mind I brought her here, do you? She won't be a bother to nobody."

"Of course I don't mind," Tobias responded. "You're most welcome, Pearlie Mae."

Frog started jumping up and down, shouting, "Yew-haw! Yee-haw! Ole Skillit's done got him a woman! They's going to be nigger babies all over the hammock, thick as junebugs!"

"Shut-up yo mouth, Frog," Skillit said, "afore I pick you up and sling you into a buzzard's nest where you belong! You scarin' the hell outen Pearle Mae. She'll think you crazy."

"He is," Tobias said. "Don't pay no mind to him, Pearlie Mae. He's just jealous. Wouldn't nothing mate up with Frog, not even a wolf."

"One thing for sure," Frog said, "ain't no woman going to get the chance. I'd as soon be in a buzzard's nest as be tied to some woman's apron strings."

"You men hush up now!" Emma admonished. "You're chattering on like a bunch of jaybirds drunk on China berries." Then she turned to the girl. "You got a fine man, Pearlie Mae, real fine. Come on down off there and let's take a look at you."

The girl climbed down reluctantly, looking as if she might yet bolt and run. She was about twenty, two feet shorter than Skillit, and fifteen pounds overweight for her size. Her head was wrapped in a red bandanna, and a feed-sack dress came down to the top of an oversized pair of brogan shoes.

She managed a feeble smile, and then she said, "I's glad to meet you, Missus Emma. Skillit done tole me all about you an' Mistuh MacIvey an' Zech an' everybody else too. I's glad to be here."

Emma put her arm around the still frightened girl and said, "We're glad to have you in the family, Pearlie Mae. Real glad. Let's me and you go in the kitchen and have some woman talk and leave the men to themselves. I'll fix us a fresh pot of coffee."

Pearlie Mae seemed to relax as she followed Emma into the house. Skillit said, "Where's the dogs? I wanted to show them to Pearlie Mae right off so they'd be friendly with her. I don't want her comin' on them sudden like and think they wolves."

Tobias glanced at Zech, and then he said, "We'll talk about that later, Skillit. The dogs ain't here just now."

Frog said teasingly, "How much a ugly nigger like you have to pay for a woman, Skillit? I bet you paid as much for her as I could buy a wagon load of Cuban rum."

"I done tole you once befo to shut yo mouth, Frog! If you don't I'm goin' to skin you out like a rabbit!" He smiled as he said it.

"When you two get done with your funnin' we need to set out them trees," Tobias said. "Ain't good for them to be out of the ground too long, and I got all the holes dug."

Zech spoke up and said, "While you're doing that, could me and Ishmael go down in the woods, Pappa?"

"Sure, go on. We don't need you with the planting."

As Zech walked toward the barn Skillit said, "Zech don't look too good, Mistuh Tobias. He been sick?"

"I'll tell you about it while we plant the trees."

NINETEEN

"The cows needs salt, Mistuh Tobias," Skillit said. "They looks poorly. Let's take 'em to that river marsh up north of here where they's salt grass."

"I been thinking about that myself," Tobias replied. "After we graze there for a while we can turn south and cross the river. Go and tell the others to turn north."

The prairie was deep brown, burned by drought, and it would take thirty acres to feed just one cow. There were more than two thousand in the herd, all of them lanky after a winter in the swamps and woods. They moved faster than on past grazing drives, clipping the ground bare and ambling on, leaving behind a dust haze that made riding in the trailing wagon a constant annoyance. Both Emma and Pearlie Mae wore bandannas over their faces to gain what protection they could from the dust.

Sun rays bore down unmercifully from a cloudless sky, creating shimmering heat waves that looked like rolling ocean surf made of smoke. It played tricks on all of them, making distance judgment difficult, sometimes blocking out the horizon. Cypress stands ahead of them moved vertically and then horizontally, disappearing momentarily and then coming back like mystic ships with masts void of sails. The entire prairie seemed to be one giant vacuum just waiting to explode.

Men and horses were sapped of strength by mid-afternoon, and Tobias' shirt was soaked with sweat when he rode to the wagon. He said to

Emma, "There's a pond fed by a spring at the stand over to the right. Pull on over there and we'll stop for the day. I think everbody needs rest and water."

The cows smelled the pond and turned to it without being herded, and when the wagon reached the stand the pond was already stomped brown with mud. Emma and Pearlie Mae filled buckets at the spring before the cattle desecrated it too.

Skillit tied his horse to a bush and said, "Lawd have mercy, I ain't never knowed it to be so hot this time of year. That ole sun puttin' out heat like a wood stove full of hickory. Way I been sweatin' today, I knows I must stink worse than any polecat ever been born."

"I can smell you from here," Pearlie Mae said, grinning. "You sho' sleep by yoself tonight, else you go in the pond with the cows an wash up some."

"I think I just do that. Move over cows, I's comin' in."

"Flies seem to like this dry heat," Emma said. "They're as thick here as molasses. I don't know how we'll keep them out of the cooking pot."

Tobias dismounted, took a dipper of water from one bucket and poured it over his head. "If I didn't know better I'd swear the tops of them cabbage palms is smoking," he said. "They look like they're going to catch fire any minute. And if they do, with the prairie so dry, we're all going to be fried blacker than coon meat."

"You think we ought to turn back and put the cows in a swamp?" Skillit asked. "We do that, they could at least keep outen the sun."

"No. We'll move on. A couple days more and we'll make the marsh flat. The grass is bound to be better there. I've never seen that flat go as dry as this place."

Zech rode in and turned Ishmael loose at the spring. He dropped to the ground and put his head under water; then he filled his hat and came back to the wagon. He sat by Emma and put the hat back on, flooding his shirt and the top of his pants. "Feels good," he said.

Tobias said to Zech, "Soon as you get done cooling off a bit, take a limb and keep the cows away from the spring. There's water enough for them in the pond, and we don't want the spring messed up too."

The sinking sun brought no relief from the heat. Emma fixed a supper of beef stew, baked potatoes and biscuits, and even Frog and Bonzo ate lightly. No one seemed interested in food.

Frog pushed his plate aside and said, "Is my eyes playing tricks on me, or is something peculiar goin' on out yonder?"

"I don't see nothin' but cows an' palmetto," Skillit said.

Frog squinted. "Maybe it's just sweat and dust in my eyes, but I swear I just seen some of them bushes pick up and move. There's something out there besides cows."

"It seen it too," Zech said. "Over to the left, about a quarter mile."

They all continued gazing, and then Zech said, "There. You see it then? It's deer."

A herd of a dozen deer stood alert, staring at the cypress stand, then darting behind palmetto clumps and coming out again.

"They act like they want to come to the wagon," Frog said. "You reckon they smell Miz Emma's biscuits?"

"Taint that," Tobias said. "It's the spring. I bet you we done blocked off the only watering hole around here that ain't gone dry. If we have, every varmint on the prairie will be trying to come in here tonight for a drink."

"If'n they do, we'll have more wolves and bears and panthers than cows," Skillit said. "Maybe we ought to move on away from here before it gets dark."

"We could build a whole line of fires around the stand," Frog said. "They sure won't come through that to get in here."

"That wouldn't help the cows," Tobias said. "We can't cram two thousand cows inside a one-acre cypress stand. They'd still be out there in the open, fair game for whatever comes off the prairie."

"If Nip and Tuck were here they could handle it," Zech said.

"They're sorely missed for sure," Tobias said. "I never knew just how much of the work them dogs did till they were gone. But they're not here now, and that's a fact. We can sit here jawin' all night and it won't help matters one bit. We best decide what to do and then do it."

Emma said, "You can't blame the animals. They get thirsty too, and it's their water, same as ours. We can fill the barrel and the buckets and leave. What difference does it make if we camp here or a few miles further on?"

"None a' tall," Tobias said. "Sometimes you the only one makes sense, Emma. Let's all saddle up and move on, and let them critters out there have their turn. Ain't no use in us starting a war tonight over nothing."

"I'd sure like to be here when all them critters come together at the pond," Zech said. "That'll be a sight to see. I'll bet the fur'll fly thicker than dandelions."

"That's their problem," Tobias said. "Ours is the cows. We'll go a few miles on and stop again."

Just before midnight, when he was relieved from watch by Bonzo, Zech did not return to the camp. Instead, he rode south across the prairie, back toward the cypress stand they abandoned that afternoon.

There was a full moon glowing, and far in the west fingers of dry lightning cut the sky and were followed by dull rumblings. Tobias would be watching this too during his guard duty, watching with concern, hoping the slender fingers from above would not spark a fire in the tinder-dry grass. This was the most feared danger they faced on open prairie, fire that could move as swiftly as deer and destroy all in its path.

A full moon was always magical to Zech, bringing a time of enchantment when all the harshness of sun-burned prairie vanished and was replaced by soft outlines of palm and palmetto. He knew this to be a time of danger, when predators roamed and ruled the countryside, but this reality did not break his thoughts as Ishmael carried him slowly across the quiet plain.

There were many times back in the hammock when he slipped from the house unnoticed and walked alone through the woods and along the river during full moon, seeing and experiencing a totally different world from that of day. There was a warmness about it on winter nights, and a coolness in summer; and always it made him feel as if he were part and parcel of nature and its night creatures, a closeness that dissipated with the coming of the sun.

When he came to within a quarter mile of the stand he tied Ishmael to a bush and walked on alone, moving slowly and without sound. Then he stopped a hundred yards short of the pond and dropped to the ground beside a palmetto.

The first forms that visited the stand were deer, and they were soon replaced by the smaller vague bodies of foxes and rabbits and raccoons. He lay there in the dry grass and watched a procession come in groups of their own kind: wolves, bears, a mother panther with a litter of cubs, all passing each other without comment, drinking and disappearing again into the night. There were no growls of anger, no warnings to move away, no snarling flashes of superiority – deadly natural enemies seemingly under a truce understood only by themselves, sharing equally a thing they all must have to survive.

Zech watched spellbound, wondering what would happen if Nip and Tuck were with him, if they too would understand and honor this truce, retreat from natural instincts and patiently await their turn; or if they would charge forward and engage in combat to run the others away without sharing. He was glad they were not present at this moment, for he did not want the scene challenged. He knew it was possible he would never again witness it.

Time passed swiftly as the strange parade continued, and he finally realized he should return to the camp lest his mother awaken and find him missing. He got up reluctantly and made his way back to Ishmael.

No one stirred as he tied the horse and unsaddled him. Off to the right, the herd stood motionless, not even the swish of a tail breaking the silence. He wondered if they somehow knew no danger would come their way this night, if they were aware of the ritual taking place a few miles to the south.

He lay on his blanket and used the saddle as a pillow, staring upward at the star-peppered sky, awed by what the night brought him. He was still awake when Tobias rode in from the herd at dawn.

Two days later they reached a low plain that stretched for five miles north and south and three miles eastward from the river. There were no trees here, only unbroken marsh, and the grass was taller than prairie grass and more wiry.

In times past when they brought herds to the salt marsh the ground was soggy, and the imprint of a cow's hoof seeped brackish water. Now there were vast stretches of cracked mud that felt powdery to the step.

They made camp beneath a grove of cabbage palms on higher land overlooking the basin, then they drove the cows into the marsh. In spite of the dryness, the grass was bountiful, and Tobias knew the herd would get salt and minerals here that were unavailable on the prairie. He figured there was sufficient grazing for at least two weeks.

The days and nights settled into a dull routine of eating and sleeping and riding guard, but there was the diversion of going to the river and catching fish that Emma either fried or made into chowder. The river was three feet below its normal level and would be no problem to cross with the wagon when the time came to turn west.

At noon on the fourth day at the marsh, black clouds formed a solid wall in the west, and the wind quickened. Tobias watched hopefully as thunderheads inched upward and closer, and by mid-afternoon the marsh was turned a somber yellow by a sunless sky.

Lightning flashes were followed by sharp, crashing thunder, scattering the egrets and herons from their feeding grounds close by the river. All of the men not on watch cut poles and hurriedly fashioned lean-tos from palmetto fronds.

The wind increased until finally the marsh grass lay flat against the ground; then solid sheets of rain blew in vertically, slashing men, horses and cattle. From the camp the plain became invisible. When they could no longer see the herd, Tobias and Zech abandoned the watch and made their way back to the wagon.

Night came two hours earlier than usual, and the cooking fire hissed and went out before Emma could prepare food. They huddled beneath the lean-tos and ate beef jerky, and soon the pounding rain found its way through the palmetto roofs and drenched them.

The rain stopped just before dawn, and daybreak came once again to a cloudless sky. Tobias stirred and said, "We needed rain real bad, but that one was almost too much. I hope nobody floated away."

He got out of the wagon and walked across the soggy ground, stopping at the rim of the basin. The herd was all there, standing in a sheet of water covering the marsh. It looked as if grass were growing from a lake.

Because the basin was low land and mucky rather than sandy, the water did not run off quickly or become absorbed. Instead, it dropped to a one-inch cover and remained that way, releasing millions upon millions of mosquito eggs attached to the grass, dormant eggs that would incubate quickly in the intense heat and turn into larvae. Each invisible larva would eat and breathe for four days, and after shedding its skin four times, become a pupa. At this stage it discontinued eating and changed rapidly, and in another two days its skin split, allowing an adult mosquito to pull itself out and dry its wings in preparation for flight. No one in the camp was aware of this natural chain of events taking place across the tranquil marsh.

Zech was at the river alone, fishing, when he felt the stinging on his neck and arms. He slapped vigorously, then he waved his hand back and forth across his face. "Damn skeeters," he mumbled as he threw down the cane pole and then mounted Ishmael.

Tobias and Skillit were with the herd, puzzled by the faint humming sound drifting across the marsh from the north. Then they saw it, a solid black cloud extending from the ground thirty feet upward, moving toward them. As they watched, other clouds formed in the west and in the south.

Skillit said, "What is it, Mistuh Tobias? Is it locusts? I've heard of a locust swarm but I've never seen one."

"Whatever it is, I got a feeling it ain't good. We might need some help with the cows."

Tobias glanced toward the river and saw Zech enter a cloud and disappear momentarily, then emerge in a full gallop. He said "I don't know what's happening, Skillit, but I think we best get the hell out of here."

Before they could turn the horses, the stinging came, setting their bodies on fire. Tobias looked down and his legs were covered solidly by mosquitoes. His horse bolted straight upward and crashed down on its side, struggling and kicking, trying to regain its footing.

Tobias felt the breath go out of his lungs, and for a moment he couldn't move. He brushed feebly at his body as he heard Skillit's horse whinny loudly and start bucking. He also heard frantic bellowing come from the herd.

Cows were bucking, kicking and falling all around him as Zech raced across the marsh. As soon as a cow hit the ground mosquitoes swarmed over it and formed a solid mass in its mouth and nose, blocking air from its lungs, causing the cow's eyes to pop out as it tried to bellow but could not do so.

Tobias finally jumped to his feet, grabbed the horse and mounted. The horse spun around and around, snorting, trying to force the obstruction from its nose; then it gained control of itself and ran blindly.

Emma and Pearlie Mae were frozen with fear as they looked out over the marsh and watched the cows running wildly in circles, jumping and falling, repeating the frenzied cycle again and again. Emma saw Tobias go down and become engulfed in blackness. She screamed at Frog, "What's happening out there? What is it?"

Frog slapped his arms and legs, and then he said, "It's skeeters, Miz

Emma! Solid skeeters! We got to leave here right away! Run for the prairie! Go as fast as you can! I'll bring the horses and the oxen!"

Zech pounded his boots into Ishmael's side, forcing him to run through the swarming mass as swiftly as possible, feeling mosquitoes pound into his face like rain. He could not see ahead and only hoped he was heading in the direction of the prairie.

Skillit stopped briefly and looked back at the spot where Tobias went down, seeing nothing. He scooped a handful of the humming bodies from his left arm, crushed them and released them, and the bloody pulp poured downward like wild honey. His horse stumbled but didn't go down; then he galloped full speed to the east.

Pearlie Mae fell constantly, her short, overweight body crashing into the bushes, and each time she could hear Emma scream, "Get up and run, Pearlie Mae! You have to!"

The mosquitoes followed them two miles into the prairie until a brisk east wind blew them back toward the marsh. No one was together except Emma and Pearlie Mae, and their bodies were stinging too badly for them to even wonder about the others. They sat on the ground rubbing themselves, scratching the welts and making them itch even worse. Emma's eyes were almost swollen shut when she heard Tobias' voice above her, "Emma. Are you all right? Have you seen any of the others?"

He then sat with her as everyone gradually came together, mutually miserable, their bodies angry red, the horses wild-eyed and still bucking but alive. All of them were dazed, and they huddled together silently until Tobias finally said, "Don't nobody go back there. We'll stay the night here. Then I'll go in the morning and see if it's safe."

"What about food?" Emma asked.

"We'll do without."

Zech climbed down from his horse and retched violently. Emma looked to him and said, "I'm sorry, Zech. There's nothing I can do to help you."

"It ain't nothing, Mamma," Zech said. "I'll be fine in a few minutes. I just got a belly full of skeeters and they ain't sittin' well. I must have swallowed a gallon of 'em."

"Don't worry none about vittles, Miz Emma," Frog said. "I couldn't work my jaws even for soup. Feels like ever bone in my body is broke and on fire."

"The cows," Tobias said, scratching continuously. "Ain't no way they could run away from it as fast as the horses, and the horses almost didn't make it. I purely hate to see what's happened to them."

"Maybe they got away," Skillit said. "But if they did, they'll be scattered all over hell and back. We'll have to start the roundup all over again."

Tobias went back to the wagon alone at daybreak, taking each step apprehensively, dreading what he might find. When he reached the marsh he saw that he no longer had a herd as such. Cows were scattered across the marsh as far as he could see, and there were many lifeless forms. Mosquitoes were still there, but not in mass as the day before.

He returned to the prairie and led the others back; then the men rode into the basin while Emma and Pearlie Mae prepared food. They counted seventy-three dead cows, and there were also bodies of rabbits, raccoons and foxes. The swift deer seemed to have escaped the death cloud.

Tobias looked sadly at the carnage, and then he said, "It don't seem to be no end to the pestilence this land can bring. Sometimes I think the Lord is warning us to go away."

"We been through worse than this," Skillit said, "and come out of it on our feet. And I don't think the Lord would turn skeeters loose on a bunch of pore cows. It must 'a been the devil instead."

"Somebody did, and the Book says everthing is the work of the Lord. If it is, I hope He gets done soon with punishing us. I don't even know what we done to make Him so mad."

"I don't either," Skillit said, "but I knows one thing. The Lord ain't going to help us round up the cows. We'll have to see to it ourselves."

Tobias looked up and watched the flights of buzzards that already circled the marsh. He said, "Soon as the sun gets to boring down real good, this whole place is going to smell pure awful. We better work fast and get away from here as quick as we can."

It took them two days to bring the herd together again. Some of the cows had run as far as five miles, and all of them remained spooked and jittery. The loss of blood also made them sluggish, and some had mouths swollen so badly they couldn't eat.

When they crossed the river and headed away from the salt marsh, the path for three miles was littered with the bloodless bodies of small animals. Buzzards were everywhere, flapping off in protest as the cows passed, then returning immediately.

Tobias knew it would take time and grass for the cows to regain their strength, so they let them wander slowly. The rain caused the prairie grass to come back to life and flourish, and they found good grazing. Day by day they drifted across the land lazily, like a summer cloud; and soon the welts and the memories faded away.

TWENTY

The two riders first appeared as black specks on the horizon. They were moving north, and then they turned west toward the herd. They rode marshtackies like Ishmael, but used no saddles.

Skillit was on the left flank of the herd, and they reached him first. Both of them were boys, ages fifteen and seventeen, and were Seminoles. Each carried a lancewood spear.

One of them said, "We are looking for a man named Tobias MacIvey. Could this be his herd?"

"You've found him," Skillit said, wondering why they would be out on the vast prairie on such a search. "He's the man right over yonder, just in front of the wagon. How long you boys been lookin' for him?"

"We went first to his hammock," the older boy said, "and no one was there. Since then we have been riding for two weeks. We thought he would be somewhere grazing a herd."

"You just lucky," Skillit said. "This is a mighty big place. You could have rode them hosses till winter and not found us. How come you lookin' for him?"

"We were sent by my grandfather. But it is not so hard as you think to find a herd. It is not like looking for just one cow. We have crossed the prairies many times and know them well, and we have also been at the MacIvey hammock once before."

"If you say so." As they turned the horses and rode away Skillit muttered, "Now when was them Indian boys ever at Mistuh Tobias' place?"

When they reached Tobias, the older boy said, "Tobias MacIvey?"

"Yes, that's me," Tobias replied, wondering also why the boys were out on the prairie.

"I am James Tiger, and this is Willie Cypress. We were sent to find you by my grandfather, Keith Tiger."

"Sure, I know Keith Tiger. I haven't seen him for a while now. How is he?"

"Not too good. That is why we are here. The long drought has dried up many ponds and streams, and most of the animals have died or gone away. We have no hides to use in trade. We also have no bullets left for the rifle, and there is little food in our village. My grandfather wishes to buy a few cows from you. He has no money now, but he will pay you as soon as he can."

"I don't care about the pay," Tobias said. "I'm just sorry to hear you're in such a fix. How many cows you want?"

"Just a few to get us by until the animals return. Whatever you can spare."

"How about a dozen? Will that be enough?"

"We did not expect so much," the boy said, surprised by the generous offer. "We were thinking of maybe four at the most. A dozen would be more than my people hoped for."

"Twelve cows ain't nothing," Tobias said. "Let's ride over there and I'll get Skillit and Frog to cut out a dozen of the best ones we got. We had some trouble a few weeks back and the cows ain't as fat as they ought to be. But they're coming along fine now."

"This will be a real help for my people, and my grandfather will be pleased. But there is one thing you must know. We do not come to you as beggers. My grandfather will repay you for this."

"Don't worry about it. Whatever he does is fine with me."

They followed Tobias over to Skillit, and after he instructed Skillit what to do, Tobias said, "How long you boys been out here looking for me?"

"Three weeks in all. Two since we left your hammock."

"How you been getting vittles with only them sticks."

"We have eaten mostly rabbit."

"Then you need some of Emma's cooking. I know how tired a man can get of eating nothing but coons or rabbits. You can stay with us tonight and fill your bellies and then leave in the morning."

Zech rode up and stopped a few feet away, staring curiously at the marshtackies and the riders. James Tiger looked at Ishmael and said, "Your horse and mine are brothers. The mother is dead now, and the stallion old, but we have others."

"Are you the ones who left Ishmael at the hammock?" Zech asked.

"It was my grandfather, Keith Tiger. But we were with him. Is that the name you gave the horse, Ishmael?"

"Pappa named him. I think he got the name from something your grandaddy once told him about the Indians."

"I know the word." James Tiger then asked, "Do you still have the wolf dogs?"

"No. They're both dead. They was shot by bushwhackers who rustled some cows from us. We named then Nip and Tuck. They were the best dogs I ever seen."

"I'm sorry to hear that. It is a cruel man who would bushwhack dogs. We will give you others to replace them. This time they will be leopard dogs."

"What's that?" Zech asked, his mind bringing forth the vision of a dog shaped like a panther.

"They are part hound and part bulldog, and they fear nothing. I have seen two of them kill a bear."

"Nip and Tuck could do it too. They wasn't afraid of anything. They once ran into a whole pack of wolves and tore one's throat open."

"Yes, wolf dogs are like that. We have no more of that kind. But you will like the leopards. They are fine dogs too."

Tobias said, "You boys could go on jawing with each other all afternoon. Zech, take them to the wagon and get some smoked beef to hold them till supper. And tell Emma to pull up at the next stand. We'll go on and stop for the day so she can fix them a whole wash tub of stew."

After supper Zech and the Indian boys rode across the prairie, talking constantly about horses and dogs and hunting and the great cypress swamp where the Seminoles lived. Even Ishmael seemed to enjoy the company of the other marshtackies as he pranced lively alongside of them.

Zech said to James Tiger, "If you wanted a few cows, how come you didn't just go out on the prairie and round up some 'stead of coming so far to find us?"

"We are not allowed to do this," Tiger responded. "We are not supposed to even own a cow anymore, and there are men who would do us great harm if we took them off the prairie. They would say we are stealing, although the cows have no marks on them. It is best that we have cows with your mark. That way, no one can say that we stole them."

"It still don't make sense to me," Zech said. "Wild cows are no different from deer. They belong to whoever takes them."

"That is not so in our case. Many of our people have been beaten and even hanged for having just one cow. It is dangerous for us to drive your cows back to the swamp, but we have no choice. Our people suffer from hunger and have great need of the meat."

Zech said, "I'll ask Pappa if I can leave the herd and help you drive the cows to your village. Three of us would be better than two, and nobody would bother us for driving cows with the MacIvey mark."

"I thank you, but we can manage. Your father would have need of you with such a large herd, and we'll be safe once we reach the south shore of Okeechobee. From there our people will help us."

When they returned to the camp Zech lay on his blanket wide awake, thinking of the things James Tiger told him, wondering why anyone would kill an Indian over a few scrub cows when they were numerous everywhere. He could also not comprehend some people denying the Indians the right to even own a cow. None of it made sense to him, and he felt a deep sympathy for James Tiger and Willie Cypress and all the others who suffered hunger because of what he could only see as gross stupidity and greed. Even the animals were willing to share if it meant survival for all.

He was saddened at dawn when the two Seminoles left, and he watched after them until horses and cows disappeared behind a distant cypress stand. He hoped their paths would cross again someday.

For four more weeks they stayed on the prairie, going wherever there was grass; then Tobias rode ahead and purchased cows that were added to the herd. By the time they reached the Caloosahatchie River the herd numbered over three thousand.

The price this time was twelve dollars per cow, and once again a steamer trunk was purchased to carry the sacks of gold doubloons.

As Tobias was leaving the store, the clerk called to him, "Mister

MacIvey, I almost forgot to mention this. We just got in a shipment from New Orleans that might be of interest to you."

"What's that?" Tobias asked.

"Come on in the storeroom and I'll show you. We haven't even put them out yet."

The clerk took a crowbar and pried open a wooden crate; then he removed a rifle and handed it to Tobias. "It's the new Winchester repeater," he said. "You put the bullets in this magazine under the barrel and it'll shoot as fast as you pump the lever."

Tobias turned the rifle over in his hands, examining the octagon barrel; then he sighted it. "How many times will it shoot?"

"Seventeen bullets per load. Most all the cattlemen who've come in lately have heard about it and asked could we get them in stock. They say rustling and bushwhacking is really getting bad everywhere. One man had three drovers killed up south of Arcadia, shot in the back, and a whole herd stole. This rifle ought to could settle a rustler's hash in nothing flat."

"I expect it could," Tobias said, clicking the lever as fast as he could pump it. "I just hope the rustlers don't get ahold of these things first. We done had a little taste of bushwhacking ourselves. They killed both our dogs and winged one of my men. How much do the rifles sell for?"

"Fifty dollars each."

"That's a mite steep, ain't it?"

"Well, not really. If you've got a single shot rifle, owning one of these is like having seventeen single shot guns all loaded and ready to go at once. And you're not paying near as much for this Winchester as you would seventeen single shooters."

"I see what you mean." Tobias counted on his fingers, and then he said, "I'll take seven of them."

"How many?"

"Seven. One for everybody in my crew, including the women. Next time anyone in my bunch gets bushwhacked we'll make some butts sing with guns like this."

"That you will. How much ammunition you want?"

"How does it come?"

"Twenty-four bullets to a box, twelve boxes to a case."

"I'll take four cases. That ought to do us for a while, including practice. We'll have to learn how to operate these things. It sure beats my old one-shooter."

"I'll have everything ready when you come back with the wagon."

Tobias hesitated for a moment, and then he said, "Make that nine rifles instead of seven, and two more cases of bullets. I've got some friends down in Indian country who can make good use of guns like these. You got saddle holsters to fit the Winchesters?"

"Yes, we have them."

"I'll need five. I'll be back with the wagon in about a half hour and pick all this stuff up."

Zech held the rifle proudly, sighting it and then pumping the lever, pulling the trigger and making the hammer click again and again.

Tobias watched him for moment, and then he said, "You ought not be doing that, Zech. It's bad on the firing pin. Don't ever pull the trigger on an empty gun."

"Can I put some bullets in it?"

"You better wait till we get out of town. That thing could blow a hole in the dock if you accidently shot it that way. Let's go on out to the camp first and pay everbody off, then you can fire it."

"I wouldn't be afraid to face a whole pack of bears with this rifle," Zech said, putting it into the holster. "It's the purtiest gun I've ever seen. I sure thank you for it, Pappa."

"You just be careful with it," Tobias cautioned. "One of them things can fire as many shots as a whole army squad used to could. It ain't no play toy. You got to handle it like a man."

"I will, Pappa. I'll be real careful. Soon as we get to the camp I'll fire off a few rounds and see how it works."

Emma popped the reins and started the oxen, and the men followed her. Skillit held the Winchester in his hands, pretending to shoot from the saddle.

As they passed one of the holding pens Tobias suddenly froze in the saddle. He stopped his horse and gazed intensely at the herd. Three of the cows closest to him had the mark MCI on their sides. Then he noticed others had the same mark.

He shouted, "Hold up, Emma! Stop for a minute!"

Skillit and Zech came to him, and Zech said, "What's the matter, Pappa?"

"Look yonder," Tobias said, pointing. "Look at the brand on them cows."

"It's ourn," Skillit said, puzzled. "How come you reckon they in there? We didn't lose no cows out on the prairie for somebody to find."

"No, we didn't. Let's see what this is all about."

Four men were standing at the gate, and one of them Tobias recognized as a counter for Captain Hendry. The others he had never seen before.

Zech, Skillit, Frog and Bonzo followed Tobias as Emma looked back from the wagon, perplexed by what was happening. Tobias stopped just short of the huddle of men and said, "Who owns this herd?"

"I do," one of the men said. He was the same age as Tobias, lanky too, with a bushy black beard. "How come you want to know?"

"My name's Tobias MacIvey. Captain Hendry knows me well, as do others in Punta Rassa. Some of them cows in there has my mark. Where'd you get 'em?"

"Oh, that," the man said, cautiously eyeing the mounted riders facing him. "Is it the ones with MCI?"

"That's my brand."

"I got a dozen of them. If they're yours, you can have 'em. I ain't got no use for some other man's cows. I just didn't know who they belonged to."

"Where'd you get 'em?" Tobias demanded again.

"Took 'em off some rustlers, over near Okeechobee."

"What kind of rustlers?"

"The worst kind. Indians. Them bastards will steal anything they can get their hands on."

"Were they men or boys?"

"Boys. Seems like they're starting real young nowdays."

"What did you do to the boys?" Tobias then asked apprehensively.

"We hung 'em."

"You what?"

"We hung 'em," the man repeated. "That's the only way you can teach Indians a lesson. If you don't, they'll do it over and over again, and there won't be no end to it."

"I *gave* them the cows!" Tobias roared, his face crimson red, his hands trembling. "They were my cows, and I gave them to them! You killed them boys for nothing!"

Zech leaped from his horse and spilled bullets over the ground as he tried desperately to load the rifle, shouting, "I'll kill 'em Pappa! I'll shoot every one of them!"

He was on his knees, snatching bullets from the dust, when Skillit grabbed him and threw him back into the saddle, holding the rifle away from him.

Captain Hendry's men started backing away hurriedly, and before any of the men could go for a gun, hammers cocked as Frog and Bonzo aimed Winchesters at them.

Tobias said harshly, "You stay out of this, Zech! I'll handle it! I should of sent someone with the boys 'stead of laying them wide open to vultures like these!"

"What you aim to do?" one of the men asked, backing up against the fence. "How was we to know they didn't steal the cows? They was marked, and we knew it wasn't no mark of a Indian."

"I ain't going to kill you like you done them boys," Tobias said, dismounting, "but I'm going to make you wish I did." He snatched the whip from his saddlebag and unfurled it. "I'm going to rawhide you bastards till you ain't got one piece of skin left on you. Frog, if one of them tries to run away from it, you and Bonzo shoot him right betwix the eyes."

"Yes, sir, Mister MacIvey. We'll do that."

The whip cracked, and the nearest man fell to the ground, cringing. Then it cracked again and again, spraying the air with cloth fiber mixed with blood. Tobias slashed frantically until finally Skillit grabbed his arm and shouted, "That's enough, Mistah Tobias! If you wants to kill 'em, do it with a gun, not a whip! They gone suffer plenty from what you done already! I know! It remind me of what happened to me! Shoot 'em, but don't beat 'em to death!"

Tobias stopped, his eyes glazed, his heart pounding, then finally he said, "You're right, Skillit. I done enough. Go in there and cut out our cows. I'll go to the wagon and wait. I don't want to even look at this vermin again."

One of the men tried to stand, then he dropped back to his knees, his shirt and trousers in tatters. He said feebly, "We'll get you for this, mister. It ain't ended yet."

"You know my name," Tobias said calmly. "It's MacIvey. And if you're interested, I live over on the Kissimmee. You're welcome to come to my place anytime you want to, but if I ever lay eyes on you again I'll kill you on sight. That's a promise, not a threat. Just keep that in mind next time you decide to lynch a couple of boys, or come looking for me." With that he mounted and rode to the wagon.

Tobias was still trembling with anger as he counted out the coins and handed them to Frog and Bonzo. He said to Skillit, "You want me to leave your share with the rest till we get back to the hammock?"

"That'll be fine. We can split it up then. What we goin' to do with these other cows? You want to sell 'em here or take 'em back with us?"

"Neither. They'll end up where them boys was taking them. I'll drive 'em myself."

Emma was standing nearby, listening, watching Tobias and hoping the anger would subside. She said, "Tobias, you don't even know where the Indians live. How can you hope to find them?"

"I know," Tobias said. "Keith Tiger once told me if I ever have need of them to come to the far side of the Okeechobee and head south. They'll find me, not me find them."

"But you don't even know where the lake is," Emma insisted.

"They said it's so big I can't miss it."

Emma knew that to argue or reason with him was fruitless, that he was determined to do this thing. She said, "At least take someone with you."

Tobias turned to Frog and said, "What you and Bonzo intend to do now? You going to take some time off before going back to the hammock?"

"We'll do whatever you want us to," Frog replied. "Bonzo has been feeling poorly, so we're not going anywhere. When he turns down a drinking spell you know he ain't up to snuff."

"What's the matter with you?" Tobias said to Bonzo.

"I don't know, Mister MacIvey. Sometimes I feel like my bones is all cracked, and I been having some sweating spells. But it ain't nothing to worry about. I'll be O.K. after I rest up a few days."

"Well, you take it easy if you don't feel good. You and Frog best ride on back with the others. I'll take Zech with me."

"I'll go too if you need me," Skillit said.

"Naw, that ain't necessary. Me and Zech can handle it. And besides, if bushwhackers is getting as bad as they say, all of you need to stay close to the wagon."

"How long you think you'll be gone?" Emma asked, relieved that he was at least taking Zech with him.

"It ought not take as much as two weeks. We'll come straight back after we find the Indians. But I purely dread what I'll have to say to Keith Tiger, if he don't already know."

TWENTY-ONE

Rather than setting out blindly, Tobias decided to go into Punta Rassa and talk to Captain Hendry concerning the location of Okeechobee. He was told that the Caloosahatchie flows from the lake's western shore; thus he could follow the river to its source and then turn south toward the great swamp. From this general description of its location, Tobias figured that on one of their grazing drives they had come to within twenty miles or so of the lake's north shore without knowing it.

Captain Hendry also warned him that the land south of the lake was virtually unknown, a wilderness not yet penetrated except by Indians. He thought such a journey as Tobias proposed was foolhardy, but he made no headway in trying to dissuade him.

It was early the next morning when Tobias and Zech departed from the others at the ferry landing. Emma said a fearful good-bye, imploring Tobias to abandon the drive and turn back if the trip became too dangerous. Skillit offered once again to go with them but was refused.

The area along the river was heavily wooded, so they moved outward and chose a path parallel to a marsh, giving them more control over the cattle. This time they did not let the cows set the pace, wandering slowly, but grazed them for an hour at a time and then moved forward at a steady pace.

Zech noticed that several times during the next two days Tobias slumped forward in the saddle as if in pain, and this perplexed and worried him. Always before Tobias had been alert and attentive to the cattle, but sometimes now he seemed to drift along aimlessly without giving his horse directions. When Zech rode to him and questioned him, Tobias snapped back to alertness, assuring him that he had merely dozed for a moment because of the intense heat. Once at night Zech heard him groaning in his sleep, and when he went to him, Tobias was drenched with sweat.

On the fourth day they struck the western shore of Okeechobee, marveling at the seemingly endless expanse of water before them. The shimmering surface stretched into the horizon and gave no hint of a distant shore. Vast areas of blooming pickerel weed lined the water's edge, creating a sea of soft blue that merged gently with clumps of willows and little islands of buttonbush with its creamy white flowers. Nearby rookeries exploded with birds, great blue herons and snowy egrets, white herons and wood ibises, whooping cranes and anhingas with their wings spread outward to dry them. Cormorants dived beneath the surface and popped up unexpectedly fifty feet away, startling flocks of ducks and coots that peppered the surface. Majestic roseate spoonbills stalked up and down the shallows, swishing their long paddle bills from side to side as they raked the bottom in search of food, their pink feathers catching the sunlight and making them appear even pinker.

Zech insisted they stop for a day or two and let the cattle graze on the abundant grass, but he was more interested in rest for his father than food for the cows. Tobias agreed reluctantly, wanting to push on immediately, but in his weakened condition he allowed himself to be overruled.

After making camp beneath a thick covering of alders, they walked back to the shore and watched the unfamiliar sights with fascination, seeing an endless parade of nature's creatures. Willows were so loaded with chattering red-winged blackbirds that it seemed the tree limbs would surely break, and fish were so plentiful their fins cut the calm surface with constant ripples.

Zech took his fishing line from the saddlebag, cut a cane pole, and caught crickets for bait; and in only moments he caught more black bass and catfish than they could hope to eat. On the way back to the camp he gathered figs from a thick grove of wild trees, and for supper they had fish roasted over an open fire, followed by the sugary fruit.

That night the eerie call of limpkins blended with the croaking of bullfrogs and the grunting of alligators, forming a strange type of music never heard out on the prairie. Tobias moved closer to the warming fire and said, "I'm glad we stopped here, Zech. I've never seen a place so full of life. Not even back in the scrub. I can see now why some of the Indians they ran off from here hid in the swamps, hoping to come back someday. I hope they can, but I got a notion they won't. When folks find out what's here they'll take it over, and you won't ever again see an Indian on this lake's shore. Maybe someday we can come back and see it all."

"I sure hope so. James Tiger told me there can be waves out there taller than a man, and at some places there's sand dunes like at the ocean. He also told me that the sun sucks water from the lake, and it'll drop down several inches during the day, and then during the night it'll come right back to where it was. I'd sure like to see that too."

"Maybe someday," Tobias said again. "But right now I think I'll sleep. I feel kinda tired all through and through, like a wore-out old ox."

"You ain't old at all, Pappa. But you get some rest. I'll stay up tonight and take care of the cows."

Two days stretched into three, and Tobias gained strength from the fresh fish, wild fruits and berries. On the morning of the third day they broke camp and continued the drive, skirting the rim of the lake, but when they rounded the western shore and attempted to head directly south, they were met by a stretch of sawgrass with blades so sharp it prohibited the entrance of cows, men and horses.

At this point they turned to the southwest and entered a custard-apple forest, a jungle unlike anything they had ever encountered. Trees were so dense they formed a barrier almost as impenetrable as the sawgrass. The sky was blocked out immediately by leafy branches completely covered by a solid blanket of moon vines, turning a bright noonday sun to dim twilight.

The cows walked single file to make their way through the wall of trunks, and there was no way to drive them in a straight line. They skirted masses of dead limbs long since blown down by hurricanes, and gourd vines looping from branch to branch formed a curtain of green fruit. Trees were peppered with air plants that blossomed with brilliant red and orange flowers, and the ground beneath was totally bare except for lush beds of ferns, some ground level and others as tall as the horses.

The forest also teemed with Carolina parakeets as numerous as were the blackbirds at the lake, and low-hanging limbs were anchored to the ground by giant spiderwebs. Once Zech threw a stick into one of the webs in a useless attempt to break through; it sang like violin strings and held fast, causing the huge brown and yellow spiders to rush forward and examine the captured missile.

Every foot of the way was blocked by something: trunks, tangling vines, webs, grotesque outcroppings of roots. They turned, zigzagged and backtracked, popping the whips and cursing the bewildered cows, moving tortuously through an atmosphere so murky they couldn't determine if they were heading south or north; and in one four-hour stretch they traveled less than a mile.

There was no sunset that afternoon beneath the solid roof of the jungle, only a fleeting moment when twilight turned to instant darkness. Zech built a fire and they huddled together, hearing the chilling cry of sentinel hawks and the mournful song of whippoorwills. Screech owls then joined the chorus, making the cows also come together in a tight circle. Zech suggested time and again they turn back and seek another way, but each time Tobias shook his head in disagreement.

It was impossible to tell when dawn came, and when finally a dim yellow light drifted down through the vines, it could as well have been noon as mid-morning. They moved again, repeating the experience of the previous day, turning, twisting and probing, mile after mile of the same frustration. Even Tobias now worried about the cows and horses since there was nothing for them to eat but ferns. He hoped the lacy outgrowths were not poisonous.

Another night was spent beneath the canopy, then another morning vainly searching for an escape route. Just when they both became resigned to the fact they were hopelessly trapped, they broke free at mid-afternoon and entered a marsh. The cows and horses grazed ravenously, and Tobias agreed to stop for the night.

After building a fire Zech walked back to the edge of the forest. He stepped gingerly onto the moon vines and jumped up and down, finding the green carpet to be as solid as a bed. Then he walked upward slowly, a step at a time, until he reached the top of the trees and stood on the jungle's roof.

The vines stretched away as far as he could see, like a verdant plain splotched with blooming white flowers. He walked forward, at first cautiously and then with confidence, traveling a hundred yards before turning back reluctantly, wishing he could retrace the entire distance they had come but knowing he should return to Tobias.

As he made his way down the leafy incline and onto solid ground again, he trembled with excitement, feeling he now had a newfound secret not to be shared, like a baby eagle no longer earthbound, drunk with the exhilaration of its first flight.

The thrill of the experience carried over past supper and into the night, and as they moved away at dawn, Zech looked back with both fear and joy at the giant tent nature had created over the forest.

The marsh dissipated rapidly, and then they came to the edge of the place they were seeking, the great cypress swamp. At first the land was peppered with small dwarf cypress and pond cypress; then suddenly there loomed before them the mighty virgin bald cypress trees themselves, reaching up to a hundred and fifty feet into the air, some with bases seventy feet in circumference.

Cypress knees sprang up all around the base of the trees, like giant mushrooms, some shaped like deformed human heads, some like birds, others like small animals, creating a wooden menagerie. Wild orchids clung to every limb, turning the somber trees into colorbursts of yellow and white and green and purple. There were also gumbo-limbo trees, lancewoods, cocoplum bushes, oaks festooned with Spanish moss; and the awesome magnolias with leaf-covered limbs reaching sixty feet outward and then downward to the ground, like a mother hen protecting her brood with a covering of wing feathers. Piercing all of it were royal palms whose bare trunks towered above some of the bald cypress, forming little umbrellas of fronds high in the sky.

At first they stopped and stared incredulously, comparing the giant bald cypress to the little matchsticks that formed cypress stands on the prairie; then they moved forward again.

The ground was dry, but they could see watermarks several inches up the cypress knees where water normally reached. They passed easily over dry sloughs that once would have to be forded, and skirted around ponds covered solidly with lily pads and green slime. Cottonmouth moccasins scurried away beneath the surface and left trail marks, and the snouts of alligators poked upward like dead logs, their eyes open and blank as the intruders passed by.

They were also greeted by hordes of mosquitoes, not a solid mass like the cloud at the salt marsh, but a constant annoyance. Zech and Tobias both slapped and scratched, wondering how the Indians who lived here could stand it.

They could see areas on the bases of the trees where panthers scratched the bark to shreds sharpening their claws, and the horses stepped around holes rooted out by wild hogs searching for food. The deeper they penetrated the swamp, the thicker became the trees and other foliage, until finally they faced obstacles almost as formidable as the custard-apple forest.

Once again they zigzagged and backtracked, searching for open paths, having difficulty controlling the cows. Zech was doubly worried, wondering if there was no end to this alien land, and also noticing Tobias slumping forward in the saddle, sweat pouring from his face and staining his shirt. He did not believe there was even a bare possibility of finding the Indian village in such an overwhelming swamp, that to continue was foolish and useless; but Tobias would not relent and turn back.

For two days they passed no pond or stream where the water looked drinkable, and at night they rationed themselves to one cup from the canteens. Supper was limited to a thin twist of dried beef and rock-hard biscuit.

On the third night in the swamp they were sitting by a fire, hoping the smoke would drive away the mosquitoes, when a man stepped from the shadows and confronted them. He was dressed in a multicolored shirt that came down to his knees, deerskin trousers, moccasins, deerskin leggings, and a crossed finger-woven sash with long fringes. From his neck downward over his chest hung a georgette fashioned from silver coins hammered thin, and on his head he wore a turban crowned by an egret plume.

Both Zech and Tobias were startled, and both scrambled to their feet as the man said, "Do not be frightened. I bear no arms, not even a spear. We have known you were coming this way since you left the custard-apple forest."

Tobias calmed himself, and then he said, "My name is Tobias MacIvey, and this is my son Zech. We're looking for the village of Keith Tiger."

"I am Tony Cypress, father of Willie Cypress. We know who you are. I will come back at daybreak and lead you to the village. Your cattle would become lost in the darkness if you followed me now."

"How do you know who I am?" Tobias questioned, puzzled.

"We trust no one, and we watch intruders. You were described today to Keith Tiger and he said it would be Tobias MacIvey. He does not understand why you drive cattle into the swamp."

"Do you know what has happened to your son and James Tiger?"
Tobias asked cautiously.

"They were sent to find you and buy cattle, but they have not returned.
We sent runners searching for them as far as the south shore of Okeechobee but did not find them. Do you have news of them?"

Tobias dared not tell of the hanging to Tony Cypress alone, fearing
the reaction. He would feel safer telling the news to a friend. He said,
"We have seen them, and we can talk of this tomorrow with you and
Keith Tiger. There's no need to discuss it now."

"Do you have food?"

"Not much, but enough to do us for now."

"I will return at daybreak. Watch your cows closely. Since the deer
are scarce the panthers are hungry and will attack anything. Do not
let your fire go out." The Indian then stepped backward and disappeared
into the darkness.

Zech threw more sticks onto the fire and watched as a stream of
sparks drifted upward, glowing briefly like fireflies. Then he took the
Winchester from his saddle holster and placed it beside his blanket. He
said, "Pappa, what are we going to do if they blame us for what
happened to James and Willie?"

"I been thinking about that too. Fact is, I thought about it all the
way down here and I don't have an answer yet. I just don't really know.
We'll have to wait and see what happens. If I were Tony Cypress, and
it was you hung instead of Willie, I'm not sure myself what I'd do."

There were a dozen chickees in the village, small open-sided huts
constructed of cypress poles with roofs of thatched palmetto fronds and
bear grass. Beneath one a black cooking pot was tended by an old
woman stirring constantly with a wooden paddle. All of the men were
dressed similar to Tony Cypress, and the women wore multicolored
ankle-length dresses with a dozen strands of glass beads around their
necks. On top of each one's head was a tight ball of hair held fast by
black netting.

At the fringe of the clearing there were several clumps of banana
trees and a small garden plot containing wilted tomato plants, okra,
squash and corn that had turned brown prematurely from lack of rain.

Everyone in the village watched curiously as the cows invaded the clearing and milled about. Tobias and Zech rode in and dismounted and then followed Tony Cypress to one of the chickees.

Keith Tiger was sitting on the ground, and when he looked up and recognized the visitors, he motioned for them to sit with him. He looked older than Tobias remembered, and his hair was now completely white. Tobias said, "It's good to see you again, Keith Tiger."

"And you too, Tobias," he answered, a smile creasing his face. "I am told by Tony Cypress that you bring news of my grandson and Willie Cypress."

"Yes, I do, but first there are other things," Tobias said, wanting to delay the inevitable as long as possible. "The cattle are for your people, and we have brought gifts. Go and get them, Zech."

Zech went to the horses and returned in a moment, placing boxes on the ground and handing two rifles to Tobias. He passed them on to Keith Tiger and said, "These are Winchester repeaters, a rifle that shoots seventeen times in one load. We also brought two cases of bullets, enough to last you for a long time."

Tiger examined one of the rifles and passed the other to Tony Cypress. "I have never seen such as this," he said. "How does it work?"

"You just put the bullets in the magazine under the barrel, and when you pull the lever a bullet goes into the chamber. It shoots as fast as you pump the lever till all the bullets are gone. It will bring down a deer easily at a hundred yards and more."

Tiger stroked the stock with his hand, saying, "This will be a great help to us, and I thank you, Tobias. The bow and arrow is almost useless in the swamp. You shoot at a deer and hit vines or trees instead. It is not like hunting on the open prairie. For here we need guns and bullets. This weapon will provide much food."

"Maybe you can shoot skeeters with it too," Tobias said jokingly, pleased by the reaction to the gift. "I don't see how you folks stand it all the time."

"We have grown used to them," Tiger responded. "There are many things we have been forced to learn since hiding here in the swamp. When our people lived on the land that is now Tallahassee, the soil there grew corn and beans and squash and pumpkins in abundance. Here things do not grow so well. It is the same with hunting. When there is no rain the swamp dries up and animals go elsewhere, and when there is great rain it floods, also driving them away or drowning them. There is always something facing us we must overcome. It has been difficult, but we have survived. But tell me now. Why is it that you drive in the cattle instead of James and Willie? What is your news of them?"

Tobias knew he could delay no longer. He spoke slowly, recounting the chain of events in his mind. "They found us on a prairie north of the Caloosahatchie and explained their mission. They spent the night in our camp and left at daybreak the next morning. Zech offered to ride with them and help drive the cattle but was refused. They said they could handle it alone, and that was the last we saw of them.

"It was several weeks before we reached Punta Rassa with the herd. As we left the village I saw cows with my mark on them in another man's herd. I questioned him about this, and he said he took them from rustlers down close to Okeechobee. Then I. . ."

Tiger broke in and asked anxiously, "If someone stole the cattle from James and Willie, why did they not return here and tell us of this? Where are they now?"

"I asked them who the rustlers were," Tobias responded hesitantly, "and they told me it was two Indian boys. Then I asked what happened to the boys, and the man who owned the herd told me they hung them. They're dead, Keith. I told the men that I had given the cows to the boys and that they had hung them for no reason. Then I beat all of them with my whip, beat them almost to death. I'm real sorry to have to tell you this. Real sorry. I don't know what else to say."

Both Indian men sat stunned, mentally frozen, trying to accept the finality of the words. Keith Tiger's eyes misted as he said, "In my heart I feared this, but it hurts no less hearing it from you now. I hoped that somehow they would return. This is the end for me. They killed my son in the last war, and now my grandson. James was the only one left, and now there is no one to carry on my name. It is ended forever. It would be better if they would come and kill me also. I have no reason now to live."

Tony Cypress said angrily, "Do you know where the men live who did this thing? If you do, we will find them and kill them!"

"I was so mad I didn't even ask their names," Tobias responded. "After I beat them with the whip, they threatened to come after me later. They know where I live, and if they ever come to my place, I'll kill them myself. This I promise. I hope you don't blame me for what happened. If I had known I would have. . ." Tobias' voice trailed off, and he never finished. He stood up suddenly, staggered a few steps and fell.

Zech rushed to him. He shook him and said, "Pappa! Pappa! What is it? What's the matter?"

Tobias shivered as if cold, and sweat poured from his face. He tried to speak but couldn't; then his glazed eyes locked onto Zech's, begging for help.

Zech brushed sweat from his father's forehead; then he looked to Keith Tiger. "Oh Lord! Somebody do something!"

Keith Tiger said, "When you came into the chickee I thought Tobias looked ill. How long has he been this way?"

"Ever since we left Punta Rassa. I begged him to turn back but he wouldn't. He wanted to bring you the cows. Can you help him? Do you know what's wrong?"

Tiger put his hand on Tobias' forehead. "It is malaria. We have seen it many times." Then he turned to Tony Cypress. "Get the medicine man, and tell Lillie to bring blankets. Quickly! He is very sick."

"Don't let him die," Zech pleaded fearfully. "If I had known he was this sick I would have tied him with ropes and taken him home. Mamma could nurse him."

"Do not blame yourself for this," Tiger said, putting his arm around Zech, trying to calm him. "It would have happened no matter where he was. It is best he is here. The medicine man can help him more than anyone. He knows what to do. We will do all we can to save him."

The medicine man was in his fifties, tall and lean, with gray hair that came down to his shoulders. He wore a knee-length dress only, and around his neck there hung a deerskin pouch, the sacred medicine bag, a symbol of his power.

Zech watched constantly, hovering, asking questions that were ignored, becoming a nuisance, told time and again to move away but refusing to do so. A bubbling pot sat next to the chickee, brewing a deep red liquid made of roots and herbs and the bark of a gumbo-limbo tree. Lillie held the blankets tight around Tobias as the medicine man lifted him up and forced the brew down his throat. Then they packed his forehead with lily pads made cool with pond muck.

For a day and a night Zech circled the chickee like a wolf stalking a herd, until finally Keith Tiger came to him and said, "There is no need for you to do this. It will not help, and soon we will have two sick men instead of one. Go and get food and rest. Leave your father to the medicine man and Lillie. If there is a change we will tell you."

The old woman in the cooking chickee gave Zech a gourd bowl of sofkee. He went to the far side of the clearing and sat on a log alone, absently chewing the hot gruel. He was not aware that someone was beside him until she said, "Don't fret so. They will make your father well again. The medicine man has great power."

Zech put the bowl down and said, "I'm sorry. I didn't know you were here."

The girl was sixteen, slim and firm, with black hair that swirled down to her hips. She had a thin mouth, high cheekbones and oriental eyes, the look of pure Seminole. She said, "I am Tawanda Cypress. Willie was my brother."

Zech flushed with guilt when she said it, feeling uneasy, as if accused without the words being spoken. He said, "I'm sorry. I offered to ride with them but they wouldn't let me. If I had gone anyway, he would be here now."

"You don't know this to be true. It's possible they would have killed you too just for being with James and Willie. I don't judge you as I judge those men who did such a terrible thing."

Zech looked at her closer, noticing she was very pretty. Something was different about her, something he could not at once place, and then he realized what it was. He said, "The night James and Willie spent in our camp we rode the prairie together, and they told me many things about life here. You don't speak like they did or the others."

She smiled. "Does it show so much? I spent three months with a missionary and his wife who are camped west of here, near the ten thousand islands. They were teaching me to read and write, and I suppose I took up some of their way of speaking. My father says someone among us should learn to write the white man's language, that it could be helpful someday, and he sent me there. They also instructed me in the Christian way, but I'm confused about that. I cannot understand why Christians kill for cattle."

"I can't answer that for you," Zech said. "I don't understand it myself. But not all white people are Christians, and not all white men will kill for a cow. My pappa would never do it, and I wouldn't either. Pappa almost beat those men to death for what they did, and I would have shot them for sure if Skillit hadn't grabbed me and taken my rifle."

"Can you read and write?"

"No. I've never had learning. Mamma can do it some, but Pappa can't. There's no time or use for such things on cattle drives. All you need to know is how to count heads and money."

"I'll go back soon and stay a while longer. Maybe someday I'll be able to teach you. Then we'll both know how."

"How come you're not afraid to stay with strangers?"

"I was at first. But they're very kind people, and they would never harm me. Their camp is also well hidden from others. Father came on it one day while hunting, and became friends."

"I guess I ought to go back now and see about Pappa," Zech said, starting to get up.

"You love him very much, don't you?"

"Yes. We've done things together ever since I can remember. We've seen some bad times, and he brought us through it. I don't know what me and Mamma would do without him."

"You can't help him now by getting in the way of the medicine man and Lillie. Let them do what they must do. Stay here with me for a while longer. I enjoy talking to you."

"I suppose you're right," Zech agreed, "but I can't help it. If we were at the house now Mamma would run me out with a broom. But I've never seen Pappa sick like this. It scares me."

"Would you like to see the great marsh?" she asked, trying to steer his mind to something besides Tobias. "I can show it to you."

"Is that the place James and Willie told me about? They said there is nothing else like it?"

"Yes. We call it Pay-Hay-Okee, the River of Grass. It would be a shame for you not to see it while you're here. If we leave now there is time to go there and return before nightfall. I know the way well."

"Then let's do it. I'll stay out of the way for the rest of the afternoon. I think the medicine man wanted to put me in the cooking pot with that stuff he's brewing."

They walked to where Ishmael was tied, and when Zech picked up the saddle she said, "We don't need that. It's better without it."

"I'll put you on first, then get on behind you," Zech said, throwing aside the saddle.

"An Indian woman would never do such a thing," Tawanda said teasingly. "We ride behind the man, not in front."

"If that's the way you want it, it's fine with me."

Zech leaped onto the horse, then he took her hand and pulled her up behind him. As they started out of the clearing she locked her arms around him, pulling as close as possible. He could feel her pressing against him, her body moving in perfect rhythm with his as Ishmael walked in a steady gait. The female smell of her made him dizzy, like the night he rode with Glenda, only this time the scent was not flowers; it was an outdoor smell, like smoke and crushed pine needles.

Zech followed her directions, and they rode deeper and deeper into the swamp, skirting islands of ferns taller than Ishmael, passing through myriad knees surrounding the giant trees. When finally they came to a narrow stream she said, "Stop here and tie the horse. We will go on in the canoe."

On the bank there was a long dugout cypress canoe and two thin poles. They pushed the canoe into the water; then Zech stood in front and Tawanda in the rear, and they poled the slim craft down the creek. At first it was tricky for Zech, and he almost lost his balance. Tawanda laughed at him until finally he gained confidence and pushed the canoe with ease.

The stream twisted and turned, sometimes just wide enough for the canoe to pass, and several times it led into small ponds covered with lily pads where turtles and alligators moved away as they glided by. Then suddenly the swamp ended, as if a line had been drawn to separate swamp from marsh, and looming before them was Pay-Hay-Okee, a land so overwhelming in its vastness it caused Zech to blink his eyes in wonderment.

Sawgrass stretched into infinity, broken only by small island hammocks of hardwood trees and cabbage palms. Flights of egrets and herons drifted for miles, dwarfing what Zech had seen at Okeechobee or elsewhere. He continued staring as Tawanda said, "You're one of the few people to ever see this besides an Indian. What do you think of it?"

"It seems like the whole world out there. How far does it go?"

"To the sea in the south. It is many days journey from here to the end of it, and it is very difficult pushing the canoe through the sawgrass. Sometimes the grass is taller than two men. When our people make the journey they push down the grass and sleep on it at night, and sometimes snakes crawl in with you. There are also many alligators out there, and crocodiles too."

"I'd like to cross it someday," Zech said. "Would you go with me and show me the way?"

"I would if you asked, but it is not a good place for women. We'll go a bit further now. Then we should turn back."

As they poled the canoe, Zech watched with interest as an Everglades kite glided over them, its huge wings extended, moving so slowly it seemed to be suspended in midair. Then a flight of small birds swooped in and harassed it, diving and pecking, until finally the kite shot downward into the sawgrass and disappeared.

The canoe sliced like a knife through the dense grass, and when Zech reached out and touched it with curiosity, blood oozed from cuts on his hand. They circled one small island and then returned to the creek.

When they reached the place where Ishmael was tied, they pulled the canoe back onto the bank. Zech said, "I'm glad you brought me here, Tawanda. I'll always remember this place."

As he untied Ishmael they brushed together, and on an impulse his arms went around her, holding her close; then he pressed his mouth to hers. She went limp, and without him she would have fallen to the ground.

Zech's breath came in gasps as he continued holding her, feeling his heart pound harder than hers. Every cell in his body tingled as he was flooded with a sensation that overwhelmed him, blocking out everything but Tawanda's presence. Time stopped, and when finally he released her, he said softly, "I'm sorry. I've never done this with a girl before. It just happened before I knew it."

"Why are you sorry?" she asked, looking into his eyes. "Is it because I am an Indian? Does it shame you to be with me?"

"No," he said quickly. "It's not that at all. I thought you'd be angry."

"Do it once more and let's see if it makes me angry."

He kissed her again, this time longer, forgetting to breathe or let her breathe, and when he broke away they were both panting. "You see, I'm not angry," she said. "I will stay here with you as long as you wish. We can find our way back when night comes."

He pressed her close again, his body aching for her, feeling actual pain, wanting to experience something he had only dreamed about. He would lie with her in a bed of ferns or even in an eagle's nest high up a cypress tree if that was what she wanted. As he held her it seemed he had known her always, not just this one afternoon, that loving her now would be as natural as a full moon or rain in spring.

He took her hands in his and said, "I've never known anything like this, Tawanda. I want to stay here and be with you real bad, more than anything. But we better go now. I need to see about Pappa."

"I thought so," she said without anger. "But it doesn't matter. There will be other times for us."

"Are you mad at me?"

"No. I know your feeling. I cried all night when your father told the news of my brother. You are crying inside now, and I know this. We can come into the woods again tomorrow, or whenever you wish. All you have to do is ask and I will go with you."

He mounted Ishmael and lifted her behind him, and as they rode back she pressed against him, her face on his shoulder, her hands burning his chest like a branding iron.

The sun sank rapidly as they approached the village, and already nighthawks swooped about, zigzagging crazily as they chased mosquitoes. No one seemed to notice as they rode in and dismounted, Zech holding her longer than necessary when her feet touched the ground. She followed him to the chickee and stood beside him as he looked down at his father. There was no change in Tobias. The medicine man and Lillie still hovered over him, paying no heed to Zech and Tawanda. Zech knew it would be useless to question them, so he turned and walked away.

One of the cows had been slaughtered while they were gone, and the smell of roasted beef drifted from the cooking chickee. Tawanda prepared two wooden plates for them; then Zech followed her to the edge of the clearing. They sat on the ground just at the point where fire shadows faded into darkness, eating silently. Tawanda then said, "We're breaking a Seminole rule already. An Indian woman does not sit beside her man while eating."

"Where I come from they do," Zech replied. "My mamma and pappa do everything together. It will be the same with us."

He surprised himself with the statement, as if they already belonged to each other. But it did not bother him. All of the awkwardness of their first meeting was gone, and he felt as comfortable with her as he did with Ishmael.

"There are many things in your world I don't know," she said. "I am Indian, and we are different from you. I'm not sure I could ever adjust."

"You wouldn't have to. I live in the woods too. We hunt cattle, then we graze them, and after we sell them we go back to the woods and start over again. What's so different about that?"

"But there are white people who would scorn you for being seen with an Indian."

"That don't bother me either. I don't care what somebody thinks."

Tawanda got up suddenly and said, "I'd better go to the chickee now before my father comes looking for me. It is also against an Indian rule for me to sit here with you in the darkness. In the morning I'll cook something special for you to eat."

He sat by himself and watched as she walked away; then he took his blanket and place it beside the chickee where his father tossed restlessly. The medicine man was gone, but Lillie was still there, changing the pads that cooled Tobias' face.

He lay on his blanket and stared upward into the trees, thinking of the contrast between the only two girls he had ever known. Glenda's skin was white and creamy, Tawanda's brown and firm. Glenda smelled like flowers, Tawanda like smoke and crushed pine needles. One rode a horse sidesaddle, the other like a man.

Guilt suddenly flushed through him, guilt that he had enjoyed himself so much being with Tawanda while his father lay gravely ill. He should have been at his father's side, not out in the woods with Tawanda. If he had accepted her invitation he would probably still be there with her at a time when his father could be dying.

His thoughts plagued him until finally he fell asleep.

The next morning Tawanda fixed a breakfast of koonti biscuits and fried beef strips, and he ate eagerly. She watched him expectantly, hoping he would again take her away on Ishmael. But he returned to the chickee and sat by his father, ignoring her. She understood, and said nothing.

At noon the fever broke, and Tobias sat up and sipped a cup of beef broth. He smiled at Zech, then he lay back down and drifted into a calm sleep. Zech's spirits soared as Keith Tiger said to him, "Tobias will be fine now. He has passed the worst of it. In a few days you will be able to take him home. I know your people are worried."

The words caused Zech a new concern that had not come into his mind while Tobias was so ill: his mother would be frantic with worry if they did not return soon. There was no way anyone from the hammock could ever find them here in this small village in the great cypress swamp.

He continued hovering about the chickee, again making a nuisance of himself, until finally Lillie spoke the only words she said in three days, "Go away and let us take care of him. You are worse than a puppy trying to get at its mother's tits."

He left reluctantly and went into the woods with Tawanda. They held hands as they walked together silently, communicating without speaking. She did not offer herself again, letting him take the lead, understanding his concern for his father overshadowed all else. This was the Indian way also, and she accepted it without hurt or anger.

When they returned to the camp they stayed together constantly, sitting beside the chickee with Tobias, dipping food from the cooking pot, leading Ishmael to a plot of abundant grass. It did not cross Zech's mind that this togetherness would be an oddity to the other Indians, and he did not notice the curious glances that came his way, even from Tawanda's mother and father. And it did not seem to cause Tawanda concern.

Tobias gradually gained strength, getting up and walking a few steps at a time, then eating solid food. He had become even more gaunt, and his clothes hung on him like sacks. On the morning of the sixth day he said to Zech, "How long have we been here? I don't remember much since the day we arrived."

"Almost a week, Pappa."

"A week? Good Lord! Emma will be worried sick. We'll have to leave in the morning."

"Are you sure you're strong enough to ride, Pappa? I could go to the hammock and tell them you're fine and let you stay here and rest. Then I would come back for you. I couldn't leave while you were so sick."

"No. I'll be fine. We'll go back together."

Keith Tiger spoke up, "You're welcome to stay here as long as you wish, Tobias. But if you leave, you must ride easy and not push yourself. See if you can find quinine at a trading post. It is what the soldiers use for malaria."

"I'll do that. And I truly thank you for what you've done for me."

"It is we who owe you thanks. The cows and rifles will save our people. Is there anything you wish from us in return?"

"My life is enough. But there's something Zech wanted if you can spare it. Dogs. Some rustlers killed the wolf dogs you gave us."

"That is no problem. We have puppies, and you can take your pick."

"No!" Zech said quickly. "James promised me some dogs he called leopards, but if I took them now they'd remind me of him and Willie. I couldn't stand it. I don't want dogs."

"I understand," Keith Tiger said. "It will be as you wish."

"I thank you just the same," Zech said more calmly, not wanting the Indian to think he didn't appreciate the offer.

"What's the name of the medicine man who tended me?" Tobias asked. "I haven't thanked him yet."

"His name is Miami Billie," Tiger responded. "He is out gathering roots and bark to make medicine for you to take with you on the trip home. He will return soon. Tonight we will have a celebration of your recovery, Tobias. We will roast the tail of an alligator. This afternoon I will test the Winchester against a 'gator's hard skull. You will enjoy the feast."

All of the Indians were in a festive mood as the huge chunk of meat roasted on a spit over the fire. Zech and Tawanda again isolated themselves from the others and ate together, and the alligator was as good to Zech as the first chicken he tasted in Punta Rassa.

Tobias was tired and went to bed immediately after eating, and soon the village became quiet as everyone drifted into the chickees. Zech was almost asleep when Tawanda came silently and lay down beside him. He put his arms around her, absorbing her warmth. She pressed closer, facing him, and sleep came imperceptibly as they clung together. Neither of them were aware when her father came from the shadows and looked at them briefly, seeing them asleep together like children, then turning and going away.

The next morning as they were exchanging final good-byes, Keith Tiger said to Tobias, "Do not go back the way you came. It is too difficult in the custard-apple forest. Go to the east side of Okeechobee, near the ocean. There are pine lands there, and open prairie. It will be easier for you."

Tobias mounted the horse shakily and steadied himself, still weak but determined to ride. Zech and Tawanda shared intimate glances, their eyes meeting in a silent understanding that he would return, but no tears came to her eyes. To cry at parting would not be the way of an Indian woman.

They looked back and waved as they entered the woods, and the sight of Tawanda became etched in Zech's mind. She looked small and alone as the early sunlight caught in her raven hair.

Tobias turned to Zech and said, "I woke up during the night and saw you sleeping with that girl. Did you do anything to her?"

Zech blushed, and he stammered as he said, "No. . ., Pappa. . ., I didn't do anything. We just slept together. . ., that's all."

"You're old enough to plant seeds now, Zech, and you got to be careful. Those people are our friends, and it wouldn't be right for you to ride off and leave something in that girl's belly. Are you sure you didn't do nothing?"

"Yes, Pappa, I'm sure. We didn't do nothing but sleep. We became friends while you were so sick. That's all."

Tobias stopped the horse momentarily and turned to Zech. "I don't have any objections to whatever you did, Zech. And I believe you if you say you didn't do anything with her. I wouldn't mind if you brought an Indian girl home with you for good, and Emma wouldn't either. That's not the point. Just don't ever mess up a girl and then go off and leave her to fend for herself. Do you understand what I'm saying?"

"I understand, Pappa. I wouldn't do anything to hurt Tawanda. Not ever!"

"I know it ain't natural for you to grow up in the wilderness without no young people around, especially girls. Heck, time I was your age I'd done had a few romps in a cotton patch, and I guess I was just lucky, 'cause nothing came of it. Just don't go hog-wild first chance you get to lie with a girl. It ain't that simple. But if you like her, don't let nothing stand in your way. I would 'a waded through hell fire to make your mamma mine, and you'll do the same when the time comes." Then he snapped the reins and said, "Let's ride now. We got a long way to go."

They moved slowly, stopping often to let Tobias rest and sip the medicine Miami Billie gave him, and when they rounded the east shore of Okeechobee it was as Keith Tiger said, pine scrub and palmetto prairie.

Days stretched into a week, and soon they came to the marsh where the herd drowned on their first grazing drive. From here they turned northwest, going out of the way toward the trading post at Fort Drum to see if Tobias could purchase quinine.

Zech had mixed feelings, wanting to see Glenda again but still occupied emotionally with Tawanda. The closer they came to Fort Drum, the more confused and bewildered he became. He remembered the words of his mother, "Cows won't ever smell like flowers." He had known few flowers in his lifetime, only cows and the smell of smoke and pine needles. The torment he now felt frightened him more than the presence of bears or wolves. If predators attacked he knew what to do: run, build fires, kill or be killed; but girls were yet so alien he didn't know how to handle it. He could not brush from his memory the smell of Glenda and the dizziness he felt as they rode together that night at the frolic, but this now seemed trivial compared to the experience of sleeping with Tawanda.

His reverie was broken when Tobias said, "Zech! If you don't wake up you're going to ride Ishmael into a palmetto clump. What's the matter with you? You want to stop and sleep some?"

"I'm sorry, Pappa. I was just thinking. I'm not sleepy at all."

Tobias smiled, thinking he understood the problem but not knowing about Zech's experience with Glenda at Fort Drum or the conversation Zech once had with Emma.

When they entered the settlement at noon the street was deserted, and there was no one in the store except Turner. Zech hovered in the background as Tobias inquired about quinine and was told they had none but it was on order and should be in soon. He waited until his father started out before going to the counter and saying hesitantly, "Hello, Mister Turner. I'm Zech MacIvey. Is Glenda here?"

"No, she's not. She's up in Jacksonville staying with her aunt so she can go to school." He then looked closely at Zech and said, "I remember you now. You were here last spring during a frolic. Glenda has spoken of you."

Although he wanted to see her, Zech felt relief that Glenda was not there. This would give him time to sort out his feeling for her and for Tawanda before seeing her again. He said, "Will she be coming back soon?"

"She'll be here for the Christmas frolic. Are you coming? I think she expects you."

"Well, I don't know, Mister Turner, but I'll try. Next time you write

Glenda would you tell her I came by to see her?"

"Why don't you write yourself? I can give you the address. I know she'd be glad to hear from you."

"No, you tell her for me if you will," Zech responded, not wanting to admit he couldn't write. "I don't know when I'll be back here to post a letter. I better go now. Pappa is waiting outside."

Turner was amused by Zech's awkwardness as he almost fell over a pickle barrel while walking rapidly from the store.

Emma ran to them immediately when they entered the clearing, her cries of "Tobias! Tobias!" bringing the others outside.

Tobias dismounted quickly and hugged her, and then she said, "You've been gone so long. I was worried about you. But I'm glad you're back now. We had a bad thing happen while you were gone."

"What's that?" Tobias asked anxiously, alarmed by the gravity in her voice.

Frog spoke up first, "Bonzo died, Mister MacIvey. He took real sick on the way back from Punta Rassa. It was malaria. We done everything we could for him, and for a while it seemed he got better, but on the first night back here he just up and went away."

"That's too bad," Tobias said regretfully. "I'm real sorry to hear it. I wish I could have at least been here for the funeral."

"He's down by the river," Frog said. "Miz Emma said words, and it was a proper burial. It surprised us all, and I sure hated it. Me an' ole Bonzo went through a lot together."

Zech said, "Pappa had it too, and that's why we're so late getting home. He was so sick he like to have died. The medicine man cured him."

"Tobias!" Emma exclaimed, grabbing his arm. "You had it too? Oh Lord! I should have been there with you!"

"There's nothing to fret about now," he assured her. "The Indians looked after me real good. I still got some medicine Miami Billie made for me, and they're getting in some quinine at Fort Drum. All I need is a few days rest and I'll be fine."

"Did you have trouble findin' the Indians?" Skillit asked. "We all figured you'd end up down in Cuba."

"It wasn't easy," Tobias said. "There were times I didn't think we'd make it."

"We seen things you won't believe," Zech said excitedly. "I walked on vines right over the top of the woods, and the cypress trees down there are so big they make everthing here look like nothing. And I went to Pay-Hay-Okee."

"What's Pay-Hay-Okee?" Emma asked curiously.

"It's a place like nowhere else. We went there in a dugout canoe. Tawanda took me."

Emma said, "Let's go in the house and I'll fix something to eat. Then I want to hear all about your trip and everything you saw."

The entire troupe followed Tobias and Zech inside.

TWENTY-TWO

A cold December wind stung his face as Zech rode alone across the prairie. There had been no change of seasons here, no brilliant colors to signal the coming of fall, no bare trees surrounded by decaying leaves to herald winter, no ice-covered bushes or frozen ponds. The cabbage palms and palmetto clumps and cypress stands looked the same and stayed the same, and the biting wind was the only indication of the dormant season.

Zech shivered as he pulled the jacket collar tighter around his neck; then he put Ishmael into a canter, hurrying along because the days were now shorter and sundown would come two hours earlier than usual. Mile after mile of brown prairie all looked the same as he headed for Fort Drum and the Christmas frolic.

The sun was not brilliant as in summer, and there was a desolate yellow glow across the land, a mid-afternoon twilight made even dimmer by an overcast gray sky. There were no long flights of birds winging their way casually toward distant feeding grounds, and the cypress stands were flooded with white and gray specks as egrets and herons sought refuge from the wind and cold.

It was three days before Christmas, a festive time Zech had never really known. Emma always tried to fix something special for Christmas dinner, baking sweet potato pies covered with wild honey, a turkey if Tobias could kill one, or whatever else was available to mark this one day from all the others. But there had been no gaily decorated tree, no exchange of colorfully wrapped gifts, no frolic or church services. When they lived in the scrub the only gifts he received were made with Tobias' hands, a chinaberry slingshot or a little windmill or a toy gun carved at night while he was sleeping. For the past three years Tobias purchased things at a trading post, hiding them in the barn loft until Christmas morning: a bolt of cloth or a bonnet for Emma, a hunting knife or a canteen for Zech; but there was no gathering of a family clan with joyous singing and a yard full of excited children.

Several coins jingled in Zech's pocket, and he wanted to reach the settlement in time to purchase gifts before attending the frolic. For his mother he wanted lilac water, remembering when she said she once smelled like flowers but no more; and for his father a pocket watch with a long chain, something he had seen men wearing in Punta Rassa.

As he drew nearer to Fort Drum, Zech's spirits rose and fell as unpredictably as winter weather – high and soaring one moment, downcast the next; excited by the reality of seeing Glenda again, but remembering Tawanda. Each one took turns occupying his thoughts, and to him each was as different as marsh land from prairie. He couldn't picture Tawanda at a Christmas frolic, or Glenda in a chickee. Both were equally fascinating yet so very far apart, in totally different worlds.

Night beat him to the trading post, and the glow of coal oil lamps spilled from the old building when he rode up and hitched Ishmael. The frolic would not be held in the open this time since the barnlike meeting hall was now completed.

Turner was starting for the door to lock up as Zech entered. He said, "Hello, Mister Turner. Looks like I just made it in time. I need to buy a few things before you close up."

"Sure, Zech. I was just leaving to get ready for the frolic. What you got in mind?"

"Lilac water if you have it. If you don't, something else that smells good, like flowers. It's for Mamma."

"I got something better than lilac. It has the scent of peach blossoms. What size bottle you want?"

"The biggest you got. And I want a pocket watch too, one with a chain."

Turner took the items from a case beside the counter and put them into a brown paper sack. "Is that it?"

"I need to get a little something for Skillit and Pearlie Mae and Frog. Maybe a couple of pipes and tobacco, and a sun bonnet. And I need a bundle of red ribbon."

Turner added these to the sack, his interest raised by the strange names. "Be anything else?"

"A dozen apples. Ishmael needs a Christmas treat too."

"Ishmael? Who's that?" he asked, his curiosity getting the best of him.

"My horse."

"Oh. That's mighty thoughtful of you. Wouldn't many men spend money buying a Christmas gift for a horse. That'll be a total of twelve dollars."

Zech put money on the counter, picked up the packages and turned to leave. Turner said, "I'm glad you made it for the frolic, Zech. It ought to be starting about now. I'll be a bit late, but Glenda's already over there."

Zech went outside and put one package in the saddlebag, then he started feeding apples to Ishmael. He watched as Turner walked away down the dark street; then it dawned on him he should have purchased something for Glenda.

Ishmael had eaten four apples when the sound of fiddles drifted from a nearby building. Zech put the remainder in the saddlebag and walked slowly to the meeting hall. When he entered and looked about, he felt embarrassment. He was dressed in faded jeans, dusty boots and denim jacket, and all the other men and boys wore black suits, startched white shirts and string ties.

Chairs were lined against two walls, and the fiddle players were on a raised platform in the rear of the room. Adjacent to that a table covered with a white cloth held a large punch bowl and glass cups.

Glenda was behind the table, her red hair standing out like a flag. She wore a blue dress decorated with white lace, with a blue ribbon in her hair. When she glanced toward the door and noticed Zech she waved at him. He stared, seeing her almost as a stranger, even more beautiful than he remembered.

For a moment Zech hesitated, feeling the urge to walk backward to the door and run for Ishmael, then retreat to the prairie where he belonged. Had he known about Christmas frolics he could have purchased suitable clothes somewhere, but no one told him. He had never seen his father in a suit or his mother in a blue dress with lace, and because of this he blamed them for his present situation and felt anger at them for allowing him to come to the frolic dressed as he was. Then it came to him they wouldn't know either. Perhaps they once did, but that was too long ago in the past. In his memory he knew there had been no Christmas frolic in Florida for his mother and father and none now, and the sudden anger at them for something beyond their knowledge shamed him.

His self-consciousness was his alone, for no one paid him even the slightest attention for the way he was dressed. The black suits in the room were worn only for funerals and weddings and the Christmas frolic, and by morning every man and boy would become a duplicate of Zech. If he had looked closer he would have seen moth holes, torn seams and frayed collars and cuffs, outgrown pants four inches short, missing buttons, and coat sleeves that came halfway to the elbow when an arm was bent.

A pot-bellied stove at the left of the door grew ripe and turned red, overheating Zech and causing him to move away. He walked across the open floor to the table. One of the ladies in attendance said, "Would you like punch?"

"I'll serve it," Glenda said. She poured a cup, came around the end of the table and handed it to Zech. "I'm sorry I haven't come to you sooner. I had to help mother. It's really good to see you again. I've thought about you often and hoped you'd be here tonight."

"I came by the store this fall to see you."

"Yes, I know. Daddy told me. I wish I would have been here. I like Jacksonville, but it's good to be home."

"You like it better than here?"

"Not better, but there are a lot of things to do there that we don't have here. They have cafes and little parks and theaters. Every Saturday night there's a dance, and on Sunday afternoon people dress up and ride in their carriages. It's all a lot of fun for a change, but I like Fort Drum too."

"We go to a cafe in Punta Rassa. They make good fried chicken and fish. But there's not much else to do there. It's just a place to ship cattle to Cuba. We own a hundred and fifty acres on the Caloosahatchie, and someday I'm going to build a cabin on it so we won't have to camp out ever time we take cows there."

"That would be nice. Maybe someday you can take me with you. I'd like to see Punta Rassa. It's such a lovely name."

"You'd be disappointed. Like I say, it's just a cowtown. Wouldn't be nothing like Jacksonville."

The music started again, and soon the room thundered with the sound of leather pounding the wooden floor. Glenda said, "Would you like to dance with me?"

"You know I don't know how."

She grabbed his arm. "I'll teach you!"

Zech pulled away. "I'm not dressed right, Glenda. You can see that. I ought not even be here, much less out on the dance floor. If I'd known everybody else had on a suit but me, I wouldn't have come inside."

"Oh pooh!" she said, taking his arm again. "You look fine. Mother has to practically hog-tie Daddy to get him in a suit, and he'll probably show up tonight dressed just like you are. And besides that, every girl here has her eye on you and would stand in line to dance with you. I know I would, and I'm sure not going to let them. You're not going to get away from me that easy, Zech MacIvey!"

"Well, O.K.," he agreed reluctantly. "But if it don't work out, let's quit."

Zech tried vainly to imitate the others, watching constantly and as stiff as a cypress pole, kicking when they kicked and turning when they turned. He was beginning to get the hang of it until they changed partners and swung down the line; then his boots grew as large as a wild steer's horns, tripping him up and staggering him sideways. He righted himself clumsily and retired from the floor.

Glenda continued the dance, and Zech watched from the sideline as she skipped from partner to partner, floating down the line as light as a feather. She glanced at him as she passed by, motioning for him to come back, but he backed further away and leaned against the wall.

When the music stopped she came to him immediately. He said, "I'm sorry. I must have looked plumb awful out there."

"You didn't either. You were doing real good, better than most people when they first try."

"I guess dancin' isn't my strong suit. Maybe I better stick to horses."

"You can learn. And I'll bet you didn't know how to ride a horse first time you got on one. We'll try again in a little while. Would you like more punch?"

He said, "Maybe that would help get the frog out of my throat. That scared me out there worse than a pack of wolves."

Glenda sensed he was more shamed by his performance than he would admit. She said, "Let's go outside for some fresh air. We can have punch later."

The cold wind struck them as they left the building and started up the street. They walked silently until Glenda said, "It's cold! Put your arm around me."

He put his arm around her waist as they continued, and then he said, "It's going to be bad out on the prairie tonight. I'll have to build a big fire to stay warm."

"The prairie?" she exclaimed, stopping and facing him. "What do you mean? You're not going home this late at night, are you?"

"Yes. Soon as we get back to the hall. I'll go out a ways and make camp, then go on in the morning."

"Zech! You can't do that! It's too cold, and there's no need of it. You can stay at my house tonight. We have an extra room."

"Your house?" he questioned, not sure he understood the invitation. "Your daddy would probably take a whip to me if I even showed up there."

"He wouldn't either! He wouldn't mind at all. I've told my mother and father how I feel about you."

"Told them what?"

"That I love you, more than anything. They know about us."

Zech gulped. "I'd like to stay, Glenda, I really would, but I just can't. It don't seem right."

"It would if we were promised."

"Promised? What's that?"

"You know, going steady. Promised to each other."

"How can we go steady with you up in Jacksonville?"

"I won't be there forever. School ends in May. And if I'm promised to you I won't even look at another boy. Will you do it?"

"I guess," he agreed reluctantly, still not sure what it meant; and then he said with more fervor, "Yes, I'd like to. But you'll have to tell me what to do."

"You can start by kissing me."

He took her in his arms and pressed his lips to hers gently, trying not to be overly eager and hurt her, and the smell got to him again. His senses reeled as he breathed deeply of her, his hands feeling flesh as soft as goose down. She clung to him firmly, then she looked up and said, "Will you stay now? Mother and Daddy will go to bed and leave us alone together."

He relaxed his grip but still held her. "Don't be mad at me, Glenda, but I can't. Next time I will. I have to be home real early in the morning.

Pappa needs me to help him with something, and we have to be in Kissimmee before noon tomorrow."

"Well, I guess if you have to, you have to," she said, disappointed. "But don't you forget we're promised! You hear? I mean it, Zech MacIvey! You're promised to me now!"

"I won't forget. I could never forget something like that."

"You can kiss me again if you want to."

"I want to," he murmured, pulling her back to him, once again overwhelmed by the smell of lilacs.

A full moon could be seen fleetingly as clouds raced across the sky. Zech galloped Ishmael during brief moments of light, then slowed to a walk when darkness rushed back in. He was ten miles out of the settlement when he stopped at a cypress stand and built a fire.

He searched himself for a reason why he lied about his father needing him, why he refused to stay in Fort Drum with Glenda. He had not hesitated to sleep with Tawanda in his arms within fifty feet of her mother and father, yet Glenda's invitation frightened him beyond his understanding. Other things also bothered him, his ease with Tawanda and his shyness with Glenda. He wondered if his father had ever been so tormented by girls, or if this anguish was his alone.

He liked Glenda very much, this he knew; but it puzzled him why she had chosen him so quickly over boys in Jacksonville who could make him look like nothing more than the prairie hick he took himself to be. She was the most beautiful girl he had ever seen, or probably would see, and he should be overjoyed by her love; yet he couldn't comprehend her choice of him, which made accepting it more difficult.

He got up and fed Ishmael an apple, and then he said, "I like you best of all, Ishmael. We go where we want to go, and there's no fuss about what to wear or where we're going to sleep or nothing else. Maybe I best stick with you and let the rest of it go. It just ain't worth it." The horse whinnied and nudged him, wanting another apple.

He lay close to the fire and rolled himself in his blanket, shivering as the wind sang through the cypress trees. He said aloud, "Lordy, I wish Tawanda was here now. She's so warm to sleep with." He no sooner said it than he wondered why. It was Glenda he was promised to, not Tawanda. And if he hadn't been so stubborn he would know by now which one was the warmest. He had not even given Glenda a chance to prove anything. But why? He asked himself this question over and over again and received no answer.

No one was in the house but Emma when Zech rode in. As soon as he entered she said, "I'll bet you haven't eaten a thing since you left Fort Drum. Sit at the table and I'll fix something for you."

She noticed he seemed agitated, and she watched him closely while fiddling with a spoon, stirring a pot unnecessarily. Finally she said, "Did you have a good time?"

"Yes, Mamma. It was real nice."

"Maybe when your father gets to feeling better we can go to the next frolic with you."

Zech toyed with the food, and then he said, "Mamma, do you know what it means to be promised?"

"Yes, I know. Your father and I were promised. It means you intend to get married someday, and you're not supposed to be with anyone else."

"Can a man like two women at the same time, and like one just as much as the other?"

"I suppose so. But there'll come a time when he has to choose between them. No man can have two wives. It's against the Lord's way."

"How do you choose, and how do you know you've chosen the right one?"

Emma sat at the table and faced Zech. "I can't answer that. I knew the moment I met Tobias. I didn't have any doubt, and he didn't either. Each person must choose alone. If there's doubt, be careful and don't make a hasty decision and a mistake. There's more to being married than just liking someone. You have to love too. And one of them will be the mother of your children."

Zech noticed she had shifted from 'he' to 'you' and suspected she somehow knew he was talking about himself. Perhaps his father had told her about Tawanda. He said, "Mamma, it hurts bad, and I don't know how to handle it. Me and Glenda got promised last night. She wanted me to spend the night at her house, and it was fine with her mother and father, but I didn't. I slept out on the prairie. There was a girl in the Indian village. Tawanda. Me and her. . ."

"You don't have to tell me," Emma broke in. "I knew something happened with you down there. A mother doesn't have to be told. Tobias said nothing, so don't think he gave away your secret. It's up to you, Zech. It's your choice, and you'll have to make it. I can't help you. I'll say only one thing. Choose wisely. And don't end up hurting one of them real bad for nothing. Don't make either one of them think they're the one if they're not. That wouldn't be fair."

"They're so different, Mamma. Tawanda is like Ishmael, and Glenda is more like you. I don't see why Glenda even likes me. She's going to school, and she knows how to dance and do all kinds of stuff like that. I can't read a book or dance or do nothing but chase cows. I even looked like a fool the way I was dressed at the frolic. Tawanda wouldn't have cared. They've got me so mixed up I wish I'd never seen either one of them."

"All you're doing is feeling the pain of growing up," Emma said gently. "I know it hurts. Everybody goes through it. There's nothing like the torment of boys and girls discovering each other for the first time, trying to make a choice. But Zech – you don't have all that much to choose from out here. But you will choose. When the time comes, you will. So don't fret about it. Sooner or later you'll know."

"I hope so, Mamma. And I thank you for listening. I just needed to talk to someone about it." Then he said enthusiastically, "I bought you a Christmas gift! You'll like it!"

"Let's see! Let me see what it is!"

"Oh no! You'll have to wait. It's a surprise for Christmas morning."

Emma put her arms around him and said, "I love you, Zech, and I can see why any girl would want you. Girls want a man, not some fancy dancer who couldn't skin a rabbit if his family was starving. You don't understand this, but girls do. That's why I chose Tobias. You've got strength like your father, and that's what girls look for in a mate. Glenda has more sense than you give her credit for. She knows what she's doing."

Zech suddenly realized something he should have known all along: there is more to life and survival than frolics or black suits or bowls full of punch. The Kissimmee and the Caloosahatchie and all the prairies and swamps between are not Jacksonville with its parks and cafes and theaters, and never will be; and someone must round up the cows and blaze the trails and fight the wolves and bears and plant the orange trees like his father had done. He was schooled not in reading and writing but in survival, and this was not something he should be ashamed of. His teachers were the best, and he loved them for it. He vowed he would never again make excuses to himself or to anyone for what he was or who he was. He was a MacIvey, and proud of it.

He jumped up suddenly and said, "I think I'll go down in the woods and see can I shoot a turkey; then I'll cut us a tree. I bought a big bundle of ribbon at the store to decorate it. We've never had a Christmas tree, and it's about time we did."

TWENTY-THREE
February
1880

"Emma! Emma! Come and see! You got to see!"

Tobias was running through the woods as fast as his lanky legs would carry him, shouting again, "They're blooming, Emma! They're blooming!"

Emma rushed from the house and said, "What on earth is the matter with you, Tobias? The way you're hollering you'll scare the life out of everybody in Kissimmee!"

"The orange trees. . ." Tobias panted, "they're in bloom! They finally done it! Millions of buds, bustin' out all over! And the smell. . .Lordy, the smell! You got to see it!"

"You know you ought not get so worked up," Emma admonished. "If you don't calm yourself you'll have another spell."

The shouting attracted the attention of everyone else, and they poured from the barn and the cabins. Pearlie Mae had given birth to three boys in three years and gained an additional thirty pounds in the process, and she waddled like a duck as her brood followed close behind her. Skillit scooped up two of the toddlers and put them on his shoulders as he ran for the sound of the commotion.

Three more times Tobias had replanted the orange trees and expanded the plot, and now there were one hundred acres inside the fenced area.

He said to the assemblage, "We gone have enough to fill a whole schooner at Fort Pierce! It'll take ten wagons to haul 'em there. That's what the future is – oranges! We don't have to round 'em up or brand 'em or do nothin' but pluck 'em off the trees!"

"Calm yourself, Tobias!" Emma cautioned again. "Let's all go and see before he gives himself a stroke."

Tobias took the lead, stepping lively, and halfway through the woods it came to them, seeping from the grove a quarter-mile distant, an overpowering fragrance. They all stopped, feeling intoxicated by what hit them. Emma breathed deeply and said, "Oh my! Oh my, Tobias! I've never smelled anything like it in all my life. It's like the Lord has turned the rain to perfume and it's come down over everything. I wish I could figure out a way to put it in a bottle."

When they left the woods and came into an open area, they were greeted by a sea of white blossoms, row upon row of trees that seemed to be covered with snow. There was a steady drone as bees darted from blossom to blossom, gorging themselves on nectar.

Skillit said, "Lordy me, Mistuh Tobias. It sure is a sight. Will all them little flowers turn into oranges?"

"They surely will. I done told all of you! There's as much gold on them trees as a whole herd of cows."

"We ought to build some bee hives," Zech said. "We could get lots of honey out of here."

"If it would taste as good as the blossoms smell," Emma said, "it would be a gift of the Lord. Orange blossom honey. It even sounds pretty. I'm real proud of you, Tobias. You stuck with it all this time, and now it's finally happened."

"There's been times I wanted to quit and give it up," Tobias said, "especially when the cows kept eating the trees. But they can't do it no more 'less they can fly. And that's thanks to you, Emma. I wouldn't have ever bought taller trees if you hadn't told me to. I'd a just gone on forever planting cow fodder."

"I could stand here the rest of my life and just sniff," Emma said. "I hope heaven smells like this. But I've got things to do at the house. I'm just getting started with my dress and the wedding is almost here."

"I'll bet ole Ishmael'll be glad when that wedding is over," Frog said teasingly. "Mister Zech done wore that pore hoss out runnin' him from here to Fort Drum."

"Ah, shut up, Frog!" Zech said. "I haven't been over there that much and you know it. You just running on like you did when Skillit got married."

"What I said come true, didn't it?" Frog chuckled. "I said the woods would be full of nigger babies, and just look. Pore ole Pearlie Mae ain't much more than a brood mare."

"Don't pay no mind to him," Skillit said. "He don't close that big fly trap, I'll put so many knots on his head he'll look like a sack of hickernuts."

Zech and Glenda had finally set their wedding for the last week in February, having honored her father's request that they wait until she finished four years of schooling in Jacksonville. She now helped her father in the store and tutored area children in English and math.

Skillit and Frog followed Tobias into the grove for a closer look as the others went back to the clearing. As soon as they were in the house, Zech said, "Mamma, I'm glad to see Pappa so happy with his grove, but there's something about it that worries me real bad."

"What's that?"

"He's worked so hard all these years and finally it's about to pay off. But somebody could come along and take it all away from him, even the house and everything. We don't own this land."

"That worries me too. Tobias thinks it's ours because we live on it, but I know it isn't. If somebody did take the grove it would just about kill him. The malaria spells are coming so often now he can't go on riding herd much longer. Sometimes when he walks down to the garden he comes back panting like a horse that's been run. He needs something like the grove to stay here and look after."

"We've got to own this land and a bunch more too," Zech said. "It's getting harder all the time to find wild cows, and if we stay in the cattle business we'll have to start raising our own or buy them off other folks and fatten them up. Somebody has bought a big piece of land up north of here and built a house on it, and if they want to, they got a legal right to stop us from grazing there anymore. And it's soon going to be the same everywhere."

"You want me to talk to Tobias again?"

"It wouldn't do any good. I'm going to handle it myself. Last time I was in Kissimmee I went to the land office and inquired about this place. All the land here was once owned by a timber company that never did anything with it. It was too much prairie and not enough trees, so they let it go back for taxes. I can buy it now for twenty cents an acre. I'll tell Pappa I'm going to Kissimmee for supplies. Then I'll take the buckboard and some of the money in those trunks and buy the land. Pappa won't know the money is gone. He hasn't looked in those trunks in years."

"Just go ahead and do what you need to do. I'll never tell him."

"While he's at the grove, I'll take the money down to the barn and hide it. Then tomorrow morning I'll set out for Kissimmee. I know it would break Pappa's heart if somebody took his grove, and that's sure to happen sooner or later if I don't do something about it."

"You're doing the right thing, Zech, and don't ever let it bother you because your pappa doesn't know. It's not like you're going behind his back for something you want. It's for his sake. And money isn't the reason why Tobias hasn't bought the land himself. He's just too stubborn to admit he's wrong, and he is wrong about this. He thinks the land is a gift from the Lord for everybody's use and it's not right for anybody to lay claim to it. Maybe it ought to be that way, but it's not. You go on now and hide that money before he gets back. Someday he'll be thankful you did this."

"I hope so, Mamma. I don't want to see him hurt, and there's nothing the Lord can do if somebody shows up here with a deed. That would be the end of it."

Zech came from the land office smiling, clutching the deed firmly as if it might fly away. The title was in three names, his and Tobias and Emma, and later he would add Glenda's name after she became a MacIvey.

He unhitched the horse and drove the buckboard down the street, overwhelmed by the fact they were now landowners. He felt like shouting it for all to hear, MacIvey land, cattle and oranges. They were no longer squatters but rightful owners, free and clear with no debt owed.

He stopped at one of the mercantile stores and went inside, telling the clerk he was interested in a black suit. There was a rack of them, all identical, double-breasted and scratchy looking, large mother-of-pearl buttons and baggy pants. He held one in front of him and looked in a mirror, thinking that a man would have to be crazy to wear such an outfit except for absolute necessity. For Glenda, he would do it, but he would not suffer alone. He also purchased one for his father, surmising they would all have to hold Tobias down and force it on him, like saddling a wild horse. He also bought white shirts and string ties and a tin of boot polish.

There was a rack of dresses next to the men's department, and he examined them reluctantly, hoping no one would come in and see him in the ladies' section. The rack was next to a counter piled high with corsets and bloomers and brassieres, and he glanced at them warily and at the female clerk who watched him with amusement. He finally selected a dress he thought would fit Emma. It was pale blue, like the one Glenda had worn at the Christmas frolic, and it was decorated with white lace.

He put the packages in the buckboard and started down the street, wanting to hurry home and show the deed to Emma, and surprise her with the dress. At first he just glanced at it as it glinted in the sunlight, strapped to the saddle as a man rode past; and then it dawned on him what he had seen, a double-barreled ten-gauge shotgun, half the length of the horse, its weight pulling the saddle sideways. He stopped the buckboard abruptly, turned and followed the rider until he hitched the horse in front of a saloon.

Zech reached beneath the seat, picked up the Winchester and pumped a bullet into the chamber; then he walked quickly to the man and shoved the barrel into his back, saying, "Mister, if you so much as breathe, I'll blow the backbone slam out of you."

"What the hell?. . . ."

"The shotgun. . .I want to see the stock. Just ease over there with me and don't make any sudden moves."

Zech turned the shotgun over with his left hand, and there it was, carved into the wood, MCI. He said, "That's my pappa's mark. This gun was stole from him a long time ago. Are you the one who took it?"

"I don't know what this is all about, but I didn't steal no gun. I bought that thing early this morning and paid fifteen dollars for it. The man who sold it to me said he was tired of hauling it around 'cause it's so heavy. He had a new Winchester, one like you got there."

"Don't you lie to me!" Zech said, shoving the rifle harder. "Can you prove you bought it?"

"Naw, I can't prove it! Can you prove you bought that buckboard? I paid cash money, and that's all I can say. I got a place just north of here, and everybody in Kissimmee knows me. They also know I ain't the kind to steal a gun or nothing else. Only reason I bought that blunderbuss is to shoot wild hogs that keeps tearing up my pasture. If it belongs to your daddy you can have it. Just take that damned rifle away before you bust my ribs with it."

Zech lowered the rifle and said, "You don't seem like a bushwhacking rustler, so I'll take your word for it. But I'd sure be interested to know where the man is who sold you the gun."

"They was camped three miles east of here, down by Panther Creek. But if I was you, I wouldn't go there alone looking for a fight. There was nine of 'em, the meanest lookin' bunch I ever seen. I was scared myself till I rode away. I thought for sure they was going to rob me."

"Maybe I'll shoot them in the back, like they're prone to do with men and dogs."

"Fellow, I ain't joshin'. I wouldn't go after that bunch 'less I had a army with me."

Zech took a doubloon from his pocket, handed it to the man and said, "Here's your money back. I want the gun. It used to mean a lot to my pappa. And I'm sorry if I scared you."

"Well, you sure as hell did! I'm not used to having a Winchester shoved up my butt. I'll just go on in here now and drink myself fifteen dollars worth of whiskey to settle my nerves."

Zech put the shotgun in the buckboard. "Which way is it to Panther Creek where they were camped?"

"About three miles out along the main east road there's a trail that goes off to the south into some thick woods. That's where they was early this morning. But you're a fool if you go there."

"Much obliged for the directions," Zech said as he drove off.

"Didn't need that damned cannon noway," the man muttered as he went into the saloon.

Zech trotted the horse until he found the trail; then he tied Ishmael to a bush and walked into the woods, the rifle in his hands. He stayed to the left of the path, moving slowly from tree to tree, listening for any sound that might indicate the men's presence. Nine to one was bad odds even for a Winchester, and he wished Frog and Skillit were with him. But if he could slip up on them undetected, he could draw down before they had a chance to go for their guns. What he would do next he didn't know.

He covered a hundred yards and then came to the remains of a camp beneath a live oak. Empty bean cans were scattered about, and the fire coals were still warm. An empty gallon jug with a corn cob stopper lay at the base of the tree. He kicked the jug and watched as it tumbled over the ground, down the bank and into the creek. He said, "Bastards! I'll catch up with you someday!" Then he turned and went back to the buckboard.

Tobias was at the grove when Zech drove in, and Emma was in the house. When he saw that she was alone, he grinned and waved the deed; then he hugged her and said, "It's done, Mamma!"

"How much did you buy?" she asked curiously.

"Twenty thousand acres."

"Twenty thousand? That's an awful lot, isn't it, Zech? Will we ever have need of so much?"

"Mamma, at twenty cents an acre, it was only eight sacks of coins. It didn't even make a dent in one trunk, and that gold's not doing anything but gathering dust."

"Well, it's for sure Tobias will never know the difference."

"The land is ours now, clear and legal. Nobody can ever come along and take it from us."

"I'll sleep better knowing that."

"Where's Pappa?" Zech then asked. "I've got a real surprise for him in the buckboard."

"He's been up at the grove all day, just sitting and looking. I think he expects to see oranges pop out right before his eyes. What did you get him?"

"His old shotgun."

"Really? How on earth did you do that?"

"I saw a man with it, and sure enough, it had Pappa's mark on the stock. He bought it off another man, and I gave him his money back and took it. I went looking for the man who sold it but he was already gone."

"It's a good thing he was. You ought not be around folks like that. You could get yourself killed. It's best you forget things that happened a long time ago and let it be."

"I don't forget easy, Mamma. Just don't worry about it. When the time comes I'll handle it. I got Pappa another surprise too. I bought both of us a suit for the wedding."

"That'll be a sight to see," Emma snorted. "It'll take a team of oxen to drag him into it. Only time I figure to see your daddy in a suit is at his funeral, and then he'll probably pop up in the casket and put on his overalls."

"I got something for you too," Zech said, smiling. "I'll bring it in now."

He went to the buckboard and returned with a brown paper bag. He held it behind him and teased, "Guess what it is and you can have it. Guess wrong and it goes to Pearlie Mae."

She snatched at his arms but he backed away. "You've got to guess first, Mamma."

"Oh, Zech, what is it? You're too big for me to spank anymore. Stop teasing and let me see!"

He handed her the bag, and when the dress came tumbling out she said, "Oh, Zech! It's the prettiest thing I've ever seen! I love it! Oh, it's so pretty!" Then she sat at the table and cried, the dress held gently in her lap.

Zech was startled. He said anxiously, "What's the matter, Mamma? What is it?"

She looked at him through misted eyes; then she took his hands in hers and said, "Oh, Zech, you've got a lot to learn about women, and you about to marry one. A women cries when her heart is filled with joy, and that's the kind of crying I'm doing now. You've made me so happy! I've never had a dress like this. I'll wear it proudly at your wedding."

"Put it on and let's see how it looks," he said, relieved. "And don't scare me like that again. I sure hope Glenda doesn't cry when she's happy."

"She will. And when she's sad too. It's a woman's way. You might as well get used to it."

Emma took the dress into the bedroom, and when she returned Zech stared at her, seeing someone other than his mother. He exclaimed, "Mamma! You're the purtiest woman I've ever seen! You look even better than Glenda did when she wore a dress like that at the frolic. Pappa's got to see too! I'll go bring him back to the house. You hide behind a door and step out in front of him. I'll bet his eyeballs pop out and roll around on the floor. I'll run get him now."

Emma stepped out on the stoop and watched as he dashed away through the woods. Then she ran her fingers over the dainty lace and cried again.

TWENTY-FOUR

"Tobias MacIvey! You put on that suit! If you don't, I'll never cook another bite of food as long as I live."

"Well now. That would be bad, wouldn't it? I guess I'll just have to learn to make stew."

"For God's sake, Mistuh MacIvey, put it on!" Frog urged. "You heard what Miz Emma said. You want us to all suffer because you so stubborn?"

"I'll hold him down," Skillit said, "and you jerk off them overalls. Then we'll hang him by his feet in a tree, like a hawg at scrapin' time, and dress him up real purty."

Tobias backed away as the two of them came toward him threateningly. He said, "All right! All right! I'll do it this once, but I still don't see why a man's got to dress up like a circus clown to go to a wedding. Back off now! I'll do it myself."

"That's better," Emma said. "And as soon as you get done in the wagon I'll put on my dress."

They were camped three miles west of Fort Drum. Zech had insisted that everyone come to the ceremony, including Pearlie Mae and the three boys. It was to take place at high noon that day in the town meeting hall.

Zech stood off to one side alone, watching and grinning, remembering what his mother said about Tobias and the suit and a team of oxen. He had been up since dawn, shaved twice, and slicked down his tousled sandy hair. His broad shoulders and muscled arms filled out the suit to perfection, and he was quite pleased with himself although the rough wool made his legs itch, causing him to scratch constantly. When Frog laughed at him he threatened him with a hickory club; then all the attention was shifted to Tobias.

Tobias finally came from the wagon, scratching also, and Frog put his hand over his mouth to suppress a giggle. Emma said, "You look pure handsome, Tobias. I don't see why you made such a fuss over it. And all you men stop this foolish joshing! This is Zech's wedding day, and you're all acting like a bunch of silly children. Now stop it, you hear!"

Frog's grin vanished quickly as Emma went into the wagon, and when she came out wearing the blue dress they all gasped in admiration. Pearlie Mae said, "Lawsy me, Missus Emma, you sho' a sight to see! Everbody at the wedding going to stare at you."

Tobias was seeing Emma in blue for the second time and with just as much excitement as the first. He said, "You look so purty, Emma. It seems more fittin' for you and me to be getting married today instead of Zech. Maybe we'll just take that honeymoon trip for them and let them go on back to the hammock."

"Hush up, Tobias!" Emma said, felling radiant from the compliments. "We're too old to even think of such a thing. This is Zech and Glenda's day, not ours. Now let's get started! We surely don't want to be late."

The procession then set forth, Tobias and Emma leading with the buckboard, followed by Skillit and his brood in the ox wagon and Frog and Zech on horseback. After the wedding Zech and Glenda would take the buckboard and the others would return to the hammock in the wagon.

As a wedding gift Glenda's father had purchased round-trip passage for them on an inland schooner from Fort Pierce to Jacksonville, and they were to leave the buckboard at a livery stable in Fort Pierce.

They arrived in the settlement a half hour before noon and found the street deserted. The store was closed, and tacked to the door there was a wreath of white flowers. They went directly to the meeting hall since Emma cautioned Zech not to go to the Turner house beforehand and see Glenda prior to the ceremony for it would bring bad luck.

Horses, oxen and wagons were hitched in front of the building, and when they entered they were confronted by the same moth-eaten black suits Zech saw at the frolic. Most of the women had on hats topped with artificial fruit and flowers. Every head turned and stared as the MacIvey clan marched single file up the center aisle and filled the seats at the front of the room. Pearlie Mae whispered, "Now the fust one of you youngens so much as open yo mouth, I'll blister yo hiney good when this over."

All of the bodies were overheating the room, and Zech was sweating profusely when a fat woman in a pink dress stood up and started singing. The ceremony was to be performed by an itinerant preacher who conducted services in the meeting hall once a month. As soon as the song was finished, the preacher came up the aisle and motioned for Zech to come forward and stand to his left. An usher conducted Glenda's mother to a front seat; then there was a commotion in the rear as Glenda and her father entered, causing another bout of neck-stretching and staring.

Zech stared wide-eyed, seeing Glenda in a flowing white dress, her red hair covered by a veil of white lace. She floated up the aisle, her face beaming, her eyes sparkling and transfixed on Zech as her father guided her to his side. Blood pumped through him so vigorously his face turned white and then crimson, flushing back and forth, and his legs wobbled as if he would pitch forward and fall flat.

The ceremony was a blur, incomprehensible words flowing from the wool-draped preacher, sweating and scratching, all of it unreal until he felt himself slipping the ring on her finger, a simple gold band made from a Spanish doubloon. Then the veil came up and he was aware of kissing her, a flood of people pressing them, pumping his hand and hugging Glenda, then a loud wail as Pearlie Mae's hand struck flesh.

Zech followed Glenda outside where they were greeted by a spring day come early, a pale blue sky, emerald trees flooded with soft sunlight. She took his arm and clung to him as they led the gathering down a dirt street, stirring up puffs of dust, heading to the Turner house for punch and cake.

Once again there was hand pumping, back slapping and hugging, until finally he said to himself, "Please Lord, no more. Let it end." He was not aware Glenda was gone and was surprised when she came from the bedroom wearing a pink cotton dress and white ribbon in her hair. She took his hand and whispered, "It's time now, Zech. We can go."

He picked up her bag in the hallway; then everybody spilled from the house to watch as they headed for the buckboard. He lifted her to the seat, jumped in and slapped the reins, causing the horse to bolt forward. Glenda looked back and waved, but all Zech could see was the wreath on the store front as it flashed by.

The horse ran full gallop for two miles, bouncing the buckboard over ruts, until finally she shook his arm vigorously and said, "We keep going like this, Zech, that poor horse won't make it to Fort Pierce! There's no hurry. The schooner doesn't leave until tomorrow."

He slowed the horse to a walk, put his arm around her and pulled her close to him; then he turned the buckboard toward a cypress stand off to the right. When he reached the trees he stopped and said, "I've got to get out of this wool suit. I'm about to die, and I feel like I've got the itch. I don't see how somebody like that preacher can wear one of these things all the time. It just ain't natural."

He took off the tie, coat and shirt and threw them into the buckboard, revealing a chest covered with beads of sweat; then he took denim pants and shirt from a bag and walked into the stand. In a few moments he shouted back, "There's a spring in here, Glenda. I'm going to splash myself down some. I'll only be a minute."

When he returned she wasn't there. He stood by the empty buckboard, puzzled, noticing that her valise was gone. He glanced across the prairie and saw nothing. Suddenly feeling panic, he wondered if she had decided the marriage was a mistake and was making her way back to Fort Drum. He said, "Glenda. . . Glenda. . ."

The voice came from behind a palmetto clump. "Over here, Zech. I'm here."

He walked rapidly into the trees and found her, sitting on a blanket spread over a bed of fronds. The white ribbon was missing, and a cascade of red swirled down over her shoulders. The dress was also missing, and the petticoat too, all of it. He stared at her, spellbound; then he dropped down beside her. "Don't you do that again! You scared the heck out of me."

"It's the only way I can keep you off that buckboard. Don't you realize we're married now. We don't have to wait any longer."

He reached over and touched her soft shoulder, and then he said, "Glenda, I'm about to bust wide open from just the sight of you, but I don't want to go about this wrong. I've never been with a woman before, but I've seen many a bull be rough and nearabouts kill a cow. I don't want to be that way and hurt you."

"The only way you'll hurt me is to ignore me, Zech MacIvey! So stop that foolish talk right now. You're not a bull and I'm not a cow.

Come on over here where you belong!"

When he moved closer the sweet smell of her came to him like orange trees in bloom, at once intoxicating and exhilarating. He kissed her, and then he took her into his arms gently, ever so gently.

Zech lay on his back and stared upward, feeling comatose, as if the blood had been drained from him. Glenda snuggled closer to him, and he rubbed his hand over her shoulders and into the mass of soft hair. He said, "What would you think if we didn't go to Jacksonville? I don't care anything at all about those theaters and parks. I just want to be with you. We could go into Fort Pierce and buy supplies and a little tent. Then we could drift around the prairie, camping out like this."

"I'd like that. I don't want to go to Jacksonville either. It was Daddy's idea, not mine. I didn't enjoy being there when I was in school."

"I thought you did."

"You were wrong. And there are a lot of other things you don't know about me yet." She raised up on her elbows and looked at him. "You think I can't be a strong woman like your mother, don't you?"

"I've never said that," he answered defensively.

"Well, I can! I'll do everything I have to. All I want is to be a good wife and make you happy. And I will, too. You'll see."

"You've already made me happy."

"Not as much as I will. I can be all the woman you'll ever need."

Zech kissed her, this time a lingering kiss; then he murmured, "I've got an idea we're not going to make it to Fort Pierce tonight."

"Who cares?" she said, drawing him to her.

TWENTY-FIVE

"Damn!" Zech said, looking down at the cow with its stomach slit open. "That's the fourth one in two days."

Skillit dismounted and examined the carcass. "All they took again was the heart and liver. They must have a powerful cravin' for that kind of meat. It sho' is a waste."

"I sure would like to get my sights on whoever's doing this," Zech said.

Skillit remounted and said, "They keep this up we won't have much to brand."

"Or sell either. Let's take what we got on back to the corral."

Zech and Skillit popped their whips, causing the cows to lurch forward. Far in the distance smoke drifted upward as Frog heated the branding iron, waiting.

It was late May, a month later than they usually completed the roundup, but Tobias had been sick again and insisted they wait until he could help. No amount of persuasion by Emma or Zech could keep him at the house, and Zech worried constantly as he watched his father become more gaunt from the hot sun and the hard work of branding.

Frog opened the gate at the sound of approaching hooves, then slammed it shut when the cows rushed inside. Tobias said to him, "How many did you count?"

"Nineteen."

"That's what I got too. I thought there would be more than that."

Zech reined his horse and said, "They done it some more, Pappa. All shot in the head and the bellies slit open. That makes about forty so far."

"How long you figure they been dead when you found the last ones?" Tobias asked.

"Not long. No more than a day, maybe less."

"Them bastards is getting awful brave. They must be out there sommers right now, watching us. This keeps up we might all have to go hunting, but this time it won't be for four-legged varmints. I can't understand why any man would shoot a cow for the heart and liver. He could get as much meat out of a rabbit."

"Just pure meanness," Skillit said. "Maybe they move on soon and let us be. They don't, we ought to set some asses on fire with the Winchesters."

"You want us to go looking for them?" Zech asked. "Me and Skillit and Frog could ride the woods at night. They bound to build a fire, 'less they eat raw meat, and that ain't likely."

"No, better not," Tobias responded. "I got a notion that sooner or later they'll come to us. And besides that, we got to get ready for the grazing drive. We're late already."

"If it suits all of you," Frog said, "let's quit the jawin' and get done with the branding. I don't like to be late for supper since Miz Glenda started making them huckleberry pies."

"She's spoiled us all, pure and simple," Tobias said. "First thing you know we'll be taking baths before having vittles."

"That wouldn't be no bad idea for Frog," Skillit said. "If he'd wash up some every month or so them buzzards wouldn't follow us all the time like they do. Pearlie Mae asked me just the other day if we had skunks in the barn, and it was Frog feedin' his horse."

"Ain't nothing in the world stinks worse than nigger sweat," Frog said. "It was you she smelled, not me."

"No wonder Glenda thinks everbody out here is crazy," Zech said. "Let's go on and get done with the work. I got a chore to do at the house."

"I know what chore you got in mind," Frog said. "I peeked in your window the other night and I ain't never seen such carryin' on. You so weak now you can't pick up a branding iron. You better stay away from that house, you know what's good for you. I knowed a man once who got hitched and done like you doin'. Then first thing you know he'd got so skinny a dog buried him, thinkin' he was a bone."

Skillit suddenly grabbed Frog, lifted him off the ground and pointed his backside upward. He said, "Get the brandin' iron, Mistuh Zech! See can you pick it up! Then stick it to him and we'll see how loud a frog can holler!"

Zech took the glowing iron from the fire and held it three inches from Frog's rear, singeing his pants. Frog shouted, "I was just kiddin', Mister Zech! Don't put that thing to me! I didn't peek in no window! I swear I didn't!"

"He bellers loud, don't he?" Skillit chuckled, releasing his grip. "He'll draw all the 'gators outen the swamp fo' a chomp of frog meat."

Frog stood up and rubbed his pants as Tobias said, "Lordy, Lordy, I hope them rustlers ain't watching us now. If they are, they'll think this outfit is run by a bunch of loons. No wonder they ain't scared of us."

"Don't you worry none about that, Mistuh Tobias," Skillit said. "We jus funnin' now. We come on them polecats, the funnin' stops. Ain't gone be no play time with them."

"That's right," Frog agreed. "It's gone be a whole lot worse than a brandin' iron and singed britches."

"I still think we ought to go after them," Zech said. "If we don't find them first, they'll do us just like somebody did the dogs."

Glenda became a member of the MacIvey clan with ease, and Emma liked her immensely, finding in her the companionship of a daughter she always wanted. Glenda refused to stand idly by as Emma and Pearlie Mae prepared meals. She peeled potatoes and chopped onions, reddening her eyes, and when there was nothing more to do she went alone into the woods and gathered berries for pies. In her spare moments she transformed the bare cabin Zech built for them into a home, putting up curtains and covering the bedroom floor with a braided rug, decorating the walls with little nicknacks she brought from Fort Drum. Zech enjoyed her pampering more than he would admit, and each evening as he headed for the hammock he ran Ishmael faster than usual.

She also convinced him to spend one hour each night beside a coal oil lamp, learning to read and write. At first he resisted, but as the words gradually took on meaning he went at it eagerly, realizing a previously unknown world was opening for him.

Emma watched it all with deep satisfaction, knowing that when children came Glenda could give them something more than she had been able to offer Zech, a chance to break free and do something more than grub for survival. There were other things in the world besides planting collards and skinning coons and herding cows and fighting wolves, things such as books and music and church services, and Glenda would lead the way. These things were now beyond Tobias, and maybe Zech too, but her grandchildren could sample them if they so desired. At least they would have the opportunity to choose.

It was not that Emma regretted any part of her own life. The sacrifices she made she made willingly, and if the choice were offered to her anew, she would follow Tobias into the wilderness again with only a frying pan and the clothes on her back. This was her destiny, an avenue life offered which she accepted without hesitation, and she never looked back or complained about things she might have missed along the way. Each step she took, each hardship overcome and each valley of fear transgressed intact, brought her closer to the realization of a hope she never abandoned: a better life for Zech and his lifemate and for those yet to come. If someday she could be surrounded by grandchildren whose faces were filled with joy and anticipation rather than just a grim determination to survive, then the long and difficult journey would have been worthwhile.

Emma took the coffee pot from the stove, poured two cups and put them on the table. She said to Glenda, "Come and sit with me. Those men will be coming in soon with their stomachs growling. We can have a few minutes of peace and rest before they get here."

Glenda sipped the coffee, and then she said, "I don't see how you cooked for so many before you had Pearlie Mae to help. It must have been a chore."

"Oh, it wasn't so bad. It's as easy to cook for six as it is for three. You just add a little extra to the pot. And there were times when the only things I had to cook were cattail flour and coon meat. That makes it simple. You should have seen poor old Skillit when he came to us. He was so hungry he would have eaten boiled cypress bark. Frog and Bonzo were just about as bad off too."

"We knew hard times too, but not that bad," Glenda said. "When we first came to Fort Drum it was nothing but wilderness. Daddy brought the lumber down from Jacksonville in an ox cart and built the store himself. It was a long time after that when the little settlement began to grow up around the store. I can remember Daddy going to Fort Capron to meet the schooner and bringing back goods a piece at a time, whatever he could get. Sometimes he traded a few turns of cloth for deer meat, and a sack of nails for potatoes. Zech doesn't know this about my family and I haven't told him. He thinks the store has always been there, stocked with food and other things. But it hasn't."

Emma put down her cup and took Glenda's hand in hers. "Glenda, I know why you're helping me so much in the kitchen, even doing the wash when Pearlie Mae could do it. Just don't try so hard. You don't have to prove anything to Zech. If you asked him how I spend each day, he couldn't tell you. He knows I always have food ready when he's hungry, and I wash his clothes, but that's all. He's not here during the lonely times. What he needs now is a wife to love, not a cook and housekeeper. He's had that all his life, and that's all he's ever had. I've given him those things, but I can't give him the kind of love you can. Don't put yourself against me. We're two different people and two different things to him. He needs you as a wife, not a mother."

"I'm not sure love is enough by itself," Glenda said. "I know it has taken hard work as well as love for you to do the things you've done to keep your men alive. When we first met, Zech thought I wouldn't be up to it, that all I wanted was to be in Jacksonville and go to theaters and dances. I've never wanted such things, and I can't even imagine myself married to some bank clerk in Jacksonville who plays the piano. I want to be here, riding with Zech, being his companion and partner as well as his wife, chasing cows if he wants me to, doing whatever he wants and being whatever he wants me to be. I love him that much. He's all I've ever wanted, and I thought for a long time he didn't want me. I felt there was someone else and I had lost out, and I had almost given up when he finally asked me to marry him."

"Zech will make you a kind and loving man, like Tobias, in his own way," Emma said. "But there's one thing you'll have to remember. He was brought up in the wilderness, and that's all he's ever known. It's inside him. He didn't shy away from you because he thought you couldn't live out here. It was because he thought he wasn't good enough for you, and that if he married you, you would make him abandon the wilderness and go elsewhere. This he will never do. You'll have to understand that, Glenda, and be patient with him. Zech will do the best he can to make you happy. He may not always show it, like his father sometimes doesn't show it, but he will."

"You know," Glenda said, "I'm glad you're you, Emma. I could never talk like this with my mother."

"You'll never know how many times I've yearned to just sit and talk with another woman, like we're doing now. That's what I've missed the most. I'm so glad you're here, and I'm proud to have you as my daughter."

"While we're talking woman talk, I have a secret to share," Glenda said, smiling. "I'm pregnant!"

"Oh, Glenda, that's wonderful!" Emma exclaimed. "I'm so happy for you and Zech! When is it due?"

"I think I'm about two months along. It must have happened real soon after we were married."

"Have you told Zech? He hasn't mentioned it, and I know he couldn't keep it inside."

"No. I'm not going to for a while yet. And I don't want you to either."

"Glenda, I don't understand," Emma said, puzzled. "Why would you keep it from him? He'll know sooner or later. Women do swell up, you know."

"I want to go on the drive with all of you. If Zech knew about this he wouldn't let me go. I just know he wouldn't."

"The drive isn't as important as this," Emma reasoned. "I have to go because I'm the cook, but Pearlie Mae can stay here and look after you. You shouldn't hide this from Zech."

"Going with Zech this time is important to me. I've got to prove to him I can do it. I know it would be foolish to take the baby out there next summer, and that's why I must go now. I just have to, Emma!"

"I've already told you. You don't have to prove anything to Zech! If you'll stay, I'll stay with you. The men go on roundups by themselves and take along smoked beef and hardtack. They can do the same thing on a drive. It would be hard for Pearlie Mae to go by herself and look after her boys and cook too. And besides that, Zech and Tobias know how to cook rabbits and coons. They'll do fine without us."

"No, I want to go," Glenda insisted. "I won't stay behind!"

"Is it really that important to you?"

"Yes, it is."

"Well, I'll say one thing," Emma said, resigned, "you're a MacIvey for sure. You're as stubborn as Tobias or Zech ever hoped to be. I'll share your secret under one condition."

"What's that?" Glenda asked, glad that Emma was about to agree.

"If you get to feeling poorly you and I will turn back. This baby means more to me than all the gold in Punta Rassa, and I know it would to Zech too. Will you promise me this?"

"Yes, I promise. But I know I'll be fine. I may not even be showing by the time the drive ends. Then I'll tell Zech."

"When we get back this time we'll really have something to celebrate," Emma said. "We'll have a party, the first one we've ever had out here. You can make the pies, and I'll do the rest, and we'll invite your mother and father."

"That would be wonderful," Glenda said. "And when the baby comes, we'll have another. It should be close to Christmas. We'll have our own Christmas frolic and birthing party at the same time."

"I don't know how I'll be able to keep this to myself, but I'll try. And I'm so happy, Glenda. I've wanted a baby around this place for such a long time. I just might take it away from you."

"We'll share," Glenda laughed. "And if it's twins, you can have one and I'll take the other."

TWENTY-SIX

One thousand and eighty sets of six-foot horns bobbed in unison as the herd was prodded from the main corral and turned to the northwest. The men were on horseback to the rear and on the flanks, followed by Emma and Glenda in the buckboard and Pearlie Mae with her load of jumping jacks in the ox wagon.

Tobias decided they should take the herd to the salt marsh for grazing, but if heavy rains came or mosquitoes appeared in numbers beyond their usual annoyance, they would avoid the place like plague. The memory of their disaster there was far too fresh in their minds to approach the marsh with anything but extreme caution.

By noon of the first day Glenda's skin was burned tomato red by the relentless prairie sun, and she retreated from the open buckboard to the protection of the covered wagon. Emma greased her neck, face and arms with lard to ease the stinging pain, and she did not complain. The next morning she was back on the buckboard wearing long sleeves, a bandanna around her neck and a sun bonnet.

She also adjusted to the fact the others would be watching as she used a palmetto clump instead of an outhouse, and her first trip to such a toilet ended in pandemonium when she unexpectedly stepped into and flushed a covey of quail, their wings sounding like thunder claps as they roared upward from their nesting place. Zech watched and tried vainly to suppress a giggle as she bolted from the palmetto and ran for the buckboard, her skirt flapping.

Emma watched Glenda constantly, beseeching her not to carry buckets heavy with water from nearby springs when they made camp, Glenda doing it anyway. No one seemed to notice this extra attention Emma was giving Glenda as she insisted on doing her share of camp chores.

Zech brought along the tent he purchased for their honeymoon trip, giving them this one small measure of privacy. He pitched the tent away from the group and took first watch so he could be with her most of each night.

One morning he awoke to find Glenda sitting upright, frozen with terror, her eyes transfixed on a rattlesnake coiled at her feet. He whispered, "Don't move. It just came in to get warm. I've found them in my boots and in the bedroll with me. If you stay still it won't strike."

She watched horrified as Zech reached slowly for the rifle, aimed it and blew the snake's head ten feet from the tent, its headless body then thrashing violently as blood gushed onto the blanket.

She screamed, "Get that thing out of here! Get it out!"

He said calmly, "It can't hurt you now. I'll skin it out for breakfast."

"You'll what?"

"That's good eating, Glenda. Taste's like chicken. We have it all the time on drives when we get tired of beef."

Glenda was about to gag when Emma rushed into the tent, alarmed by the gunshot and screaming. "What is it?" she asked anxiously. "Are you all right, Glenda?"

"Snake," Zech said, pointing. "I'll have it ready time you get the frying pan hot."

"Oh. You sure you're all right, Glenda?"

"I'm fine. It just scared me, that's all."

"I won't tell you what happened first time one of those varmints crawled in bed with me," Emma said. "It'd ruin your breakfast."

Glenda dressed shakily, came outside and was greeted by the smell of meat sizzling in the cast-iron skillit. She sat by Zech as he put a chunk of fried snake onto a tin plate and started eating. The cooked flesh was white, like chicken breast, and she accepted the bite he handed her. She put it in her mouth reluctantly, chewed and swallowed; then she said, "Not bad. It does taste something like chicken. I know you like it, so you can have the rest of it. I'll just have coffee and a biscuit."

Zech gulped down the chunk and took another piece from the frying pan. He said, "Just wait till you try some of Mamma's fried rabbit brains for breakfast. It's even better than snake."

"Not now, Zech," Glenda said, nibbling the biscuit. "Tell me about it later. I've got to go to the tent for a minute. I forgot something."

He kept munching as she went around the side of the tent and then ran for the nearest palmetto clump, clutching her stomach.

They drifted lazily, finding abundant grass and remaining until it was cropped short, spending days under clear blue skies not torn asunder by violent thunderstorms; enjoying gentle, cooling rains in late afternoon, Glenda enthralled by brilliant rainbows forming glowing arches over the flat prairie land. This was her first trip inland, and she was fascinated by seemingly endless flights of herons and egrets and ibises, and by herds of deer galloping close by, stopping momentarily to stare at them curiously, then bounding away.

One night the cry of wolves pierced the stillness, causing the cattle to low nervously. Glenda stayed up all night, watching wide-eyed as glowing fires pushed back the darkness, the men like roaming shadows as they circled the herd. She did not fully comprehend the danger involved and was unaware of how quickly disaster could strike, but the sight and sound of it thrilled her because this was what she wanted to be a part of. Here things were happening, things beyond human control; and there was no house to take refuge in for protection, no doors to lock or windows to close. It was them against nature, winner take all, and the reality of it both frightened and enchanted her. She was beginning to respect Tobias and Emma and Zech even more for having survived a lifetime of this, facing it again and again without trepidation, then coming back for more.

When they reached the edge of the salt march, they were met by four armed riders who charged the lead steer, turning the herd away from the basin and toward the river. Tobias and Zech rode forward as Frog and Skillit popped their whips, regaining control of the herd and holding them in a circle.

Tobias noticed cows scattered across the marsh as he rode to the line of men. He stopped directly in front of them and said, "What the hell you mean turning my herd like that? You could 'a caused a stampede!"

One man moved his horse forward and said, "You can't come in here.

You'll have to go sommers else."

"How come?" Tobias asked. "We been here ever time we wanted to and nobody stopped us. Who says we can't come in now?"

"This says," the man answered, waving a Winchester. "We got here first. 'Less you want to risk getting your ass shot off, you'll move on away from here. I got six more men down there, all armed."

"You ain't got the right!" Tobias said angrily. "This place belongs to us as much as it does to you, and my cows needs the salt. We're coming in!"

Four levers pumped as four Winchesters were pointed at Tobias and Zech. Tobias looked at the barrels and said, "This ain't going to do nobody any good. I got more riders and guns too. There's grass enough for everbody."

"I say there ain't. The first cow you move in here gets shot, and ever one that follows gets shot, and ever drover too. You just better back off, mister, and think about it."

Tobias wheeled the horse without further comment and rode back to the buckboard, popping his whip two times as a signal for Frog and Skillit to come in. Emma immediately noticed his stern expression and said, "What's happening, Tobias? Who are those men?"

"They're trying to turn us away."

"We got as much right to be here as anybody, Pappa," Zech said. "We ought to start us a war."

"You don't know what a war is," Tobias responded. "If I have to I will, but it ain't a pleasant thing to see. We'll talk first."

As soon as Frog and Skillit rode in, Tobias said, "Only way we're going to get in down there is to shoot our way in. What does everbody say we do?"

"How many men they got?" Frog asked.

"There's four over there, and they claim to have six more."

"Well, they's four of us," Frog said, "and if the women shoot from up here, that cuts down the odds some. I say we have at it."

"What about you, Skillit?"

"I don't know, Mistuh Tobias. Me, I don't mind goin' after them, but I sho' don't want Pearlie Mae an' the boys gettin' shot up. How come jus' us men can't do it?"

"We can. We'll leave the women out of it. First thing we'll do is stampede the herd right at them. Then we'll come in behind the cows and shoot everthing we see on a horse."

"No, Tobias!" Emma exclaimed loudly. "This has gone far enough! It's not worth it! We can go somewhere else!"

"If we back down now, Emma, it will happen again and again. Someday the range is going to get crowded. We just been lucky so far. We're going to have to fight for what belongs to us."

"Belongs to us?" Emma questioned. "We don't own this marsh, Tobias. If you got here first would you do the same thing those men are doing?"

Tobias didn't know exactly how to answer, never having faced such a situation. "Well, I don't know. But at least we ought to share."

"I'm not saying we shouldn't," Emma said. "But those men don't want to, and all the cows in the world aren't worth one of us getting killed. If somebody has to die for that grass down there, Tobias, which one of us do you say it is? Which one? Is it me, or Zech, or Skillit? Who? If you have the right to choose, which one of us do you want to see killed?"

"Aw, Emma, I don't want nobody killed," Tobias said meekly. "You know that. I don't have the right to say somebody has to die, and I wouldn't say it even if I did have the right."

"That's right, Tobias! You don't have the right! So stop this foolishness and move the herd across the river and away from here. I don't want to hear any more of it unless you say I'm the first to die. Do you hear me, Tobias?"

"Yes, Emma. I hear. And I'm sorry to have riled you up so. Sometimes us men are like frogs, we jump before we think and land right in a 'gator's mouth." Then he turned to the men and said, "What the hell you staring at? You heard Emma! Get them cows moving toward the river!"

Frog said, "If that's what you want, Mister MacIvey. But I hope it comes a pure flood and them sons a' bitches gets et up by skeeters."

Emma breathed a sign of relief as the men rode away. She said to Glenda, "That was close. And I couldn't have blamed them too much if they had charged in. There's grass enough to share, but some folks just don't want it that way."

"I'm learning," Glenda said. "I couldn't have pulled that off like you did no matter what. I would probably have pleaded with them. But I'm learning."

"You best. Things like this are going to happen more and more as time passes. It frightens me to think of it. If the men had been here alone, somebody would be dead by now. Maybe all of them."

Zech and Skillit rode ahead, buying cows and bringing them into the herd, and when they reached the Caloosahatchie the total was just over two thousand.

Tobias seemed disinterested as the sacks of gold coins were placed on the table. Zech took them out to the buckboard alone and gave Frog and Skillit their share. He told his mother and Glenda to take what they needed to buy supplies for the return trip and for whatever else they wanted.

When the two women came from the store both were dressed in jeans, denim shirts and boots, and Glenda had on a black felt hat. Her hair was tied in a pony tail that hung down her back.

Frog was the first to notice, and he said loudly, "Whoo-ee! Just look at that! Miz Emma and Miz Glenda got on britches!"

Glenda turned around and around, showing herself, and Zech said, "What's all this? You two look like drovers."

"It's silly for us to wear dresses on a drive," Glenda said. "This is much better. And Emma agrees. We've got as much right to wear britches as any of you."

"You have for a fact," Frog said, giggling. "And I think I'll just go on in there and buy myself a dress. What color you think would look best on me, Zech?"

"Red. And you ought to get yourself some pink bloomers too. I'll help you put 'em on."

"Next one who makes a crack like that has dipped his last time in the cooking pot!" Emma snapped.

"I think you look just fine, Miz Emma," Frog said quickly. "You ought to have bought them things a long time ago. Now you an Miz Glenda can ride a hoss without sittin' sidesaddle."

Emma turned to Pearlie Mae. "You want some britches too?"

"No ma'am, I better not," she responded, glancing at Skillit. "It take a pair big enough to stretch over a ox for me, more like a tent. I better not, Missus Emma."

Zech said, "If you don't mind, all of you go on back to the camp in the buckboard and leave me the wagon. I got something to haul. You can take Ishmael, Glenda."

"I'd like that," Glenda beamed. "It'll give me a chance to ride in my new outfit."

Emma frowned as Glenda mounted the horse, but she said nothing. The red pony tail swished from side to side as she tested Ishmael down the street and back. Then she trotted the horse ahead of the buckboard.

Zech went into the store and purchased tools; then he drove the wagon to a lumber yard on the north edge of town. When he arrived back at the camp the wagon was stacked to capacity with lumber, its wheels groaning, and a load of cypress shingles was ordered for delivery the next morning.

Tobias stared as the oxen struggled in, puffing, and then he said, "What in thunder is all that for? You aim to pull that load slam across the prairie?"

"No, Pappa," Zech answered, climbing down. "It's for here. I'm going to build a cabin. If everbody pitches in and helps, we can do it in a couple of days."

"How come you want a cabin in Punta Rassa?"

"Just some place to stay when we come over here. And it would let folks know we own the land."

"I don't think nobody cares," Tobias said. "But we'll do it if that's what you want. It don't make no difference if we start back a couple of days later. Just so I get back pretty soon to see about my oranges."

Hammers pounded and saws pinged as the task took on the festive air of a barn-raising. The women abandoned the cooking pot and supervised, telling the men to extend a wall here, put the stoop there, windows here and the door over yonder. By late afternoon the floor was down and all the framing up, and they went back into the town and ate the cafe completely out of fried chicken and fish.

Glenda enjoyed all of it, thrilled to be a part of people doing things, already planning in her mind where the bed should go, the color of curtains, a rug here and a shelf there.

That night after they had gone to bed Glenda still reeled with excitement and was unable to sleep. She aroused Zech and said, "Will you buy me a horse?"

"Huh?" he responded sleepily.

"A horse, Zech. I want one of my own."

"Sure. What kind you want? A green one or a blue one?"

She shook his shoulder. "Be serious!"

"You want a horse, you got a horse. Would you like a marshtackie, like Ishmael? A little horse would be better for you. It's like riding in a rocking chair."

"I'd love a little horse, but I've never seen another like Ishmael. All the horses at Fort Drum are big, like the ones all the other men here have."

"The Indians have more like Ishmael down in the swamp where they live. Sometime this fall when we don't have much to do I'll take a trip and get one for you."

"Will you really?"

"First chance I get."

She leaned over and kissed him. "I love you, Zech."

"Oh my," he groaned, putting his arms around her. "You do that again I'm liable to come back with a whole passel of horses. Maybe we ought to talk about it some more."

"Let's do. I'm not sleepy anyway. But I don't need a passel. Just one little horse will be fine."

The shingles arrived at mid-morning, and by late afternoon the cabin was completed, a day sooner than Zech anticipated. That night he and Glenda slept in it, and an hour after dawn the next morning the MacIvey caravan reached the ferry landing, crossed the river and headed east.

They journeyed leisurely, stopping often in mid-afternoon so the men could hunt deer that would be roasted whole on sweetgum spits over beds of hickory coals. Glenda traded places with Tobias, riding the horse with Zech while Tobias drove the buckboard, Emma disapproving and cautioning Glenda to go easy, but retaining the secret.

They were five days out of Punta Rassa, turning to the northeast toward the lower Kissimmee, when they entered an area of scrub pine and thick palmetto. Glenda and Zech were riding ahead, with Frog and Skillit at the rear, behind the wagon.

The first shot came from a thicket on the right, striking Glenda's horse in the shoulder, sending it tumbling forward instantly. She tried to jump from the saddle as the horse crashed down on top of her. Zech wheeled Ishmael just as a bullet exploded the horse's brain, peppering him with blood and bits of tissue. He too hit the ground beneath the horse.

Tobias stared disbelievingly as Glenda and Zech struggled to break free; then he shoved Emma from the buckboard and jumped on top of her, shielding her from a spray of splinters as bullets ripped into wood. The horse bolted forward, taking the buckboard past the dead horses and directly toward the line of fire.

Pearlie Mae jumped from the wagon and ran for a palmetto clump, dragging all three boys with her, screaming, "Oh my! Oh my!"

Frog emptied his Winchester in less than ten seconds, firing into bushes and palmetto, aiming in the direction of smoke puffs and fire belches. Then he jumped to the ground, struck the horse to make it move away, and started reloading.

Skillit followed Pearlie Mae, making sure she was safely hidden in the brush; then he too fired the rifle as fast as empty cartridges spewed from the ejection chamber.

Zech struggled and kicked, finally freeing himself from the mound of lifeless flesh. He pulled the rifle from the saddle holster and used Ishmael as a shield, lying flat and shooting over the horse, then glancing back and seeing Glenda still penned. He crawled over the ground to her, untangled her foot from the stirrup and pulled her into the palmetto.

Tobias and Emma also crawled for cover, hopping quickly, Tobias cursing because his rifle was in the buckboard. Then he remembered the shotgun, lying in the wagon bed. He dashed forward, grabbed it and a sack of shells, and retreated into the brush.

The bewildered horse stopped the buckboard at the edge of a thick line of trees. Tobias watched as two men scrambled into the wagon bed and struggled with the trunk, sliding it toward the rear. He said to Emma, "It's the gold! Them bastards are trying to kill us for the gold! They must 'a followed us all the way from Punta Rassa!"

The buckboard was fifty yards away, and Tobias calculated in his mind how much the shots would spread in that distance. He put a shell in each barrel, aimed at the space between the two men, and pulled both triggers simultaneously. The boom overwhelmed all other sound, drowning the sharp pop of rifles. Both men screamed as they were knocked backward from the buckboard, peppered with buckshot, one jumping up and running blindly, blood gushing from both eyes. He ran no more when a bullet from Frog's Winchester smashed through his rib cage and blew parts of his heart out the other side.

Tobias reloaded the shotgun, waiting for a sign, watching for a puff of smoke or fire to give him direction. He fired one barrel, aimed quickly to the right and fired again, hearing more screams as bits of palmetto fronds and pine limbs exploded into instant sawdust.

The barrel of Frog's rifle became too hot to touch as he loaded and fired again and again, covering the ground with empty shells. He was not even aware of Skillit beside him, also firing rapidly at any sign of life across the open space.

None of them knew the precise moment the opposite firing stopped as they continued pouring lead into bushes and trees; then one by one they lowered their rifles and listened, hearing no sound except their own heavy breathing.

Tobias ventured out first, going to the wagon and squatting behind it; then Zech walked to Ishmael and knelt beside him, his face ashen, shaking the body as if to awaken it. Frog jumped on his horse and charged across the open area, Tobias shouting, "No, Frog! No! Don't go in there yet!"

Frog paid no heed as he galloped full speed into the woods and disappeared.

Emma rushed to Glenda, having seen her go down with the horse, finding her lying in the bushes, clutching her stomach and moaning.

"Glenda? Are you all right?"

Glenda's face twisted with pain as she said, "It hurts, Emma. It hurts real bad. I think it's going to come out of me."

"Oh Lord!" Emma exclaimed, touching Glenda's face, then shouting, "Pearlie Mae! Come quick! Bring cloth and water from the wagon!"

Tobias and Skillit walked into the edge of the woods, finding tree trunks and bushes splattered with blood, one horse down with its stomach blown out. Skillit said, "I knowed we was bound to have hit something, all that lead we put in here. They's some men out there sommers sho' hurtin'. That cannon you got damn nigh blew down the trees."

"I wouldn't want to be on the receiving end of it," Tobias said.

"What we gone do with them two you blowed out of the buckboard, leave 'em for the buzzards or bury 'em?"

"They'd probably make the pore buzzards sick. We'll bury 'em."

They heard Emma's voice, "Zech! Come here!"

Zech walked to her slowly, muttering, "Damn them! Damn them!"

Emma said, "Get your tent and put it up here! Hurry!"

"They killed Ishmael," Zech said absently, still shocked.

"Forget the horse!" Emma snapped sharply. "Glenda's hurt! There's no time left! Move quickly!"

"What's the matter with her?" Zech asked, brought back to reality by Emma's urgency. "Was she hurt when the horse fell on her?"

"Stop asking questions and move!" Emma insisted. "Just do what I tell you! I'll explain later!"

As soon as the tent was up, Emma and Pearlie Mae moved Glenda inside. Zech hovered outside, hearing the moans, temporarily forgetting the downed horse as concern for Glenda pushed all else from his mind. He paced back and forth until Emma finally emerged carrying a small cloth-bound bundle. She went behind the tent and then returned empty-handed.

Zech said, "What's the matter, Mamma? Tell me now! I want to know."

Emma's eyes filled with tears as she said, "She's had a miscarriage, Zech."

"A miscarriage? What's that?"

"She was pregnant, and she's lost the baby. It was a little girl."

"Baby? Glenda was going to have a baby?" Zech's face was first puzzled, then contorted with anguish as he realized what Emma was saying. "I didn't know, Mamma! Why didn't she tell me? I wouldn't have let her come if I'd known! She had no right to keep this from me!"

"Now don't you start that!" Emma said harshly. "I don't want to hear a word of it! She told me, and I promised not to tell you for the very reason you just said! She kept it a secret because she wanted to come along and be with you and with all of us! She loves you that much! Can't you understand this?"

"I wish she had told me."

"She's the bravest girl I've ever known, and you ought to be proud of her. Now you go on in there, and don't you say one damned word to make her feel worse than she feels now! Do you understand me, Zech? This is not her fault! She didn't shoot that horse out from under herself!"

"I understand now, Mamma. It's just hard for me to take all at once."

Glenda was lying on a blanket, her face white and sweating, her blue eyes not sparkling as usual. She looked up when Zech entered, and then she pushed herself up and cried, "I'm so sorry, Zech! I'm so sorry! I would have told you as soon as we got back to the hammock."

Zech dropped down and put his arms around her, holding her close. He said gently, "It's all right, Glenda. I understand. We'll make another baby as soon as you're well enough. I'm just glad you're fine."

"Oh, Zech. . . .I just wanted to be with you. . . .I'm so sorry. . . ."

He brushed warm tears from her cheeks, feeling the dampness of her hair; then he pushed her back to the blanket and said, "Just rest now, Glenda. Everything will be fine. We'll give the baby a proper burial. There'll be others."

When he came outside he said to Emma, "Where'd you put the baby?"

"Behind the tent."

"I'll get a shovel."

Emma put her arms around him and stopped him for a moment. "Oh, Zech. I'm so sorry this happened to you and Glenda. Just don't blame her. It wasn't her fault."

His face was sober as he pulled away. "I'm not blaming Glenda anymore, and I know whose fault it is. It's those bastards out there somewhere. They won't stop till they kill us all, unless I kill them first. And I will."

"Don't say that, Zech! And don't feel that way. The Lord will punish them. The Lord. . . ."

He turned and walked away before she could finish, moving rapidly to the wagon, snatching up a shovel and banging it against one wheel, beating the spokes again and again until finally the startled oxen bolted forward and ran across the clearing.

Zech then saw Frog come from the woods and stop beside Tobias and Skillit. A man trailed the horse, a rope around his neck, his hands tied behind him. He was tall and gaunt, his clothes filthy, a matted black beard covering his face.

Frog said, "This must be the one whose horse was shot. I found him hiding in a bush. He shore is a purty sight for a bushwhackin' killer, ain't he?"

Zech went to them as Frog dismounted. Tobias said, "Now that you got him, I don't rightly know what to do with him. There ain't no law out here to turn him over to."

"That's for sure," Frog said. "I ought to have just shot him out there in the woods."

Zech dropped the shovel and sprang catlike onto the horse, startling the others because they were not aware of his presence. He grabbed the rope attached to the saddle and kicked the horse's flanks, bounding away into the woods, dragging the man through the brush. He heard his father shout, "Zech! What the hell you doing? Come back here!"

He raced full gallop for fifty yards, feeling the rope jerk as the body bounced off the base of trees; then he stopped and threw the rope over a hickory limb. There was no struggle or cry for mercy as the horse moved forward again, snatching the body upward, dangling it just beneath the limb.

Zech was not aware of where he was until he felt Skillit pull him from the saddle and back the horse, lowering the lifeless body to the ground. He stared blankly as Frog said, "You sure settled that in a hurry, Zech. All we got to do now is plant him."

Tobias said nothing as he looked into Zech's glazed eyes, knowing that any comment now would be useless and wasted. He surmised that something must have happened other than Ishmael's death to make Zech take such a drastic action. He said to Skillit, "Bring him on back to the others and we'll bury 'em in one grave." Then he turned and ran through the woods toward the place where he saw Emma rush to Glenda.

One grave was only two feet long, the other huge. Zech insisted they bury Ishmael too. Crosses made of hickory limbs were at the head of each mound.

All of the men were soaked with sweat from digging, their shirts dust-covered and clinging to their bodies. Zech held Glenda up, his arm tightly around her, bringing her from the tent although Emma advised against it. Tobias turned to Zech and said, "You want me to say words, or you want to do it yourself?"

"I'll do it myself. It's my baby."

Zech took off the black felt hat and pressed it to his chest. Then the others did likewise. He said, "Lord. . .bless this little girl. . .and see to it the wolves don't dig her up. Make her to be a fine woman. . .like Mamma and Glenda. And Lord. . .forgive me for what I done. . .but the bastard deserved it. Amen."

Then he led Glenda back to the tent and went inside with her.

At Emma's insistence they camped for two more days, letting Glenda rest and regain strength. Zech roamed the woods, finding wildflowers and putting them on the grave each day. On the third morning they put Glenda into the covered wagon, Emma riding with her and Zech driving. Tobias rode with Skillit and his family on the buckboard.

Zech glanced at the graves one final time; then he popped his whip and moved the oxen forward.

TWENTY-SEVEN

September passed into October as the men made trip after trip into Fort Pierce, purchasing and stockpiling barrels to be used when the oranges matured later that year. February's blossoms turned into green globes that grew larger each week and would eventually inundate the trees with balls of gold.

Glenda recovered fully, and the nightmare was gradually overshadowed by the everyday routine of living, not forgotten but looked upon as one more tragedy endured.

It was the end of October when Zech set out alone for the cypress swamp to purchase a marshtackie for Glenda and another to replace Ishmael. This would be no leisurely trip, camping often and shooting game along the way. His saddlebag contained smoked beef and biscuits, and he cantered the horse more than he walked it. He was expected back as soon as possible to help with the orange harvest.

As he rounded the eastern shore of Okeechobee and turned southwest, something came back to him that had been pushed far back in his memory, Tawanda. During those years Glenda remained in school in Jacksonville, and he knew he would eventually marry her, he gradually forgot Tawanda, thinking he would never see her again, or even visit the Indian village.

He did not think of Tawanda now with the passion and yearnings that once tormented him. He wondered if she were still there, if she had married and had children, but he could no longer smell the smoke and crushed pine needles or feel the warmth of her body or the softness of her hair. She was only a vague shadow from the past, and he was not sure he could even recognize her.

He skirted the eastern edge of the custard-apple forest and entered the swamp, searching for something familiar, some landmark that would jar his memory and point the way, but he found none. It had been too long, and now all trees looked the same, all ponds and sloughs the same, all trails the same.

For two days he wandered, becoming more discouraged as he zig-zagged from east to west and moved southward, penetrating deeper into a forest that seemed even more awesome than he rememberd, sometimes plodding the horse through shallow coverings of water that lasted for miles before finding firm ground. He was considering abandoning the quest when he was confronted by an Indian armed with a rifle.

Zech was startled when the man stepped from behind a palmetto directly in front of him, blocking the way. His eyes were hostile, and they both stared silently until Zech said, "I'm looking for the village of Keith Tiger. I've been there but I'm lost now. Can you give me directions?"

The Indian made no answer except to motion with the rifle for Zech to follow him. One hour later they entered a clearing dotted with chickees.

Other than two old women in the cooking chickee, the village seemed deserted. As Zech dismounted, his guide pointed with the rifle but still did not speak. This puzzled Zech, for the reception his father received from the Seminoles had been so different from this, friendly and with genuine affection.

He tied the horse to a bush and walked to the edge of the clearing, finding two old men sitting beneath one of the chickees. Again he searched his memory for recognition but found none; then he said, "I'm looking for Keith Tiger. I have business with him."

One of the men said, "I am Keith Tiger. What is your business?"

"You don't remember me, but my name is Zech MacIvey, son of Tobias MacIvey. I was here once with my father."

The old man smiled, Zech's first sign of welcome, making him feel more at ease. "It is good to see you, Zech MacIvey, and you are welcome. You have grown so much I did not know you. When you were here before you were a boy, and now you return as a man. How is Tobias?"

"He's doing pretty good at times, but he still has spells of malaria.

He's not as strong as he used to be."

"None of us are as we grow older. It is a pity of time passing. But I worried about Tobias when he left here so sick. It is good to know he survived. What brings you on such a long journey to find me?"

"I want to buy horses," Zech responded, sitting in front of Keith Tiger. "Two marshtackies, like the one you gave us a long time ago. I didn't know anywhere else to get them but from you."

"They are yours for the asking, but I will accept no pay. We still owe you for the cows. I will have the horses brought here in the morning. They are at a place deeper in the swamp. We do not keep our horses and cows here in the village where they might be seen."

"Tomorrow is fine, but I'll be glad to pay."

"You have paid already for much more than two horses. Your father is a friend we will never forget. And do not be troubled by your reception here. No one knew who you were, and there has been much trouble lately between our people and some bad white men in the ten thousand islands. It will be different when you are known as a MacIvey. Our people will come back into the village soon and I will tell them. Are you hungry?"

"Yes, I am," Zech admitted. "I was in a hurry to get here and didn't cook along the way."

"Then you must eat now. Come with me and I will get food for you."

Zech followed the old man to the cooking chickee were he was ladled a large wooden bowl of turtle stew and given a chunk of koonti bread. He sat on the ground outside the hut and ate as Keith Tiger returned to the chickee. He thought of asking about Tawanda but decided against it, thinking she no longer lived in the village and was elsewhere with a family of her own. It disappointed him that he would not see her even briefly or at least know what happened to her.

After eating he unsaddled the horse and then returned to the chickee, finding Keith Tiger asleep. He didn't want to disturb the old man so he went back to his horse, mounted and rode bareback into the woods, following a trail to the south. He would like to see Pay-Hay-Okee again but knew it was too far a journey for an afternoon; and even if there were time, he was unsure of the way.

He walked the horse slowly, killing time, feeling uncomfortable alone in the village without even the old man to talk to. He wished the hours would pass quickly so he could take the horses and leave.

The voice came from behind him as the trail turned to the left. "It is you, isn't it, Zech?"

He stopped the horse immediately and looked back, seeing her standing there, the same brown skin and deep-set eyes, the flowing black hair, a still youthful body now mature.

She said, "I watched you as you came into the village. Can I ride with you?"

He reached down, took her hand and pulled her up behind him. "Why didn't you come forward and speak? I thought you didn't live here anymore."

"I was too surprised. I didn't think I would ever see you again, and there you were."

As the horse stepped forward she put her arms around him and drew close, pressing against him, bringing back a flood of memories so vivid it seemed to Zech it happened only yesterday, that he never left the swamp at all.

He put his right hand on her arm, feeling the firm flesh as his hand moved back and forth, his mind suddenly blocking out all things but her presence there with him on the horse, riding a trail he once rode with her when they were both too innocent to know what love can be.

He did not know if he turned the horse or if it turned itself. They moved off the trail and stopped beneath a bald cypress surrounded by a ground-covering of green moss. She slipped down first, and as he dismounted she wilted to the ground, speaking to him with her eyes. There was no timidity this time, no hesitancy. He dropped down into the moss and took her in his arms, and it happened so quickly he had no time to cast doubts about what he was doing. There were no thoughts of Glenda or the marshtackies or why he was there or anything but Tawanda.

She put her face against his and said, "Why did you wait so long to come back? I watched the trail each week until I finally gave up."

"I wanted to come back, but too many things happened with my family. I thought of you a lot."

"I thought of you too. All the time at first, and then I tried to forget. But I couldn't. I'm glad you're here now. I've waited so long for you."

"There's something I must tell you, Tawanda," Zech said hesitantly. "I'm married now."

The words did not shock her or anger her. She said, "It doesn't matter. I would want to be with you anyway. Is she pretty?"

"Yes. Her name is Glenda. We were going to have a baby but she got hurt in an ambush and lost it."

"That is sad. You deserve many sons, and I'm sure there will be others. You have not told me why you're here."

"To buy horses. I want marshtackies, and I can't find them anywhere else. I have to start back in the morning and help Pappa harvest his oranges."

"We'll spend the night here together!" she said with excitement. "I'll go to the village and get food and blankets, and you can rest while I'm gone."

"What will everyone think if we do this?" Zech asked doubtfully.

"I don't care what anyone thinks! I'm not promised to any man because I choose not to be, and no one will come looking for us. I'll go now and return soon."

Zech watched as she jumped up, put on the dress and ran down the trail. He felt as if he were caught in a hurricane, sucking him backward in time, powerless to control what was happening even if he wanted to. He was not the leader but the follower, doing what she wanted him to do, and if she had resisted he would have backed away. It happened because they wanted it to happen and made it happen, and no one would be hurt by it. Then he wondered why he was reasoning with himself, why he felt the necessity to explain it away to himself or to anyone. All he cared about at this moment was for her to come back and be with him. His other world seemed very far away.

When they rode into the village together at dawn, Tawanda's face beamed with fulfillment, her emotions so obvious he knew that everyone would notice. But no protest was made, not even by her father or mother as they watched Zech and Tawanda take food and go off alone. Zech was glad they accepted it, for he wanted no trouble with them or anyone in the village, no ill feelings among people who were his father's friends. And there apparently were none.

The marshtackies were waiting, and after a final farewell he tied them behind his horse. He put a loaf of koonti bread Tawanda prepared for him into the saddlebag; then he kissed her, undisturbed that others were watching them. Once mounted he rode away quickly, not looking back for fear he would return and stay longer.

With each mile he traveled, bringing him closer to the hammock and his real world, Zech felt pangs of guilt. He tried to push Tawanda from his mind and pretend it had not happened at all, but he knew it had. It was all too real to be make-believe.

He thought that what he had done made him no different from a bull going from cow to cow, planting seed indiscriminately in all of them; then he salved his conscience by reasoning it could not have been prevented under the circumstances, that it was a natural act between a man and a woman who cared for each other. What he had done with Tawanda belonged in the swamp and would remain there, and had nothing to do with his life with Glenda. These were two separate worlds, one real and one fantasy, and there was no reason for them to ever meet.

He knew Glenda would never do the same when away from him, and this bothered him the most. Her love and commitment was total; yet his was broken at the first opportunity. It was unfair to her and he admitted it, but it happened only with Tawanda. He wasn't a bull, and he had not gone from cow to cow, only to the one other woman he had ever wanted. This made a difference. It was not something he had run away seeking, like a bull bursting through a fence to get at six cows, not caring which was which, and it would never happen again.

His final rationalization was that Glenda deceived him once and once only, about the baby; he would deceive her this one time only with Tawanda, equalizing things back to zero, and also being the end of it.

As he approached the hammock he looked back at the marshtackies, the purpose of his trip, trying to decide which he should keep for himself and which would be Glenda's. Keith Tiger had selected a stallion and a mare, telling him that marshtackies were becoming rare and would someday soon die out and vanish forever, that if he wanted more he should raise his own from this pair.

He would take the stallion and give Glenda the mare, for the mare would be more loving and gentle. When the time came, and the mare went into heat, they would mate the two and perpetuate the breed. He was sure Glenda would approve of his decision and be happy with the mare, for she wouldn't know how to handle a stallion as well as he.

TWENTY-EIGHT
1883

Solomon MacIvey was born March 12, 1883 in a flurry of activity as Emma and Pearlie Mae bounded about, shouting orders for more hot water and towels, the bewildered men stoking great fires under two cast-iron washpots, filling the clearing with smoke.

Zech thought they had boiled enough water to scald and scrape a dozen hogs, and he wondered if his mother and Pearlie Mae were drowning Glenda and preparing the same fate for the baby.

It was a breech delivery and very difficult, and Zech winced with horror each time he heard screams coming from the house, making him vow he would never again inflict such pain on Glenda if this was what birthing was all about. He had seen calves born wrong, making it necessary to cut off the calf's head in order to pull the twisted body from its mother and save her life, and the thought of it turned his stomach sick. But after six hours of constant turmoil, Emma and her assistant extracted a healthy, wailing boy from Glenda.

Two days later they chose the name Solomon because Zech had been reading the Bible and discovered that Solomon, son of David and king of Israel and Judah, was noted for his wisdom. Sol, as they would call him, would be a very wise man indeed, since he would be the first MacIvey to have his own private tutor from birth. Glenda would give him knowledge beyond all things Zech and his father could ever know, and he would be the one to build a MacIvey temple rather than a frontier house made of rough cypress long since turned black by exposure to the elements.

When it came time in April to move the herd for grazing, Emma and Pearlie Mae both refused to go, telling the men to fend for themselves while they stayed behind to look after Glenda and the baby. Under protest, Skillit was elected cook by a vote of three to one.

Zech left the hammock reluctantly, fearing that in his brief absence the baby would grow up and not know him as the father. He was puffed with pride but would not hold the baby, convinced that such a small and delicate thing would surely break in his rough hands. He cautioned Glenda and his mother to be very careful with Sol, causing them to smile knowingly and assure him they would do their best while he was gone.

Tobias decided not to move the herd too far from the hammock and send a rider back every two days to make sure the women were fine. They moved south, heading for the lower Kissimmee valley where the marsh and prairie grass should be plentiful.

It was mid-week of the second week when six riders came out of the southwest and approached Skillit on the right flank. One said briefly, "Who owns these cows?"

"Mistuh MacIvey," Skillit answered, pointing. "That's him over there, just behind the herd."

Zech noticed the riders and came over to see what they wanted. One said to Tobias, "Where you taking this herd?"

"Nowhere in particular," Tobias responded. "Just grazing wherever they want to go. We do it every summer."

"Well, you can't go any further in this direction."

"How come?" Tobias asked, thinking it was another situation like the one they encountered at the salt marsh. "I don't see any more cows any-where."

"This is private land, all the way from here down to Lake Okeechobee. You're trespassing right now."

"Private land? How come all of a sudden it's private land? It's always been open range."

"Not any more. This is Disston land. Mister Disston bought four mil-lion acres here."

"How many?" Tobias questioned, baffled by the figure.

"You deef? I said four million. Bought it from the state for a million dollars. Mister Disston has done run all the squatters off, and he's got plans to drain all this land and develop it. He's already got dredges working. He don't want nobody driving cows in here, and that includes you."

"What if I want to drive a herd through here to Punta Rassa? What could I do if he closes the land?"

"I don't give a damn what you do. You can take them cows slam around the south end of Okeechobee, you can go back north and find another way, or you can shove 'em up your butt. But you're not going through here."

"What if I do it anyway?" Tobias shot back, his anger beginning to boil.

"I got a hundred and fifty men working on this place, and all of them are armed. We'll shoot ever cow that enters. Now if you want to convert them cows to carcasses, you just go ahead and push 'em in the direction you're going. That's all I got to say."

With that the men rode off a hundred yards and stopped, forming a line facing the herd, rifles drawn.

"Damn them!" Tobias cursed. Then he said to Zech, "Go tell Frog and Skillit to turn 'em. We can't fight a hundred and fifty men. We'll go back north and then cut to the west, toward the salt marsh. But ain't nobody got the right to close off the land!"

"Pappa, this is just the beginning," Zech said. "Someday there won't be any open range left. Last time I was over at Fort Drum and talked to Mister Turner he said men are out everwhere now, surveying land for new railroads, and the railroad companies are buying everything they can get. The lumber companies and turpentine men are doing it too. Someday it's coming to an end, Pappa, and there's nothing we can do about it."

"You're wrong!" Tobais responded. "It ain't coming to an end, and it never will. But if this kind of crap keeps up, we'll just put in more orange trees and run less cows. Prices keep going up like they been doing we ought to be able to clear a thousand dollars a acre on oranges."

"Maybe so, Pappa. But if we stay in the cattle business we're going to have to own the land and fence it too."

"Fence it? That's the best way I know to start a range war. I know what I'd do if I came to a fence. I'd cut it."

"And maybe get yourself killed for doing it."

"Whose side are you on? You sound more like a landlord than a cattleman."

"I'm not talking sides, Pappa. I'll always be with you, and you know it. What I'm talking is sense."

"We'll see," Tobias said, dismissing the conversation. "Go on now and help Frog and Skillit turn the cows. We'll find grass elsewhere. There just ain't no way we can face a hundred and fifty men."

As Zech rode off he thought about the deed lying in a drawer in his cabin, MacIvey land that would never be closed to them. He must plan soon to convert more of the gold doubloons into land.

TWENTY-NINE
1888

The cattle drives were reduced to one every two years, and much of the grazing was done on MacIvey land. More and more they encountered other herds on the prairies, landless men searching for open range and free grass; and often the sound of Winchesters could be heard firing point-blank at quarter-mile distances, warning intruders away. Had it not been for Emma they would have already engaged in at least a half dozen all-out gun battles over grazing rights. Others were not so fortunate as range wars broke out everywhere.

Tobias gradually increased his orange grove to three hundred acres, and if they never owned another cow, the grove would provide a good living. But cows were in their blood, especially Zech's, and they refused to give it up. It was a way of life too deeply ingrained to discard easily. The days of driving herds across open land where nothing could be seen but endless wilderness were vanishing rapidly, but there was still profit in cows. Tobias wanted to fight for it, but Zech was formulating other plans. First he would fence the MacIvey land, which he had increased to thirty thousand acres; then he would look to the south for additional land. The last great manless frontier lay to the south of Lake Okeechobee, and it was there he felt his future destiny lay. Someday he would explore this possibility.

Skillit left the caravan as they returned from Punta Rassa, telling
Tobias he had a "chore" to tend to in Kissimmee. Tobias wondered
about this, remembering that Skillit's previous "chore" of finding himself a wife had taken several years. There were now five boys riding
in the wagon with Pearlie Mae, and their wailing had been the only
sound of babies born in the MacIvey hammock since Sol. Glenda had
become pregnant twice more, each one ending in a miscarriage, and
Emma feared that complications caused by Sol's difficult birth might
prevent Glenda from having another child.

It was just before noon when Skillit came into the clearing, driving
a wagon hitched to two oxen, his horse trailing behind. Tobias watched
curiously as Skillit tied the oxen and came to the stoop; then he said
to him, "Where'd you get that outfit?"

"In Kissimmee. They's good oxen, ain't they?"

"They look right fine, but we don't need another team, 'less you
plan to fill another wagon with babies. And you're getting kinda old
for that."

"I jus' thought I wanted 'em," Skillit said, casting his eyes downward.

Tobias noticed that Skillit was not looking at him as he spoke,
avoiding his eyes, and this puzzled him. He said, "Are you feeling
poorly, Skillit? You don't seem right to me."

"I's fine, Mistuh Tobias. Must be something I et on the trail."

Zech rode up on the marshtackie stallion which he had named Tiger,
and Sol was in the saddle in front of him, his red hair tousled down
his forehead. Zech said, "Sol rode Tiger by himself down in the woods,
and he did right well for the saddle not to have a horn. I've got to get
him a western saddle so he can have something to hold on to. You
should 'a seen him go, Pappa. He looked like a frog on a rabbit's back."

Glenda had come outside unnoticed. She said, "I don't doubt that
one bit, but you shouldn't turn a five-year-old boy loose on a horse.
First thing you know you'll have him branding cows."

"Next year," Zech said, dismounting and putting Sol on the ground.
"One more year and he can ride herd as good as anybody. We'll have
us another drover."

"I can do it now, Mamma," Sol said excitedly, scurrying to Glenda.
"I can ride as good as Pappa."

"Let's see how good you can wash your face and hands," Glenda
said. "Dinner's ready. All of you hurry on up before it gets cold."

They gathered at the long cypress table where they still shared common meals, continuing the practice although the clan had grown larger. New planks were added to accommodate new arrivals.

Frog popped a fried pork chop into his mouth and said, "Where you been to, Skillit? I figured you'd done wore pore old Pearlie Mae out an' gone after a new wife. Where you got her hid, out in the woods? Pearlie Mae gone kill you for sure."

"There you go again, Frog, always teasing," Emma said. "And don't talk with your mouth full. It doesn't set a good example for the youngens."

"Sorry 'bout that, Miz Emma," Frog responded, "but Skillit sure looks like he's been up to something."

Skillit suddenly pushed his plate away and started sobbing. All of the others were startled, and Frog said in a subdued voice, "What's the matter, Skillit? You ain't never took offense before when we jawed each other. I didn't mean nothin'. I'm sorry."

"It ain't that," Skillit said, his voice choked. "I done a thing I ain't proud of."

"What the devil is it?" Tobias demanded. "I've never seen you carry on so, Skillit. You done killed somebody?"

"Nawsir, it's more than that. I been with you more than twenty years, Mistuh Tobias. You been the onliest family I ever had, but it's time to go now. I got to leave."

"You what?" Tobias asked, totally baffled. "How come you say that? You're family, Skillit. You can stay here as long as you want to."

"I's gettin' old, Mistuh Tobias, an' I got five boys to look to. I got to see to them. I took some of that gold you been givin' me all these years an' bought me some land south of Kissimmee. I got to start my own place so them boys can have somethin' goin' for them after I's gone. I hope all of you ain't too mad at me. It would kill me if you is."

"Nobody's mad at you, Skillit," Emma said, absorbing the meaning of the words. "You done the right thing. I'm proud of you."

Tears formed in Tobias' eyes. He was shocked by the news but he understood. Skillit's desire for his own place was the same he had known all his life. He said, "Couldn't nobody be mad at you for what you done. You got a right to do what you want, same as anybody. But I'd like to help. You need more money?"

"Nawsuh, Mistuh Tobias, I got enough. You done give me more than I ever dreamed of. I got plenty left after the land to build me a house an' buy some cows an' hogs an' chickens an' start a little farm too.

We'll make do fine. But I done something else you might want to shoot me for."

"It would have to be powerful bad," Tobias said.

"When I went to the land office the man tole me he couldn't record the deed jus to Skillit, that I had to make up a last name if I didn't have one. I put it down as Skillit and Pearlie Mae MacIvey, an' all the boys too. I done took yo name, Mistuh Tobias. If you wants me to I'll go back an' change it to something else."

The shock and grief flushed out as Tobias said, "Hell, that's fine, Skillit! We're proud you took the name. You're welcome to it."

"Don't swear in front of Sol!" Emma admonished. "It's not nice. But you know what you've done, Skillit? You've given me six grandsons instead of one. I'm right proud too."

Skillit felt relief that he had revealed his decision without ill feelings. Had the response been otherwise he might have backed away and stayed at the MacIvey hammock. He said, "Lawd, you sho' fine folks! I done got me my own place an' a name too! An' it won't be like we's gone. It's close enough we can come back an' visit whenever we want to. An' if you needs me on a drive I'll go."

"And if you have need of us we'll come," Tobias said. "If anybody hassles you they'll answer to me. MacIvey's stick together, white or black. When you aim to set out?"

"Soon as we get our stuff loaded in the mornin'," Skillit responded.

"Then we'll have a celebration tonight," Emma said. "I'll cook the biggest meal you ever saw."

"If she's gone do that, you ought to come back and leave ever week," Frog said.

Zech listened to it all but said nothing, too many memories cropping up at once. His voice choked as he said, "Y'all excuse me a minute. I'm not sure I tied my horse." He went behind the house and stood there alone, staring at the little cabin where Skillit and Pearlie Mae lived, thinking of all the things Skillit had been an intimate part of, good and bad. Then he washed his face at the stoop and went back inside.

Pearlie Mae stood by the loaded wagon, crying so hard she could only croak, "Missus Emma. . .Missus Glenda. . . ."

Both hugged her, and then Emma said, "God bless you, Pearlie Mae.

We'll miss you."

Frog said to Skillit, "Nigger smell ain't so bad after all, Skillit. I got kinda used to it. I'll miss it for sure."

Skillit gave Frog a bear hug, pressing the breath from him. "Bless you, Frog. . .you old buzzard bait! An' you take care of yo'self. You gettin' old too, like me."

"Ain't no use bustin' my ribs over it," Frog said. "You need me to help out with something you let me know."

Skillit then hugged Tobias and Zech, afraid to say more lest he would unload the wagon and stay. The boys clambered into the wagon bed as he helped Pearlie Mae to the seat. He tried to speak again but couldn't; then he popped the whip, moved the oxen forward and said, "I got to go now. . . ."

The others drifted away silently as Tobias and Emma continued watching the wagon until it disappeared into the woods. Tobias said, "It's breaking up, Emma."

"Yes, it is. But it has to sooner or later. Nothing lasts forever. Everything ends."

"Us too. Our time is coming. But it's sure been something while it lasted."

"It rightly has."

She took his hand in hers and they walked back toward the house, trudging slowing as if tired, Tobias looking down at the deep ruts the loaded wagon cut in the sandy soil.

THIRTY
1892

"I wish I could have made Pappa stay at home," Zech said, eating alone with Glenda. "He'll soon be sixty years old, and he's too sick to be out here on the prairie."

"The spells are coming more often," Glenda said, "but you can't tie him up with ropes and leave him behind."

"I will next time if I have to. I'd rather tie him up than see him die out here in a cypress stand."

"Does there really have to be a next time," Glenda asked seriously. "Won't the orange trees make enough money without us driving cows all over the countryside to Punta Rassa?"

"I suppose so. But the whole thing of shipping from Punta Rassa is going to be settled someday. There's trouble brewing in Cuba, and sooner or later there'll be a war down there. When it happens, there won't be any more Cuban market. Someday all the cows will be shipped up north on the railroad."

"That would surely be better than this," Glenda said. "I hope it happens soon. And we've got enough land of our own now to fatten cattle for market. We don't have to roam around out here looking for grass. If you would just go ahead and fence our land we could stay at home until shipping time."

"I'm going to do that, but it'll sure cause trouble with that Allister family up north of us. Every time I go up that way they're on our land.

I've warned them but they don't pay any more attention to me than they would a jaybird. They're as stubborn as Pappa about open range."

Sol came galloping in on Tiger and was followed by a new man Zech hired named Lester. He was in his early forties and a typical cracker drover, rail-thin, beard-covered and somber, like Frog. But also like Frog, inside he was both gentle and tough when he had to be.

Sol was stamped from his father's mold except for the red hair. He was already taller than most boys at age nine, broad-shouldered and lanky. He said, "Is Grampy feeling better?"

"I suppose," Glenda responded. "We'll be moving on soon, so you and Lester better eat now."

"I'll see to Grampy first," Sol said, bounding off toward the wagon.

Tobias was sitting beneath the shade of a palmetto, mopping his forehead with a damp cloth. His hair and beard were now completely gray, his body even leaner than ever. Sol threw his arms around him and said, "How you feeling, Grampy? You missed a good one this morning. We saw a bear over by the edge of the woods, and when I charged toward him with Tiger he ran away."

"I seen enough bears already," Tobias said. "But you best be careful. There was a time when a bear would snatch you off that horse and eat you, and then eat the horse for good measure."

"Here, swallow this," Emma commanded, shoving quinine into Tobias' mouth.

Tobias grimaced, then he said to Sol, "Boy, don't ever let yourself get into the mess of having a woman around always shoveling crap into you. It ain't worth it."

"Hush up and go eat!" Emma snapped. "You get more cantankerous every day. You're worse than an old billygoat. You need food for strength."

"See what I mean," Tobias said, smiling. "She's like a crow sittin' in a tree, squawking at everything that passes."

"You can ride in the wagon with Granny if you want to," Sol said. "Me and Pappa and Lester can handle the cows. I could do it by myself if they'd let me."

"I suppose you could," Tobias said, getting up. "You're a MacIvey through and through, for sure. And I might just ride with Granny for a day or two and let you prove yourself."

"That's the only thing you've said that makes sense," Emma said. "You don't need to be out there in the sun on a horse. Them cows can chomp grass without you staring at every bite they take."

"We'll do it!" Sol said enthusiastically. "We'll handle the cows while you rest up some. But come on now, Grampy, and let's eat! I'm about to starve."

Tobias took the boy's hand and felt himself tugged hurriedly toward the cooking pot.

Emma smiled at both of them as she followed.

The herd grazed in a northwesterly direction, eleven hundred cows, mostly home-grown rather than popped wild out of swamps. By not driving to market each year the calves were given time to grow on land closer to home. Some were still rounded up wild but not so many as in days past.

One morning they could see the railroad in the distance as the sun reflected off shiny steel rails. It was the new line into Tampa. Zech and Frog had come upon a section of it under construction while scouting grazing land, and the foreman contracted with them for delivery of two dressed steers each day for forty dollars per steer. They followed the workers for over a month, killing and dressing beef at the corral and taking it to the site in the wagon. When the construction crew moved too far away for the dressed meat to be transported safely in the heat, they followed the crew for two more weeks, driving cows with them and butchering on the spot. Then they abandoned the project and returned home.

When the lead steer reached the rails they could see smoke boiling up on the horizon, painting a black streak in the sky. Soon afterwards a tooting sound broke the silence of the prairie.

The cows poured halfway across the rails and stopped, oblivious to the engine puffing toward them. Zech and Frog popped their whips frantically, trying to move the balking herd.

Tobias jumped from the wagon and watched as the train came closer without slowing, and then he shouted, "That damned fool is going to plow right into 'em!"

Zech and Frog wheeled their horses and got out of the way as the engine smashed into the herd, its iron cowcatcher scooping up three cows, crushing and killing them instantly. The train then came to a stop a hundred yards down the rails.

Zech looked at the mangled bodies; then he and Frog rode quickly to the idling engine, its stack belching soot over the grass. Zech shouted,

"What the hell you mean, fellow? Can't you see a herd of cows a mile away? If you'd stopped that damned thing, we'd 'a got them out of the way!"

The engineer leaned out the window and shouted back "If you hadn't 'a had them friggin' yellowhammers on company property it wouldn't 'a happened anyway. You're going to make us late!"

"That's no excuse for what you done!" Zech said angrily. "The railroad's got no right to keep us from passing. You know that as well as I do. You could 'a stopped for a few minutes. Who's going to pay us for the cows you killed?"

"File a claim with the headquarters office in Tampa," the engineer said. "But don't try to charge us a hundred dollars each for buzzard bait worth fifteen. We won't stand for it no more! I ain't never seen so many hundred dollar cows till we hit some flea-bit varmint out here on the prairie, then all of a sudden it's worth its weight in gold. Who the hell you crackers take us for anyway, a bunch of fools?"

None of them noticed Tobias as he walked on the side of the engine, carrying the shotgun. He aimed at the boiler and pulled both triggers, blowing an eight-inch hole in the steel plate. Steam shot out and hissed loudly, like angry rattlesnakes, spewing a white cloud over the engine.

The engineer and the fireman hit the deck as Zech and Frog's horses bolted away. Tobias lowered the shotgun and walked calmly back to the wagon.

The engineer finally peeked out the window and said, "What the hell?. . . ."

Zech brought the bucking horse under control and returned to the edge of the billowing steam cloud. The engineer jumped from the cabin and came to him. "Do you know what the old fool has done?" he shouted. "It'll take us a half day to patch the boiler and get up steam again! Who's going to pay for this?"

"We'll swap out," Zech said, trying hard to be serious. "We'll trade you our dead cows for your hole. That ought to about even things up. We'll see you. And good luck with the patchin'."

As Zech and Frog rode off the engineer shouted after them, "Damn you! Idiots! Cracker jackasses!"

Zech made no comment to Tobias as they moved the herd on across the tracks and to the west. Frog rode up to him and said, "The old man's still got fire in his guts, ain't he?"

"Sure seems that way," Zech said. "That breech loader has killed everthing but a train engine, and now it's done that too."

After crossing the railroad they turned due north and grazed unmolested for a week; then one morning another herd was spotted on the horizon. Wishing no confrontation, Zech ordered them to move south again. They recrossed the rail line without incident and drifted to the southwest.

At noon one day a week later they were once again approached by armed riders. Off to the right of the herd, no more than two miles away, Zech could see men digging frantically with both machines and shovels, cutting wide gashes in the earth. As soon as the riders reached him he said, "What's happening over there? It looks like the biggest fishbait digging contest I ever seen. Must be some kind of worms them fellows are after."

"Tain't worms," one man said. "It's phosphate. You'll have to turn away. There's no way you can get them cows through here, and it's the same slam over to the coast and for fifty miles south. You best go east and around."

"Appears to me they're just digging up dirt," Zech said, puzzled. "How'll they ever get all them holes filled back up?"

"They won't. As I said, it's phosphate. Folks has gone plumb wild over it, as bad as the forty-nine gold rush. Speculators are jumping around like rabbits, buying land and filing claims and jumping claims and shooting at each other, raising pure hell like you never seen. If I were you I'd cut a wide path away from here afore some fool cracks down at you from behind a bush. The mine over yonder belongs to a company out of Chicago, and they aim to fence the whole area. We got orders to turn everbody away."

Zech felt no anger as he had when they were denied entrance to the Disston land. He said resignedly, "I guess you're just doing your job. We'll cut east and find another way to Punta Rassa. But it sure seems the whole prairie is going to hell in a basket. I don't know what use they'll ever make of them big holes once they're done with the mining."

"Beats me, but I think nobody gives a damn. I'm paid to ride guard, and that's all. I ain't in the hole business. But if I were you, mister, I wouldn't come this way again. We done had two gun battles this week over that stuff they're digging up, and there's four men dead 'cause of it. You best stay away."

"I'll do that," Zech said. "And I thank you for the advice."

They turned the herd eastward for several days, and then south again, finding land that seemed like times gone by, endless stretches of palmetto prairie and scrub pine shared only with herds of deer and flights of birds.

One night as Zech listened apprehensively to the lonesome cry of a wolf, realizing it was a harmless lone voice and not a pack, he wondered what the future held for old adversaries like wolves and bears and for all the other creatures that depended on the land for survival. He remembered that night years ago when he had witnessed the ritual of animals peacefully sharing the life-giving water, some inborn instinct telling them they must share and conserve to survive. Perhaps animals are smarter than men, he thought, taking only what they need to live today, leaving something for tomorrow. Even the hated wolf kills only for food and only for immediate need. Maybe it is man who will eventually perish as he destroys the land and all that it offers, taking the animals down with him.

As he thought of these things and the unknown future, he realized one thing was certain: if the wilderness shrinks, pushing more and more men together, there will be explosions without end. Some will yield but other's won't, and someone will be hurt. It will never be like the animals sharing water.

THIRTY-ONE

After they had bought cows from several small ranchers, the herd numbered two thousand when they reached Punta Rassa at the end of the summer. The market price had gone up to twenty dollars per head, and Zech collected forty thousand dollars in gold doubloons. Tobias was not present when the accounting was made.

After loading the gold on the wagon, Zech went into the office of Jacob Summerlin, the present owner of the Punta Rassa shipping facility. He said to him, "I'm interested in buying some land south of Okeechobee. Is there a land office down there anywhere?"

"There's a small trading post on the southwest shore," Summerlin replied. "Mostly does business in 'gator hides and egret plumes, but the man who owns it is a land agent. What you gone do, go in the bullfrog and wildcat business? I don't know why anybody would want a piece of that place."

"Oh, I don't know, Mister Summerlin. I went through there once a long time ago and just thought I'd like to have some of it."

"I imagine you can get all you want. Most folks don't even know where it is, but there's beginning to be activity over that way. There's some commercial fish houses dealing in catfish, but they're mostly on the north shore and the east side. I don't know of a thing to the south."

"Last time I went there from Punta Rassa, we followed the river to the lake and then turned south. It seems that's pretty far out of the way if I'm heading straight for the south shore. Is there a better way to get

271

there?"

"Well, if you go straight east from here you'll run into a place called the devil's gardens. If you go in there, you're liable not to come out again. Some folks claim it's haunted. Past that is another swamp just about as bad. If you swing down south from here don't go too far in that direction. That's outlaw country. I wouldn't go in there with nothing less than General Grant's army. Best thing to do is follow the river again for about thirty miles and then turn southeast. If you ride steady you can make it in a day more or less, depending on how good your horse is."

"Thanks for the information," Zech said. "I'll see you next drive we make."

As he walked away Summerlin shouted after him, "Hey, MacIvey! Don't let nobody down there sell you a 'gator farm!"

Emma suggested to Zech it would be wise to let Tobias rest at the cabin for a week before setting out on the return trip, and it was during this idle time Zech contemplated making the trip to Okeechobee.

When he arrived at the cabin, he called Glenda aside to discuss what he intended to do. He said to her, "If we stay here for a week I'll have nothing to do but sit, so I thought I'd ride over to Okeechobee and see about buying some land. Mister Summerlin told me where to go. Would you mind being here without me?"

"No, I don't mind at all. We'll be fine. How much land are you thinking of buying?"

"I don't know. I'll stuff both saddlebags with doubloons and buy whatever I can get with it. We may never need land down there, but again we might. And I'd rather have the land than more gold sitting in trunks back at the house. We'll pretty soon have to start storing it in the barn."

"How long do you think you'll be gone?"

"I'm sure I can make it there and back before we start home. I'll leave at dawn tomorrow and take Tiger. He'd be faster on a trip like this than the roan. Whatever time it takes, I'll be back as soon as I can."

"Don't kill yourself or the horse by hurrying. There's no need of that. It's good for Tobias to rest for as long as we can keep him here. I sure hope you can talk him out of making any more of these trips."

Zech cantered the marshtackie for two hours at a time and rested him when they encountered thick woods, then cantered again. Moving steadily without stopping to eat, he covered the sixty miles to the lake shore and found the trading post before sundown.

The owner was a relatively young man of forty, dressed in blue overalls and brogan shoes. He seemed mildly surprised when Zech entered the store. "Kinda late to be pushing a horse way out here," he said. "I don't see many riders near to sundown. Where you coming in from?"

"Punta Rassa. I've been riding steady all day. You got some cheese?"

"Nope, sure don't. It's too hot here to keep cheese. I tried it once and it spoiled before I could sell it, a whole fifty-pound block. Turned plumb green. I gave it to some Indians and they et it anyway. Last I seen of them they was down by the lake, pukin' to beat all hell. Sounded worse than a bunch of whoopin' cranes trying to mate. Next time I seen one of 'em he told me he couldn't shit for a month. Turned plumb green too. You ever seen a green Indian? You didn't ride slam over here from Punta Rassa for cheese, did you?"

Zech ignored the question. "What've you got to eat? I didn't have room in my saddlebags to bring food."

"Tinned beef. How many you want?"

"Two cans will do for now."

He took the meat from a shelf, handed it to Zech and said, "Where you headed? You sure don't smell like a hide trader. If the wind's blowing this way, I know when they're coming when they're still ten miles away."

"Right here. I'm interested in buying land and was told you're an agent."

"Yeah, that's right, I am. But it's just a sideline. My main business is trading. If I had to depend on the commission I get for handling land sales in these parts, I'd 'a starved to death a long time ago. What keeps me in this hell hole is 'gator hides and egret plumes. Them damned feathers is bringing two bucks each now. Ain't that something? Two bucks for something growing out of a bird's rear. What you interested in?"

"Land to the south of the lake."

"How much you got in mind? It comes in eighty-acre sections. You want a whole section?"

"How much is it an acre?"

"Going price right now is fifteen cents. But as I say, you can't buy no less than eighty acres. Anything less than that ain't worth my time to make the deed. Hell, I've had fellows come in here and want to buy five acres to put a cabin on. Can you imagine me going to the trouble of making out a deed and recording it for seventy-five cents? Crap!"

"You got a pencil and a piece of paper?" Zech asked.

"Sure. But I can tell you right off what a section is worth. It's twelve dollars."

"I'd like the pencil anyway."

Zech figured for a moment, scratching his head along the way. He rechecked his figures and said, "I want sixty thousand acres."

"Would you repeat that again?" the man said, staring with deeper interest at Zech.

"Sixty thousand acres. Way I figger it that's nine thousand dollars."

"Well, you figger right. But listen, fellow. We don't sell no land on credit. You got to pay at least half down and the rest in a year."

"I'll pay cash. I've got nine thousand in gold in my saddlebags. I'll bring it in now."

Zech went to the horse, came back and threw the bags on the counter, creating a dull thump. "You can count it whenever you want. It's all there. When can you get the deed ready?"

"For a chunk that size it'll take me the best part of a day, and I'm ready to close up now for the night. My missus don't like to be alone with the youngens after the sun goes down on account of all the riffraff we got around here. I can have everything for you first thing day after tomorrow. Does that suit you?"

"It does if it's the best you can do. I hoped to start back right away, but I'll kill the time somehow."

"You pretty good at counting katydids? If you ain't, I can loan you a fishing pole."

"Don't worry about me. I'll be here day after tomorrow."

"Here's a receipt for your money till it's counted and the deed is done," the man said, handing Zech a slip of paper. "Come on over here and look at this map on the wall. It shows the whole general area, and you can point out where you'd rather have your land."

Zech studied the map for a moment; then he put his finger to it and said, "Right in there to the southeast will do fine."

"That area is the best of the lot," the man said, marking it with a pin. "It ain't all swamp like some of it. I'll make sure the description is right for whenever you want it surveyed."

"I'd appreciate that."

The man took a ring of keys from a nail and said apologetically, "I'd ask you to stay the night at my place but we don't have no spare room at all."

"That's all right. I'll be fine."

"Lordy me!" he then said, popping his fingers. "You shook me so with that land order I plumb forgot to ask your name for the deed."

"Zech MacIvey. And I want three names on it, my wife and boy too. I'll write it down for you."

The man accepted the printed names and said, "I'm Jasper Thurmond. It's been a pleasure doing business with you, Mister MacIvey."

"You too," Zech responded, turning and leaving the store.

He mounted Tiger, rode a short distance to an oak tree, dismounted and opened one tin of beef. As he ate hungrily, he wished he had brought Sol along just for company. After finishing the beef he built a fire, spread a blanket and fell into a tired sleep.

At dawn Zech ate the remaining canned beef and washed it down with water from his canteen. For a while he watched the rising sun burn the sky and tint flights of egrets heading out over the lake; then he lost interest and mounted the horse.

At first, he rode south aimlessly, bored already with waiting for the deed, not at first aware he was heading in the direction of the Seminole village. Realization came slowly as he plodded onward, and then he calculated he was no more than twenty miles from the village. It would be a good day's outing and something to do while killing time, and also a chance to see Keith Tiger again.

He had not thought of Tawanda when he planned the journey to the south shore of the lake, so close to her and the village. The purchase of land had been his only reason for coming. It had been too many years, too many happenings, and surely she would be married now with children of her own. Perhaps he would at least be able to speak to her briefly and learn her fate since their last meeting.

This time he did not become lost and wander vainly as before, hoping to be discovered rather than discover. On his last trip he studied the landscape carefully, making mental notes in case he ever did return; and now when he encountered changes from meadow to slough to swamp he knew the direction he wanted to take.

He reached the village at noon and found it to be the same as the last time he rode in, deserted except for two old women beneath the cooking chickee. No one challenged him as he approached. He tried to talk to one of the women but she couldn't understand him, making signs toward the south of the clearing and chattering in a tongue unknown to him. Then he looked into all of the chickees and found them empty.

He sat on a palm stump, trying to decide what to do, to wait longer in hopes of someone returning soon, or leave now and reach the trading post before nightfall. Then he was startled as a marshtackie ridden by a young boy bounded out of the brush, dashed full gallop a yard from him and disappeared into the woods.

Several people then ran into the clearing as if chasing the horse, and before Zech regained his composure from the near miss by the dashing rider, Tawanda stopped suddenly in front of him, staring wide-eyed.

"Zech? Zech? Is it really you? I don't believe it!"

"Yes, Tawanda, it's me," he replied, getting up. "I almost got run over by a horse just now. Who was that boy flying through here on the marshtackie?"

"It was my son, Toby. The men are breaking horses at a corral in the swamp and we've all been watching. Toby rides well, doesn't he?"

"I'll say," he answered, thinking of the words "my son," knowing now she was married. "That horse barely touched the ground going by here. He rides like the wind. You must be real proud of him."

"Yes, I am."

He was still as surprised as she, and for the first time he looked at her, seeing that she was as he remembered, not yet touched by the years, still firm and youthful with sparkling eyes and flowing black hair.

For a moment more neither of them spoke, as if waiting expectantly for the other to make the first move, and then Tawanda said, "What are you doing here? I still can't believe it's really you."

"I had some business at a trading post on the south side of the lake and just decided I'd try to find the village. This is the first time I've been back down this way since that time I came for the marshtackies."

"It's been over nine years, Zech! I think I can truthfully say that you don't visit very often. This time I had really given up hope of ever seeing you again. Come with me and we'll talk."

Zech followed her with trepidation, fearing what an Indian husband would do if he found them together, knowing there were surely people yet in the village who remembered seeing them together as lovers. They made no effort to hide it the last time he was here, but now he was not the only man in her life, and he wished to cause her no trouble by his presence. He regretted even making the trip to the village.

They sat on a palm bench beside a chickee, Zech tapping his fingers nervously against the fibrous wood. She watched him for a moment, and then she said, "Why are you so agitated, Zech? You are as nervous as a horse saddled for the first time. Is it because of something I have said?"

It embarrassed him that it was so obvious. He said, "Well, yes, it is, Tawanda. Your husband. Where is he now? Will he come here soon?"

"So that's it," she said, smiling. "If that's what's bothering you, you can relax. I have no husband."

"No husband?" he questioned, puzzled. "But you said the boy is your son."

"He is. And yours too."

"My son too?" Zech's face drained white. "Tawanda. . .what are you saying?"

"Toby is our son. He is of both of us. We made him that night we spent together in the woods."

Zech was shocked, trying to grasp the full meaning of what she was saying. He finally said, "Why didn't you send word to me? Why didn't you let me know about this? I would have done something if I had known."

"That's why I sent no word. There was no need of it. You gave me what I wanted, and I didn't want to risk having it taken from me."

"I wouldn't have taken the boy, Tawanda. You should know better than that! But I would have done something, not just left you here alone with a baby."

"What would you have done? I have need of nothing but Toby."

Her calmness about the whole thing exasperated Zech. He then exclaimed, "Damn! All this time I've had a son down here and didn't know it! I could have come back to see both of you, Tawanda. I would have! I'm not an animal. But I didn't know."

"There's no need for you to become so excited," Tawanda said, taking his hand in hers. "We're not the first man and woman to make a baby. And I'm sure by now you have others."

"A son. . .only a son. . . . His name is Sol. He's about the same age as Toby."

"That's good. Now you have two."

"Does Toby know?" Zech asked.

"Yes. Everyone here knows. At first Toby was scorned as a half-breed. He was picked on by other boys because of his birth, and it was hard on him, but no one does this any more. He's accepted now, and many say he will someday become the leader of our people. Everyone admires him. He's really a fine boy, Zech, and you can be proud of him too."

"This is going to take some time getting used to," Zech said. "It's not like coming on a stray calf in the woods. Lord, I wish I'd known! What do you want me to do for him? I'll do anything you say."

"Do for him?" she questioned. She thought for a moment, and then she said, "Yes, there is something you can do for him. You can promise me you'll never interfere in his life. Never! In no way. You must let him grow up here among his people where he's happy and where he belongs. He will never be a part of your world and you must know this, and you must never tell anyone in your world about Toby. Do you promise, Zech? This is all I ask of you."

"If that's what you want, I promise. I'll never interfere, and I'll never tell anyone. But I wish I could do more."

"When he comes back, you must meet him. After that, I'll fix food for the three of us. Would you like that?"

"Yes, I would. I would very much like to know Toby."

"Now that this is all settled, aren't you going to do it?"

"Do it? Do what?"

"Kiss me. I haven't been kissed for nine years, and you haven't touched me since you've been here."

"Yes, I would like that too. Very much." He leaned over, put his arms around her and kissed her gently. Then he repeated it.

The second kiss was interrupted by a marshtackie digging its hooves into the dirt and stopping just short of entering the chickee. Toby jumped down, ran to Tawanda and said excitedly, "Did you see it, Mother? He's the best of the lot! I'll keep him for myself!" His features were all Seminole except for Zech's deep brown eyes and the sandy tint to his hair.

"Yes, I saw," Tawanda said, trying to calm him. "But forget the horse for now. There's someone here you must know. This is your father, Zech MacIvey."

The boy wheeled around quickly and stared at Zech, his eyes wide and boring into the stranger. Zech tried to smile but couldn't, and then he said, "Hello, Toby. It's good to know you. You're a fine-looking boy, and you ride as good as anyone I've ever seen."

"You really think so?" Toby said hesitantly, unsure of himself and what to say or do. "Would you like to ride the horse?"

"Yes, but not now. I'd like to be with you first. Tell me about yourself. What do you like to do best?"

"Ride horses."

"It was the same with me when I was your age. I rode a marshtackie too, and his name was Ishmael. He was given to us a long time ago by Keith Tiger. He was killed, but we have two others like him. One of them is tied over there."

Toby glanced across the clearing at the horse. "What's his name?" he asked.

"Tiger. I named him after Keith Tiger."

"You named him for a Seminole?"

"Yes, and I'm proud of it. The Seminoles have always been our friends. And I want to be your friend, too."

"Will you go hunting with me?"

"I'll do anything you want me to do. And I have presents for you. Wait right here and I'll get them."

Zech walked quickly to his horse and returned carrying the Winchester and a hunting knife with a nine-inch steel blade. He handed them to Toby and said, "These are for you."

Toby's eyes widened again as he turned the rifle over and over in his hands. "You mean this is for me? I can keep the rifle and the knife as my own?"

"They're yours now. And before I leave I'll teach you to shoot the rifle. It's loaded, so be careful with it."

The awkwardness and the timidity suddenly vanished as Toby put the rifle down and ran to Zech, throwing his arms around him, seeking a relationship he hungered for. He said, "Thank you, Father! I've never had such presents!"

Tawanda watched both of them, and when she heard the word "father" she smiled. Toby turned to her and said, "Can I go now and show the rifle and the knife to Billie Bird? He won't believe what I have unless I show him!"

"Yes, go and show everyone you wish, but come back soon. We'll all eat together."

Zech smiled too as the boy bounded off, shouting, "Billie! Billie! Come see! Come and see what my father brought me!"

Tawanda said, "You have made him very happy, Zech. He never expected to own such things. But wasn't it foolish to give away your rifle and face the return trip unarmed?"

Zech thought of how little the rifle now meant to him except as a killing tool, and how much it seemed to mean to Toby, the same feeling he had when Tobias first presented it to him. He was also touched by the proud shout, ". . .what my father brought to me!" He finally said, "It doesn't matter about the rifle. I have a pistol in my saddlebag. I hope I don't need a gun. But there's something you maybe can answer for me about this trip. A man at Punta Rassa warned me not to go too far south coming here, that it's outlaw country. Do you know anything about this?"

All traces of a smile disappeared quickly as Tawanda said, "Yes, I know. We all know. There are very bad men in the area of the ten thousand islands. They have sugar cane fields there, and they keep slaves, white men they capture. They keep them in chains and work them like oxen. One of our men was held like this but managed to escape. They also go out and roam the land, stealing cattle and driving them back there. Some they slaughter, and others they take by boat to Key West to be sold. They have killed several of our men and boys who wandered too close while hunting or fishing, and they think no more of killing a man than a snake. I hate to think what has happened to the women they take too. I have warned Toby to never go that way."

"Could be they're the same ones who attacked us and have stolen our cattle. How many are there?"

"No one knows for sure."

"Well, I'd like to wipe them off the face of the earth, and someday I will."

"Don't be foolish, Zech!" Tawanda exclaimed with alarm. "Never go there! If you do, you may not return. My people know that instant death awaits anyone who comes too close to those men. Please, Zech, do not even think of what you have said!"

Tawanda's seriousness startled Zech, and he wished he had not asked the question. The possibility of his going into the area was remote, and even so, he wouldn't attempt it without help. He said in a calming voice, "Let's just forget that I even asked, Tawanda. I'll go back the same way I came, far to the north of them."

"When do you have to leave?" Tawanda asked, relieved that Zech apparently dismissed the subject from his mind.

"The deed to some land I'm buying will be ready in the morning, and I'd planned to leave as soon as I pick it up. But I'll stay here tonight and tomorrow and tomorrow night so I can spend some time with Toby. One more day won't make any difference in getting back to Punta Rassa."

This pleased Tawanda, and she said, "We will have you then for two days, but won't you spend some of the time with me as well as Toby?"

"All that I can," Zech replied. "But what will your people think of our being together again?"

"They will think nothing. They know you are Toby's father. Toby is known as Toby Cypress, but he is also half MacIvey, and the name MacIvey is respected here. I wouldn't be ashamed if he were called Toby MacIvey. So forget what is bothering you about this and let's make the most of the time we have. Can you do this?"

"I just did. We'll enjoy the next two days together, the three of us."

That night Zech spread his blanket beneath the chickee adjacent to the beds of Tawanda and Toby. It still bothered him to be so open, for he knew such as this would never be accepted or understood in Fort Pierce or Fort Drum or back in the MacIvey hammock. It was against all things he had known.

When Toby was asleep Tawanda abandoned her bed and came to him without hesitation. Later on they both lay awake, and Zech said to her, "Tawanda. . .there's something I must say to you, and I hope I say it right. I've loved you since that first time I came here with my pappa, but I love Glenda too. I hope it doesn't hurt you for me to tell you this, but it's something you should know. I'll never leave Glenda for you. I remember after I met both you and Glenda, I asked my mamma if it's possible for a man to want two women at the same time, and love them both. She said yes, but a man must choose between them. I chose Glenda, but it doesn't mean I wanted you less. No matter what happens with us in the future, you and Toby will always be a part of me. It will pain me less if you know this and accept it."

"I accepted it long ago, Zech, the first time we met. I knew you would never be mine. When you chose Glenda you chose wisely. It could never have been for us to be together except like this, and I knew it from the beginning and accepted it. I am Indian, and you are white, and these are two worlds that have never come together, and never will. Had you chosen me you would have been scorned for it, and you may have come to hate me for it. This way is best for both of us. What part of you I can have is all I expect. You have already given me the one thing I sought since the first time you rode into this village. . .your son."

"I wish I had known about Toby. There are things I could have done for him during those times he was treated badly by the other boys. It makes me sad to think of it."

Tawanda pushed herself up and said, "Zech. . .never grieve for me or for Toby. We're happy here now, and this is where we belong. We love you and will share whatever we can of you. . .whatever part of yourself you give. . .but don't grieve for us. It would be tears wasted. Think only happy thoughts, not sad ones. That is what we do of you. But enough of this now! We have talked enough! Even an Indian woman likes to do something with her man besides talk."

He said no more as she dropped back down beside him.

The next morning Zech took Toby into the woods and taught him to shoot the Winchester. After this they took a long ride together, prancing the horses, galloping single file down narrow trails, laughing together when the marshtackies snorted at each other, each one trying to outperform the other.

Toby marveled at Zech's ability with the horse, watching with admiration as Tiger leaped a five-foot fern without touching even one leaf. When Toby tried the same thing, he brushed the top but swelled with pride when Zech told him he was as good a rider as he had been at his age.

When they returned to the village Toby took Zech by the hand and led him constantly, going to other boys his age and telling them he could now shoot the Winchester his father brought him, that he knocked an orchid from a cypress limb fifty feet up the tree. He was trying to make up instantly for all those years something was missing from life, all those times he stood by alone and watched enviously as other fathers took their sons hunting or fishing, times when he had no one to follow through the woods with pride. Others had taken him along sometimes, but it was not the same. He was always the outsider, always the one who had only a mother in the chickee. Now he had a father who could ride like no one else, could outdo even an Indian on a marshtackie, and could shoot the eye out of a spider with a Winchester. It was a father in visible flesh rather than a phantom nobody believed, and he wanted to make the most of it while he could.

The afternoon they all spent together, going deep into the swamp and building a fire beside a small creek. Now it was Toby's time to show Zech how to do something he had never done, and he took the stance of teacher as he slammed the lancewood spear into the side of a bass, repeating it again and again until he had more fish than Tawanda could roast on sticks over the coals. He also caught a snapping turtle and cut out the meat with his new knife, and this Zech liked best of all.

Tawanda bubbled with happiness as she watched Zech and Toby enjoying each other, having the two men she loved with her at the same time. If nothing else good ever came her way this afternoon was enough.

Zech spent a few minutes that night visiting with Keith Tiger before he hurried back to the chickee to spend his remaining time with Tawanda and Toby.

Dawn came all too soon, and Zech knew he could stay no longer. After breakfast he saddled his horse reluctantly, feeling as if he were leaving a part of himself here in the swamp he might never see again. As he started to mount, Tawanda looked to Toby and said, "Now, Toby."

The boy stepped forward and said, "I thank you again for the gifts. . .and Father, I love you. Will you come and see me again?"

Zech couldn't hold back the tears. He took Toby in his arms and said, "Yes, Toby. . .I will. And I love you too. Very much. There is one thing I ask of you. . . . Please take care of your mother for me. Will you do this, Toby?"

"I will look after her as you would if you were here with us. Whatever she asks of me I'll do."

He could take no more of it. He looked deep into Tawanda's eyes; then he mounted and rode away quickly.

As he made his way back to the trading post there was no prolonged guilt as there was the last time he had been with Tawanda. He knew now that fate had given him two lives and two families, and he accepted it without question. As Tawanda said to him, the two worlds would never come together; yet they were there.

Rather than comparing Tawanda and Glenda as he often did in the past, he now compared Sol and Toby, finding them alike in many ways. Had they been allowed to grow up together as a pair, they would have been unstoppable, capable of accomplishing anything they desired; but because they were born of different races and cultures they were destined never to share the same hopes and dreams, or to even know each other. This saddened Zech, and he pondered the why of it.

When he reached the trading post and picked up the deed, he didn't purchase even one tin of beef for the return trip. Instead, he put Tiger into a steady canter and headed nonstop for Punta Rassa, intending to travel all night if necessary.

A rising sun was just streaking the sky as Zech rode the last mile along the Caloosahatchie and approached Punta Rassa. He skirted the cabin and went to the store, buying a new Winchester and hoping that no one would notice it was not the same as the one he left with. If they did, he would say he lost his old rifle crossing a river and replaced it at the Okeechobee trading post.

Glenda came to him as soon as he rode into the clearing and hitched the horse, and he watched each step she took, reacquainting himself with everything about her, the still lithe body, the perpetually excited eyes, the red hair yet untouched by any sign of gray. Before she could greet him, he took her in his arms and said, "I love you, Glenda. I really do. . .and I want you to know it." Then he kissed her.

"Well!" she said, putting her arms around him. "If you come back like this each time, I should send you on trips more often. A woman needs to feel she's missed and wanted."

"You've been missed and wanted," he assured her, trying to brush from his mind all that happened during the past few days.

"Did you get what you went after?"

"Yes, I did. And even more than I expected."

"What do you mean?" she asked curiously.

He realized he had almost made a slip in spite of his determination not to. He said, "Even more land than I thought I could buy. It was fifteen cents an acre, and the gold I took was enough for sixty thousand acres."

"That's a lot of land, isn't it, Zech?"

"Yes, it is. But it's sixty thousand acres a Disston can never touch. If we ever have need of it, it's there."

"Are you hungry?"

"I'm about to starve. I didn't eat along the way. How's Pappa?"

"He seems fine now. We can leave whenever you say. As soon as you eat and rest we'll decide what to do."

They walked hand in hand to the cabin, and just as they reached the door, Sol bounded by on the other marshtackie, galloping full speed.

THIRTY-TWO

It was just past noon when the MacIvey caravan crossed the Kissimmee below Fort Basinger and turned north. Although Tobias had gained strength and seemed normal, they stopped early each day on the return trip to ensure his rest. The closing days of summer were the hottest of the year, and Emma fretted that the stifling prairie heat would bring back the chills and fever. And there was no need to hurry. The orange crop wouldn't be ready for harvest for two or three months and there was little to do until then.

They stopped an hour later at the edge of a large hardwood hammock and made camp in the cooling shade of a live oak. All but Tobias and Emma rode away to hunt deer or turkey for the evening meal.

Emma built a fire and put the cast-iron pot over the flames, making preparations to cook whatever the evening meal offered. If the hunters failed to bring back wild game, she would make her usual stew of smoked beef and potatoes. There would also be biscuits and an unlimited amount of hot coffee. Frog alone could drink a quart with each meal.

Tobias spread a blanket at the base of the tree and fell asleep. Until recently, afternoon napping was as alien to him as the streets of Tallahassee, but now his weakened body urged the extra rest. He would have preferred to follow the others.

Emma peeled the potatoes, put them into a bowl and covered it with a cloth to keep out the flies; then she kneaded the biscuit dough, rolled it on a cypress plank and patted it into little round mounds. This too she covered and set aside, waiting always until the stew or roasted game was done before putting the dough into the Dutch oven for baking. Tobias liked his biscuits fresh from the oven and piping hot, and she always tried to please him. One of her greatest satisfactions was the meals everyone enjoyed with relish. She gave each one as much attention and care as she would a Christmas dinner.

After these chores were done she decided to go into the woods and pick the last of the season's huckleberries for a special treat of pies. This was usually done by Glenda but on this afternoon Glenda wanted to accompany the men on the hunt.

The tiny berries were now fully ripe and deep purple, and most of the bushes had been raided by birds. She picked several bushes clean of all the remaining berries, and they barely covered the bottom of the wooden bucket; then she moved on to find others. Some she plopped into her mouth and ate, staining her lips with the sweet juice.

The sun-blocked darkness of the deep hammock felt good to her, cooling her as she moved constantly, and when she reached the river bank the berries were four inches up the side of the bucket. One more inch and there would be enough for four pies.

She turned south and picked along the bank, soothed by the rippling sound coming from the river, enjoying this brief moment of solitude. She loved Tobias and the others, but there were times when she regained her own inner strength by being away from those she loved and served. At such times the lonely woods became a sanctuary and a cathedral, a place of spiritual resurgence.

Time passed swiftly, and finally she realized she must start back to the camp. She had gone but a hundred yards from the river when the pain hit her, causing her to stumble and fall to the soft ground. She tried to get up but could not do so, and then it came again, a searing hot flash that burned into her chest like a branding iron. At first she was too stunned to realize what was happening to her, and then she knew. Her only thought was that she was going to die alone in the woods without once again seeing Tobias and all the others.

Sweat poured from her face, and when she wiped it away with her hand, she discovered that her flesh had no feeling. For several minutes she lay on her back and looked upward into the trees, her eyes focusing on a squirrel that squatted on a limb and barked at her.

She finally forced herself to a sitting position but could not rise further. Her mind was coming and going, aware and then unaware of where she was, one moment resigned to dying alone and the next moment back at the camp putting biscuits into the oven; then floating upward into the trees, feather-light, drifting peacefully, wanting to abandon any attempt of survival and become pain-free.

Her will to return to Tobias proved stronger, and she struggled to her feet and walked shakily, her view clouded by glazed eyes. She stumbled constantly, falling and then righting herself, stopping often to lean against a tree trunk, step by step making her way by instinct and determination back to the camp.

Tobias was awake now, and when she staggered from the woods he took one look at her and screamed, "Emma!. . . Emma!. . . What in the name of God is wrong with you?"

She said feebly, "The pain, Tobias. . .it hurts so bad. . . .It came on me sudden. . . ." Then she wilted and fell to the ground.

Tobias ran to the buckboard and snatched up his whip, popping it three times; and then he fired both barrels of the shotgun. He rushed back and dropped down beside her, panic-stricken, his heart pounding so wildly it formed a tight ball of spit in his throat. He gagged as he put his hand to her forehead and wiped sweat from her eyes, and then he said, "Oh God!. . . . Emma. . . . Emma. . . . Don't you leave me, Emma. . . . You hear me!. . . . don't you leave. . ."

She looked up at him, her eyes momentarily clear; then her hand went to his, gripping his flesh. She said, "Tobias. . .Tobias. . .I'm sorry. . . ." Then the last flicker of life went out of her.

Tobias shook her, gently at first and then violently, crying, "Emma!. . . . You can't do this. . . . Emma!. . . . Emma!. . . ."

He was not aware when Zech rode in and jumped from the horse, taking one look at the lifeless form and then shouting, "Pappa! What has happened? Did someone do something to Mamma?"

Tobias sat by the body, shocked speechless, swaying back and forth as he chanted, "Emma. . . . Emma. . . ."

Zech grabbed his father's shoulder and demanded harshly, "What has happened, Pappa? You've got to tell me! Did those goddam bush-whackers do something to Mamma?"

Tobias finally looked up and said, "No, Zech, it wasn't that. . . . It was her heart. . .or apoplexy. . .or maybe she was just wore plumb out from this hard kind of life. . . . I don't know. . .but she's gone from us, Zech, and it ain't fair. . . . It just ain't fair."

"Oh Lord," Zech moaned as he dropped to his knees beside his father.

Glenda cooked the potatoes Emma had peeled, knowing the men should eat, but the food was ignored. Zech took Tobias off alone and said to him, "Pappa. . .you want to dig the grave now?"

At first Tobias made no answer, as if his thoughts were elsewhere and he didn't hear the words; and then he said, "We'll not bury Emma out here alone on the prairie. We'll take her back to the hammock where she belongs."

"The heat, Pappa," Zech said hesitantly. "We're several days from the hammock. . . . The heat. . . ."

Tobias suddenly snapped awake and said harshly, "I don't give a damn about the heat! If I have to I'll shoot every goddam buzzard along the Kissimmee River! Emma's going home, Zech! We'll not stop till we get there! Do you understand me?"

"Yes, Pappa. I understand. We'll leave right away and not stop till we reach the hammock."

Zech went back and wrapped Emma in a blanket, then he and Sol placed her in the wagon. Glenda helped Tobias onto the buckboard seat, and as soon as all were mounted, Zech said to Frog, "You and Lester ride on ahead of us and build a coffin. Make it of cypress, not pine. And have it ready time we get there."

"Yessir, Mister Zech," Frog responded solemnly, grief-stricken too, his tired eyes dripping sorrow. "We'll do that, and we'll make it good. It's got to be a fine coffin for Miz Emma."

Zech then popped his whip, moving the oxen and the horses forward.

By traveling steadily and as fast as the animals could be pushed, they reached the hammock at nightfall the next day. The coffin was waiting, and Tobias directed it to be placed on chairs in the main room.

Glenda removed Emma's clothes and bathed her with damp cloths, and with Zech's help, they dressed her in the blue dress she had worn but once at the wedding. After placing her in the coffin, Zech removed the bottle of perfume from Emma's dresser drawer and poured it over the body.

Glenda came back into the room and said, "What is that smell, Zech?

It's gone all over the house."

"Peach blossoms. Mamma always smelled good to me, and now she does again. It's what she would have wanted."

Tobias took up a vigil at the table, sitting statuelike as he gazed absently across the room, getting up and looking into the coffin and then sitting again. Zech suggested that he sleep while others rotated the vigil throughout the night, but he would have none of it, refusing to leave even for a moment.

Zech went to his cabin and lay down, bone-tired, but sleep was beyond even the realm of possibility. He went back to the house and sat by his father in the dim glow of the coal oil lamp.

Tobias turned to him and said, "You know something, Zech. It was your mamma who held this family together when times was roughest. Hadden been for her you and me would 'a probably starved. She could cook pine tree roots good enough to keep a man alive. And I never did nothin' for her. With all the gold in them trunks I could 'a bought her fancy dresses and shoes and such as a woman likes, but all I ever gave her was that goddam cook stove. And now it's too late to do anything. I waited too long."

It bothered Zech that his father was feeling guilt about Emma, and he said, "She didn't want stuff like that, Pappa. It wouldn't have meant anything to her. All she wanted was to be with us and help out all she could, and you made her as happy as she could be. She told me that several times when me and her talked. She loved you, Pappa. More than anything."

"She told you this?" Tobias questioned. "You really heard her say it?"

"Many times, Pappa. Me and her used to talk a lot before I got married, like a mother and a son. The kind of talk me and you couldn't do. It's the God's truth, Pappa. I swear it."

The words soothed Tobias, and he said, "I'm right beholden to you for telling me now. I was afeared she might have held it against me for keeping her out here in the wilderness. But you listen to me now, Zech, afore you have cause to regret it. Don't ever take a woman for granted as nothing more than a cook. A woman gives her man a heap more than biscuits, and he ought to know it. She gives herself. Do something good for Glenda without her asking. Emma would 'a waited till hell froze over before asking for anything, no matter how much she wanted it. I should'a done a lot for Emma, but I didn't. And it wasn't because

I didn't love her. I did that truly. But I put it off and let it slip my mind till now it's too late. Don't make the same mistake, Zech. If you do, it will pain you more than any varmint can ever hope to do. It pains me now just as much as that awful thing that struck down Emma, only I'm still here to live with it and she ain't."

"I'll heed your words, Pappa. But don't you ever worry none about Mamma being happy. She was. She was the most happy woman there ever was. Now why don't you go in the bedroom and get some sleep? I'll be right here with Mamma."

"I'll rest after Emma is at peace in her own ground. Not till then, and maybe not ever. So don't waste your breath by askin' me again, Zech. I ain't going to budge from here till the sun comes up. This is the last night I'll ever get to spend with Emma in the house and I intend to make the most of it."

As soon as daylight invaded the hammock the grave was dug. Glenda greeted the returning men with a hearty breakfast of fried pork, grits and biscuits, but it seemed eerie to all of them sitting at the table without Emma's bustling smile as she went from table to stove and back again, replenishing plates and waiting until she was sure all were satisfied before sitting down to eat herself. Tobias refused food altogether, taking only coffee as he glanced constantly at the crude coffin resting just ten feet from the table. It was still impossible for any of them to accept the fact that Emma would never again occupy the chair that now sat empty beside Tobias.

Zech wanted to delay no longer and prolong his father's grief, so as soon as they finished eating he closed the coffin lid and nailed it shut.

Ground fog hazed the clearing as they came outside, Zech, Frog and Lester carrying the coffin with Tobias, Glenda and Sol following.

This was Sol's first encounter with death and it frightened him, the fear overwhelming sorrow. Tears were mixed with sheer horror as he looked at Emma for the last time before the coffin was closed, seeing his beloved Granny lying still and unable to speak or return his glances, knowing in a boy's own way that he would never again feel her warmth and strength as she put her arms around him and whispered just for the two of them alone, "I love you, Sol." And now as the procession moved slowly to the grave, he hovered close to Glenda, holding her hand and casting his eyes downward, trying desperately not to break down and cry like a child in front of the others.

They put ropes around the coffin and lowered it into the awaiting earth; then Tobias stepped to the foot of the grave. For a moment he bowed his head in silence, and then he said in broken words, "The Good Book says the Lord giveth. . .and the Lord taketh away. . .but this time, Lord, You done took back an awful lot. We ain't been no churchgoin' folks like we ought to, but it was because there wasn't no church to go to out here in the wilderness where You directed us. But Lord. . .there ain't never been no finer woman put on earth than Emma. I thank You for the time we spent together. . .and I wish You had let her stay here with me longer. I'll miss her powerful. . .and I don't understand why she had to go 'stead of me. I don't think it's fair, but that's Your judgment. . .but take her to You with the same love she had when she was here. Amen."

At this point Tobias stopped momentarily, then he spoke again in a tone barely audible to the rest of them, as if the words were meant for Emma alone: "Emma. . .I say to you truly. . .you may be gone in the flesh. . .but you'll always be right here with me. . .always. . . . I love you, Emma. . .and happy sailing. . . ."

Zech had never heard his father use the saying before. It surprised him, but he knew the meaning. He echoed, "Happy sailing, Mamma. . . ."

Tobias threw in the first shovel of dirt; then he stood by and watched as the grave was filled. Long after the others had gone back to the house he was still there. He had not changed positions when Zech came back an hour later and placed a bundle on the head of the grave, a large fragrant bouquet composed of white pond lilies, wild white roses, wild yellow senna and purple deer tongue.

THIRTY-THREE
1894

For over a year Tobias grieved, seldom leaving the clearing and having no interest in cows or anything. After this period of mourning he gradually focused his attention back on the orange grove, his one personal pride and satisfaction, and he spent most of his time there, often just sitting alone among the trees. Zech often said that Tobias counted each tiny orange as it evolved from a blossom, knowing in advance exactly how many barrels the crop would fill. And this was more fact than jest.

Zech, Glenda and Sol moved into the main house to be closer to Tobias, and Glenda assumed all of the chores that once were Emma's domain, the cooking and washing and housecleaning, never complaining or asking for help. Several times Zech offered to hire someone to come live on the place and assist her, but each offer was refused. Whenever the men were tending herd close by, she went out each day in the buckboard with a hot meal for them, and often she rode horseback alongside Zech and the others as they drove cows into the corral for branding. Zech could not remember the last time she wore a dress, seeing her daily in the jeans and chambray shirt and the wide-brimmed black hat. Without the flaming red ponytail hanging down her back, she could have passed for just another cowhand.

Zech and the men started fencing the MacIvey land, going to Kissimmee and bringing back wagon loads of barbed wire, cutting cypress posts in the swamp and stringing the unfamiliar barrier yard by yard across the open range, coming back week after week and finding it cut, then stringing again. He knew this would eventually lead to a violent clash, but he was determined to see it through.

There had been no drive to Punta Rassa in two years, and this was the reason Zech wanted to fence the land. He planned to accumulate herds, abandon the practice of wandering with them all summer, and fatten them on MacIvey land before driving them to market; and there was no way to contain the cattle except with the hated wire.

They were still plagued constantly by rustlers, often finding cows slaughtered on the range or driven away. During the previous summer they took turns riding armed guard both day and night, but it did no more good than looking for invisible sand flies. The raiders were indeed ghosts, killing and stealing and then vanishing. Only now, Zech felt sure he knew where they were coming from. His thoughts turned more and more to the ten thousand islands area and what Tawanda said about the outlaws there.

There were many times when Zech thought of Tawanda and Toby, wondering about them, regretting that he could not see Toby grow into early manhood as Sol was doing. He surmised that Toby was beginning to take his place among the men of the tribe and fulfill the prophecy of leadership; but no matter how much he yearned to see them, there had been no reason or opportunity for him to return to the Indian village. And even if there had been a reason during this past two years, he dared not leave Tobias alone for an extended period of time. His health was becoming more and more fragile.

Zech also remembered the things Tobias said to him the night before Emma's burial, and each time he went into Kissimmee or Fort Drum or Fort Pierce he brought back gifts for Glenda, dresses still hanging unused in her closet, ribbons and bottles of perfume, aprons with lace borders, silk underthings it took all his courage to buy – all of them useless on a wilderness homestead but nevertheless appreciated by Glenda. His mother's death and Glenda's willing assumption of Emma's role brought them even closer together, forming an unbreakable bond between them.

December 28

"Pappa! Come down off there before you sail away like a kite! The wind's too strong for us to pick any longer!"

Tobias paid no heed to Zech as he continued to perch on top of a wooden ladder leaning against an orange tree, a canvas sack slung over his shoulder.

Zech shouted again, "Dammit, Pappa! Come on down before I come after you!"

"I'll finish the sack first!" Tobias shot back. "Go on about your business and let me be!"

"Stubborn old billygoat," Zech mumbled as he walked away and started loading filled barrels onto the ox wagon.

Glenda's special Christmas dinner with roasted turkey and mincemeat pies was still fresh on everyone's mind as they put the holiday behind them and worked the grove. There was a bumper crop of juice-filled globes, and the harvest was about a third finished.

The wind started early that morning, and the sky far in the north was totally black, signifying a coming northern. this was the time of year when brief storms and cold fronts rushed across the land and then disappeared as quickly as they arrived, making the temperature go up and down rapidly, often changing as much as thirty degrees in one hour. it was not a thing of dread but something to look forward to, not only for its temporary cooling effect but also because it sweetened the winter crop of collards now full grown in the garden and made the oranges even juicier.

Everyone else went back to the house as Zech waited for his father to finish picking and empty his sack into a barrel. As soon as this was done he drove the oxen to the barn and stored the barrels in the adjacent orange shed.

By mid-afternoon the wind took on more authority and roared instead of growling. It lashed the hickory and oaks and popped the palmetto as the temperature dropped sharply, causing Zech to shiver as he left the house and went to the small corral attached to the rear of the barn. Frog and Lester were already there, driving the horses and oxen inside where they would be given a feeding of hay and bedded down for the night.

Frog pulled the light-weight jacket tighter around his neck and said, "Feels like the devil's stingin' me. This storm gone be a humdinger if it gets much colder. I think I'll build a big fire in my cabin and bring out a jug of rum. That ought to keep a old man like me warm."

"I guess it would," Zech said. "But before you do that we need to chop more firewood. And what we need is firewood, Frog, not firewater."

"Ever man to his own choice," Frog smiled. "And you ain't even near about as old and wore out as me. Young man don't need extra fuel like a old man does, especially when it gets cold in winter."

By the time Zech got back to the stoop, the outside thermometer attached to the wall showed only three degrees above freezing. He brought an arm load of stove wood into the kitchen and returned for another, and in this short time the mercury had dropped to thirty-one degrees.

Tobias was sitting close to the stove when Zech brought in the last load of wood. "How's it doing out there?" he asked.

"Getting colder, Pappa. It just went to a degree below freezing."

"If it keeps this up and holds for long, it'll sure play hell with the oranges. I wish we'd got done with the pickin' before this came."

"It'll probably ease up and pass by. It always has. If the wind keeps up like this it'll blow the cold over the tops of the trees anyway. There's no need for worry."

"Maybe so," Tobias said doubtfully, "but if the temperature drops much more, everbody better pray it don't rain. If it does, we'll have the damndest ice storm you ever seen. I seen it happen a many a time in Georgia when I was a boy, and it always started out just like this."

"Well, it didn't really hurt nothing, did it, Pappa?"

"Not so much that nature didn't cure in the spring, but we sure didn't have orange trees up there."

At supper time the kitchen was cozy-warm, and the meal took on a festive air. After a sweltering summer and the sultry dog days of early fall, a cold snap was a welcome relief. It thickened the blood and invigorated everyone to a point of exhilaration. No one except Tobias seemed to be particularly concerned as the wind pounded the side of the house and rattled the cypress shingles.

Frog helped himself to a second portion of collard greens and corn pone and said, "If it's still cold in the morning we ought to go out and shoot wild hogs. There ain't no better time for the killin' and dressin' of hogs. It makes the meat taste sweet as honey."

"That's not a bad idea," Zech agreed. "We could cook some fresh, smoke some and salt down the rest. We might could get enough pork to last all winter."

"Can I go too, Pappa?" Sol asked, excited by just the mention of a hunt.

"This time you can. If you're not old enough now to face a wild boar you never will be. Way before I was your age I'd done killed a bear with Pappa's old shotgun."

"That's for sure," Tobias said. "Zech done it when we lived up in the scrub. Two bears tried to get in the barn one night when I was off driving Confederate cattle up to Georgia during the war. When they hemmed your granny up, Zech blowed one of them bears slam across the clearing and into the woodshed."

Sol's eyes widened as he said, "Really, Grampy? Did Pappa really do that? You're not funning me again, are you?"

"He sure enough did."

"Will you tell me about it sometime? Please, Grampy, will you?"

"I'll tell you about it when we ain't got nothing better to do. So just hush up about it now. And I'll tell you a lot more besides that. We seen some things and done some things folks nowdays wouldn't believe."

"Would you believe your big brave daddy tripping over his own boots and falling flat on his face at a square dance?" Glenda said to Sol.

"Did you do that, Pappa?"

"Can't say as I did," Zech laughed. "Leastwise, I don't remember. But your mamma once ate some rattlesnake meat and threw up all over the prairie."

"That's enough!" Glenda snapped. "Not at meal time anyway. We started out talking about hog hunting, so how did we get around to all this?"

"Well, Miz Glenda," Frog said, "when you get a bunch of dodo birds perched on the same fence, like they is in here now, there ain't no telling which way the conversation will go. But getting back to hogs, are we goin' in the morning or not? If we ain't, I won't come out at sunup and freeze my tail off for nothin'."

"We'll go," Zech said. "Come first dawn we'll eat and leave."

"Not me," Tobias said. "My days of chasin' some scrawny varmint all over the woods is long gone. I'll stay here and help later with the scrapin' if you get anything to scrape."

"Fair enough," Zech said, relieved that Tobias did not want to go. "We'll meet here in the kitchen at dawn."

Before going to bed Zech stoked the fire to keep the room warm during the night; then he took the coal oil lamp and went out to the stoop. The wind made the flame flicker and nearly go out as he held the lamp in front of the thermometer. It now read twenty degrees, a temperature drop of fifty-five degrees since morning, and for the first time he shared Tobias' concern. But he learned long ago they were all powerless and at the mercy of their most fickle and deadly adversary, the weather. It couldn't be shot or hanged or roped or corraled or harnessed in any way. It rendered them helpless against all onslaughts, and whatever was to come would come, regardless of worry or concern. He glanced once more, and then he turned and went back into the house.

Dawn was late in coming because the sun couldn't penetrate a low covering of black clouds boiling just over the treetops. There was an eerie gray gloom permeating the clearing when Zech came outside and looked anxiously at the thermometer. It read fourteen degrees, and the cold slapped into his face like ice water. He shivered violently and went back into the house.

He went to the stove and backed up as close as he could get to it, shivering again, feeling the heat tingle his flesh as it drove away the cold. Glenda put on the coffee pot and said, "What's the reading now?"

"Fourteen degrees. The water bucket is froze solid. If it wasn't for the wind still blowin' we'd be knee deep in frost. I've never seen it so cold."

"Are you still going hunting?"

"I guess. It's up to the others. If they want to, I will, but we'll all have to wear two pairs of britches."

"It's foolish to go out in this. You'll make yourselves sick."

"Well, if we do go, I don't think we'll have to shoot any hogs. They'll be so froze we can pick 'em up like cord wood and bring 'em on back to the house."

Tobias came into the room and poured himself a mug of coffee. He said, "I heard what you said, Zech. Fourteen degrees. That means the oranges are gone. And if it holds for much longer, the trees'll go too."

Zech knew the truth of this, but still he didn't want Tobias upset. He said, "Don't count them out yet, Pappa. This may blow over by noon. If it does I don't think it'll leave much damage."

"If you believe that you also believe a jaybird can play a fiddle."

There was nothing more Zech could say, and he was relieved when Frog and Lester came into the house and interrupted the conversation.

Frog backed up to the stove and said, "Lord have mercy. What a feelin' it is to drape your bare bottom over one of them outhouse holes on a mornin' like this! I think my butt is froze solid. It's probably goin' to crack when it thaws."

"It's already cracked," Zech chuckled.

Frog rubbed himself vigorously. "It may be, but I'm goin' to have more than one crack time this is over. Next time I take a crap I'll have to spread myself over two seats."

Glenda smiled and shook her head as she continued the task of making fried hoecakes for their breakfast. She mumbled, "You men!"

After the meal was finished they took the rifles and went to the barn to saddle the horses. The cold rushed through the double layers of clothing like they weren't there, burning the skin and making the bones feel like they were being crushed. If any one of them had backed out the others would follow gladly, but no one made the suggestion, each waiting to see what the others would do.

Zech said, "Any hog with good sense is going to be buried as deep as he can get in some bushes. I don't think we'll have much luck without dogs, 'less we riot them out ourselves."

"Well, I ain't goin' to stick my foot in no damned bushes for sure," Frog said. "They'll be rattlers in there too. Maybe we ought to just ride for a spell and see what it looks like, if the horses don't freeze under us."

"Me and Sol'll go down by the garden and cut north. You and Lester go west. If you need help pop your whip."

"It may be too froze to pop," Frog responded. "And if I'm stuck to the saddle when we get back I'll just ride my hoss into the kitchen."

The horses blew white clouds of icy breath as they trotted away. When Zech and Sol reached the garden they paused and looked over the split-rail fence. All of the plants were flat on the ground and had taken on the death color of yellow. Only a few hardy collards were still upright, but the fringes of each leaf were curling. Tomatoes, beans, squash and peppers lay in lifeless heaps.

They turned north and rode into the grove. Zech dismounted, picked an orange and cut it in half with his hunting knife. The inside was solid ice, and when he squeezed it a blob of frozen juice plopped to the ground and bounced like a steel ball. He knew now the remaining crop was a total loss, and he dreaded telling Tobias.

From the grove they went into the creek bottom and found a flight

of twenty Carolina parakeets dead on the ground, all frozen. One
remaining bird was on a tree limb, swaying drunkenly. As they watched,
it fluttered to the ground, flapping its wings in one last desperate gasp
of life, and then it too lay still.

The sight of the colorful bodies dotting the ground in motionless
heaps saddened Sol. He said, "Pappa, are they all going to die?"

"I suppose so. They can't stand this much cold. It'll kill a lot of fish
too, and other things."

Sol then said, "Pappa, I'm not trying to back out of the hunt if you
want to keep going, but ever time my hand touches metal it sticks to
it. It feels like it's going to pull my skin off. I don't think I can hold
my rifle and aim it without some gloves."

"I'm having the same trouble. We best go on back to the house now.
There's no need for us to stay out here and freeze for nothing."

Shortly after they reached the house, Frog and Lester returned too.
The rest of the day was spent in the room by the stove.

The cold lingered on for two days as they all huddled inside for
warmth. A clear sky and brilliant sun greeted the third morning, and
the temperature rose rapidly to seventy-five degrees.

Tobias and Zech went to the grove and found the trees not green but
brown, each already surrounded by piles of fallen dead leaves. Tobias
cut into the trunk of one and said, "It ain't dead all the way. They just
might make it if it stays warm like this. I just thank the Lord we didn't
get no rain and ice with all that cold."

"They'll make it, Pappa. We may never have another cold snap that
bad. What I need to do now is replant the garden. There's not a single
thing left in there alive, and I sure don't want to go back to eating wild
poke two meals a day."

"Poke ain't so bad. We lived off it for years when we had to."

"I know, Pappa. But tomatoes and beans and collards is better. Soon
as we get back to the house I'll put out the seeds."

A month later Tobias came running through the woods, shouting as
loud as he could, "They done it! They done it!"

Everyone poured out of cabins and house, and Zech scrambled from
the barn and raced to meet his father as he came into the clearing. He

said, "What in the world is all the shouting for, Pappa?"

"The orange trees," Tobias panted, "they're puttin' out sap and new growth! They're goin' to bloom, Zech! They done made it!"

"That's great, Pappa! Just great. I knew they'd come through."

"I sure thought for a while it was all gone, but the Lord's done smiled down on us. I got to go now and tell Emma."

Zech stood by Glenda and put his arm around her as they watched the frail body lumber across the clearing toward the small plot of ground bearing the grave.

February 6, 1895

Zech was in the garden, driving thin stakes into the ground beside the tomato and bean plants that were thrusting up from the soft soil, when he felt the first rush of cool air. It was a moist breeze, not hot and dry, and he said to Sol who was working close by, "Goin' to rain soon. It'll be good for the garden. We better hurry and get done with this."

A thunderhead formed in the north, layer upon layer of black clouds that spread rapidly and soon covered the horizon. The wind then came in gusts, blowing leaves from the nearby woods and scurrying them across the garden.

Rain was just beginning to pelt down when they reached the clearing and ran for the stoop. Zech stood there for several minutes, watching the blue sky disappear as clouds raced to the south like galloping horses, turning early afternoon into twilight.

The rain came steadily all afternoon, pattering against the cypress roof, and when Zech finally left the house and ran for the barn to tend the livestock, there was a strange coolness in the air and the rain. It felt like little drops of ice rather than water.

Shortly after dark the wind increased to a howling fury, rattling the windows and making the walls creak. The temperature dropped rapidly, and they put more wood into the stove to warm the room.

Tobias paced back and forth, his face creased with worry. He said to Zech, "I don't like the sound or the feel of this. It's more than a rain storm for sure."

"Don't go seeing buggers in every cloud," Zech said. "You're just gun-shy, Pappa. There's just no way we're goin' to have another storm like that last one. It'll pass over before the sun comes up."

"Don't never say 'no way'," Tobias admonished. "Whatever the Lord wants to do He'll do. And He's not goin' to ask our advice about it."

The wind didn't abate, and Zech could hear it continue pounding throughout the night. When he crawled from beneath the warm quilts at dawn he was greeted by a room as cold as an ice cavern.

He dressed hurriedly and rushed outside, and what he saw stunned him. The temperature was at eleven degrees, and what had been rain the day before was now sleet. Every tree was ice-covered, and the ground was one solid sheet of ice.

Zech and Sol brought in as much wood as they could pile in the kitchen, and the frozen wood made loud hissing sounds as it was put into the fire.

At mid-morning the sleet stopped, and an hour later snow came, a blinding, swirling blizzard that erased the earth and turned the clearing and the woods into a sea of white.

Sol was fascinated, seeing such a phenomenon for the first time, not realizing it was also the first glimpse of snow for all except Tobias, and he had not seen it now since leaving Georgia almost forty years ago.

Tobias again paced the room. He went to a window and looked out, grimacing as the flakes hit the ground and froze immediately, piling deeper and deeper. He turned to all the others in the room and said, "The Lord's done treed us for sure this time, like a wildcat with no place left to go but down, and the ground full of dogs. There ain't nothing what can survive this. It's all gone now."

Zech did not even try to console Tobias this time, knowing full well his father spoke the truth. Nothing would survive, not even some of the small animals with a covering of fur.

As the day wore on, the air was filled with cracking sounds that came like thunder as overburdened tree limbs gave way from the weight of ice and crashed to the ground. In late afternoon Zech and Frog fought their way to the barn to feed the horses and oxen, and Zech could see that the woods were becoming impassable from cluttered limbs. There were great raw gashes on trees where limbs had broken away.

They had been caught by surprise without an adequate supply of chopped wood, and in order to conserve what they had, Frog and Lester abandoned their cabins and came into the house, sleeping that night on blankets spread on the kitchen floor.

The next morning the snow still came, not a blinding blizzard as the day before but a steady falling of white flakes. At noon it stopped and was replaced by sleet once more, frozen rain that formed a hard crust over the seven inches of powdery snow. The thermometer rose only one degree to twelve and hovered there.

There was no festive mood in the house this time, no joviality as the grim-faced captives looked out windows at the ice-encased earth, wondering when and if it would ever stop. It was an almost impossible challenge to slide and stumble to the barn and give each animal a short ration of hay. The outside pile of the precious fodder was now a frozen mass rendered useless.

Tobias went out to the stoop constantly, looking anxiously at the thermometer and coming back inside, repeating the cycle again and again until finally Zech warned him that all he was accomplishing was turning cold air into the house, icy gusts that did not dissipate without adding more wood to the fire.

Just before nightfall Zech and Frog and Lester went into the yard and brought in more wood, almost exhausting the supply, each dreading the possibility they might have to go into the woods and chop a fresh supply from the ice. Tobias insisted that he help, and in spite of Zech's protests, he brought several loads to the stoop, turning his thin hands blood red and making them sting like fire.

It was when Glenda put supper on the table that Tobias was first missed. All of them paid no heed to his absence from the kitchen, thinking he had gone into his bedroom to rest after helping with the wood.

Zech went for Tobias and found the room empty. He came back into the kitchen and said anxiously, "Pappa's not in there. Did anyone see him come back in the house after the last load of wood?"

"I wasn't paying any mind to him, Zech," Glenda said, becoming frightened too.

"I saw him after that," Sol said. "He was putting some pine kindling into his coat pockets. But I didn't see him no more."

"Oh my Lord!" Zech moaned. "He's slipped out and headed for the grove. I'll go after him."

"I'll go with you, Pappa," Sol said, scrambling for his jacket.

"No! There's no use for but one of us to freeze. I'll see to it myself. The rest of you stay here."

Zech went down the stoop and paused for a moment, letting his eyes adjust to the darkness, then looking ahead at the ghostly forms of ice-covered trees. He made his way forward one cautious step at a time, sliding over the hard crust, entering the woods and moving gingerly through a jungle of shattered limbs, hoping that no more of them would come crashing down and land on top of him. When finally he reached the outside edge he could see it ahead of him, a fire glowing like a beacon, giving him direction to the edge of the grove.

Tobias was standing there, trying to warm himself as smoke and flames leaped upward into the shriveled tree, his frozen beard glistening with ice. Zech emerged from the darkness and said harshly, "Pappa! What the hell you mean coming out here? It'll be the death of you!"

Tobias turned to him and said calmly, "I had to come here, Zech. I've got to save at least one tree, and heat from a fire is the only way. If I don't save one tree there won't be nothin' left to take cuttin's from and start the grove again. I've got to save one tree."

"Damn them trees, Pappa! After this is over we can grow another tree somehow, but we can't grow another you! Come on now and let's go back to the house before we both turn into chunks of ice!"

"I'll not leave here and let the fire go out!" Tobias said defiantly. "Don't you understand what I'm doing, Zech? There won't be one tree left standing nowhere, not here or anywhere! Can't you understand? I'll not. . . ." the fire went out of his eyes and the words stopped as his lanky body suddenly folded and toppled backward into the small circle of slush caused by the heat of the crackling pine.

"Oh, Pappa. . .Pappa. . ." Zech said as he picked him up, surprised by how light the frail form was. Then he went back into the darkness, groping his way as quickly as he could toward the clearing.

Tobias' flushed face poured sweat as they put him into the bed and covered him with quilts. He came awake and said, "You got to promise me something, Zech. You'll replant the trees. Oranges is the best way to go. Better than cows. Don't have to chase 'em. You got to promise."

"I promise, Pappa. Just be quiet and get some rest. We'll talk about it later."

He drifted away again as Glenda put her hand to his forehead and said, "He's burning up with fever. I'm afraid he's got pneumonia as well as a malaria spell. He's real sick, Zech. Real sick."

"I know. . .I know it, Glenda. He may not even last out the night. If I'd known he'd do something foolish like this I would have nailed the door shut. You'd think them trees are the only things on earth that count."

"Maybe they really do mean that much to him."

"Maybe so, but they're not worth this. It's just that when a old man gets something on his mind there's no way to make him let go of it. No way! But he sure did what he thought he had to do. You can't fault him for that."

Zech and Glenda both sat with him throughout the night, Glenda bathing his face with damp cloths, trying vainly to bring the fever down, Zech just sitting and staring, feeling helpless and useless. At daybreak Glenda went back into the kitchen and prepared breakfast.

Sleet still came down from a slate-gray sky, and Zech did not even bother to go out and look at the thermometer, knowing what it would say without seeing it. The windows were now frozen over, making the rooms almost as dark as at night.

Glenda went into the bedroom to lie down and rest while Zech continued the vigil. Everyone else sat by the stove, stone-faced, afraid even to ask what was happening behind the closed door.

Just before noon Tobias became conscious again. He looked up at Zech and smiled, and then he said, "Did you keep the fire goin'?"

"Never mind the fire, Pappa. Just keep still and you'll feel better. You'll be fine soon."

"I ain't goin' to be fine, Zech. . .and I know it. . .and I don't mind none at all. . .so don't fret. It's been a long trail but I'm done with it now. And you know something, Zech. . .I ain't tryin' to run down Glenda. . . . She's a fine woman and a fine cook and I truly thank her for all she's done for us. . .but I ain't had a biscuit like Emma's since she left us. . . . Maybe Emma's got a cook stove up there with her and she'll make me a batch. . . ."

Tears came to Zech's eyes as he said, "Just hush up now, Pappa, and don't talk like that. You're going to be fine. Glenda will make you some biscuits for supper."

Tobias drifted away again; then he snapped back and said, "We done some things, didn't we, Zech."

"Yes, Pappa, we done some things. We surely did."

His eyes then turned upward, staring right through the cypress roof, remembrance flooding from them as he smiled and said again, "We done. . .some things. . .Zech. . .you and me. . . . We done. . .some. . .things. . . ." The voice trailed off as the tired body went limp and lay still.

"Oh, Pappa. . .why'd you have to do it? . . .Damn trees!. . . ."

Zech sat on the edge of the bed for several minutes, physically and mentally stunned, feeling that a part of him had died also. Then he touched the eyelids and pulled a quilt over his father's face.

When he came into the kitchen his stricken look said it all, and no one had to ask. Glenda came to him immediately, put her arms around him and said, "I'm sorry, Zech. So sorry. We all loved him."

Sol jumped up and ran into his room, shutting the door so no one could see as he dropped down on his bed and sobbed, "Grampy. . .Grampy. . . ."

Frog sat immobile, struggling to retain his composure. "They ain't never goin' to be another like him," he finally said. "Not ever. Ole Skillit would sure like to know. I'll go an' fetch him when the sleet lets up."

Zech poured himself a mug of coffee and sat at the table. He stared at the steam rising upward, drifting like summer fog from a swamp at dawn. He said to Glenda, "You know what one of the last things he talked about was? Mamma's biscuits."

"Would you like something to eat?" Glenda asked, concerned with the devastation in his voice. "You haven't had a bite since yesterday."

He suddenly felt a tremendous need to be alone. Without answering he put on his coat and went outside, walking silently toward the grove, not feeling the cold or hearing the crunch of ice beneath his feet.

Every tree was now dead, killed right down to the ground, forlorn and foreboding in the somber gray glow, a brown sea of death replacing what had been lush green foliage and golden globes. Sleet piled up on his hat and shoulders as he looked down at the black stain, all that was left of Tobias' futile fire. He picked up a piece of half-burned wood and sailed it high into the air, as far as he could throw. It crashed down into the top of a tree, causing frozen leaves and fruit to shoot outward and scatter across the snow.

He said, "Don't you worry none, Pappa. I'll put it all back." Then he turned and walked away.

The next morning the sleet stopped, but the sky was still overcast. The three-day storm left far more damage than any of them yet realized.

Frog saddled his horse and rode away alone to inform Skillit, insisting he could move steady and return by the next day. Zech worried that he wouldn't make it at all through the ice and snow, but he didn't protest. It was a thing Frog was determined to do and would attempt regardless of any warning against it from anyone. And the delay would cause no problem since the grave couldn't be dug in the frozen ground. It would have to thaw first.

Zech walked into the woods beyond the garden, awed by the strange silence, hearing not one bird call to another or one animal move. The only sign of life he could find was a lone robin perched on a bush, its breast feathers puffed into a red ball.

He stopped several times and kicked at lumps in the snow, uncovering the frozen bodies of rabbits and raccoons and foxes, their mouths open as if crying out for help that didn't come. Then he went back to the barn and measured cypress planks stored in the loft. There would be enough for a coffin, and he would build it himself that afternoon.

When he returned to the house he sat at the table, silent again until Glenda joined him. He said to her, "It's down to just you and me and Sol now, and from what I've seen out there so far, we're back to where this family was twenty-five years ago. I hope there's a few rabbits and coons still alive, 'cause it might be all that's left to eat. We'll have to grub for it again, Glenda, and it's going to be a long time before we get over this."

"We'll make it, Zech. We'll do whatever we have to do."

"You know something else," he said, reaching out and touching her hand. "All that gold we got in those trunks can't be stewed or fried. It's not worth a damn for anything unless I can find supplies. And everybody who's got a dime in cash is going to be out buying everything they can find in the way of food. Rations is going to be real short, so as soon as all this ice goes away, I better hightail it to Kissimmee or sommers and get all the flour and cornmeal I can find. If it's all gone time I get there, I hope you know how to cook cattails."

"I'll cook whatever I have to, even rattlesnakes if it comes down to that. We'll make do. But you ought to go to Fort Drum first. Pappa will let us have whatever he can spare. Then you can try elsewhere."

"That's a good idea, and I'll do it." Then he got up and said, "I think I'll go back out and gather up some of the frozen animals. I can smoke 'em and store the meat away. We may have need of it."

Soon after he left the house the clouds dissipated and the sun came through, reflecting a brilliant, blinding glare and causing ice to crack from limbs of trees. It crashed down thunderously, preventing him from

entering the woods again to gather the carcasses. Like the digging of
the grave, the gathering of meat would have to wait until the sun won
the battle and thawed the earth and woods.

Frog made good his vow, and before noon the next day he came into
the clearing, leading the ox wagon through what was now a sea of
slush. After a round of greetings and hugging and no small amount of
tears on the part of Skillit and Pearlie Mae, the men went to the south
edge of the hammock to dig the grave beside that of Emma.

They first raked away the remaining snow, and then they dug into
the mushy ground, spade by spade of dirt thrown aside until the proper
hole was formed. It looked so final to Zech that he walked away quickly
when the task was finished.

Frog and Skillit helped Zech dress Tobias in his one black suit,
complete with white shirt and string tie. They all could not help but
remember the time they forced him to put it on for the wedding, threat-
ening him with all sorts of dire things until he finally retired into the
wagon and then emerged looking like an itinerant preacher. The suit
had not been worn since.

As soon as they placed him in the coffin Zech nailed it shut, wanting
all of this to end as soon as possible, also knowing that Tobias would
not want it dragged out any more than necessary.

After reaching the grave and lowering the coffin, Zech stepped forward to say last words. This was a new duty for him, and he was unsure
of himself. He spoke slowly, "Lord, bless Pappa. . .and see to it he's
with Mamma again, where he wants to be. Since You seen fit to take
both of them away from us in such a short time, You ought to at least
do this. Pappa was a good man, Lord. I never knowed him to do a bad
thing. . .not ever. I'll be hard put to measure up to him, but give me
strength to try. And one more thing, Lord. . .please don't throw nothing
more like this at me any time soon. . .I don't think I can stand any
more for a while. . .Amen."

Skillit, Pearlie Mae and the boys moved into their old cabin for the
night. When they all gathered for supper, Zech at first sat in his usual
place; then at Glenda's urging, he moved into Tobias' empty chair at
the head of the table. He did it reluctantly, feeling like an intruder, and
then he realized he would have to assume the position either now or
later. It was a thing he had to do, just as Glenda was forced into the

position of Emma. There would be no more Tobias or Emma to take responsibility and lead the way. It was now up to himself and Glenda alone.

They made small talk, remembering things past, incidents long-forgotten but now brought back vividly – all of them trying to brush death from their minds. Skillit told of the success of his farm and ranch, pleasing everyone by the news, and the strained conversations went on for an hour; then fatigue hit all of them and they retired early.

Final farewells were said just past dawn; then the two oxen pulled Skillit's creaking wagon across the slushy clearing and along the trail leading northwest past the orange grove.

THIRTY-FOUR

Zech made trips to Fort Drum, Fort Pierce and Kissimmee, finding the land devastated everywhere, trees downed, prairie grass dead, cypress stands filled with the decaying bodies of animals. Only buzzards profited from the freeze.

News drifted in from north and south, and Zech learned that orange groves were almost totally destroyed everywhere. Not one tree was alive north of Lake George, and trails leading north out of the state were filled with steady streams of families abandoning the land and heading into Georgia or Alabama or the Carolinas or wherever else they could go and start a new life. On his trips he witnessed long processions of ox carts and wagons plodding north past Fort Pierce and Kissimmee, loaded with only those possessions the families could carry along.

He also learned that the one place the freeze didn't devastate was a small village at Fort Dallas, at the extreme end of the eastern coast. It was said orange trees could be obtained there for cash, and it was there he would seek trees to rebuild the MacIvey grove.

Food supplies of all kinds were short everywhere, but he managed to purchase enough flour to see them through the rest of the winter with careful rationing. Another month and spring would come, turning the woods and prairies green again, and things should improve. But for all those people who were abandoning their homesteads, there was no hope and no future. Without a reserve of cash money there was no way to purchase food supplies or replace orange trees or plant new

310

gardens or do anything but pack up and leave, taking with them bitter memories of the great freeze and of what might have been. Those who were lucky enough to get anything at all were selling homesteads they had owned for fifteen or more years for one Spanish doubloon or whatever else was offered, even a sack of cornmeal to eat along the way.

It was six weeks after the freeze and the burial of Tobias when Zech was at the corral, helping brand what few cattle the spring roundup produced. The cows were scattered worse than he had ever seen them, foraging for miles in search of anything they could eat, and there was hardly a calf left alive. Those that survived the ice storm were slaughtered by marauding packs of hungry wolves as well as bears and panthers whose food supply of small animals had been severely depleted. Wolves even invaded the corral one night, killing and dragging away a steer. It seemed to Zech that all of the creatures had gone mad, driven to a bloody frenzy by the ice and snow and the death that lingered because of it. But he did not begrudge them the taking of an occasional steer, knowing they too must eat to survive a situation not of their own making.

Zech was pressing the branding iron to a half-starved cow when he noticed a caravan approaching from the south. At first he thought it was just another family heading north, but as it came closer, he could see it was not. There were no wagons or carts, and all of the people seemed to be adults.

He continued to watch curiously until he distinguished them as Indians; then he mounted his horse and rode out to meet them. At the head of the procession was Keith Tiger, looking like a mummy astride a horse. The old man was now beyond age, his white hair capping a face as gnarled as a cypress knee.

Keith Tiger raised his hand in salute, and then he said, "It is good to see you again, Zech MacIvey. You look more like your father each time we meet."

There were thirty men and women in the group, some mounted but most walking. Zech searched them quickly, seeing that Tawanda and Toby were not among them. He said, "It's good to see you, Keith Tiger. But what are you doing way off up here with so many of your people? Are you abandoning the land like so many others are doing?"

"We have come to pay last respects to Tobias."

"You've come all this way to do that?" Zech said, surprised and puzzled. "How did you even know about Pappa's death?"

"We learned of it at the Okeechobee trading post, and word was left there by a man who deals in oranges at Fort Pierce. It saddened our hearts to hear of it. Tobias was our friend, and this is what we wish to do."

"You're most welcome," Zech assured the old man. "Pappa would be real pleased. He thought a lot of you and all the others. I'm glad you've come."

"If you would show us the grave now we would thank you. We will camp nearby for the night and leave in the morning. You and I can talk later, after the respects are paid."

"I would be honored to do that. Just follow me."

Zech led the caravan to the house and across the clearing, past Glenda's curious glances and into the oak grove where the graves were located. He said, "Pappa's grave is the one on the right."

Keith Tiger dismounted and said, "You will leave us alone now if you will. We wish to do this in our own way."

"Take all the time you want. I'll come to your camp later."

As he rode back to the house to tell Glenda what was happening, he glanced back and saw Keith Tiger break a lancewood spear in half and place it on the grave; then he heard chanting, a wailing, mournful sound that chilled him as it increased in intensity.

As Zech rode through the oak grove he saw gifts scattered over the grave, a pouch made of deer hide, a carved wooden steer, a piece of alligator hide and a cluster of egret feathers. The broken spear was placed across the head of the grave.

He continued through the woods until he came to the camp site. Keith Tiger was sitting on a blanket, eating sofki and beef jerky. Zech dropped down in front of him as he said, "Would you join me in food?"

"No thanks. My wife will have supper ready soon. You're welcome to join us if you want to."

"We have enough with us, but I thank you. We have brought you a sack of koonti flour. We thought you would have need of it. Since the freeze we have sold great amounts of it to the trading posts. People are hungry everywhere. The storm did not hurt us so much as it did to the north."

"It was bad here, and I appreciate the flour. We can sure use it. If you want I'll round up a few steers for you to take back with you. They're real scrawny, but maybe you can fatten them up."

"We have no need of them at this time. The rifles Tobias gave us have provided food. I hate to think what would have happened to our people without them. And we are still getting calves from the cows you and Tobias drove to our village those many years ago. We will never forget all you have done for us."

"Well, I'm sure you can use some bullets. I've got several cases of them stored in the house. I'll bring you a case later this afternoon."

"That would be appreciated. It would take much koonti for us to earn a whole case of bullets."

Zech then got up and said, "I'll come back and talk more in a few minutes. I'd like to visit around some."

Keith Tiger looked at him knowingly as he walked away, a sudden sadness coming into his face. He watched until Zech reached the cabbage palm where Tawanda's father and mother were sitting; then he turned his eyes away.

Zech dropped down to the blanket and said, "I came to ask of Tawanda and Toby. How are they?"

At first the man made no answer, avoiding Zech's eyes, and then he said hesitantly, "Tawanda is dead, Zech. She died in childbirth."

The words dumbfounded Zech, shocking him. He said in disbelief, "Dead? Tawanda is dead? When did this happen?"

"After the last time you were there. She never knew another man but you."

Tears came into Zech's eyes as he said, "Then it's my fault! I the same as killed her, and I wasn't even there to help her when she needed me!"

"No! Do not say that, and do not blame yourself. The medicine man and the women did all they could to save her and the baby, but there was nothing they could do for either. She would have died even if you were there."

"But I'm the one who put a baby inside her," Zech said in anguish.

The man put his hand on Zech's shoulder and said, "Do not feel this way. We do not hold you responsible, and we have no hate for you in our hearts. You did not force yourself on Tawanda. She accepted you willingly. You did only what she wanted you to do. You made her happy, and we thank you for this, not hate you. This may seem strange to you, but it is our way. Tawanda died happy, and that is what counts most.

We believe that one who dies in sadness can never rest easy in the afterlife that comes to all of us."

Zech often wondered why Tawanda's parents made no protest when they so openly loved each other in the village, and now he knew. He said, "I thank you for what you're saying. If you felt otherwise I don't know what I'd do. If it helps any, you should know I loved Tawanda, and I told her so."

"We know this. That is why we never interfered in what little life you had together. And she knew it could be no other way than what it was. Remember what you had with her in happiness, not sadness. She would not want you to be sad. The last words she spoke were, 'When you see him again, tell Zech I leave this life in happiness.' "

"What of Toby?" Zech then asked. "What has happened to him?"

"We have taken him as our own. We did not bring him here because Tawanda would not wish it. He is a fine young man. Someday you should come and see him again. He has never forgotten your last visit, and he speaks of you often with much pride."

"I'll do that," Zech said, getting up. "I promise you I will, and you tell him so. I must go and speak again with Keith Tiger."

Zech walked back to Keith Tiger and said, "I'll go to the house and get the bullets and take the koonti flour to Glenda. She'll be real pleased with it."

The old man looked deep into Zech's eyes and said, "You know now what happened, my son, and I am sorry it had to be. But we are not sorry that your blood runs in Seminole veins. It is good blood, MacIvey blood passed on to you by your father. We are glad a part of you is Seminole. Do not forget this, Zech MacIvey."

"I won't forget. And I'm proud that Toby is my son. It's just that so much grief has come to me lately. The Lord must be punishing me for what I did to Tawanda."

"That is not so! It is not a punishment to have a fine son, and loving a woman and giving her love in return is not a thing for punishment in the eyes of an Indian. If this is your white man way of thinking, you are wrong. There are more ways for a man to join himself with a woman than standing before a white man's preacher and having him say it is so. This is a great fault of your people, thinking that your way in everything is the only way. You have no reason for punishment or for the guilt in your words. Remove this from your heart and replace it with happy memories. Will you do this for me and for Tawanda?"

"I'll try to remember only the good of it."

Zech tied the sack of flour to his saddle, and as he rode away he thought of those two days he spent with Tawanda and Toby, seeing again the joy in her heart just from his being there with them. He also remembered her saying that he should never grieve for her or for Toby, no matter what came their way. He vowed to himself he would see Toby again soon.

THIRTY-FIVE

Nature slowly heals itself of its own transgressions, and a warm June sun and gentle rains once again splashed the forests and prairies with green. Pine trees still stood forlorn and denuded, their tops snapped away by ice, rosin oozing down bare trunks like rivers of solidified tears; but scars on the sturdy oaks were sealing themselves and showing signs of new growth.

The men of the MacIvey hammock spent two months clearing the orange grove, chopping down dead trees and burning them in great piles, then pulling lifeless stumps from the ground with ropes and oxen. The holes were filled back with shovels and indented, waiting for new trees to replace the old. It was a repeat of nature's own perpetual cycle, life replacing death, the world moving on.

Zech put Frog in charge of the homestead as he and Glenda and Sol set out for Fort Dallas to make good his promise to Tobias to replant the grove. Zech and Glenda rode in the buckboard pulled by two horses, Sol mounted on Tiger. In addition to supplies for the trip, the buckboard contained one steamer trunk loaded with sacks of Spanish doubloons.

From Fort Pierce they headed south on a narrow dirt road paralleling Henry Flagler's railroad, stopping to watch as smoke-belching steam engines labored down the steel rails, causing great flights of birds to flap away in terror. Alligators stalked long-snouted garfish in canals dug by the road builders, and turtles sunning themselves on mudbanks paid no heed to any of it. Zech marveled that anyone could have ever pushed such a ribbon of crushed rock and steel through what once had been impenetrable jungles of palmetto and Spanish bayonet and swamps where even a horse could not pass.

The trip down the coast took five days, leisurely days that turned into a holiday outing, the first such venture for Zech and Glenda and Sol. Always before there had been cattle to drive and predators to fear and daily chores to do and nothing unusual to see except endless miles of brown prairie and palmetto plains, cypress stands that all looked the same, murky swamps that warned them to turn away. Now they drank in unfamiliar sights along the coastline like revelers, sometimes crossing the tracks and making their way to the beach where they camped on soft sand and cooked sea turtle eggs in the coals of a fire. And then Zech would remember the purpose of the mission and push south at a faster pace.

They finally reached a settlement of shacks west of Palm Beach where the railroad ended. It was in these clapboard houses where servants lived, black mostly but Spanish and white also, people who worked in hotels and dining rooms, cleaned the shops, tended flower gardens and cut grass, performing menial labor by day and streaming back to the shacks at night like ants returning to a hill.

When they crossed over to Palm Beach proper it was like entering a make-believe fantasy world to Zech and Sol. Glenda had seen some of it during her years in Jacksonville, but nothing on such a grand scale as Palm Beach. Stores along the main thoroughfare displayed elegant gowns from Paris, men's fashions from London, delicate pastries of all shapes and sizes, fine wines and champagne, sausages and cheese from New York. Women walked from store to store beneath dainty parasols, and men wore three-piece vested suits and bowler hats, and some were dressed in knickerbockers with gaily colored socks coming up to their knees. Couples rode down sandy streets in two-seater wicker chairs on wheels, hooked to bicycle devices pedalled by sweating, puffing Negroes dressed in black knickers and white knee-socks with red tams capping their heads.

They turned down another street leading to the beach, both sides heavily lined with stately royal palms. Then they came on it suddenly, the Royal Poinciana Hotel, one of the largest wooden buildings in the world and the largest resort hotel anywhere, a monumental goliath drawing wealthy patrons like bees attracted to an orange grove in bloom. The 1,150 guest rooms were made possible by five million feet of lumber, 1,400 kegs of nails, 360,000 shingles, a half-million bricks, 4,000 barrels of lime, and 240,000 gallons of paint. The grounds were aflame with red poinsettia and blue plumbago.

Twelve hundred windows blinked back at him as Zech stared open-mouthed and exclaimed, "God 'a mighty, just look at that! I didn't know there were enough trees in all the world to make that many boards! Where you reckon Mister Flagler got it all?"

"I don't know," Glenda responded, "but it's sure something to see."

"Let's stay in it tonight, Pappa!" Sol urged, bouncing up and down in the saddle. "Go on in there and get us a room!"

"Shoot, Sol, we go in there in these wore-out jeans, they'd kick us out faster than a rabbit taking off in front of a wolf. This place is for rich fancy folks, not prairie dogs. They wouldn't even let us eat in the kitchen with the hired help."

"You're probably right," Glenda said. "But let's do go inside and look. We may never come this way again, and it won't hurt anything just to look."

"All right, we'll give 'er a shot," Zech said, getting down and tying the horses.

They crossed the wide veranda and entered two huge oak doors with stained glass panels, coming into a cavernous lobby lined with satin-covered chairs and couches. Overhead, a gigantic chandelier with hundreds of French crystal prisms sparkled brightly with the soft glow of electric light bulbs.

"How in the world do they do that, Pappa?" Sol asked, staring upward. "Them's not candles, or coal oil either. How they make it shine just sitting up there?"

"It's electric lights," Zech responded, staring too. "I heard about it in Fort Pierce once. They say it's coming there too someday. A fellow named Ed-sun made it, and he also made a thing that makes music come out of a box. I'll bet there's one of them around here sommers."

"I'd sure like to see it if it is," Sol said, becoming more excited.

"Why don't you go over and at least ask about a room?" Glenda said. "Surely we can afford to stay here for one night, and Sol would really enjoy it."

"I'll do that, but I got an idea it's not going to come out too good."

Glenda and Sol continued touring the lobby as Zech crossed the room to a counter on the far left side. A man in a white suit watched curiously as he approached, then gave him a more penetrating look as he said bluntly, "I'd like a room here for the night. I can pay cash."

"Do you have a reservation?" the man asked.

"Reservation? What's that?"

"Did you write or wire ahead and request lodgings?"

"No, I didn't. We're just passing through, on the way to Fort Dallas. I didn't know this hotel was here till we seen it. And we just want to stay for a night."

"Well, I'm afraid nothing is available," the man said, wishing to end the conversation. "There are several boarding houses to the west of here. I suggest you give them a try."

"Thanks anyway," Zech said, disappointed for Glenda and Sol. "But in case we come back this way from Fort Dallas, how much does it cost to stay the night here? I might could make one of those reservations."

"Rooms start at fifty dollars a night and go up, and suites start at three hundred."

"God a'mighty!" Zech exclaimed. "It's fifty cents a night at the boarding house in Punta Rassa. It's a good thing you sold out before we got here. A man would be crazy to pay three hundred dollars just to sleep. Hell, that's as much as I get for eight or ten cows."

"We're not in the cattle business. And there's no need for you to try here coming back. We're booked solid for the rest of the year. You'll have to look elsewhere."

"I'll do that!"

When he came back across the lobby Sol ran to him and said, "Pappa, you ought to see in that room over yonder! It's a indoor outhouse, and they got stools with lids you can sit on. When you pull a chain it flushes everything away with water. You ought to see it, Pappa! It'll do the same thing when you take a leak. I pulled the chain six times, and it worked ever time!"

"I seen enough in here without something stupid like that. Go and get your mamma and let's leave before they charge us for the water you used."

Glenda came to them and said, "Well, what did they say?"

"You got to have something called a reservation. The man said we ought to try a boarding house."

They went back to the main street and tied the buckboard again, walking sidewalks and gazing into storefronts. One shop sold only birds, colorful macaws and parrots and small canaries. Sol went inside, pointed to a parrot and said, "How much you get for a bird like that?"

"Two hundred dollars," the clerk said, supposing that Sol would not be a customer.

"He's not as pretty as a Carolina parakeet," Sol said, looking in other cages. "But they're all dead now. The freeze killed them."

"Yes, I know. We used to sell them too when we could get them."

"How much is that little yellow bird?"

"Twenty-five dollars each. They're canaries."

"Wow! He's awful little to cost that much. Birds must sell real good here. What do folks do with them?"

"Carry them back up north and keep them as house pets. We sell everything we can get in the store. Are you interested in buying something or just asking questions?"

"Well, maybe I'll buy something," Sol said, his mind racing. "What about those wooden cages? How much are they?"

"Just a cage?"

"No, a bunch of 'um."

"How many would you want?"

"Two dozen."

"I've never sold just cages alone, but for that many I could let you have them for a dollar each."

"Can I pick them up first thing in the morning?"

"I come in the shop at six o'clock. Just knock on the door and I'll let you in."

Sol went back to the sidewalk and ran to catch up with his mother and father. He said, "Pappa, can I have a couple of coins to spend myself?"

"Sure. I'll give them to you when we get back to the buckboard."

"Can I use the buckboard for a little while first thing in the morning?"

"I suppose so. But why do you want it?"

"I've got a thing to do, and it won't take long. I'll be real careful with it, Pappa. I just want to go back out of town a ways."

"You can do whatever you want tomorrow, but come sunup the next day we've got to push on. We best go on now and find us a place to stay. I don't believe folks here would look kindly if we camped out on the street."

Had it not been for Glenda wanting to stay another day and enjoy browsing through the shops, Zech would have preferred to leave right then and camp in the woods. To him it seemed impossible that such splendor could exist just a few miles from the wilderness. People and animals out there were starving, scratching desperately for survival; yet here there was an abundance of everything. Just the thought of it was repulsive, and he wanted no more of Palm Beach.

Sol ran on ahead to the buckboard, and as Zech and Glenda walked together he said absently, "All this is just the start of it."

"The start of what, Zech?"

"Someday the damned railroads will haul folks in here thicker than deer flies, and it'll spread elsewhere. I'm glad pappa never saw such as this. It would 'a killed him quicker than the malaria and the cold."

"You're not making sense to me."

"I suppose not. Maybe someday all this will make sense to Sol, but not to me. I've lived too long out yonder to change now. I guess I'm just a dumb cracker, like Pappa."

"Well, it just so happens I like dumb crackers," she said, taking his arm in hers. "What say after we get a place to stay we find a cafe that serves fried chicken? We haven't had that since Punta Rassa."

"That would be fine. There's bound to be some place here that don't require a reservation just to eat. Fried chicken sounds good to me."

Sol left before breakfast the next morning, and by nine o'clock he still had not returned to the boarding house. Glenda was worried about him, but Zech assured her he was old enough to look out for himself and would return soon.

They left the boarding house and crossed the bridge leading back to the main section of Palm Beach, enjoying the cool breeze that came in from the ocean and the scent of flower gardens that bordered houses.

Soon they came to the shops again, and Glenda went into each of them, not wanting to buy anything but fascinated by the items imported from Europe and the Far East. There were statues and bowls of silver and brass and solid gold, and gowns of silk and satin.

Zech soon became bored by it and walked on alone, idly watching carriages pass by and the funny little bicycle carts driven by black men, wondering what the tourists paid them to peddle the streets all day.

At the next corner he stopped and stared at his own buckboard tied there. Sol was accepting money from an elderly man dressed in knickers, and he continued staring as the man walked away briskly in the direction of the Royal Poinciana, carrying a caged bird in his left hand.

There were six more cages on the buckboard, each containing a small bird with frizzy white fuzz and feathers. Zech walked over rapidly and said, "Sol, what the hell are you doing?"

Sol grinned, and then he said, "I'm selling birds, Pappa, just like the shop down the street."

"Selling baby buzzards?" Zech said incredulously.

"They ain't buzzards," Sol said defensively. "They're kookabens, brought over from Cuba on a schooner. They'll turn green and red when they grow up, and they'll sing just like them little yellow birds in the shop."

Zech stared at the cages again, and then he said, "Son, don't try to bullshit your daddy. Them's buzzards! I seen a million of 'em in my day."

"All right, Pappa, they're buzzards," Sol admitted. "I done sold eighteen at twenty-five dollars apiece, and I didn't have to climb but six trees to get 'em. One man was so glad to get his that cheap he gave me an extra ten dollars. I only got six more to sell, Pappa. Please let me finish it."

"God a'mighty!" Zech exclaimed, shaking his head. "Me an' Pappa thought we'd done something when we sold our first wild cows for fifteen dollars each. What you're doin' seems downright dishonest to me, but I guess if a man's fool enough to pay three hundred dollars for a hotel room for one night he can afford another twenty-five for a buzzard."

"I'm not making nobody buy 'em, Pappa. They all seem to want one real bad 'cause mine are cheaper than the ones at the bird store."

"Kookabens! Lord help me! What you reckon them folks will do when they get back home and them things turns black and gets so big they flap right off, carrying cage and all?"

"I don't know, Pappa. But I won't be there to find out."

"You sell the rest of them things, that's six hundred dollars for a batch of buzzards. I guess you're going to make out all right, Sol, but I sure wouldn't want to do business with you. Maybe I ought to go out to the woods and shinny up a tree myself. But I best go on back and steer your mamma in another direction. If she sees you on the street sellin' buzzards, she'll most likely have a faintin' spell. You hurry up and get done with it, and don't you do it no more!"

"Thanks, Pappa. It won't take long. Everybody who comes by wants to buy one. I wish I'd got more of them but I only had twenty-four cages."

As Zech turned and walked back up the street a man and a woman stopped at the buckboard, looking curiously at the fuzzy birds. He glanced back as the man picked up a cage and handed it to the woman; then he muttered, "Kookaben birds! Lordy, what some folks won't buy!"

Zech was at the livery stable at dawn the next morning, hitching up the buckboard to resume the trip. He said to the stable owner, "Is there any special way a man ought to go to get down to Fort Dallas?"

"Yep, sure is. Leave that rig here and take a schooner. That's the best way."

"Well, I don't want to do that. I've got to take my trunk along, and it's too heavy to lug on board a boat and then off again."

"Too heavy for a schooner? What the hell you got in there, gold bars?"

"Nope. Coins."

The man gave Zech a queer look. "You can make it in the rig, but you'll have your work cut out for you. Just follow the only trail going that way. But I still say if I was you I'd take a schooner. How come you want to go to that godforsaken place anyway?"

"Got business there. And thanks for the information."

"Must be going into the skeeter business," the man said as Zech drove off.

As soon as he got back to the boarding house they set forth again, Zech gladly leaving Palm Beach behind. Sol was still exuberant with his sack of buzzard money safely tucked into his saddlebag.

At first the dirt road was easily passable, running a few miles inland from the ocean. Just before they reached Lake Worth at noon, they passed through an area planted heavily with pineapples, stopping briefly to gather some for their next meal.

They could not pass between the lake and the ocean because someone had cut a canal from the beach into the fresh water lake, turning it to salt; so they skirted the west shore and then turned south again.

Later that afternoon they stopped and made camp in a hardwood hammock and were immediately introduced to mosquitoes that would plague them for the rest of the trip. They came in clouds, swarming over arms and faces, attacking constantly. Zech and Sol built two huge fires, throwing on green wood to create as much smoke as possible, but still they came. All of them slept that night with blankets pulled over their heads, suffering the heat in order to get as much protection as possible.

From this point south the passable area gradually narrowed to a thin strip separating ocean and palmetto jungle in the east from the vast Pay-Hay-Okee that stretched away endlessly to the west. Zech had seen the River of Grass when Tawanda took him there, and he was not so surprised by it; but its majesty overwhelmed Glenda and Sol. From far out in the marsh they could see smoke boiling upward from great fires that raged across the sawgrass each spring and summer, tongues of flame and soot-saturated smoke blocking out the horizon and staining the blue sky with gray. Zech hurried along for fear the fires would turn their way and trap them with no possible escape route.

The further south they moved, the worse became the trail, and after three more days they came into a veritable jungle of trees and vines, reminding Zech of the custard-apple forest on the western shore of Okeechobee.

They were all beginning to believe there was no Fort Dallas when finally they came into an area planted with oranges, lemons, limes, figs and guavas, mangoes and bananas and avocados – the first sign of human habitation since leaving Lake Worth. The vegetation and the trees here were indeed unharmed by the freeze, and they had never seen such lushness. This pleased Zech, for the word he received at Fort Pierce about this southern tip being untouched by the freeze was, so far as he knew, only rumor or speculation and not fact. He had talked to no one who had actually been there.

When they made camp for the night, Sol ate bananas as quickly as he could zip the peels off, unconcerned that he was harvesting someone's fruit. They were so plentiful that a few wouldn't matter, and the evening meal also included abundant bowls of ripe figs and guavas.

At mid-morning the next day they came to the remains of the old fort, finding that someone had converted part of it into a private dwelling. Just past this there was a scattering of shacks and a weathered building that served as a post office, land office and general merchandise store. Across from this were the schooner docks.

Zech paused and said, "It sure don't look like much. Reminds me of the first time I saw Punta Rassa. Only this place is not even near as big as that."

"I just hope we get what we came after," Glenda said. "I would hate to make a trip all the way down here for nothing. It seems like the end of the world, and I can't for the life of me see why anyone would ever want to live here."

"Me neither," Sol said. "The skeeters is big enough to suck a horse dry."

"There'll be people aplenty when they find out it didn't freeze here," Zech said. "You can count on that. It won't stay like this forever. After we buy the trees, I think I'll spend all the gold that's left on land."

"I don't know what we'd ever do with land here," Glenda said, "but I guess buying it would be better than carrying coins all the way back to the hammock."

They chose an area beneath a thick growth of coconut palms to make camp, and Sol immediately shinnied up the thin trunk of one tree, trying to reach the green nuts.

Glenda shouted up to him, "Come down from there, Sol! You're not a monkey!"

"Sometimes it seems he is," Zech said. "While you're trying to get him back on the ground I'll walk over to the store and ask about the trees."

"Could you buy something there for us to eat? It's just too hot right now to build a fire and cook."

"I'll see what they got," Zech replied, walking off.

The proprietor was a short fat man in his late forties, wearing a huge straw hat and brown leather sandals with no socks. His thin cotton clothes hung loose over his body and looked more like pajamas than a shirt and pants.

Zech entered and said to him, "Howdy. Name's Zech MacIvey."

"Sam Potter. I seen you come in with that rig. You drive it all the way down here or did the wind blow you in from sommers?"

"Drove it from Palm Beach. And before that, the Kissimmee River."

"You got guts. What can I do for you?"

"I'm interested in buying orange trees."

"Got caught by the freeze, eh? We heard about it. Felt real sorry for you people. How many trees you got in mind?"

"How much they cost?"

"Can let you have cuttin's for five cents each. Trees cost a quarter. When the trees are bigger you can make your own cuttin's."

"I'm not interested in nothing but trees. Cows eat them cuttin's right up. I'll take eight thousand trees for a start."

"How many?"

"Eight thousand to begin with, and as many more as I can get ever month or so. I aim to end up with about ten thousand acres in trees."

"That's a heap. But you sure can't get many trees in that buckboard. Best way is for me to ship 'em up the coast to Fort Pierce by schooner and you pick 'em up there."

"That'd be fine. I'm not too far out from Fort Pierce."

"Eight thousand trees is two thousand dollars. What you got to pay with?"

"Spanish gold doubloons."

"Good enough!" Potter said, smiling. "Can't do better than that. Most folks tries to pay me off with coconuts. That's why I always ask the manner of payment before striking a deal. I ain't seen gold in a coon's age."

"Can you ship me a thousand more ever month till I send word I got enough?"

"No problem."

"How will I pay you?"

"The skipper is a friend of mine. You can pay him when he brings the trees. He docks at Fort Pierce twice a month on a Monday, 'less the weather messes him up. I'll ship 'em so they'll arrive the first Monday ever month and you can meet him there."

"That's real fine. As soon as we eat I'll come back and pay you for the first batch. I might be interested in buying some land too. How much is it?"

"Well, right now the going price is a dollar an acre, but it won't stay that way for long. We're trying to get Flagler to run his railroad on down here, and if he does, the price is sure to go up. It'll go to five dollars an acres, maybe more. Now's a good time to buy."

"I'll think it over and let you know. What you got to eat my wife don't have to cook?"

"Fresh smoked fish, canned beans and tinned beef. You want some fruit, hell, just go out and pick it. Folks here don't care."

"We done that already. I'll take a big batch of smoked fish and a half-dozen cans of beans. I been hankerin' for some beans lately, and my son Sol likes 'em too."

Potter put the items in a sack and said, "You don't owe me nothin'. It's on the house. I ain't traded none for gold in a long time. It's a pleasure dealin' with you."

"Same here, and thanks. I'll see you again in a short while."

The fish was delicious, thick slabs of king mackerel and amberjack, and Sol capped it off with three cans of beans, followed by Zech with two. All of it was washed down with thick, creamy milk from several coconuts Sol brought down from the tree.

Zech sat on the ground, savoring the aftertaste and figuring in his mind; then he said to Glenda, "I'm only going to have to put out two thousand in cash for the trees, and I'll pay for the others as they come to Fort Pierce. There's over eight thousand in gold in the trunk, so I might as well go on and spend it down here. I'll keep enough for us to get home on and buy land with the rest."

"Whatever you say, Zech. I know there's plenty more gold at the house, and it just takes up room in the buckboard. Maybe land here will be worth something someday."

"It ain't too bad a place except for getting here and the skeeters. But it looks like things sure grow good down here."

"I want to buy some land too," Sol said, listening to the conversation.

"What for?" Zech asked, surprised. "How come you'd want to do that? I'll put everybody's name on the deed and it'll be yours as much as mine."

"I just want to do it myself, Pappa," Sol insisted. "I've got the money I made in Palm Beach."

"What money?" Glenda asked.

"Never mind about it," Zech said to Glenda quickly. "He sold some stuff he gathered in the woods. It's your money, Sol. Just do what you want with it and shut up."

"What kind of stuff?" Glenda then asked curiously.

"Just stuff, Glenda," Zech said. "That's all. It didn't amount to nothin'."

Glenda wasn't satisfied, but she dropped the questioning and said, "While you two are over at the store I'm going to walk to the old fort and look around. I'll meet you back here later."

"Come on, Sol, let's go talk to the man and see what we can do," Zech said.

As they led the buckboard to the store, Sol said, "Thanks, Pappa."

"You're welcome. But next time you better think before you talk in front of your mamma. You'll get yourself in trouble if you don't."

Zech tied the horses and then removed four sacks of coins from the trunk. He and Sol carried them inside and put them on a counter, and Zech said to Potter, "There's more here than I owe for the trees, so just count it later and hold on to the rest. We want to talk now about land."

"You decided what you want to do?" Potter asked.

"Yeah. I want six thousand acres, and Sol wants to buy a little on his own."

"Six thousand acres," Potter repeated, visualizing the sacks of coins that much gold would be. "That's real good, Mister MacIvey. Any particular place you want it?"

"I wouldn't know one from the other. You got any suggestions?"

"All the land from here south would be real good if it was cleared. Would make a fine farm. Let's block it out there."

"Suits me. What about you, Sol? You want him to just pick out some for you?"

"What's on that land you can see over yonder across the bay?" Sol asked.

"Well, there's a right nice beach over there if you can push through the mangrove swamps to get to it. Plenty of skeeters too. It ain't fittin' to plant crops on, but if you want some land over there, I can drop the price to fifty cents an acre."

"That's what I want, over yonder on the beach," Sol said. "I've got enough for twelve hundred acres."

"You sure about this?" Potter questioned. "I don't want you to come back later and think I cheated you."

"It don't look like much from here," Zech said, "but it ought to be worth twenty-four buzzards. Go on and sell it to him if that's what he wants. It's his money, free and clear."

"Ain't no buzzards over there I know of," Potter said, puzzled by the remark. "It's mostly pelicans and gulls."

"Never mind," Zech said. "I don't think Sol's going in the bird business again. When can you have the deeds ready?"

"I'll try to get it done this afternoon. If I don't, sometime tomorrow. And I'll tell you for a fact, Mister MacIvey. You ain't making no mistake. We're putting in for a state charter to make this place Dade County, and when that goes through we're going to name the village Miami."

"Miami? I know a Indian medicine man first name of Miami. He saved my pappa from dying of malaria. But I never asked him what the name means."

"It's Seminole for 'very large'."

Zech laughed, and then he said, "That's kind of a joke, ain't it? I haven't seen a dozen people since I been here."

"You will if you stay long enough. As I say, you ain't making no mistake. That railroad comes here, your land will be worth at least five bucks an acre and go up from there. Even that land over across the bay might be worth something someday. It's got a right pretty beach if you can find it."

"Can you help us bring in the gold?" Zech asked. "It's kinda heavy."

"My pleasure. And after we get done with it, I want to give you some red snapper for your supper. Friend of mine brings it to me fresh ever day. I'll tell your missus how to cook it like we do down here. It's been soaking in coconut milk all morning, so it ought to be real good come supper time."

That night Glenda cooked a supper as instructed by Potter. He gave them two whole snappers of five pounds each, and she wrapped them in banana leaves and baked them at the edge of the fire. Avocados were cut in half and stuffed with crab meat provided by Potter, then steamed in an inch of water in the Dutch oven. There was also fresh boiled shrimp, and mangoes so ripe they poured juice when opened.

By the time the meal was finished all of them were stuffed. Zech leaned back against a palm trunk and said, "As far as vittles goes, this place ain't bad at all. Not bad. That supper was real fittin'. A man could sure get plenty to eat here without working so hard at it like we have to do back at the hammock."

"I met a real nice lady this afternoon when I went for a walk," Glenda said. "Name of Julia Tuttle. She lives in the old fort and has fixed it up real nice. She said it's not bad living here once you get used to the isolation, and that's what most folks here want anyway. Flowers grow all year long, and vegetables too. She said there's so many fish in the bay you just scoop out what you want with a net. And they have mail service too. A man walks barefooted all the way down the beach from Palm Beach and brings it here."

"He must have the biggest set of clod-hoppers in the world to walk that far over sand," Zech said. "I'll bet his feet looks like barrel lids."

"She sure told me a lot of things," Glenda said. "She sent Mister Flagler some orange blossoms up to Palm Beach to show him it didn't freeze here, and because of it he might run his railroad down here."

"I don't know why the folks here would want that," Zech said, his voice reflecting distaste. "This place ever gets like Palm Beach, it's ruined for sure. Why would they want to bring hotels and them wicker bicycles and all that other cruddy stuff down here?"

"That's not what they want at all," Glenda said assuringly. "She said they just want folks to come here and build nice little houses and clear the land for planting. It is a real pretty place once you think on it."

"Don't matter what she wants, or the others either. If that engine comes puffin' in here with people packed in like sardines, it's going to mean nothin' but ruination. It'll end up just like Palm Beach. But it sure sounds like that woman done a sellin' job on you. You want to come down here and live?"

"Oh no!" Glenda said quickly. "I wouldn't leave our hammock for anyplace! But maybe someday we could build a little cabin here like the one in Punta Rassa. We could come down by boat from Fort Pierce. It might be fun to come back once in a while and eat the fish and mangoes. And I could visit again with Julia."

"Let's do it!" Sol exclaimed. "Next time we're here I want to see my beach. I want to see what's over there, Pappa."

"We'll think on it," Zech said. "But soon's we get the deeds tomorrow we got to clear on out of here. We still got cows to mark and more holes to dig in the grove. We sure want to be ready when the orange trees get to Fort Pierce. I aim to build Pappa the biggest grove in the whole damned state."

It was not until noon the next day when Potter handed Zech the deeds, repeating again, almost apologetically, "You ain't made no mistake, Mister MacIvey."

After farewells and promises to return, Zech turned the buckboard north, now much lighter because of an empty trunk.

The first night they camped again at the edge of a lush grove, gorging for the last time on bananas and mangoes, and also tormented by mosquitoes. Then they moved slowly back up the coast.

Zech skirted to the west of Palm Beach, avoiding it as he would Sodom and Gomorrah, not wanting even the sight of it to come back in his mind. He was also anxious now to reach the lower Kissimmee and that final stretch toward home.

As the horses plodded slowly across the open prairie, bringing back the familiar sights of cypress stands and palmetto and cabbage palms and herds of deer and great flights of birds, Zech was troubled by the things he had seen, contrasting such a place as Palm Beach with the land that was still wilderness, unconquered but threatened, some of it yet untouched by a white man's boots.

There was no doubt in his mind there would be other Palm Beaches, the next most likely at Fort Dallas, but he hoped they would be confined to the coastal beaches and never turn inland, never come even close to his Kissimmee River hammock.

THIRTY-SIX
Spring
1896

Zech stood by the empty holding pen, which was located seventeen miles south of the main corral. He followed tracks for a hundred yards toward a line of hickory, stopping several times to feel the indented earth; then he turned and went back to where his horse was tied.

Frog rode from the woods and came to him, saying, "I found where they was camped, Mistuh Zech. They's empty bean cans a mile over yonder. Couldn't 'a been more than two days ago."

"A hundred head!" Zech exclaimed, exasperated. "Damn! This keeps up we might as well let them drive the herd to Punta Rassa and sell it themselves."

Rustling had become rampant, not only with Zech but with other cattlemen throughout the area. A month earlier Zech and Frog followed the trail of sixteen stolen cows as far south as Fort Pierce. Three miles outside the town they found the hides and heads in a palmetto grove, indicating the rustlers had slaughtered the beeves and sold the meat to someone in Fort Pierce. There was no way for them to find out who bought the beef since dressed cows carry no brand. The trail of this herd led to the southwest.

Frog said, "You want to go after them? 'Less they're runnin' them cows full gallop we can catch up with 'em in a few days."

"Wouldn't be no use just you and me doing it. I counted almost a dozen horse tracks. They'd bushwhack us for sure. But I got a idea how to stop it. Let's ride on back north and we'll talk about it later."

That night at supper Zech was strangely quiet, and Glenda suspected something was bothering him more than usual. She knew about the stolen cows, and shared his concern, but she had never seen him as angry as he was when he rode in that afternoon.

Zech toyed with his food, and finally he turned to Frog and said, "You been around more places than me, Frog, what with all them trips you've taken after drives and when we don't have much to do. What's the roughest town there is, with the meanest men you can find anywhere?"

"There ain't no doubt about that one," Frog mumbled, his mouth full of roast beef. "It's Arcadia. That's the wildest place this side of hell. They's about fifty fights a day there, and as many as four killin's 'tween sunup and sundown. Last time I was there some fellows whupped the stew outen me just 'cause they didn't like the cut of my britches. You aim to go there and give it a shot?"

"No. That's not what I've got in mind. Can you hire gunslingers there?"

"You can go into Arcadia and get anybody you want killed for two shots of likker."

"What would a man there do for five hundred dollars?"

"For five hundred dollars, Mistuh Zech, he'd slit his mammy's throat an' turn his pappy into a steer. What you leadin' up to?"

"I want six men to ride south with me. I'll pay five hundred dollars each for the job."

"What on earth are you talking about?" Glenda asked, alarmed by the conversation. "You sound like you're going to start a war somewhere."

"I am. I'm going to settle it once and for all with them rustlers. I know who's doing it, and I know where they're at. If we don't stop it now, we might as well get out of the cattle business and turn the whole damned prairie over to them."

"I still don't understand," Glenda said. "How could you know these men? You've never seen even one of them."

"Indians told me a good while ago there's a nest of outlaws down south of Punta Rassa, at the edge of the ten thousand islands. I heard it too in Punta Rassa last time we was there, and also in Kissimmee. Other folks has been hit by the same men. It's said that a man named Wirt McGraw is the leader, and everbody is afraid to go after him.

Well, I ain't. I don't mind poor folks livin' out in the woods taking a few cows to eat, but that's not what these sons a' bitches is doing. Unless they done passed on by now, some of these men are the same varmints that killed my dogs and Ishmael and caused me and you to lose a baby. I'm going after them, and I should 'a done it before now."

"That's the most foolish thing I've ever heard you say!" Glenda said, even more alarmed. "You'll get yourself killed!"

"Maybe yes, and maybe no," Zech replied calmly. "But I'm tired of wondering if somebody hiding behind a bush is going to blow my head off ever time I ride through the woods. There ain't no law out here to do anything about it, and you know that; so if we don't do something ourselves, nobody will. I know of at least six cattlemen who'll join me, and with six gunslingers, that ought to even the odds. We can ride in real quiet and pop them bastards good before they know what's happening. They think nobody's got the guts to come after 'em. I know there's always going to be rustling, so long as there's men and cows, but if we can put a stop to this bunch it'll be a warning to others. At least it'll make 'em think twice. But as long as we just sit by and do nothing it's an open invitation to any varmint with a horse and a gun. They'll know they can get away with it, and it'll never end. Not ever."

"What you want me to do?" Frog asked, glancing at Glenda.

"I'm not asking anybody here to go with me that don't want to," Zech said. "That's not what you and Lester is being paid for. All I want you to do, Frog, is take the money and hire the men in Arcadia. Then you can come on back here if you want to. I'll pick up the other ranchers and meet your men at the cabin in Punta Rassa. We'll ride south from there."

"You can count me in all the way," Frog said, almost gleefully. "I'd purely enjoy bein' a part of this trip. We'll wipe out that buzzard's nest as clean as a whistle."

"What about you, Lester?" Zech then asked.

"Well, I don't know, Mistuh Zech. I don't want you to think I got no guts, an' I'm willin' to do whatever you say, but I'm sure not much good with a gun. All I ever done is punch cows."

"Then you won't go, and there's no hard feeling at all. You can stay here with Glenda and Sol."

"I want to go too, Pappa!" Sol said. "I can shoot a rifle good as anyone!"

"No way!" Zech said emphatically. "You'll stay behind with your mamma. And that's that!"

"I'll not stay here either!" Glenda snapped. "Not while you're way off down there getting yourself shot at! Sol and I'll go with you to Punta Rassa and stay in the cabin. That way we'll know real soon if you'll ride back with us or if we bring you back in a box. I'll not sit here all that time wondering!"

"You can do that if you want," Zech said, "but nobody's coming back in a box. I'm not a fool. We'll be real careful and do this thing right. Frog, you go to Arcadia and come on to Punta Rassa soon as you can. I'll round up the other cattlemen and go straight there. Lester, you stay here and look after the place. We'll leave at sunup."

"I still think this is stupid!" Glenda said. "But I can see there's no way to talk you out of it."

"It's a thing that's got to be done, either now or later," Zech replied. "There's no way out of it, so what's the use of putting it off any longer."

Frog arrived in Punta Rassa one day later than Zech. After taking one brief look at the group Frog was leading, Glenda retired immediately into the cabin and shut the door.

Each man was over six feet tall, slim as a rail, filthy and bearded, wearing a black felt hat and clothes that hadn't been washed since the previous year. They were all hungry-looking, hollow-eyed and expressionless, and the only thing separating them from the dead was the apparent fact they were breathing. None of them acknowledged or returned Zech's greeting as they dismounted in front of him. They simply walked off to a nearby tree and squatted.

Zech said in hushed tones, "God a' mighty, Frog. That's the meanest looking bunch I ever seen."

"That's what you wanted, ain't it?"

"I guess so. But Lord, the smell. We'll have ever buzzard on the west coast following us."

"Just watch where you ride," Frog said. "If the wind comes from the south while we're headed down that way, go in front of them. If it's from the north, ride behind. That way it ain't so bad. I found that out comin' here. But if there ain't no wind, Lord help us. We're in a heap of trouble."

"Maybe we can stand it for a couple of days," Zech said.

"I done things a little different from what you wanted, Mistuh Zech. I only gave 'em two hundred each to begin with, and promised the rest when the job is done. That way they won't hightail it off before we even get there."

"That's a good idea. I wouldn't trust that bunch with a bucket of slop. They'd probably be in the hog business and make off with it."

"Where's your men?" Frog asked.

"At the boarding house. I got seven ranchers from Kissimmee. Word spread here what we're going to do, and when they found out about the men you're bringing, they all seemed to get courage they ain't never had. Six more cowmen wants to join up. That'll make twenty-one of us altogether. I'll go on down there now and bring the rest back here."

Zech returned in a half hour leading the troop. He went into the cabin briefly to say good-bye to Glenda.

"Please be careful, Zech," she pleaded. "I feel better now with so many of you, but don't take foolish chances."

"We won't. I promise you. And we ought to be back here day after tomorrow. It's only about sixty miles down there, so we'll probably hit them first thing in the morning."

He kissed her; then he went outside and mounted. The group rode away briskly, cantering the horses, looking like a small army, however ragtag.

They had been gone no more than ten minutes when Glenda heard a horse come galloping past the front of the cabin. She rushed outside, seeing Sol jump a split-rail fence and head toward the holding pens where the men disappeared.

She shouted frantically, "Sol! Sol MacIvey! Come back here! You come back here this instant!"

He merely waved back at her, then went past the pens and turned south.

She leaned against the outside cabin wall, staring after him, and then she said, "You men! MacIveys! Damn you! I hope Zech has the sense to send you back!"

The men rode steadily all afternoon, staring straight ahead, grim-faced, each knowing the danger they faced and the possibility of disaster. When night came they continued on for an hour; then they stopped and made a fireless camp beneath a grove of oaks, eating cold beans from cans.

Frog's recruits still had not spoken one word to anyone, huddling together and shunning all offers of camaraderie from the other men. Zech speculated they were just as mean as the men they were setting out to kill, and they displayed no more emotion than they would have if hired to castrate bulls or slaughter hogs. Their only concern seemed to be the money they would receive, not what they would do to earn it. Just their presence made Zech uneasy, and he would be relieved to end this thing and see the last of them. But he was glad they were riding with him and not against him.

At dawn they ate more beans and set out again, but this time they rode slowly, suspecting they were right at the threshold of what they were seeking. Zech finally signaled everyone to stop, and then he said, "We must be awful close now. Me and Frog'll ride out a ways and see what's ahead. Everbody else wait here till we get back."

They moved cautiously through a thick hardwood hammock that ended abruptly at an open field; then they dismounted and crept forward, hiding behind a clump of cocoplum bushes. Sugar cane in the field had come up to a height of one foot. Across from the field there were several cabins, a barn, and a corral filled with cattle. Off to the right a dock ran out into a bay heavily dotted with small mangrove islands.

A fire blazed under what looked at a distance to be a whiskey still, and over another fire, close by one of the cabins, a whole steer was roasting on a spit. Zech counted twenty-three men moving about the compound, one of them hobbling on a wooden leg.

After studying the compound and outlying areas closely, they eased back to the horses and returned to the waiting men. Zech said, "Best as I could tell, there ain't no more of them than there are of us. And them bastards is so sure of themselves they don't even have a guard out. We'll catch 'em by surprise for sure. The whole area around the compound is open land, so we'll divide into groups and ride in from three sides. In the west there's water. Frog, you take your men around to the south. Six of you stay here with me, and the rest can come in from the east. Watch the line of woods over this way, and when you see me start across the cane field, ride in like hell and we'll have the whole bunch right in the middle."

As the men broke into groups Zech said, "Good luck, fellows. We'll give you about fifteen minutes to get in place."

Zech led his group of silent men to the edge of the cane field and again used cocoplum bushes as shields. One of the men plopped a huge plug of tobacco into his mouth, chewed nervously, and spat a brown stream onto the ground. Ants converged on it immediately, investigated briefly, and then turned away.

A lump came into Zech's throat as he stared across the field, watching one man turn the steer as flames licked the meat. He wondered who these men were, where they came from, why they were here and what drove them to do what they were doing; he knew that soon now someone would die, maybe them and maybe himself. Is it really worth all this, he asked himself, all this approaching death because of cows? But he knew it was more than cows that brought him here, remembering the dogs and the horses and the bullet in Bonzo and the bushwhacking and the firefight and the murder of an unborn baby and the absolute need to take these men's lives from them in order to stop it. But why had they started it in the first place? This he couldn't answer, knowing only the fact that some men would rather take than share and would indeed as soon kill another man as a snake.

He was so deep in thought the man next to him had to shake his arm and say, "Ain't it time to go now?"

"Yes. It's time. Everybody ought to be in place. Lord help us. . .and watch over us. . . . Let's go!"

The horses bolted forward, and they were halfway across the field when other groups rushed from woods in the east and south.

They were within one hundred yards of the compound before they were noticed. Then men scrambled frantically into cabins and popped out again, firing rifles, dodging behind whatever was available as bullets pounded into every building and across every foot of ground. Zech aimed the Winchester as best he could on the bouncing horse, pulling off three shots in rapid succession, then seeing the man at the spit topple forward into the fire and scream wildly as he rolled across the ground, consumed in flames.

The three streaking groups had the surprised men in an inescapable vise. They could conceal themselves momentarily from north riders, but this exposed them to those coming from the east and south. Before the three groups converged in the middle of the compound, nine men lay dead, three more wounded and crawling in dirt like stricken dogs.

Frog saw one man jump from behind a woodpile and aim a rifle at him. He dodged sideways as a tiny speck of fire erupted from the barrel; then he felt a sharp pain in his left shoulder, knowing he was hit. He said, "Aw hell! . . .you sons a' bitches done it now, damn you!" He charged straight forward, pumping six bullets into his assailant, four of them hitting the man after he lay dead on the ground.

It ended as quickly as it began, men throwing down rifles and holding their arms upward, some with terror in their eyes, others still hostile, horses now running around them in circles. Zech brought his horse to a halt in front of the captives and said, "Which one of you varmints is Wirt McGraw?"

The man with the wooden leg hobbled forward. He was in his late sixties, bald and bearded. He said gruffly, "I am, if it's any of your damned business! And who be you?"

"Zech MacIvey."

"MacIvey, eh. I'll remember the name. When you fools get done with whatever you're here for, I'll take care of you, MacIvey. You can count on it."

"Only thing you can count on is the fires of hell!" Zech shot back harshly. "We're goin' to hang the whole lot of you!"

"For what?" McGraw asked belligerently. "You can't prove we done nothin' to nobody!"

"We'll see about that. A couple of you men go look in the barn and then see what brands them cows has. Then we'll talk more about why you're going to do a rope dance."

None of them noticed the black marshtackie as it came across the canefield and stopped at the edge of the clearing. The rifle blast caught them by surprise, but before they could turn and see where it came from, a man staggered from the corner of a cabin, a gaping hole in his forehead spewing blood. He staggered four steps forward and fell, firing the rifle as he went down, the bullet striking Zech's right foot like a hammer, knocking him out of the saddle.

Zech jumped up quickly and looked behind him, seeing Sol's horse trot forward, the Winchester smoking. Sol said, "I had to shoot him, Pappa! He was drawed down on you! I had to do it!"

"What the hell are you doing here?" Zech demanded. "I told you to stay in Punta Rassa with your mamma!"

"I wanted to come, Pappa! I wanted to be here with you!"

"Well, what's did is did," Zech said, his voice calmer. "And I guess it's a good thing you did sneak along. If you hadn't, that bastard would 'a blowed my head off 'stead of my foot. I thank you for that, Sol."

Zech limped to his horse as one man rode into the circle and said,

"They's four men chained in that damned barn, and them cows has got ever brand on 'em you can think of, including MacIvey."

"That's it!" Zech said. "Somebody take the chains off them men and set 'em free, and the rest of you herd these varmints to the nearest tree and string 'em up. Then we'll set fire to this whole stinkin' place and burn all of it to the ground."

McGraw spoke up, "You fellows wouldn't do something like that to a old army buddy, would you? I lost my leg fightin' for the Rebs in the war."

"That ain't what they say in Punta Rassa," Zech said. "Word is you were a damned deserter and plundered ever homestead you could find without a man there to protect it. And you been at it ever since. Backshootin' included. You can take what's coming to you now like a man, or you can whine like a baby, whichever you choose. It's up to you."

"To hell with you!" McGraw bellowed. "Damn all of you! You'd 'a never took us hadn't you snuck in here like shittin' wolves! Go on and do it and be done with it!"

"We will!" Zech retorted. "And you'll be the first! I'd put the rope on you myself if I could walk!"

As the men started herding the captives away, Frog said, "I need a little help, Mistuh Zech. I got a hole in my shoulder."

"And I got a foot that pure hurts like hell," Zech said. "Sol, get down off there and see to Frog. Then help me tie a cloth to my leg to stop the bleeding. Then we better hightail it back to Punta Rassa. They got a doctor there now."

Sol tore up his shirt and made a compress for Frog's wound. Then he bound Zech's foot and leg. Fires leaped up all around them as they mounted the horses, and at the edge of the east woods, men dangled from the limbs of an oak.

One of the men from Arcadia rode up and spoke for the first time, "We'll take the rest of our money now. Everbody's dead. Anything else you want us to do?"

Frog handed him a sack of gold as Zech responded, "Naw, that's it. We done what we came for. You can leave anytime you want."

"Thanks," the man said, before he galloped away.

"That bunch will all probably kill each other before it's over," Frog said. "I sure wouldn't want to be the one totin' the sack of money."

"Me either," Zech said. "But right now let's make these horses burn dust. My foot feels like ever bone in it is broke."

As they rode off, the men from Arcadia came back into the compound, drew knives and started hacking huge chunks from the roasted steer; then they turned their attention to the nearby whiskey still.

Zech lay on a cot as the doctor examined his foot. Frog was already bandaged, and Glenda hovered over Zech as the doctor shook his head and said, "I've never seen one like this before. That bullet is buried in bone, with just a tip showing. There's no way I can get it out. I just don't have the tools to do it. Only thing I can do, if you say so, is take off the foot part way up your leg."

"Hell fire no!" Zech roared. "You ain't goin' to do no such thing! Where's a doctor who can do what needs to be did?"

"Not anywhere around here. Maybe in Jacksonville, and you might have to go all the way to Atlanta to find one. It's going to take a bone specialist with the proper knowhow and tools. But you better do something. That bullet stays in there, you'll never walk on that foot again. And you'll probably get lead poisoning."

"Damn!" Zech shrieked as the doctor poured whiskey into the open wound. Then he said, "There ain't no way I can stand this much longer. I'd never make it to Jacksonville, much less Atlanta."

"You've got to try, Zech!" Glenda pleaded. "We've got to do something!"

For a moment Zech dropped into deep thought, and then he said, "I know what I'll do. I'll go to the same doctor what saved Pappa. The Seminole medicine man."

"What the hell?" the doctor said. "A medicine man? What's he going to do, dance around in a circle shaking rattles? You best either let me take the foot off or head straight for Jacksonville or Atlanta. Medicine man!"

Zech ignored the doctor as he said, "Sol can ride down there with me, and Glenda, you stay here and tend to Frog till he can ride. Me and Sol'll come straight on back to the hammock from the Indian village."

"Your friend ought to be able to ride in a buckboard in four or five days," the doctor said. "His bullet went clear through but it busted some ribs. He'll have to be careful for a good while."

"Don't worry 'bout us, Mistuh Zech," Frog said. "We'll be fine.

Soon's I can move about, me and Miz Glenda'll go on back to the place. We'll see you there."

"Zech, are you sure this is what you want to do?" Glenda asked, deeply concerned. "If the doctor here can't help you, what can a medicine man do?"

"He saved Pappa. That's for sure. And he'll do the same for me. I sure as hell ain't goin' to hobble around the rest of my life on a wooden stump. I'd look just like that bastard we hung down there in the woods. Sol, get the horses ready. We need to get on with it."

"Yessir, Pappa," Sol responded. "I'll give 'em a good feedin' and some water. It won't take but a few minutes."

As Sol went out Zech said to Glenda, "Don't get on him no more for what he done. If he hadn't followed us I'd be dead for sure. He saved me, Glenda. So just don't say nothing more to him."

"I won't. But he sure gave me a fright shucking out of here the way he did."

The doctor picked up his bag and said, "I've done all I can, so I'll leave now. I think you're doing a foolish thing, but it's your foot and your life. You better pray that thing don't get infected. If it does, you're in bad trouble. Medicine man! Good Lord!"

As the doctor left, Zech said, "Glenda, go on out there and hurry Sol up. I don't think I can stand this but just long enough to ride from here to the village. It's a good thing I know the way now."

There were times when Zech didn't know who he was or where he was, the pain shooting up his leg like boiling fire, but he rode doggedly, galloping and then walking the horses to rest them. At dawn they passed by the Okeechobee trading post, and in another two hours they came into the village.

Zech slumped forward in the saddle as Keith Tiger came to him first and said, "Zech?. . .Zech MacIvey?. . .What is the trouble?. . . . You seem to be in much pain."

"My foot. . . ." Zech muttered. "Bullet. . .the medicine man. . . ."

Toby Cypress then came scrambling from a chickee and said, "Father! It is you! What is the matter?"

"He's been shot," Tiger said. "Help him to the chickee while I get the medicine man. Quickly!"

Sol's eyes widened as he watched the strange boy help Zech from the horse and carry him gently to a cypress table, the words ringing in his ears, "Father. . .it is you." Then he jumped from the horse and helped place Zech back down on the rough planks.

The medicine man was now as old and stooped as Keith Tiger, and he seemed to float as he came across the clearing. He took the foot in his hand and stared at it; then he drew a long hunting knife from his belt and pushed the blade into a fire.

Toby's grandfather and three older men came to the table and held Zech down as Miami Billie said, "This will hurt you, but it will be over soon. Put this piece of hickory in your mouth and bite down on it."

Zech bit the stick viciously as the medicine man leaned down to the wound, his mouth groping, teeth grinding until they took a firm grip on the tip of the bullet; then the knife was inserted into the bone and shaken back and forth, loosening the lead, teeth locking on again as the old man sucked and grunted. Slowly but surely the bullet moved outward, Zech feeling like he would pass out from pain; then suddenly it popped free and Miami Billie stood straight, his face blood-covered, the bullet firmly gripped in his teeth. He spat it out and said, "I will make the poultice now. You may limp, my son, but you will walk."

Those were the last words Zech heard before he fainted, ". . .you will walk."

When Zech looked up an hour later, Sol and Toby were standing by the table, Sol's eyes both puzzled and hostile as he glared at Toby and then looked to his father. Zech knew why, and he said to Sol, "You heard what Toby said, didn't you?"

"I heard him call you 'father'. What does this mean, Pappa? Do Indians call everbody that?"

"No, they don't. No more than you. Toby is my son, Sol, and your half-brother. His mamma was Tawanda, and she's dead now. I promised her that you and Glenda would never know about this, but what's done now can't be helped. You got to promise me you'll never tell your mamma, Sol. You got to do it. Promise me now!"

"All right, Pappa, I promise. I won't ever tell."

"And I know what you're thinking," Zech said, troubled. "I can see it in your eyes. It wasn't no bad thing, Sol. I knew Tawanda before I married your mamma, and I ain't done nothing like that with nobody else. Tawanda was a good woman, a real fine person, and it wasn't no bad thing like with somebody I didn't hardly know, just for the hell of it. I don't want you to think hard of me. Do you understand what I'm saying?"

"I'm trying to, Pappa," Sol said, tears forming in his eyes. "Honest I am. But I never knew I had a Indian brother. It'll take some getting used to."

"I'm going to be flat on my back for a few days," Zech said, looking down at what appeared to be a mud pack encasing his foot and leg. "And I don't want you two standing here gawking at me all the time. Go off and do something together. Hunt or fish or ride horses. Get to know each other while you got the chance. You might find out you like each other."

"I can show you Pay-Hay-Okee, the River of Grass, if you would like to see it," Toby said hesitantly, watching Sol's reaction.

The ice suddenly broke. Sol smiled and said, "I'd like that. And I'll bet my marshtackie can outrun yours."

"We'll see," Toby responded as they both scrambled for the horses.

Zech smiled too as he watched them gallop away. He said, "I wish I could go with you. I'd like to see it again myself."

Toby's grandfather came to the chickee and said, "It's good those two have gone away together. I was afraid they would hate each other."

"I was too. Maybe boys can accept things grown folks can't. They might end up friends."

"That is the way it should be. But tell me now. How did you come to have that bullet in you?"

"We wiped out that pack of varmints in the ten thousand islands and one of 'em put it there. They're all dead, so you don't have to worry about them no more. You can tell your people to go there now whenever they like and they won't find trouble."

"I will do this gladly. It took great courage for you to go against those men. Nobody else would."

"It wasn't no big deal at all. We took 'em by surprise and ended it real quick." Zech became silent for a moment, and then he said, "I been thinking of something ever since you came to my place to pay respects to Pappa and told me about Tawanda. You'll have to help me with it."

"What is that?"

"I'm goin' to give money to the man at the Okeechobee trading post so he can hire a stonecutter to make a marker for Tawanda's grave. I'll draw a map, and he can bring it down here in a ox cart. You'll have to show him where to put it."

"Tawanda is resting in the Seminole way, in a casket on top of the ground."

"Then you'll have to bury it. I want you to do this for me. I want her buried like my pappa and mamma. That's the way I want it to be."

"If that is your wish I will do it. I will see to the grave this afternoon, and then watch for the stone to arrive."

"It'll probably be a good while before it gets here, but I sure thank you for letting me do this. It will give me peace of mind knowing it's done."

Zech suddenly felt overwhelmed with tiredness. He said, "I hope them boys has a good time together. Maybe they. . . ." Before he finished, he fell into a deep sleep.

Zech stayed in the village for six more days, the medicine man and two women tending him constantly, changing the poultice and giving him a strong brew made from herbs. The swelling subsided rapidly, and on the fourth day he hobbled around with the aid of a hickory cane.

Sol and Toby spent all of each day together, racing the horses and fishing in creeks and ponds. One day they killed a deer and cooked it themselves, feasting with Zech on venison steaks and swamp cabbage prepared by Toby's grandmother.

At daybreak on the seventh day, the medicine man bound Zech's wound for the final time, cautioning him to be careful on the return trip and rest often. Sol and Toby said warm good-byes, promising to see each other again someday. Then Zech and Sol mounted and rode away slowly, stopping at the edge of the woods and raising their arms in a final salute.

THIRTY-SEVEN
March
1898

"Mistuh Zech, how we gone ever put a mark on that big mother?" Frog asked, looking inside the pen.

"It'll take some doing," Zech replied, scratching his head doubtfully. "It's for sure he's not going to stand there and let us poke him with a hot iron. What we need is ole Skillit to put him on his back."

Inside the pen was a Brahma bull, its huge hump quivering with fury, fifteen hundred pounds of hostility wanting to get at the men who put him there. Zech had purchased him the previous week from a Texan who brought six of them into Kissimmee by rail and sold them for five hundred dollars each. But he hadn't warned the buyers that these were wild range bulls, not domesticated ones. The bull was delivered to Zech's corral that morning in an iron cage mounted on wagon wheels, drawn by three oxen.

"He's ugly," Glenda said distastefully, astride her horse by the fence. "Mean ugly. I don't see what you want with such a creature."

"He ain't pretty, I'll admit," Zech said, "but they say he gets by on less grass than any critter and can stand the heat and ticks better. It's the coming thing, Glenda, and all the cowmen are turning to Brahmas. Besides that, when one of them things is dressed out for beef he's going to look like any other skinned cow. Folks don't buy meat for its looks.

And you won't ever see a yellowhammer that big. Beeves his size bring twice as much money. It's like having two grown steers on four legs 'stead of eight."

"Just the same, I think he's disgusting. That hump makes him look like he's deformed."

"You want me and Lester to go in there and see can we get a rope on him?" Frog asked.

"Let's just cool him down a bit first," Zech responded. "Maybe by tomorrow he won't be so cantankerous. We'll let him simmer awhile and try him in the morning."

"I don't think he likes it here, Pappa," Sol said. "I bet if you opened the gate and turned him loose he'd be in Punta Rassa before sundown."

"Maybe so, but I'm not going to find out. He's here to service female cows, not to run a race slam across the state. Them young heifers will take the starch out of him."

The bull wheeled around constantly, nostrils flaring angrily as he snorted, pawing his front hooves menacingly. Saliva streamed from his mouth as he charged forward, shaking his head up and down, then ramming the fence with his horns and backing away.

Frog watched fearfully as the bull rammed the fence again and again, and then he said, "I ain't sure them heifers can do the job, Mistuh Zech. It might take a cypress pole right betwix his eyes to settle his nerves. You let me bash him two, three times, he'd stop carryin' on so."

"If we had some dogs we could do it," Zech said, limping to his horse. "Else he'd get his hind legs and his nose ripped out. Just let him be for now and we'll try again tomorrow. And Sol, don't you be teasin' him. You'll just make him madder."

"I won't Pappa. But if I could get on his back I'd break him."

Zech and Glenda rode off together, and when they were past hearing range Glenda said, "Frog's too old to fool with such things as that bull."

"I know," Zech replied. "I worry about him a lot. I've told him a hundred times he can feed the horses and tend the garden but he won't have none of it. An old cracker like him'll keep doin' what he's doin' till he drops dead in the saddle. There's no way to stop him, and I'm sure not going to run him off the place after all the years he's been here with us. If Pappa was alive he'd be the same way. You'd never get Pappa to sit in a rockin' chair and take it easy. He'd be out there doin' something."

"I suppose. But I'd feel better if Frog would slow down. It's time he rested some. And you don't have any business either trying to brand cows with that bad leg. You couldn't get out of the way quickly if you had to. It's downright dangerous."

"I can still move fast enough to look out for myself," Zech said, not wanting to pursue this line of conversation. "I guess I'm lucky to walk at all, but no damned cow's going to catch me flat-footed. So you best forget that."

They crossed through the hammock and came to the open area of the grove. Zech had gradually increased it to eight thousand acres, just short of his ten thousand acre goal; and now the deep green trees marched over the land like rows of silent soldiers. Fruit was no longer carted to Fort Pierce and put on slow schooners with rampant spoilage but taken to a nearby railhead and shipped rapidly to northern markets. Zech had long since admitted the truth of Tobias' prediction that oranges would become like gold growing on trees. The acreage was now so extensive it was necessary for him to hire pickers from St. Cloud and Kissimmee and Fort Pierce to come in during the season and harvest the crop.

Zech stopped beside one of the trees and examined the acorn-size fruit. "These trees are a lot better than the ones killed by the freeze. We're going to have oranges running out our ears come fall. I wish Pappa could see how well they're doing. He'd be right proud."

"I'm sure he would," Glenda agreed. They moved on silently for a moment, and then she said pensively, "The mangoes should be ripe at Fort Dallas now. I wish we could go back down there. Maybe this time we could build our little cabin."

"We'll go soon as the branding's done. The railroad has been run to Miami now, so we can ride the train all the way. One time before I die I'd like to ride one of them smoke-belchin' devils. Just once, and that'd be enough."

They continued on through the grove, enjoying being alone together, a thing that was impossible back in the hammock where cooking and washing and tending the men's needs took all of Glenda's time. She said, "Zech, why don't we go away together this summer and take a trip. Just the two of us. We've never done anything like that, and it's about time we did something just for pleasure. We've got the money to go anywhere we want to go. We could ride the train up north. Wouldn't you like to see places like Washington and New York and Boston just once? They seem so foreign to us here, they could as well be in Europe."

"I've never given it any thought, but we could go there if you'd like to. Sol could look after things while we're gone. Fact is, he could take over this place now and run it by himself."

"That's another thing I've been thinking on," Glenda said. "Sol will be fifteen next week, and I've taught him everything I can. He can read and write and work figures as good as anyone, but there's more to learning than that. Maybe we should send him off for more schooling. There's a college now in DeLand."

"Send Sol off to college?" Zech questioned, amused by the thought of it. "How'd we do that? Hog tie him and drag him there? If he ever got to one he'd probably get kicked out for riding his horse into the classroom."

"Be serious, Zech!" Glenda admonished. "It's something to consider. Someday he'll need to know more than riding horses and herding cows and what little I've taught him. You've said yourself Florida is changing."

"It's doing that for sure, and I wouldn't want Sol to be any part of it. I'd hate to even think of him living someday in a place like Palm Beach. Out here is where he belongs, just like you and me and Pappa and Mamma."

Glenda decided not to pursue it. "At least think about it," she concluded. "We could do without him here this fall. He could go for a while just to see if he likes it. It's worth considering."

"I'll think on it, and if that's what Sol wants to do I won't stand in his way. But it's up to him, Glenda. It's his choice, and I don't think he'll want to do it. He's where he wants to be."

"Maybe so," Glenda sighed, "but there are other things in life besides horses and cows."

Zech remembered hearing that before, and it brought back painful memories. He regretted being so adamant. He stopped his horse and said, "Glenda, I didn't mean to sound the way I did. It's just that I fear for the kind of life we've lived. It's slipping away. I don't want to hold Sol here if he wants something else. I'm sorry for all I said. I got no right to say where he can live and how he can live. Pappa never said that to me. Come fall we'll speak to Sol about more schooling. I'd hate for him to grow up dumb and stupid like me."

"You're not dumb or stupid!" Glenda said, smiling at him. "You're just the way I want you. And it's time we turned back to the house. I don't want those hungry men to come in and think they'll get no supper.

That would make me the one who's dumb and stupid."

Zech shouted, "Sol, stay out of there and let us handle it! And Glenda, keep your horse well away from the fence. If that critter comes bustin' out of the pen, give him a wide berth."

The bull had not settled down as Zech hoped, and now he dashed from one side of the pen to another, his eyes wild and his mouth foaming with rage.

Frog said to Zech, "Me and Lester'll go in there and try to get him on the ground. If we do, we can tie his feet and we'll have him for sure. I'd like to be the one to stick a hot iron to him. Only I'd like to ram it up his rear."

"Be careful," Zech cautioned. "If we can't get a mark on him we'll just turn him loose without one. I don't think nobody can catch him and steal him. That Texan must of had some kind of fun catching him and putting him in a boxcar."

"If he did it, we can," Frog said. "I ain't never seen a bull yet that couldn't be throwed one way or another. But I'd sure like to see ole Skillit standin' here now. He'd have that thing down in nothin' flat."

Frog and Lester eased through the gate, and the bull turned to them immediately, pawing his feet and snorting. Frog said, "Move over to the right real slow and draw his attention. If he comes at you, dodge out of the way and I'll put a rope on him."

The bull watched both men for a moment more; then he was attracted to the movement. He snorted again and charged directly at Lester. Frog shouted, "Get outen the way, Lester! Hurry!"

Lester hit the split-rail fence scrambling. He went up the side like a frightened lizard and rolled over the top just as horns crashed into wood. Frog threw the rope, and the noose dropped down over the neck and became taut. Then all hell broke loose. The bull wheeled and charged away, dragging the struggling Frog in the dirt.

Zech shouted, "Turn loose, Frog! Let go and get the hell out of there!"

Frog didn't let go. He made one circle of the pen behind the flying bull and jumped to his feet when the movement stopped momentarily. It took less than two seconds for the bull to sight its prey and charge again, surprising Frog by its quickness, coming at him full bore with no chance to jump aside. One horn smashed through his rib cage and sent him hurling eight feet backward.

Zech opened the gate and ran for the rope, his bad leg tripping him up and sending him sprawling beside Frog, knocking the breath from him. He glanced up as the bull rushed past him and out the gate; then he watched helplessly as it wheeled about and charged the horse, hearing the thud as horns met flesh, then seeing the horse and Glenda topple to the ground.

Zech scrambled to his feet and watched horrified as the horns rammed into Glenda, going into her stomach and ripping upward, staying there. He heard her scream, "Zech!. . . . Zech!. . . . Help me!. . ."

The bull raised its head upward, lifting her into the air, suspended on the horns as she screamed again, "Oh God!. . . .Zech!. . ."

The first bullet caused the bull to stagger, and the second brought it down. As it hit the ground Glenda came loose and tumbled away. Zech ran from the pen as fast as he could, snatching the smoking rifle away from Sol, firing into the dead animal again and again until the chamber was empty, then falling down beside Glenda.

Blood gushed from her mouth and from her open stomach as she tried to speak, "Zech. . . Zech. . ." It turned to a gurgle, and then silence came as her head rolled to the side.

"Oh no. . ." Zech moaned. "Oh no. . . Glenda. . . ."

He fell across the body, soaking himself in blood, unaware as Lester shook his shoulder, saying urgently, "Mistuh Zech! Mistuh Zech! Frog's hurt real bad! What you want me to do?"

He finally looked up and said, "Go and get the buckboard. Hurry! And bring blankets from the house."

Sol leaned back against the fence, his face white and his legs rubbery as he retched; then he staggered forward and said, "Is she dead, Pappa? Is Mamma dead?"

"She's gone from us, Sol. Get on your horse and go to the house as fast as you can. Fetch back the shotgun and a sack of shells."

Sol looked at his father in astonishment, puzzled by such an order at such a time; then he jumped on his horse and galloped away.

Zech was still holding Glenda in his arms when Sol and Lester returned. His eyes were glazed with anger as he got up and took the shotgun from Sol. He inserted shells and fired pointblank into the bull, doing it again and again until the carcass was cut in half, its entrails blown ten feet over the ground. Then he put the shotgun into the buckboard and went inside the pen to Frog.

Frog was lying still, his eyes hazed but seeing, and when Zech dropped down beside him he said, "Ain't this some crap, Mistuh Zech. All the things I've done and got by with, to be did in now by a friggin' bull."

"Don't talk," Zech said, pulling Frog's shirt away, seeing a six-inch hole where Frog's side had been. "We'll get you to the house as quick as we can. Then I'll send for a doctor in Kissimmee."

"I'm old enough to know better than that," Frog said weakly. "There's no need for a doctor. Did that critter hurt Miz Glenda when he went for her horse?"

"Yes, Frog, he did. He hurt her real bad."

"Lordy me. . . I'm sorry to hear that, Mistuh Zech. I wish I could 'a kept him here in the pen, but there wadden no way. He was just too strong to handle."

Zech and Lester lifted Frog up gently and carried him to the buckboard. Then Zech picked up Glenda and place her beside him. He said to Sol, "Leave that varmint right there where he's lying till the buzzards pick him clean. When there ain't nothin' left but bones, I want you to throw 'em in the river. I don't want to ever see nothin' more of him again."

Sol nodded in agreement as Zech climbed onto the buckboard and drove away.

When they reached the hammock Zech and Lester put Frog on his bunk; then Zech carried Glenda into the house alone. He came back out and said to Lester, "Go down to the barn and start a coffin. I just can't bring myself to do it, Lester. You'll have to. And while you're at it, you might as well make two."

"I know, Mistuh Zech. Frog's not goin' to last long. I doubt he'll be here at nightfall. I gave him a big shot of rum to ease the pain, and I'll go back in an hour and give him some more. And don't worry about the coffins. I'll take care of it."

Zech sat on the stoop, his face buried in his hands, remembering, thinking of things done and not done, said and not said, hearing vividly the conversation of only yesterday and the plans that were now canceled forever. He also remembered the day of Emma's death when Tobias urged him to do things for Glenda before it was too late.

He was unaware of Sol sitting beside him until he heard the sobbing.

He looked up and said, "Sol, don't ever get yourself tied up with a woman. It's like owning dogs. You get to liking them, and it hurts powerful when they go away. And they all go away. If you get to lovin' a woman too much, it'll bring pain and sorrow when she leaves you. It's done hurt me twice, and the pain of it is pure awful. It'll never go away. Don't let it happen to you."

"I don't understand, Pappa," Sol said, wiping away the tears. "Wasn't you glad to live with Mamma?"

"That's just it, son. I liked it too much. And now that it's all done, I'm not sure the joy of it can overcome the pain and sorrow."

"I still don't understand," Sol said, perplexed.

"I hope you don't ever have the feel of it and have to understand. Maybe it won't come to you like it has to me. And besides that, I know I'm not makin' sense. I didn't expect nothin' like this to happen, Sol. I don't know what I'm going to do without your mamma. I don't rightly know if I can make it or not, or even if I want to try."

"We'll be fine Pappa," Sol said, putting his arm around Zech's shoulder. "Mamma would want us to try. She wouldn't give up on nothing, and you know that. I'll learn to cook and wash and do all the things she did for us. We'll make out somehow, Pappa."

"That's not exactly the part of her I'll miss," Zech said, knowing now he would have to carry on for Sol's sake, whether he wanted to or not. "But the stuff you're talking about we can't do and run this place too. We'll need a man to replace Frog and a woman to do the rest of it. I'll go first to Fort Drum and tell Glenda's folks about this. Then I'll go to Fort Pierce and see if I can hire somebody with a wife to come live with us. If I can't get somebody there I'll try Kissimmee. But we can talk about this later. Right now I need to look in on Frog."

Frog had moments of delirium and moments of rationality, and it was just after dark when he emerged from the fog and opened his eyes, seeing Zech sitting beside the bunk. He smiled, and then he said, "Mistuh Zech, I want to ask a favor of you."

"Sure, Frog. Anything you say."

"I come here to help on one cattle drive, the first one your Pappa made to Punta Rassa, and I been here ever since. This hammock's the only home I've had since before the war. I'd like to be buried right alongside Mistuh Tobias and Miz Emma. Don't put me way off in the woods by myself, Mistuh Zech. Please don't do it."

"You'll rest right next to Mamma and Pappa, but I would have done that even if you hadn't asked."

"That's not all of it, Mistuh Zech. I got a good bit of gold over yonder in my locker, and I want you to take it and get me a headstone, like the ones over the other graves. I been here so long now I feel like part of the family, and I'd like the stone to say Frog MacIvey. When ole Skillit dies his is goin' to say Skillit MacIvey, and that's what I want too. Would it be too much of a shame to you if you did this for me?"

Zech reached down and touched the gnarled hand. "It wouldn't be a shame at all, Frog. You're as much family as anybody, and I'll be right proud to get the stone just the way you want it. Mamma and Pappa will like it too, and so will Glenda."

"I thank you, Mistuh Zech," Frog said, smiling again. "I'll tell Mistuh Tobias you done a good job here after he was gone, and about all them trees you planted. He'll be right pleased. . . ."

He drifted away again, and fifteen minutes later he was dead.

It took Zech and Lester and Sol two hours after daybreak to dig the holes, and then the coffins were brought to the gravesite one by one and lowered into the ground.

The three of them stood there silently as birds chattered above them, Zech's eyes now dry because all the tears had flooded out of him the night before as he struggled alone to put the wedding dress on Glenda. A red fox suddenly popped out of a bush, stared at the subdued assembly for a moment, and then scurried away.

Zech finally said, "Lord. . .I'm not going to say much about this, because if I do, I'm not sure I can stand it. It seems a man is born into life just to suffer and bear grief, and I done suffered enough of it. I want You to forgive me for buyin' that damned bull, 'cause all I done it for was to make money, and I'll never do nothin' like that again. So help me, Lord, I promise it, but it's too late now to help Glenda and Frog. They suffered because of what I done. Lord. . .bless Glenda. She was as fine a woman as You ever made, and I loved her truly, although I done a thing that might make it look otherwise. But that was my doing, not hers, and I'm glad she never knew about it. And bless old Frog too. He done the best he could, Lord. . .the best he could. Make them a home with Mamma and Pappa. . .and see to it they're happy now. . .Amen."

Zech then turned to Sol, "I'm going to go now, son, to Fort Drum first and then to Fort Pierce. When you and Lester get done covering the graves, I want you to get all the flowers you can find in the woods and put them on your mamma's grave. She liked pretty things, and she'd appreciate you doin' this. And I would too."

After talking with Glenda's father at the store, Zech turned the horse south, counting each step, measuring the distance of two miles. It was still there, just as it was eighteen years ago, the cypress stand where he stopped on their wedding day to wash sweat from his face. He dismounted and walked beneath the trees, dropping down and dipping his hands into the same spring. Then he walked to the palmetto clump, the one where Glenda sat on a blanket waiting for him to find her, then beckoning him. He heard the words, as strongly as if just spoken, "Don't you realize we're married now, Zech? We don't have to wait any longer."

He sat on the ground, on the exact spot they spent their wedding night, remembering, seeing her on Ishmael with him at the Fort Drum frolic, overwhelming him with the smell of lilacs, feeling her softness as he locked his arms around her, holding her gently in the saddle.

It suddenly came out of him, all the tears he thought were gone forever, all the pent-up grief that numbed him as he stood looking down at a cypress box that would someday rot and become only a minute part of this vast earth he had roamed since boyhood.

He said softly, "Oh God, Glenda. . .I'm sorry. . .I'm so sorry. . . ." Then he got up and rode away.

THIRTY-EIGHT
Summer
1905

A thunderhead formed in the north as Zech plunged his horse into Turkey Creek, heading for the north corral some five miles from the hammock. He rode with anticipation, wanting to see the new purebred Hereford bull that had been picked up at the railroad and taken straight to the corral for branding before release on the north range.

He watched the sky as he rode briskly, hoping to beat the rain, and soon he came to a small pen off to the left of a barn. Sol and Lester were there, along with the man who replaced Frog, Tim Lardy. Sol watched his father ride up and dismount; then he came to him and said, "He's a real beauty, Pappa. He ought to be worth ever cent we paid for him."

Zech walked to the pen and gazed at the polled bull, a sleek creature weighing fifteen hundred pounds, deep red with white splotches on its head and legs, hornless, with a ring in its nose so it could be led easily. Compared to the Brahma that wreaked such havoc and death, the Hereford was as docile as a house cat. It paid no heed as Lester ran a curry comb across its back. The letters 'MCI' were freshly burned on its left rear flank.

"He's sure a fine one," Zech said, "and I think you're right, Sol. He's worth the money. Beeves bred from him ought to bring a mighty fair price. I'm glad we've got all them young heifers to put with him soon's they come in heat."

Thunder rumbled across the prairie as lightning flashed in the north, and soon the wind picked up, blowing loose hay from the barn door. Sol said, "Going to rain soon, Pappa. We best head back to the house else we get a drenching."

"You and the rest go on," Zech said. "I'll stay here a short while and ride in after you. I want to look some more. After we turn him loose he'll be interested in them heifers, and he won't be as easy to catch up to. It starts to rain I'll put him in the barn and ride on in as soon as I can."

"All right, Pappa. We'll see you back at the house."

The drive in the summer of 1898 had been the last for MacIvey cattle, and it was the one that set Zech on a new course, concentrating on smaller numbers of quality beeves and abandoning the scrawny yellow-hammers. All shipments to market were now made by rail, and the old trails leading to Punta Rassa were a thing of the past, bush-covered but not forgotten.

It was during the trip after Glenda's death to find a new hand and a housekeeper that Zech learned in Fort Pierce of the sinking of the U.S. battleship *Maine* in Havana Harbor and the impending war. He was advised to get his cattle to Punta Rassa as soon as possible since the war would put an end to the market there. Although consumed with grief and not really caring, he knew he must do something with the cows; so he decided to make the drive as soon as the herd was assembled.

Before the roundup was half finished, war was declared on Spain, and when finally they set out for Punta Rassa it was too late. A rider on the prairie told Zech to turn away, for no further shipments were being made and the market was closed, but that the army was buying cattle at Fort Brooke outside Tampa, the embarkation port for troops being sent to Cuba.

It was a small herd of nine hundred beeves, and when they reached Fort Brooke in June, all were sold at an inflated government price of forty dollars each, more than twice what they would have brought in Punta Rassa. The beef would be used as food for soldiers stationed there and in Tampa.

A great wall of smoke blocked the sky in the west, making Zech think the port city was burning, and when he asked a soldier about this he was told it came from fires set to drive flies from the army camps and corrals. The boom of cannon fire was constant, and this, he was told, was to disperse germs. Malaria, typhoid fever and yellow fever had broken out in the camps, and all the smoke, fire and commotion were used to battle the diseases.

They decided to ride into the port to see the ships assembled there to transport the troops to Cuba, and along the railroad tracks they passed hundreds of boxcars backed up one to another, filled with war supplies, rotting food and men, army volunteers who were there without uniforms or guns, sweltering in the torrid heat and throwing up all over each other. The tracks were also lined with prostitutes, beckoning the miserable men to come into tents dotting nearby fields.

The army camps stretched from Ybor City into Tampa, and streets there were also crowded with prostitutes competing with men and boys selling everything from stale lemonade to Cuban cigars. Barrels of burning tar lined the streets and again were used to drive away flies and germs.

They rode past the port docks, seeing lines of steamers awaiting the troops; then they went onto the grounds of the Tampa Bay Hotel, now occupied with army officers and their wives, curious tourists who had come to gawk at the war activities, newspaper correspondents, hucksters of all kinds, and more prostitutes doing a brisk business with all of them. The huge garish building with its strange turrets reminded Zech of what he had seen at Palm Beach, and the entire city seemed to be a repulsive, grotesque circus, not a place of serious preparation for war. He turned away in disgust, and they made a hasty retreat from Tampa back into the countryside. Zech swore he would never again go into any town other than Fort Pierce or Kissimmee, and this was a promise he would keep.

The year after this final drive, Zech finished fencing all of the MacIvey land, finally putting an end to the fence-cutting by hiring eight men from Arcadia to patrol the property with orders to shoot to kill. After two months on the job and the wounding of five would-be cutters and the killing of two, it all stopped; then the gunslingers rode away.

Twenty thousand acres were eventually put into orange trees, and the other ten thousand used for cattle. Zech upgraded his herd by mixing the range cows with Herefords, gradually breeding his cows to seven-eighths pure Hereford blood; but he never again purchased a Brahma, the bitter memories lingering on.

He planted winter grass for the cows and supplemented the summer feeding with hay and grains, discontinuing the practice of letting herds graze freely across the prairies and following them, although other cowmen still roamed constantly until market time. And because he isolated his cattle from wandering range herds he escaped the devastation other cowmen received when tick fever first became rampant, wiping out entire herds. He was the first to build his own dipping vat to kill ticks, doing it voluntarily at a time when most ranchers bitterly resisted such a practice because of its cost and the fact that tax men would come to the vats and count cattle for tax roles, a thing they could not do with wandering prairie herds and those kept wild in swamps. Zech figured it was best to spend the dipping money and pay the cattle tax rather than risk losing everything, and it paid off for him. When other cowmen were losing herds, giving up and abandoning the land, his healthy steers brought forty and fifty dollars each.

He made four trips back to Okeechobee to see Toby and also to buy the land where the custard-apple forest was located. For ten thousand five hundred dollars in gold he purchased seventy thousand acres stretching from the lake's southwest shore to the edge of the great cypress swamp. Glenda had been fascinated by his tales of the place, and wanted to see it, but he had never taken her there because of the nearby Indian village, fearing that she would somehow learn of Tawanda and Toby. He bought it because of not taking her there, wanting to leave it in its natural state and be sure that no one ever put axes or machines to it, destroying it as the land was destroyed around Palm Beach. He suspected this was also happening at Miami, but he had not returned there to see.

All of the improvements he made to the orange grove and the cattle operation he made for Sol, not for himself. After Glenda's death he had no use for money or any desire for anything except to build something better for Sol, his only remaining link with Glenda and all things past. Surplus money from oranges and cattle still went into trunks stored in the old house.

He also offered to send Sol away to college as he promised Glenda, but the offer was firmly refused. Sol had no interest in further schooling, wanting only to stay on the land and be with his father.

As the first drops of rain pelted down Zech hooked one finger through the nose ring and led the bull into the barn, guiding it as easily as he would a horse. He put it in a stall with fresh hay; then he went to the door and looked out. The soft shower turned into a downpour, blocking his view of the nearby corral, causing him to retreat further into the barn to escape the pounding water.

Rain always brought memories of Glenda, for some of their happiest times were spent inside the old house, listening to the patter on the cypress roof. And if it was winter, they snuggled together for warmth, hoping it would continue throughout the night; then awakening at dawn still together, relaxed and refreshed as sunlight streamed into the room, signalling a new day washed clean.

It also reminded him of wildflowers in spring, prairies splashed with green, orange trees bursting with new life, and plains scorched the yellow color of death when it did not come down from cloudless skies.

Black clouds boiled angrily overhead as the rain continued for another hour, tempting him to stay inside the dry barn for a time longer, but knowing that this kind of summer thunderstorm could last well into the night. Sol would be worried, and possibly come out into the storm looking for him, and the worst he could do was soak himself on the return trip.

He mounted his horse and rode away, straining his eyes to see through the deluge, feeling water pour from the brim of his hat and stream downward inside his shirt.

He soon came to the bank of the creek and gazed across it, seeing that the level had risen two feet, watching brown bubbling foam rush past him as the creek water surged toward its distant rendezvous with the river.

The horse slid and then stumbled as it went down the muddy bank, plunging headlong into the water, causing Zech to be jolted from the saddle as the horse and rider went under and then surfaced a few yards downstream.

Zech thought he had come free, but then he felt a tugging as the horse swam desperately against the current. He knew now that his lame foot was caught in the stirrup, dragging him downward. He held his breath as he went under, trying vainly to free the foot, feeling water rush over him, holding his breath until his lungs could stand it no longer and screamed for mercy; then he let go and sucked for air, pulling a flood of brown water inside him.

A rapid succession of faces and things suddenly rushed through his mind, Tobias and Emma and Glenda and Tawanda and Toby; Ishmael tied to the garden fence, Nip and Tuck baying, Skillit in a clump of palmetto; Frog eating ten biscuits and asking for more; all of them looking at him, beckoning him to come and be with them; and then he was free, free of the pain in his leg, free of the struggling horse and the rushing water. Sol then came before him, and his last conscious thought was, "Don't grieve, Sol. . . . Don't ever grieve. . . ."

The horse kicked frantically, pulling its load yard by yard across the creek, and when it reached the far bank and struggled upward, Zech's lifeless form dangled from the stirrup, the lame leg twisted grotesquely.

After resting for a moment the horse started home, moving automatically in the right direction, paying no heed to the saddle pulled sideways by the trailing man, thinking only of the hay stacked in bales in the barn.

Sol was standing on the stoop, beyond reach of the rain, watching, worried because Zech had not yet returned. In a few minutes he would go after him, wishing now he had insisted that his father come back with the rest of them, but not expecting such a flood. Then he saw the horse, moving slowly through the woods, at first seemingly alone; but when it came into the clearing and turned toward the barn, he saw a form being dragged through the mud, the body of a man.

Sol jumped from the stoop screaming, "Pappa! Pappa!"

He could not untangle the foot, so he ran into the house and returned with a knife, cutting the stirrup from the saddle and then carrying Zech inside.

THIRTY-NINE
1908

Jessie Lardy, Tim's wife and MacIvey cook and housekeeper for the past eight years, came bustling into the kitchen before sunup. She looked like a white Pearlie Mae, short and overweight, an apron strapped to her, a red bandanna covering her hair.

Sol was sitting at the table, studying a pile of papers in front of him. Jessie put more wood in the stove and said, "I can't sleep when Tim's not here. He should 'a been back two days ago with the load of barrels. He must 'a gone to Jacksonville 'stead of Fort Pierce. I'm goin' to skin that man alive when he gets here!" Then more calmly, "I seen the light and decided I'd come on over. Have you been sittin' there all night, Mister Sol?"

"No, Jessie. I just got up a few minutes ago. I thought I'd go over these deeds and land descriptions one more time before I go."

Jessie picked up the coal oil lamp and looked at it; then she put it back on the table. "That ain't so, Mister Sol! I filled this lamp when I left here last night, and now it's almost empty. You ain't even been to bed. A trip like you got ahead of you today, you ought to have rested. I'll fix us some coffee, and then I'll make breakfast for you."

"Just coffee, Jessie. I'm not hungry."

Jessie put the pot on one lid of the stove and said, "Lordy, Mister Sol, I sure hates to see you leave. I know it's lonely here for a young man like you, without no girls or other young people around. But how

362

come you can't go up to Kissimmee and get yourself a good woman and come on back here to live?"

"It's not that at all," Sol said, pushing the papers aside. "I can stand it being lonely out here, but every time I ride through the woods or go into the grove or tend cows, there's a ghost looking at me. It's like Mamma and Pappa never left. And Grampy and Granny too. I just can't take it any longer, Jessie. I've got to get away from all these faces staring at me. I've got to try something different."

"I understand that, Mister Sol. I just hates to see you go. It won't be the same here without you."

"You'll like the Clayton family. They're good folks. They'll be moving in sometime this afternoon."

Sol had hired a Kissimmee man named Ron Clayton, his wife and three teenaged boys to come live on the place. Clayton would take over as manager of the citrus and cattle operations and be paid a monthly salary plus a percentage of the yearly profits. He had already made several visits to the homestead to study the operation.

Jessie set two cups of coffee on the table. "Maybe so. But they're still not you, Mister Sol."

Sol took a sip of the steaming brew and said, "One thing's for sure, Jessie. I don't have the problem most folks have when they move. There's not much to take with me. Pappa and Grampy had only one suit, and they're buried in them. There's a few dresses of mamma's still in there. You can have them if you want and see if you can let them out and make them fit. I'm taking Grampy's old shotgun and the rifles, Pappa and Grampy's whips, and a few other small things. And that's about it. I'll store it all in the cabin at Punta Rassa. All that stuff's not much for two lifetimes of MacIvey's, is it?"

"I guess not, Mister Sol. But they sure left behind a heap more than the mess of junk some folks leave. You can't haul memories in a buckboard, but they're sure there. And they left you enough to last a lifetime."

Lester came in, poured a cup of coffee and sat at the table. Sol noticed how much he had aged so quickly, or perhaps he was just taking a close look at him for the first time. He was as frail and stooped as Frog during his last days.

Sol watched him saucer and blow the coffee, and then he said, "When you get done with that, Lester, I'd appreciate it if you'll go down to the barn and hitch up the buckboard. Put two horses to it, and throw in my saddle. I want to leave soon after sunup."

"Not before you eat!" Jessie said emphatically. "I'll fix you a whop-pin' big breakfast that'll hold you for a while."

"Coffee's fine, Jessie. I couldn't eat a bite this morning. Honest I couldn't."

"You want me to tie Tiger behind the buckboard?" Lester asked.

"No. He's too old now to go with me. But I want you to see to him real good. Turn him loose in the north range and let him do what he wants to do, and give him plenty to eat. I hate to leave him, but he's just too old. He'll be happy here."

"What about your mamma's horse?"

"Do the same with it." Sol sipped the coffee, and then he said, "I've talked to Clayton about you, Lester, and about Tim and Jessie. All of you have a home here as long as you wish. If it gets to a point where you don't do nothing but tend the garden or just sit on the porch that's fine with me. You'll stay on the payroll. I've told this to Clayton, and he understands. None of you don't ever have to leave unless you want to."

"I appreciate that, Mistuh Sol," Lester said gratefully. "I wouldn't have no idea what to do if I left. We'll all look after things real good. Me and Tim'll keep the graves up like you said, and never let no weeds get to them."

"And I'll put fresh flowers on them ever week," Jessie said. "You don't have to worry about that."

Jessie then started sobbing, and Sol said, "Now stop that, Jessie! I don't want no blubbering. It's hard enough for me to leave as it is. And it's not like I'm going off forever. I'll come back as often as I can to check the books and the sales receipts and see how things are going. So you stop that or you'll have me doing it!"

"I couldn't help it, Mister Sol," she said, wiping her eyes. "I won't do it no more."

Lester got up and said, "I'll go on now and bring the buckboard up here, then we'll load your trunk and the other stuff."

Sol was taking one trunk of money with him. The others had been put in one room of Tim and Jessie's cabin and padlocked, Sol cautioning them not to give the key to anyone or let anyone in the room.

Sol followed Lester outside and turned south toward the oak grove and the graves. A dim light was just coming into the hammock, and the eastern sky was tinted red.

He stood before the five stones, all marked MacIvey, two of them covered with wilted flowers. Then he said, "I'm sorry, Pappa, to be leaving, but I just got to go. It's not that I'm afraid to keep on my shoulders what you had to take from Grampy, or what he took himself from the wilderness. I don't know how to explain it, but it's a thing I've got to do.

"And Mamma, I remember that time you wanted to stay in the fancy hotel at Palm Beach and they wouldn't let Pappa have a room. I'll stay there for you someday, Mamma. I promise you I will.

"Grampy, Granny, Frog – all of you – rest easy. I'll come back to see you again soon."

Then he turned and went back to the house.

As soon as the buckboard arrived they loaded the trunk and the few other things Sol was taking. As he climbed to the seat Jessie said, "God bless you, Mister Sol!"

"You too, Jessie. Tell Tim good-bye for me, and don't be too hard on him because he's late. And Lester, you take care of yourself. You're about the last oldtime cracker left."

The horses trotted away, vanishing quickly in the early morning mist. He headed east first, going to the site of the original corral. When he reached the split-rail fence he stopped and gazed at it, into the empty pen, remembering all those things that had taken place here during his lifetime and before, so much MacIvey blood and sweat and tears staining the ground. The corral was no longer used since there were no more spring roundups of wild cows, but he had given orders to Clayton to maintain it and never tear it down for any reason.

He could almost hear the whips popping and the shouts and the pounding hooves of cows and the smell of scorched flesh as hot irons burned into hides. For a moment he saw it all, thundering out of the mist, becoming alive and real again, then vanishing as suddenly as it appeared. He looked once more, seeing only an empty corral; then he turned the buckboard west toward Punta Rassa and left hurriedly.

FORTY
South Okeechobee
1911

The two tracts of land Zech had purchased south of Lake Okeechobee were right in the middle of what was to become the most extensive farmland in South Florida. Sol suspected this when he rode his horse onto the section southeast of the lake and examined the rich soil and the lushness of the vegetation. As he gazed out over the land and then explored it, riding past ponds and sloughs filled with snakes and alligators and turtles, coming to areas of open glades where the shadows of egrets and herons and ibises glided over the sawgrass, his first thought was, "How the hell do you turn a place like this into a farm?"

Upon riding further south he found the answer. Dredges had already worked here for five years, cutting drainage canals across the land, carrying away the water, then using men and machines to strip the land bare and turn it into open fields.

He asked questions everywhere, slowly finding answers, learning who owns the dredges and machines and how much they cost and where to go and who to see. He built himself a small house on the lake's south shore, and then he set out to transform the land.

He hired dredges to gash the earth and drain it, paying with Spanish gold, then the men and saws and machines to rip out the giant bald cypress and the hickory and the oak and the cabbage palm and the palmetto and the cocoplum bushes, pushing mounds of dirt over the sawgrass and the seas of violet-blue pickerel weed. It took more than a year, but he gradually turned hammocks and Everglades into fields stretching as far as the eye could see, soil so black it looked like soot. Then he formed the MacIvey Produce Company and hired workers to plant tomatoes and beans and squash and celery and corn and cucumbers and lettuce and okra, eventually becoming a supplier of vegetables to the growing cities of Palm Beach and Fort Lauderdale and Miami and Fort Myers and Tampa and Saint Petersburg, also shipping vast quantities by rail to markets in Chicago and New York and Boston.

Then he turned his attention to the land southwest of the lake, attacking the custard-apple forest with more dredges and men and machines, cutting down the ancient trees with their canopies of thick moon vines, ripping out the lush beds of lacy ferns, strewing the ground with thousands of air plants and wild orchids that soon shriveled and then disintegrated, burning all of it in huge bonfires that blackened the sky with smoke, slowly transforming jungle into more fields that were destined to put more vegetables onto tables in Palm Beach and Fort Lauderdale and Miami and New York and Boston. Some of this land would also be planted with sugar cane.

Near the end of the clearing of the custard-apple area, Sol decided that since he was so near he would ride down to the Indian village. He had not been there since moving to Okeechobee, and he was sure Toby Cypress did not know about Zech's death and had wondered why Zech never again returned after his last visit seven years ago.

When Sol reached the village it was still as he remembered, the cluster of chickees, the banana trees, a small garden in an open area to the left. Smoke drifted into the thatched roof of one chickee where an old woman tended a cooking pot that smelled of stew.

Sol went to her and said, "I'm looking for Toby Cypress. Do you know where I can find him?"

"His chickee is the last one toward the edge of the woods," she replied, pointing.

A woman in her early twenties was sitting on a cypress stool, operatng a foot-pedal Singer sewing machine. Two boys, ages four and two, were playing just outside the chickee. As Sol approached, the woman stopped the machine and watched him. He said, "I'm looking for Toby

Cypress."

"I am his wife, Minnie," the woman said, eyeing him curiously. "Could you be Sol MacIvey?"

"Yes, I am," Sol replied, surprised, "How did you know?"

"Toby has spoken of you often. I guessed it because of the hair. He said you have red hair, and we do not see such as that often. Toby is hunting but should return soon. Would you sit here and wait?"

"Yes, I would. I haven't seen Toby in a long time. How is he?"

"He's fine."

"What of Keith Tiger? He was a good friend of my pappa and my grandfather. I could visit with him while I'm waiting."

"Keith Tiger died five years ago."

Sol then became silent, not knowing what more to say and feeling uneasy. He watched for a moment, and then he said, "Are those your boys?"

"Yes. And we will have another in six months. Do you have sons too?"

"No, I don't have any children. I'm not married yet. I've been too busy to give it much thought."

"If you do not marry and have sons, how can you pass on the name of MacIvey?" she asked seriously. "Nothing should be more important to you than that."

The question embarrassed Sol, and he didn't know how to answer since she seemed so concerned about it. He said, "Maybe someday. But I'm glad you and Toby have a family. That's real good. They're part MacIvey, you know."

"Yes, I know."

Toby suddenly came around the side of the banana clump carrying two huge cane-cutter rabbits. When he saw Sol beneath the chickee he dropped them and exclaimed, "Sol! How long have you been here? If I had known I would have returned sooner!"

The two of them clasped hands vigorously, and Sol said, "I've been here just a short time. I enjoyed visiting with Minnie."

"You have grown into a man since you were here last," Toby said, smiling. "I have to look up to you now, like a pine sapling. But for the red hair, you look exactly like Father. How is he, Sol? I have wondered about him."

"He's dead, Toby. He died six years ago."

"I'm sorry to hear that," Toby said sadly. "But that is why he never returned. How did it happen?"

Both of them sat on the bench, and Sol said, "He was crossing a creek and his horse threw him. His lame foot tangled in the stirrup and he drowned."

"That's too bad. I guess the bad foot must have caused it, for he was the best horse rider I have ever known. He was a good man, Sol, and I hate to know he's gone."

"It hurt me too, real bad, and I was a long time getting over it. But I don't think Pappa hated to go. He never seemed to get over my mamma being killed by a Brahma bull. He blamed himself for it, and after it happened, he didn't really have much interest in anything."

Sol realized immediately he should not talk further about Glenda since the two of them were of different mothers. But before he could change the conversation to something else Toby said, "The stone that Father sent for my mother was brought here since your last visit. Would you like to see it?"

"Yes, I would."

They got up and walked along a path that wound through thick woods and then widened into a clearing surrounded by cabbage palms and pond cypress. Several weathered coffins were on top of the ground and had frames of thin poles built over them. The one stone stood out like a beacon in the middle of the burial ground. Sol walked to it and gazed at the words:

Tawanda MacIvey

Beloved

He finally said, "It's real nice, Toby. Real nice. I'm glad Pappa did this."

"It is a fine stone," Toby said proudly. "I come here often to look. Mother would be pleased with the name Father put on it."

They went back to the chickee and again sat on the bench. Toby said, "Are you still raising cattle at your ranch on the Kissimmee?"

"Yes, but I don't live there anymore. I left a man in charge of it and moved to the south shore of Okeechobee three years ago."

"You've been so close by for three years and haven't come here?" Toby questioned. "Why is this, Sol? We could have hunted and fished together like we once did."

"I wanted to, but I've been too busy. Pappa owned two sections of land below the lake, and I've been clearing them for farming. We're working up north of here now."

Toby's eyes flashed surprise. He said, "You mean it is you who is destroying the land? I cannot believe this, Sol. Father would have never put an ax to the custard-apple trees. He loved that place. Why is it you are doing this?"

Sol was shocked by the reaction. He said hesitantly, "Like I said, Toby, I'm turning it into farm land. People in the new cities have to eat, and there's beginning to be more and more of them. I'm growing vegetables in the fields."

"Animals have to eat too, and so do birds, and so do we!" Toby said angrily. "Will your infernal machines not stop until they come here and crush my mother's grave? I hope they never enter this swamp, or go into Pay-Hay-Okee. If they do, you will have destroyed us too, all of us!"

Sol was totally dumbfounded, wishing he had never mentioned his work. He said, "It's just swamp, Toby. And there's plenty more of it."

"It is not just swamp!" Toby responded harshly. "It is God you are killing. He put the land here for all creatures to enjoy, and you are destroying it. When you destroy the land you destroy God. Do you not know this? Go now and stand in the middle of your fields. Count the deer you see, and the alligators, and the fish, and the birds. Count them, Sol, and then tell me how many are still there. You have crushed them with your damned machines, and if you do not stop what you are doing, there will soon be no more! They will be gone forever!"

Sol got up and said, "I'm sorry you feel this way, Toby. But it's my land now, and I have the right to do whatever I want with it."

"You are a traitor to the wishes of your father!" Toby snapped, his face now flushed red with anger. "He told me himself he purchased the custard-apple forest so no one could ever put an ax to it, and you have leveled it to the ground! He would die a second death if he knew this!"

"He told you that?" Sol asked, surprised. "He never said anything like that to me."

"Why should he? He never dreamed you would someday come down here and do what you have done. Wasn't the cattle ranch enough for you to make money? Where will you go from here with your machines? I am no longer proud to call you brother!"

Sol couldn't take it longer. He said regretfully, "I'm really sorry you said that, Toby. I've only done what I thought was right, but no matter what a person does, he can't please everybody. Someone will object.

I'm sorry." Then he mounted his horse and rode out of the village.

As soon as he was gone Minnie Cypress said, "You were too cruel to him, Toby. After all, he is your half-brother."

"I had to be," Toby replied pensively, "and it hurt me more than it did him. I only hope it makes him think. But I suppose it cannot be blamed on Sol. If it were not him doing this, it would be someone else. And many others will follow. I hate to think of the end of it."

Sol felt physically sick as he rode back through the swamp, thinking of what Toby said about the custard-apple forest, the word "traitor" still ringing in his ears. Since Zech had never mentioned this to him, he could not be sure Toby's words were true. And it was natural that anyone living off the land like Toby and his people would feel the way Toby expressed himself. Toby would soon forget it, he told himself, and they would become friends again. And what little land he had cleared would not make that much difference anyway. There was much of it left, more than anyone could ever use. He vowed he would go back someday and try to make peace with Toby.

Sol got up at dawn the next morning, still shaken and depressed from his encounter with Toby. He paced back and forth for several minutes, muttering, "Damn him anyway!" Then he went into the kitchen and made coffee.

He was hungry, but he did not have the motivation to fry eggs and eat alone again. He ate one piece of stale white bread with the coffee; then he started pacing again.

It was Saturday, and all the field hands and work crews had left for the weekend. He thought first of going fishing, but this too was no fun alone. Many times on lonely nights and weekends he wished he had never left the homestead, where at least he would have the companionship of Lester and Tim and Jessie. One of the reasons for leaving was to escape the loneliness, but instead he had trapped himself in a situation far worse than the one he left.

There was nothing in the nearby villages of Clewiston and Belle Glade but a few stores and small cafes where he often took evening meals to escape the boredom of cooking for himself. He longed for one of his mother's meals or one prepared by Jessie, good wholesome food and not something always fried in stale grease that should have been dumped long ago. The villages were also void of people his age, for all of them, except a few engaged in commercial fishing or working as field hands, migrated as soon as they could to find jobs in Palm Beach or Miami.

He went into the bedroom, put on fresh jeans and a denim jacket, and attempted to dust off his boots; then he went outside and got into one of the Ford Model T trucks he had purchased for delivering vegetables. The motor sputtered to life, shaking the fenders as if they would fall off; then he put it in gear and ambled off, the rutted sand road causing it to rattle even worse.

There was a dirt road leading directly east from Belle Glade, crossing forty-seven miles of prairie into West Palm Beach. He pointed the Model T in that direction and floored the accelerator, sounding like an approaching hurricane as he roared across the land. Terrified rabbits jumped six feet high as they bounded out of his path, competing with frightened deer that almost trampled the smaller animals as they rushed past them. Birds flew too, and buzzards circled overhead, watching all of it, sensing there would soon be some kind of disaster that provided food.

When he reached West Palm Beach he sped right through it, scattering chickens and cats and dogs, stirring up a cloud of dust until he hit the wooden bridge leading across the water to Palm Beach proper. The accelerator was still on the floor as he drove straight to the driveway of the Royal Poinciana Hotel, came to a screeching halt in front of the main entrance, and jumped out. A cloud of blue smoke drifted across the veranda, and steam made angry hissing sounds as it boiled from beneath the truck's hood.

The doorman came down the steps hurriedly, eyeing the 'MacIvey Produce Company' sign on the dusty truck's door. He commanded Sol, "Get that damned thing out of here! Are you crazy? All deliveries are made at the rear entrance! Move it, fellow!"

Sol glared back defiantly, and then he said, "I'm not delivering anything! I'm a customer, and I want a room here for the weekend! And you best let the truck sit right here till I go in and inquire about it! You so much as touch it I'll cram that fancy little hat you got on right up your ass!"

The doorman stared sullenly as Sol stalked off. Several guests who watched the brief encounter turned away, heading for the area where the bicycle wicker-chairs were parked.

Sol crossed the lobby briskly, going straight to the counter, popping his hand several times on a little bell. A man in a white linen suit came from behind a shelf of key boxes and said, "Something I can do for you?"

"I want a room," Sol said impatiently, "one with a view of the ocean if you've got it. Otherwise, I'll take anything."

The clerk looked first at the jeans and denim jacket, at the boots with mud caked to the soles; then he examined a ledger briefly and said, "If you don't have a confirmed reservation we're all full. And I assume you don't."

"That's right, I don't," Sol replied, taking a thick roll of bills from his pocket. "You folks pulled that reservation shit on my pappa when my mamma wanted to stay here. I don't have a reservation, but I've got enough money here to choke a stallion. You going to give me a room or not?"

"I've already told you," the man said indignantly. "We're full up."

"O.K.," Sol said, putting the money back into his pocket. "My name is MacIvey. Sol MacIvey. I want you to remember that. One of these days I'll build my own hotel, and it'll be a heap sight better than this dump. So damn you and your stinkin' rooms!"

As Sol turned away the man said, "Cracker hick!"

When he got back to the truck he drove it off the driveway and right down the middle of a flower bed, scattering plants in all directions, hearing the doorman run after him screaming obscenities as he swerved back onto the driveway and sped away, the truck now decorated gaily with scarlet poinsettia bracts.

It was an hour past noon when he got back into West Palm Beach, as he parked in front of a cafe, got out and went inside. It was nothing fancy but clean, with good smells coming from the kitchen. Tables were covered with checkered cloths, and several people, obviously workers from their dress, were finishing eating.

A waitress came over and handed Sol a menu. She appeared to be about twenty, with long blonde hair and blue eyes. Her figure filled the uniform to perfection, and she would be extremely pretty except for the dour look on her face.

Sol said, "You sell beer?"

"Yeah. What kind you want, bottle or draught?"

"Hell, I don't know, what's the difference?"

She gave him a queer look and replied, "One comes in a bottle. That's bottle beer. The other is drawn from a barrel and comes in a mug. That's draught. You think you can make up your mind now?"

"Draught," Sol said sullenly, the anger still boiling. "And I'll have the blue plate special."

He watched as she walked away, noticing the gentle sway of her hips, the graceful curve of her legs. When she came back with the beer he said, "You know, you'd be as pretty as a speckled calf if you'd just smile."

She did smile, and then she said, "Thanks. Most folks never give me a compliment. They just gripe about how slow the service is, and I do the best I can. But you don't look like mister sunshine yourself. You came bustin' in here like a thunderhead."

"I guess I did," Sol said, chuckling. "I had a bad experience over in Palm Beach, and it sort of got my dander up."

"It's not hard to do over there. I stay away from that place. All those old men in their knickers ever do is leer and try to get you in bed with them. I don't know what they could do if they did. Probably nothing."

Sol immediately like her, her frankness reminding him of things his mother often said to Zech. He said, "What's your name?"

"Bonnie."

"Bonnie what?"

"Bonnie O'Neil. My daddy is Irish."

"I'm Sol MacIvey. My daddy was cracker."

"Cracker?" she giggled. "What's that?"

"Men who run after cows crackin' whips. That's how come they're called crackers."

"Is that what you do, run after cows?"

"I used to, but I'm in the vegetable business now."

"We got a garden too, but Daddy won't put a hand to it. He makes me do all the work. Where's your place?"

"Over at Lake Okeechobee."

She glanced back toward the kitchen and said, "I better get your food before Mister Lumkin comes shouting at me. I'll be right back."

When she returned Sol said, "What time you get off work here?"

"Two o'clock. You're the last customer for the noon serving. But I have to come back at five and work another two hours."

"You want to go over to the beach for awhile?"

"And do what?" she asked suspiciously.

"Sit. We could gawk at the men in their knickers, like they do us. After that I'll have to go on back to Okeechobee. I don't like to be on the road at night. If my truck broke down the skeeters would eat me alive."

"Sure, why not. It would beat going home and washing clothes. I'll meet you a block down the street. Mister Lumkin would have a stroke if he saw me leave here with a customer. He doesn't allow that at all."

They sat on the small area of public beach, watching waves roll in from the ocean and sandpipers scurrying about, pecking frantically at the sand as the water rushed back. Sol said, "Those little birds sure are swift. They never get their feet wet. Reminds me of a wild bull when you trap him in a palmetto clump. You never know which way he's going to go."

"Mamma used to like to come here and watch the birds. She's dead now. Died three years ago."

"What does your pappa do?" Sol asked.

"He's a groundskeeper at the hotel. Mamma worked there too, in the kitchen, till she took sick. Since she died Daddy don't do nothing but drink. I have to cook all the meals and do the washing and cleaning and tend the garden. When Daddy gets home from work he's drunk before supper."

"If you have to do all that, how come you work in the cafe too?"

"Daddy makes me. He wants the money for likker, an' he takes all of it. He won't even give me a dollar to buy toilet water. If I get a tip I hide it in my shoe so he can't find it."

Sol became silent for a moment, thinking, and then he said, "How much you make at that cafe?"

"Twenty dollars a month."

"Would you like to change jobs?"

"I sure would, but there's nowhere else for me to go. Those people won't hire me in their fancy shops, and I don't want to work at the hotel. I tried that once, in the housekeeping department, and I just couldn't stand those old men leering at me. And I had to clean twenty rooms every day. You'd be surprised what's in some of those rooms. Some of them have mirrors over the beds."

"That's not what I mean," Sol said. "How'd you like to come and work for me?"

"Doing what?" she asked, surprised, suspicious again.

"I need someone to do the cooking and look after the house. I'm tired of being alone and having to do all the housework myself. I'll pay you a hundred dollars a month."

She turned to him and said, "A hundred dollars a month? I've never seen that much money. How much of a garden have you got if you can pay a hundred dollars a month for a cook?"

"A hundred and thirty thousand acres. And a good bit more at other places."

"Good Lord!" she exclaimed, not knowing whether to believe him or not. But he said it too matter-of-factly to be lying. Then she said, "If you're so tired of being alone, how come you haven't married? It would be a whole lot cheaper than hiring a cook at that price."

"Pappa told me once that getting married is like owning dogs. You get to liking them too much, and it pains you when they go away. I saw it happen to Grampy when my granny died, and then to Pappa too. It pained them both worse than I've ever seen. I'm just not sure yet I want to try it. Maybe someday."

"For that much money would I have to sleep with you too?" she asked seriously.

"Not if you don't want to," Sol replied, even more amused by her bluntness.

"Well, if I ever climbed in bed with you, I wouldn't take a cent. It would make me feel like one of those women who hang around the beach at the hotel. I'll never do that for money. I'm not that kind of a girl, and you better know it right from the start!"

"That's fine with me," Sol agreed. "You'll be just a housekeeper, and you don't have to do anything you don't want to do. If it turns into something else, we'll talk about it when it happens, if it happens. But we need to start to Okeechobee now. You want to go and tell your daddy, or what?"

"No way!" she said, still not sure to believe what was happening. "He'd beat the hell out of me. He's done it before, and I don't want any more of it. He doesn't work Saturday afternoons, so he's home now. I can't even get my clothes."

"Don't worry about that," Sol said, getting up. "I've got enough money with me to buy out a store. We'll stop and get whatever you need."

As they walked back to the truck Bonnie said, "I don't believe this! It's just not real. I thought I'd never get out of that cafe. You don't know how many times I've thought about running away to Miami or Jacksonville but didn't have the nerve to do it. And here you come out of nowhere, and suddenly I'm gone. Just like that. I don't believe it's really happening to me."

"It's real, Bonnie," Sol said. "I wish I had found you a long time ago. The moment I saw you in the cafe I knew I wanted to do this. I was afraid you'd turn me down."

She stopped momentarily and said, "You know, Sol, you're a real nice fellow. I mean it. And good-looking as all-get-out too. I guess I'm about the luckiest girl in West Palm Beach. Plenty others would go with you no questions asked. I'm sure glad you stopped at the cafe."

"I am too, Bonnie. You're the kind of girl my mamma would like. I'll take you to our homestead sometime. It's up on the Kissimmee River. You'll like it."

"I already do. And you too. I'm not so sure how long I'll be able to stay on the payroll. I may not even make it for one week."

"We'll see," Sol said, smiling. "But we best get on the way. That truck stops after dark, the skeeters'll suck us dry."

"Then let's go!" she said enthusiastically, taking his hand in hers and pulling him hurriedly across the sand.

FORTY-ONE
1918

The Ford touring car bounced along the road leading past the east shore of the lake, swerving when it hit sand pockets. Sol said, "If it wasn't for saving time, I'd rather be going up there on a horse. It's a lot smoother."

"Does seem a bit rough," Bonnie replied, almost shouting over the roar of the engine. "But I'd never make it that far on a horse. I don't know how you stood it when you drove those cows clear across the state."

"Sometimes I don't either. I guess I was tougher then, and surely a lot younger. But I'd like to do it one more time just for the heck of it. I remember when it took us three days to move cows as far as we can go in one hour with this flivver. But we weren't in any hurry and didn't know the difference."

"Are we going back by Punta Rassa?"

"Yes. I want to check on the cabin and see if they got the fence done like I ordered."

"When you come to a nice shady hammock we can stop and have a picnic. I've brought a real nice lunch."

"There's one just past Basinger," Sol said. "We'll make it there right about noon."

Bonnie's blue eyes sparkled as she said, "I just thought about something real nice, Sol."

"What's that?"

"We could stop some place where there's a preacher or a justice of the peace and then have a honeymoon in Punta Rassa."

"Ah, come on, Bonnie," he said, putting his hand on hers. "You wouldn't want to do that."

"Yes I would! And one of these days I'm going to trap you into saying yes."

"You probably will, but not quite yet."

"That's what you've been saying for seven years, now," she sighed, "'not quite yet'. One of these days, Sol MacIvey, I'm going to drag you to an altar. You'll see!"

"I might fool you and take you first. But preacher or not, Bonnie, you're here to stay. I wouldn't trade you for all the oranges and cows and vegetables in the whole world. And you know that."

"Yes, I do know," she said tartly, flipping her blonde pony tail over her left shoulder. Sol insisted she wear her hair this way, like Glenda did. "But it's just my cooking you're used to."

"It's a heap more than that," Sol smiled, touching her hand again. "But hush up now before you get me distracted and I ram this machine into a cabbage palm. We've got to get to the place by early afternoon. I've got a lot to do there before we go on to Punta Rassa."

"That letter has really upset you, hasn't it?"

"Tim Lardy would never have written me twice to come back in a hurry unless something is bad wrong. I should have gone after the first letter. But I'm anxious to get there now and find out what it is that's got Tim in such a stew."

As Bonnie predicted that day they left Palm Beach together, their arrangement for her to be simply a housekeeper didn't last for even one week, and from that point forward, their lives were comfortably entwined. She was a housekeeper, but she was also a companion and a lover, and much more. She became Sol's business partner as well, doing all the clerical work and offering advice when Sol was in doubt about what he was doing. And her advice always proved right. But she never let up pestering him to visit a preacher or justice of the peace and make their life together legal.

For several years after Sol left the homestead he went back every few months to check things out, but as the vegetable business continued to grow and prosper and demand more and more of his time, the visits became less frequent.

On one of his visits he loaded the remaining money trunks on a Model T truck and took them to his house at Okeechobee, and this also made it seem less necessary for him to go back on a regular schedule.

The war in Europe was a distraction too, causing him to step up the production of his fields. He registered for the army but was told his job supplying food was far more important to the war effort than being just one more soldier carrying a gun, so he took the work seriously, looking upon it as his substitute for wearing a uniform and possibly fighting for his country.

It had been over two years since he was at the homestead, handling all business matters by mail. This had not bothered him, for the old place produced more and more cash income, and Clayton's books were always in order. But a year ago Clayton wrote him that he was going into business for himself at Bartow and recommended that a man named Donovan replace him as manager. He assured Sol that Donovan was experienced with both citrus and cattle, so Sol took the recommendation and hired Donovan by mail.

Sol had no reason to doubt his decision, for the income from the place continued to increase steadily. Then came the first letter from Tim Lardy, urging him to come back as soon as possible. He knew he should have gone at once, but he put it off for one thing and then another. And than a second letter arrived, this one even more urgent. At this point Sol dropped everything, and he and Bonnie set out immediately, Sol regretful that he had not responded sooner.

Sol turned from the main road and followed a trail leading across a section of prairie, the tall grass making swishing sounds as it brushed the underside of the vehicle. When he came to an area that should have been open pasture but was now an orange grove it confused him, thinking perhaps he had taken the wrong turn.

He stopped for a moment and said, "I know damned well this is where the corral was. We never planted trees here. Something is powerful strange, Bonnie."

"Are you sure we're at the right place?" she asked.

"I think so, unless I've gone crazy. Let's go on to the house and see what this is all about."

He continued following the trail and became even more perplexed when he arrived at the spot where he thought the hammock would be but found only more orange trees. He began to wonder if he really had come to the right place, but at the same time doubting he could have forgotten so soon.

Bonnie remained in the car as Sol started walking through the grove, searching for some sign of recognition, startled once when a rabbit bounded from a clump of grass right at his feet and rushed away. And then he came to it, right in the middle of two rows of trees, five stones, all bearing the name MacIvey. He stared for a moment, at once not believing, then realizing what had been done. He screamed furiously, "Damn you! Damn you, you son of a bitch! I'll kill you!"

The sound of it frightened Bonnie so badly she jumped from the car, trembling as Sol rushed from the trees and slid beneath the steering wheel. She climbed back in quickly, her eyes terrified as Sol cranked the car and spun it around, going full speed back down the trail, crashing into limbs and showering the air with twigs and leaves.

He drove transfixed, his hands gripping the wheel. They skidded sideways when the trail split with another path leading off to the left. The Ford righted itself and roared forward again, the motor straining and leaving a trail of blue smoke that hung suspended just above the ground.

Soon he came to a small clearing containing a house and two small cabins off to one side, all of them new and made of pine. The car skidded to a stop and spun around, facing back the way it had come.

A cloud of dust boiled up as Sol jumped from the car and grabbed a Winchester from the back seat. Tim and Jessie then came from one cabin, and as soon as they recognized who it was, Jessie started crying.

Tim ran forward and said, "I couldn't stop him, Mistuh Sol! I tried, but he wouldn't listen to me!"

Donovan came around the side of the house, trotting, drawn by the sound of the unexpected commotion. He was a huge man, six and a half feet tall, gruff-looking, built like an ox. Sol knew who he was without being told. He cocked the lever of the Winchester, pointed it and said, "I'm going to blow your head off, you no good bastard!"

Donovan froze, looking at the trembling hand pressing the trigger, the barrel pointed directly at him, the rage in Sol's eyes. He spoke as calmly as possible, "You must be Mister MacIvey. How come you're in such a huff?"

"What the hell you mean by what you've done?" Sol demanded, hatred for this unknown man pouring from him like sweat.

"I don't know what you mean."

"You know!" Sol shouted, his face now as red as his hair.

"Them houses was rotting down," Donovan said, still looking at the rifle and not at Sol. "They wasn't worth a damn for nothin'. And there's three hundred acres of good land where that hammock was. Hell, I was hired to run a grove on a percentage basis, not look after some old shacks and run a old-folks home. You ought to be glad I cleared off all that stuff and put it in oranges. It'll mean more money for you."

Bonnie had never seen Sol so angry, and she knew he was going to do it. She ran to him and pleaded, "Please, Sol, don't! What's done is done, and killing him won't bring it back! It'll only bring trouble! Please listen to me!"

He looked at her terrified face, then back to Donovan, and then he said, "I want you off this place in ten minutes! You get in that goddam truck over there and go! Whatever you leave behind we'll burn! Now move it and count yourself lucky! If you're still here in ten minutes, so help me God I'll kill you!"

Sol watched as Donovan went into the house briefly and then came outside dragging a frightened woman by the arm. He did not lower the rifle until the truck sputtered down the trail and disappeared.

Tim then said, "I tried to stop him, Mistuh Sol! He just wouldn't pay no mind to me at all!"

"What'd he do with my granny's cook stove?" Sol asked.

"He give to a junk man from St. Cloud. All the old tools and other stuff too."

"Damn!" Sol then looked around and said, "Where's Lester?"

"Over in his cabin. He don't work any more, Mistuh Sol. He's been too poorly. Mistuh Donovan was goin' to run him off the place, and he would have too if you hadn't come right now."

Sol tried to calm himself and think rationally, but the overwhelming anger wouldn't go away. He said, "I can't stay here any longer today or I'll go after that bastard and kill him for sure. Tim, I want you to take over as manager and run the place from now on."

Tim's eyes widened, and then he said, "Mistuh Sol, I appreciate your saying that. I know the orange and cattle business as good as anybody, but I'm sure not a bookkeeper. I just couldn't handle that part of it at all."

"It doesn't matter. I'll hire a bookkeeper in Kissimmee to come here once a month and take care of that. That's not important, but running the place is. And you can do it, Tim. The first thing I want you to do is rip out all those trees where the graves are. Clear it all out, and then put an iron fence around it. And plant some oak back in there."

"I'll do it, Mistuh Sol. It nearbout killed me and Jessie when he done that. We knowed how you'd feel, but I just couldn't stop him."

"We're going to go now," Sol said, his voice still trembling. "I'll go to Kissimmee and talk to a bookkeeper, and I'll also hire a couple of hands to come live here and work under you. I'll come back in about a month and help you set things up."

"I'll do a good job for you, Mistuh Sol. And I'll see to the grave site right away."

Without speaking further Sol got into the car and drove off. When he reached the place where the corral had been he stopped, leaned forward against the steering wheel and cried bitterly. Bonnie put her arms around him but did not intrude, letting it all come out and be done with in his own way.

He finally straightened up and controlled himself, and then he said, "You know, Bonnie, that bastard bulldozed two whole lifetimes. Everything Pappa and Grampy did is gone now. It's a wonder he didn't pull out the stones and plant trees there too. I should have stayed here and looked after the place. Those damned vegetable fields aren't worth this. It's all my fault."

"That not true, Sol," she insisted, feeling the pain with him. "You couldn't have known this would happen. Don't feel this way, honey. Please don't."

A shocked realization came on Sol's face as something unexpected came into his mind. He suddenly understood why Toby had been so angry when he destroyed the custard-apple forest, a place that both Zech and Toby loved. To them it was much more than just another stretch of raw swamp and forest. And he had done the same thing Donovan had done, only it was for vegetables rather than oranges.

He brushed his eyes and said, "They'll never forgive me for this, Bonnie, and I know I won't forgive myself. All they left behind is gone now, and regrets won't bring it back. Toby knew this, and now I do too. Toby was right and I was wrong, but it's done now, and what's done can't be undone. I guess nothing in this whole damned stinking world lasts forever."

She did not know who Toby was, and none of it made sense to her. She passed it off as rambling grief, but the puzzled look stayed on her face as he cranked the car and drove off. When he reached a turn in the trail he stopped and glanced back briefly just to be sure the old corral was really gone.

FORTY-TWO
1924

After moving to Okeechobee, Sol made many trips into Miami, occasionally at first and then frequently as he established markets for his produce. On his first visit in 1908 the place did not even remotely resemble the sleepy little village he and Zech and Glenda rode into that summer day in 1895. As the trading post owner predicted when he sold them their parcels of land, the coming of Flagler's railroad, which arrived the next year, did indeed change the face of the area. With each visit Sol found something new, some seemingly overnight transformation.

He made no plans whatsoever for the land they owned there, merely paying the taxes each year and letting the vegetation grow wild. Twice he purchased other small plots and threw the deeds into a box with the others. During one early visit he did hire a skiff and cross the bay to see his beachside property, finding it exactly as the land agent described it, a mangrove swamp occupied by chattering birds and roaming animals, the beach itself a haven for sandpipers and gulls and terns and pelicans.

In January of 1912 Sol and Bonnie went into Miami and purchased tickets on the first train to run from Miami to Key West over Flagler's overseas railroad, seeing the old man himself dressed in a black frock coat and silk stovepipe hat, the two of them staing in Key West for a four-day celebration of the momentous event. The whole island was one big orgy of a party such as neither of them had ever witnessed, not at Palm Beach or elsewhere. Rum flowed as abundantly as coconut milk, and there was wild dancing in the streets, picking up tempo at sunset and still going strong at daybreak. Outdoor tables overflowed with conch chowder and conch fritters, a dozen varieties of fish cooked in every conceivable way, piles of raw oysters and boiled shrimp, whole pigs roasted Cuban-style with apples stuffed in their mouths, and baskets of fruit beyond count. They were both exhausted when they arrived back in Miami and then returned gladly to the sedate life of their Okeechobee home.

And then Sol began to see dredges in Biscayne Bay, pumping mountains of sand from the bay floor, building additional land on the strip that was becoming known as Miami Beach; and then it was connected by bridges to the mainland. His property soon became the only plot where birds and animals still prevailed over men and machines and building materials, and he continued to leave it that way. Unknown to him, developers searched frantically for this elusive family named MacIvey that owned this prime beachfront acreage and also the extensive tract in Miami itself. On the original deed Zech had listed the family address simply as "Kissimmee wilderness."

After the war ended, the construction activity increased at a frantic pace, and then hordes of tourists in their newly acquired flivvers streamed into the area, wanting to see and own a piece of this tropical paradise as advertised in Northern newspapers and journals, a land of beauty beyond description where the moon each night dripped honey onto silver beaches and swaying palms. Something strange was happening, some electrifying surge that charged the air with excitement bordering the irrational. Sol sensed all of this as the tempo of land sales and construction increased, but he did not really know what to make of it.

The frenzy then spread like an uncontrollable prairie fire, moving up the coast to Fort Lauderdale and Hollywood and Pompano and even into exclusive Palm Beach itself: more and more people, more and more developers, more and more real estate hucksters and swamp peddlers, more and more con artists of every type, the whole situation rapidly developing into a ludicrous circus.

Sol and Bonnie watched from the sidelines and waited, frightened by all of it, Sol knowing that day by day and week by week his property became more valuable. Each rumor and each newspaper ad and circular listing land values stunned him, and he knew he would have to do something either eventually or soon; but he continued to hold back, the potential value of his holdings staggering his imagination.

In 1923 he made his first move, hiring a contractor to build a combination house and office in Miami, the first floor to be the business area and the second floor their living quarters. It was a small, inconspicuous place compared to the Spanish-style mansions rapidly dotting the area, the ten-story office buildings and the vast hotels and apartment complexes.

Sol built his house as if building a fort, with foot-thick concrete walls and iron grills across each window. One of the first level rooms contained a walk-in vault, the same type as in a bank. The contractor thought Sol was either crazy or eccentric at best, warning him that such a monstrosity located inside a house would probably cost as much as the house itself; but Sol was adamant, insisting that it be done to his exact specifications regardless of cost.

His reason for this unusual addition was that he would keep his money himself, just as his father and grandfather had done, and trust no bank or anyone else with it. Had it not been for the MacIvey system of banking by trunk, as started by Tobias and continued by Zech, there might not have been any MacIvey land and no reserve money to purchase more or to develop what he now had. Sol figured what was good for them was good for him, only his new trunk would be a great deal stronger than the steamers purchased by Tobias in Punta Rassa. He soon owned the only house in Miami with a full-sized steel and concrete vault, and from the outside appearance of his place, no one else would know it was there.

As soon as the house-office was complete Sol hired a foreman for the vegetable business and set forth with Bonnie to participate in the great Florida Boom. The sign outside his office read, "MacIvey Real Estate and Development Company."

After having it surveyed, Sol found that the six thousand acres of mainland property covered a portion of the commerical area of the city and extended into one of the most sought-after residential areas, including waterfront. None of it was swamp or muckland, so there would be no need of drainage or filling before placing it on the market. He plotted only a small section at first just to see what would happen, breaking an acre into individual lots of seventy feet by one hundred feet in the commerical area. Then he studied current prices listed by other firms, finding that residential lots ranged from twenty to seventy thousand dollars according to location, and commercial property starting at one hundred thousand and going up from there. The Miami Beach acreage was even more valuable. He could not believe that people would actually pay so much money for such a small plot of raw land.

That morning he went to a small print shop and ordered circulars stating that MacIvey Real Estate would be offering prime lots beginning at 8 a.m. the next morning, first come first served. Residential lots valued at $70,000 were reduced to $50,000 for cash only, and commercial lots for $100,000 cash only. No paper transactions accepted. He picked the circulars up at noon, and that entire afternoon he and Bonnie distributed them throughout Miami and Miami Beach, handing them out on streets and tacking them to light poles.

All of Miami and Miami Beach was like a carnival, with people thronging everywhere. Car horns blared and were blended with the sounds of pounding hammers and machinegun riveters, all of Miami enveloped in clouds of dust. Real estate salesmen were in every door and on every street corner, dressed in the adopted uniform of white knickers and bow ties, offering free cigars and shouting like circus barkers as they held sheaths of deeds high in the air, enticing prospective buyers to examine their wares. Some pieces of property changed hands five and six times in one day, each purchaser selling it again for a higher price, most of it on option with a small down payment and mortgages. Paper empires were created rapidly on every corner.

Tents were set up on vacant lots, with belly dancers and cancan girls and jugglers used to draw in the potential customers. After the entertainment a lecture was given concerning the certain riches of the land offered. Then eager speculators lined up to plunk down their initial payments. They came from as far away as Europe, drawn magically to the land of eternal sunshine and flowers, buying lots sight unseen, some of it in swamps reachable only by canoe. Sol vowed he would never do this, that all of his offerings would be of solid value and could be inspected in advance by any purchaser who wished to do so.

Next they crossed the bridge to Miami Beach and turned south, passing Spanish-Boom houses and towering hotels, coming into areas where sweating men in white knickers held forth at tables under trees, free champagne flowing, bands playing, every palm and palmetto laced with electric oriental lanterns that burned night and day, reams of freshly printed deeds stacked neatly on other tables, awaiting the signatures of buyers.

All of it repulsed Sol, but he figured if there were this many crazy people in the world he might as well take advantage of it too. He had no other use for the land except to sell it. To Bonnie, all of it was simply amusing, like visiting a zoo; and to both of them it was not something real but a game being played in a fantasy world. Surely, Sol thought, this madness must end someday.

The next morning they did not know what to expect, whether anyone would show up or not, especially since their lots were offered for cash only while others gladly accepted paper. But when Sol opened the door there was a line outside, people shoving and cursing as they waited impatiently in the sultry heat, afraid that all the bargain MacIvey land would be gone before they reached the office.

By noon when he could not stand the shouting and mayhem any longer, Sol and Bonnie had sold and deeded four commercial lots and nine residential lots for a take of $850,000 in cash. Sol told everyone outside to come back the next day, and then he put a "closed" sign on the door. Some still pounded and demanded to be let in. One man who purchased a commercial lot sold it to another man at the rear of the line for $200,000 – half of it cash and half of it paper.

The next morning was a repeat of the first, and by week's end total sales amounted to more than three million dollars, all of it stacked on shelves inside the vault. The frenzy went for months – with each day seeing more hotels and apartments and villas, more tract houses and private clubs and swimming pools – not reaching its peak until the middle of the next year. By this time Sol and Bonnie were exhausted and decided to spend several months resting at their Okeechobee home. They loaded a Pierce-Arrow with suitcases and set forth for the peaceful country, leaving behind over $80 million in their Miami vault.

FORTY-THREE
September 15,
1928

Sol turned left at Belle Glade and headed for Lake Harbor and the Okeechobee house. It was Saturday, and they had driven up from Miami that morning, leaving the city because of advance warnings that a hurricane was approaching from the south. Memories were still too fresh of what had happened in Miami and Miami Beach two years before when a September hurricane virtually destroyed the area, bringing an end to the great frenzied land boom.

Sol and Bonnie had ridden that one out in their little concrete fortress, emerging unscathed into a devastated city littered with the trash of scattered houses, flattened hotels and apartment buildings, the harbor blocked by sunken vessels, forty-foot yachts resting forlornly on dry land a half mile inland. People had wandered the streets dazed, not believing that the great Florida Sun God could do this to them, seeing all their hopes and dreams swept away by the shrieking winds and surging tides. The storm had turned paper millionaires into paupers overnight, former tycoons now pushing wheelbarrows and working with crews on dump trucks, shoveling up litter and salvaging what little the winds spared.

Sol and Bonnie were not hurt by it, and were in fact helped. A week later they put a sign in front of their office saying, "We're Buying."

And they had the cash money to do so, paying five cents on the dollar for flattened property as people abandoned their deflated fantasies and headed back north, some sadly but gratefully accepting as little as train fare for what a year before had promised to make them into empire builders.

Sol purchased property after property, believing that someday the area would recover, undaunted personally when others gave up because he knew of all those things nature unleashed against the MacIveys during those decades of time when they suffered catastrophes worse than this and came back again and again, refusing to surrender.

But they wanted no more of a Miami-style hurricane if it could be avoided, knowing they were lucky once but maybe not twice, and the sturdy old cypress house at Lake Okeechobee offered a safe haven out of the path of whatever was coming across the Gulf or Caribbean.

They stopped at a country store and purchased supplies, making sure the house was well stocked with food for at least a week's stay if that was necessary. After the suitcases and bags of groceries were deposited in the house, Sol set out alone to inspect some of his outlying fields.

Although two years had passed since the savage 1926 storm, the area had not yet fully recovered from it, and some of the fields lay fallow. The storm spawned an aftermath of smaller disasters, and the following winter there were killing frosts one after another, seven in all, destroying crop after crop even while seed still lay buried in the ground. Flooding from the lake had always been a problem, even though temporary, sometimes drowning crops and other times washing them away; but the effects of this storm lingered on for six months after the winds passed, bringing flood after flood until it seemed endless. And the destruction of the cities along the coast greatly reduced the local markets for vegetables and all other things, bringing depression to South Florida years before it was to strike the nation's heart elsewhere. But finally it seemed to let up, and Sol now saw sprouts of winter crops creeping upward from the black soil, tiny plants that would soon grow to maturity and make the land bountiful again, providing vegetables to fill the bins of stores in the North and Midwest.

When Sol returned to the house, he and Bonnie drove along a sandy trail leading to the lake, passing cabbage palm hammocks strangely devoid of birds, huge oaks whose limbs were normally playgrounds for barking squirrels now empty and silent. As he rounded a bend there was an area of open sawgrass off to the left, and the air above the marsh churned with white specks so thick they formed a low-lying cloud.

Sol stopped the car, and they both gazed at the strange phenomenon. Bonnie then said, "What is it, Sol? Is it insects?"

"No, it's pollen," Sol replied. "It's not a good sign, either. Toby Cypress once told me that when sawgrass pollen boils like that it means a great storm is coming. They flee from the sight of it. Maybe it's just another Indian legend, but it's weird, isn't it?"

"Yes, and I don't want to look anymore," Bonnie said, suddenly shivering. "It still looks like bugs to me, and I don't want to be around it."

Sol drove on, and then he parked on the bank of a drainage canal leading eastward from the lake. Flights of herons and egrets and ibises were streaming above the water, moving northward, not floating casually as they often do with wings outspread, but flapping constantly.

The surface of the lake was deathly still, like a mirror tying together an immediate point with the horizon. In the distance they could see commerical fishermen taking their boats toward the mouth of a creek where they often sought refuge from storms.

They both got out of the car and walked along the canal, watching small explosions as bass struck minnows lurking at the edges of pickerel weed. Then there was a more violent upheaval as an alligator snapped up one of the stalking bass, chomping it into a bloody pulp and then gliding away, its powerful tail weaving slowly, sending ripples against the bank.

"That's the way it goes," Sol said as the 'gator disappeared into a clump of weeds. "Minnow eats the skeeter eggs, bass eats the minnow, 'gator eats the bass, and next thing you know he ends up as shoes and belts, his tail meat in somebody's frying pan."

"I feel sorry for the poor fish," Bonnie said distastefully. "I sure wouldn't want to be chomped up like that."

"Neither does the minnow, but nothing has a choice. Everything has to eat, Bonnie, including us. And we all eat each other. If we'd brought along our poles we could have a fish fry tonight, the way those bass are striking."

"I've got steaks," Bonnie replied. "I don't want fish after watching that. And if you don't hush up that kind of talk you won't get anything.

You make me feel like a cannibal."

"I hope you don't think the cow those steaks came from committed suicide," Sol grinned. "But we won't go into that. I'll hush."

They walked a short distance further, and then Sol said, "I've never seen the lake so still, and the birds all moving in one direction. I've got a gut feeling something is wrong here, bad wrong."

"I do too," Bonnie said. "It's eerie. Maybe we should have stayed in Miami."

"One thing for sure," Sol said, slapping his arms, "the skeeters aren't leaving too. Let's get out of here before they have us for supper."

As they drove back past the stretch of marsh, the pollen boiled even more, looking like millions of swarming gnats. Sol stopped briefly and looked again, saying, "If Toby were here he'd be cutting out for somewhere else. Next thing you know an owl will light on our roof and cry out. That's an even worse omen."

"Quit kidding me," Bonnie said, her voice serious. "This place is spooky enough without you scaring me worse with Indian tales. I don't want to hear any more of it."

The sun did not come up the next morning. Instead, it seeped through leaden skies that rapidly turned from gray to angry black, boiling like the pollen boiled. At first the wind came in gusts, banging against the side of the house and causing palm trunks to bend double and then snap back. By mid-morning it changed to a steady howl, bringing with it a sheet of pelting rain that came in horizontally, pinging sharply against the walls and window panes.

Sol looked out one of the east windows and noticed that the door on the garage had come open. It flapped back and forth violently, as rapidly as blades on a windmill, shaking the structure on its foundation. When he opened the front door of the house to go out to the garage, the door slammed back with such force it knocked him sprawling across the floor, snapping one steel hinge like it was made of matchsticks. He and Bonnie put their shoulders against the door and forced it back, and then he nailed it shut.

Bonnie backed away exhausted, soaked instantly from rain that rushed through the open space and splattered against the living room walls. She said, "I'm afraid, Sol. Really afraid! What are we going to do?"

"There's nothing we can do," Sol said, picking up the hammer and nails. "I'll nail every door and window shut and then pray the old house holds together. Looks like we jumped right out of it in Miami and landed in the path up here."

"I wish we'd stayed there," Bonnie moaned. "We could have got inside the vault and been safe."

The house cracked and vibrated constantly as Sol put his arms around Bonnie and tried to reassure her. "Don't worry, honey. We'll make it through this. We always have, and we will again."

"I hope so," Bonnie replied. "But Lord, I don't know, Sol! I just wish it would go away."

They ate cold beans for lunch, and shortly afterwards Sol looked out the window just as the banging garage disintegrated, pieces of walls and roof sailing upward and disappearing, exposing the Pierce-Arrow to the full force of the wind. It bounced up and down like a rubber ball, skipping across the ground a few feet at a time, and then it rolled over and over and crashed into a clump of palm trunks.

By mid-afternoon the area outside the house was covered with brown foam as the lake water reached the yard. Waves on the lake gradually increased, starting at two feet and going to six, crashing over the flat banks and rushing southward; and then it came like tidal waves, ten feet high, wall after wall of wind-driven water, uprooting palms and oaks and anything in its way. It inched up the house's foundation, three feet off the ground, then it touched the porch floor and slushed in beneath the doors.

Bonnie stared with horror as the water covered the floor, an inch at first and then three inches, rising rapidly. She wailed, "Oh my God, Sol! What can we do? The whole lake is coming down on us!"

"Stand on a chair!" Sol shouted above the roar. "It can't come higher than that!"

But it did come higher, lapping the top of the dining room table. Then Sol put a chair on top of the table and climbed through an opening into the roof rafters, pulling Bonnie after him, the two of them clinging to studs as cypress shingles gave way and sailed off like leaves, exposing them to the pounding rain that made breathing almost impossible.

And then it stopped suddenly, as instantly as if someone had flicked off a light switch, the night now deathly still, not a single drop of rain coming down. Sol looked up through a hole in the roof, seeing the moon and stars trapped inside a swirling mass shaped like an inverted ice cream cone, one big round area of peaceful sky surrounded by spinning madness. He said, "It's the eye, Bonnie. It's passing over us now. Are you still all right?"

She pulled herself across the stud to him, sucking air into her tortured lungs. "I don't know, Sol," she gasped. "I can't hang on here much longer. And we're only half way through it. Oh God, honey, it's coming again, only this time worse! I don't know what we'll do."

"I'll hold you," Sol responded, putting his arms around her soggy body. "We'll make it, Bonnie. We have to! Just don't give up."

Water sloshed two feet below them as Bonnie said, "Sol, I might as well say it now as ever. I love you, and I wouldn't trade our life together for anything. I'd do it all over again the same way if I had to. But we should have been married. I don't want to die in sin. My daddy wouldn't care, but my mother would. She would care, Sol, and I do too. Say you love me. If you'll tell me that now, it'll be all right."

Sol pulled her closer, feeling the fear tremble through her. "I do love you, Bonnie, and always have. The first thing we'll do when this is over is look for a preacher. I swear it! And we should have done it a long time ago. Just because my mamma and my granny died so sudden the way they did is no excuse for what I've done. It's a chance in life we all must take, and I know it now. No other MacIvey before me ran from it, and I won't any longer. I love you, Bonnie, more than anything, and I declare you right now before God to be my wife. And tomorrow we'll have a preacher say the words."

She leaned over and kissed him. "Thanks, darling. That's what I wanted you to say. I can face it now. I think I'll be forgiven."

The first gust then struck the house, coming from the opposite direction of the previous wind, signalling the passing of the eye and the coming of the second phase. It increased rapidly, now roaring, rain coming again and pounding through the open roof, making further conversation impossible.

Sol shuddered with anxiety and clung desperately to Bonnie as he felt the house being jolted from its foundation, moving off slowly, pushed along by surging water as the lake left its banks again and pounded southward. And then it exploded, sounding like a dynamite charge, sending boards and beams and window frames flying away with the howling wind. Sol felt himself ripped from Bonnie and flipped over and over like a coin, splashing down into angry, boiling water, gasping for breath as he went under and came back up again, grabbing frantically in utter darkness for something to hold to, finally locking his aching arms onto a section of roof as it swept by. His shouts of "Bonnie!. . .Bonnie!. . ." were heard only by himself as he moved rapidly over what had once been a vegetable field.

Dawn came from a sky still gray, but the violence was gone. Rain pelted down steadily as Sol opened his eyes and looked up.

The roof section had come to rest against a drainage canal dike, and above him he could hear voices as a group of black field hands sang gospel hymns and prayed. The water was clogged with the remains of shattered houses and trees, and the floating bodies of dead animals and humans. A small child was jammed into the fork of a tree limb just to the left of Sol, its face frozen into a death mask of utter terror.

He pushed away from the beams and pulled himself slowly up the muddy bank, at first unable to stand, kneeling and looking out across a brown sea. Not a tree was left standing, not a house or barn, nothing visible but water covering the earth as far as he could see. One of the field hands watched him for a moment, and then he said, "Bless you, brother, bless you! Praise the Lord for bein' spared!" And then he returned to the hymn.

Sol stared at the man blankly. Then he pushed himself up and staggered forward, seeing people further down the dike, his blistered eyes searching for some sign of a small woman wearing a blonde pony tail. He cried out, "Bonnie!. . .Where are you, Bonnie?"

Suddenly he stopped and shook his fists at gray clouds covering the sky, shouting, "Damn you! Damn you! You'll not do this again! We'll dike the lake so you can't do it again! Bonnie. . .Answer me, Bonnie!. . . ."

But there was no answer, and never would be. Bonnie was among the two thousand who died, and had vanished forever.

FORTY-FOUR
Miami
1954

Sol sat behind the massive mahogany desk in his office atop the MacIvey State Bank, waiting impatiently for the woman to keep her appointment. He did not want to go through with this, thinking it foolish and an invasion of his privacy. The call came the day before, from the executive director of the Greater Miami Economic Council, telling him he had been selected Citizen of the Year for his lifetime contributions to the Miami area and to Florida. But so little was known about his private life, which he guarded zealously, they had requested an interview to gain information for publicity and for the award ceremony to be held the next week.

Finally she was ushered in, a young woman of twenty-two, with deep green eyes and black hair, wearing shoes with spikes four inches tall. She was visibly nervous as she took a seat in front of the desk.

She took a note pad and pen from her purse and said, "I'm Alice Bryant, Mister MacIvey. I've always wanted to meet you but never thought I would. And I want to congratulate you on the honor. You certainly deserve it for all you've done for the state."

"Just what is it you want to know?" Sol asked, bored already as he leaned back in the chair.

"Oh, just everything," she replied enthusiastically. "Something about your family background, how you got your start, where you went to school. All that sort of thing."

Sol's eyes suddenly twinkled with mirth as he said, "O.K., Miss Bryant. I'll talk, and you take notes. Then you can ask questions. First, my grandaddy was a plantation owner in Georgia and came to Florida before the Civil War to establish a cattle and citrus empire. He served as a Confederate general during the war. My pappa helped Grampy buy the land and start the business, and I learned it from them. But before I took it over and expanded it, I was sent away to college. Graduated from the University of Virginia in 1906, magna cum laude. My mother was from a pioneer family too, and so was my wife. She died back in 1928. My wife's father was one of the founders of Palm Beach. . . . Now the way we really started the MacIvey empire was. . . ."

The Okeechobee hurricane of 1928 changed the face of the land forever. As Sol vowed that morning as he searched vainly for Bonnie, the lake was eventually diked, surrounded by such a high mound of dirt that its waters would never again be seen from ground level. Then drainage canals were cut, drying up the muck soil until summer winds blew it away, turning the life-giving water away from the Big Cypress Swamp and the Everglades, creating drought in dry seasons when the natural flow from the lake no longer came, and flooding in rainy seasons because the earth could no longer absorb it. It was all done with good intent and faith at the time but nevertheless created a travesty against nature that could never be reversed.

Sol played a big part in it because of his anger at the storm and Bonnie's death. He rebuilt the Okeechobee house, this time of concrete and steel, and then he went back to Miami. When the depression came in 1929, causing banks to fail, he started his own, naming it the MacIvey State Bank and stocking it with hard cash from his private vault.

His MacIvey Developing Company continued buying land during the 1930's, moving up the coast and inward, draining vast areas and then waiting for the depression to pass before developing them. He built a mansion on Key Biscayne, not because he wanted it but because he thought it to be something Bonnie would have enjoyed. He lived there alone with only his household servants, giving no thought to marriage or living with a woman again.

When World War II came he did his part by serving as chairman of war bond drives and donating money to the USO. Later on, he gave generously to numerous charities and civic projects but never attended social functions, the name MacIvey becoming associated with some elusive philanthropist hiding from public view.

After the war it started again, another boom, not as frenzied as the madness of the 1920's but boom nevertheless. MacIvey Development surged forward, dredging and filling, building tract houses with their St. Augustine lawns and transplanted cabbage palms, blocking off the ocean beaches with towering condominiums and gigantic apartment complexes, moving westward into the Everglades from Hollywood and Fort Lauderdale and Pompano and Boca Raton and Lake Worth. Sol was no longer an active part of it, turning the management of the company over to eager young executives he hired; but before he realized what was happening he had created a juggernaut that would not stop until the last swamp was drained, the last tree felled, and the last raccoon left to scrounge scraps from garbage cans or starve.

In 1952 he built his hotel, naming it the La Florida, twenty-five stories of concrete and glass overlooking the ocean on Miami Beach. Again he did it not because he wanted another business enterprise but because he remembered the vow he had made that day in Palm Beach so many years ago. When the hotel held its grand opening he did not attend the gala celebration which featured a bevy of Hollywood stars.

More and more he retreated into his private Key Biscayne world, serving as boss of the MacIvey empire in name only, knowing now what was happening but closing his eyes to it, looking the other way. He also withdrew more and more into the past, living in the world of Tobias and Zech, letting his imagination and his memories take him backward in time. The name MacIvey became a phantom, not something real but meaningless letters across bank buildings, art centers and small parks.

Sol sat at the head table, looking out at a sea of faces he did not know and did not want to know. Pounds of diamonds caught the light from glittering chandeliers and magnified it, and women were draped with furs despite the outside heat.

Sol's red hair was now sandy gray, but his lean body was still as ramrod straight as it had ever been. He was dressed in a black suit custom-made by a tailor just for this occasion, patterned after those worn by men prior to the turn of the century. He also had on a string tie, and looked like a relic taken from a just-opened 1880 time capsule. This was the way he wanted it, and he drew curious glances from everyone in the room, almost all of them seeing him for the first time.

Finally the evening neared the climax as a man droned on and on at the microphone. Sol did not listen to the introductory speech, knowing already what would be said about him, but the closing words came through to him, ". . .one of Florida's most prestigious families. . .a man who played a major role in conquering the wilderness and bringing civilization and progress to Florida. . . ."

He got up to thunderous applause and made his way to the podium. He adjusted the mike upward; then he spoke slowly and deliberately, "All that stuff you just heard about me is pure bullshit. It's all lies I made up just to see how gullible you are. And it's all a shame on the name of MacIvey. To all those MacIveys who left this earth before me I apologize for telling such whoppers."

He paused for a moment, looking out over an audience now shocked into silence, and then he continued, "My grandaddy wasn't any plantation owner in Georgia. He left there dirt poor and starving, and when he arrived here all he owned was in an ox cart. He didn't start a cattle and citrus empire. He and my granny and my pappa slept on the ground and ate coons and rabbits till he could build a shack to live in. He caught wild cows in the swamps till he had enough to sell the first bunch, and then he went from there.

"I've never been to college one day in my life, much less hold a degree from anywhere. My grampy and granny were illiterate, and my pappa was too till he married my mamma and she taught him to read and write. Everything I know she taught me at night beside a coal oil lamp.

"My grampy would never buy the land and never owned so much as a grain of sand. He was a squatter. He believed that no man can own the land, that it all belongs to the Lord, and the Lord lets us stay on it temporarily as tenants. If this is so, and I now believe it's so, then the Lord must be powerful mad at all of us for what we've done to His property. There'll be a day of reckoning for you and for me.

"The first land owned by my pappa was won in a horse race in Punta Rassa, and the first land I bought on Miami Beach was bought with money I earned selling buzzards on the street at Palm Beach.

"It wasn't me who, as was said, 'conquered the wilderness.' I am the least of the MacIveys. It was Tobias MacIvey and Emma and Skillit and Zech and Glenda and Frog and Bonzo and several others I won't even mention. All I did was cash in on what they did. They're buried right now in the middle of an orange grove beside the Kissimmee River, and that's where I'll rest too when the time comes. And it might also interest you to know that my pappa hung enough men to fill this head table. I killed too when I had to.

"The ones who got the shaft from all this so-called 'progress' were an old man named Keith Tiger and Tawanda Cypress MacIvey and my half-brother Toby Cypress MacIvey and a bunch more still living out yonder in the swamps in chickees.

"When I first started out alone after my pappa died, I didn't know what I was doing, and I thought I was doing the right thing. But you sons a' bitches knew, and you did it deliberate. That's the only thing that marks me from you. The catchword with me is stupidity. With you it's greed. More is better, bigger is better. Well, you bastards are too stupid to know there soon won't be no more. Else you haven't been here long enough to remember.

"All of you who don't like what I've said here tonight can kiss my ass. I don't give a damn about you and you don't give a damn about me, pure and simple. And besides that, you've seen the last of me you'll ever see. I'm going to hide from such as you and pray for forgiveness for what I've helped do. If I could rip out the concrete and put back the woods, I would. But I can't. Progress ain't reversible. What's done is done forever, and I'm sure as hell not proud of it. If any of you idiots had the brains of a jaybird you'd stop right now too. From what we've done to this place in just the past fifty years, what the hell you think it's going to be like in another fifty?"

He stopped abruptly, stepped back and said, "I do thank you kindly for your attention." Then he walked briskly to the nearest exit and left.

FORTY-FIVE
PUNTA RASSA
1968

Morning sunlight streamed through the east window as Sol sat in a cane-bottom rocker, staring at an old board tacked to the wall. Its white letters were badly faded but still readable: MacIVEY CATTLE COMPANY. Sunbeams seemed to catch in the ancient paint and make it glitter. The glow hurt his eyes, so he got up and closed the curtains.

Just beside the window there was a gun rack containing several Winchesters and a ten-gauge double-barreled shotgun. He picked up the shotgun and aimed it, its tremendous weight pulling his frail arms downward. He cocked one hammer and squeezed the trigger, hearing a sharp click as the firing pin popped into an empty chamber; then he put it back into the rack beside a rusty branding iron.

He crossed the room and took one of the two whips from a dresser drawer; then he went outside and popped it. The awesome sound sent a frightened rabbit bounding away. He cracked it again and again, seeing phantom cows scatter in front of him, and then he felt a hot pain sear through his chest.

There was a cypress bench beside the cabin porch, and he staggered to it and sat down. Sweat poured from his face as he watched himself race across the clearing on Tiger and jump the split-rail fence, going after Zech as he rode south seeking the outlaws. He heard his mother

402

shout, "Sol MacIvey! You come back here this instant!"

For a moment he thought of going inside and searching for the pill bottle, but Bonnie came and sat beside him, distracting him. She took his hand in hers and said, "Thanks, darling. I can face it now."

Then suddenly they were all out there looking at him, MacIveys all, burned brown by prairie sun and wind, living and loving and dying, one by one bidding him farewell as they faded back into the harsh glow of sunlight, leaving him desperately alone again.

The pain increased as his tired eyes squinted and looked after them, seeing them come and go now, Zech galloping wildly on a marshtackie, Skillit throwing a bull with just a twist of his powerful body, Frog stuffing himself with stew as Emma put more bowls on the table, Glenda in her jeans and boots, Bonnie's pony tail flapping as wind rushed through the open Model T. As his eyes glazed, the last one to appear was Tobias, looking like a living scarecrow in his faded overalls and wide-brimmed hat, leading all of them, heading westward as they searched for a Babylon called Punta Rassa.

He gazed to the west where the shipping port had once been, straining to hear the bellowing of penned cows, hearing instead the roar of gasoline engines somewhere to the north. He said weakly, "Where did it all go, Pappa?. . . Where?. . ."

The whip dropped from his hand just as a dove called mournfully for a missing mate no longer able to answer. It lay crumpled beside the nearby highway, hit and crushed lifeless by a speeding automobile.

If you enjoyed reading this book, here are some other books from Pineapple Press on related topics. To request a catalog or to place an order, visit our website at www.pineapplepress. com. Or write to Pineapple Press, P.O. Box 3889, Sarasota, Florida 34230, or call 1-800-PINEAPL (746-3275).

OTHER BOOKS BY PATRICK SMITH
Forever Island and *Allapattah*. A classic novel of the Everglades, *Forever Island* tells the story of Charlie Jumper, a Seminole Indian who clings to the old ways and teaches them to his grandson. *Allapattah* is the story of a young Seminole in despair in the white man's world. (hb)

The River is Home and *Angel City*. Smith's first novel, *The River Is Home,* revolves around a Mississippi family's struggle to cope with changes in their rural environment. Poor in material possessions, Skeeter's family is rich in their appreciation of their beautiful natural surroundings. *Angel City* is the powerful and moving exposé of migrant workers in Florida in the 1970s. (hb)

A Land Remembered, Student Edition. This best-selling novel is now available to young readers. In this edition the first chapter becomes the last so that the rest of the book is not a flashback, and also the language and situations are altered slightly for younger readers. **Volume 1** (hb & pb) **Volume 2** (hb & pb)

A Land Remembered Goes to School by Tillie Newhart and Mary Lee Powell. An elementary school teacher's manual, using *A Land Remembered* to teach language arts, social studies, and science, coordinated with the Sunshine State Standards of the Florida Department of Education. (pb)

Middle School Teacher Plans and Resources for A Land Remembered: Student Edition by Margaret Paschal. The vocabulary lists, comprehension questions, and post-reading activities for each chapter in the student edition make this teacher's manual a valuable resource. The activities aid in teaching social studies, science, and language arts coordinated with the Sunshine State Standards. (pb)

CRACKER WESTERNS
Alligator Gold by Janet Schrader. On his way home at the end of the Civil War, Caleb Hawkins is focused on getting back to his Florida cattle ranch. But along the way, Hawk encounters a very pregnant Madelaine Wilkes and learns that his only son has gone missing and that his old nemesis, Snake Barber, has taken over his ranch. (hb, pb)

Bridger's Run by Jon Wilson. Tom Bridger has come to Florida in 1885 to find his long-lost uncle and a hidden treasure. It all comes down to a boxing match between Tom and the Key West Slasher. (hb & pb)

Ghosts of the Green Swamp by Lee Gramling. Saddle up your easy chair and kick back for a Cracker Western featuring that rough-and-ready but soft-hearted Florida cowboy, Tate Barkley, introduced in *Riders of the Suwannee*. (hb & pb)

Guns of the Palmetto Plains by Rick Tonyan. As the Civil War explodes over Florida, Tree Hooker dodges Union soldiers and Florida outlaws to drive cattle to feed the starving Confederacy. (pb)

Riders of the Suwannee by Lee Gramling. Tate Barkley returns to 1870s Florida just in time to come to the aid of a young widow and her children as they fight to save their homestead from outlaws. (hb & pb)

Thunder on the St. Johns by Lee Gramling. Riverboat gambler Chance Ramsay teams up with the family of young Josh Carpenter and the trapper's daughter Abby Macklin to combat a slew of greedy outlaws seeking to destroy the dreams of honest homesteaders. (hb & pb)

Trail from St. Augustine by Lee Gramling. A young trapper, a crusty ex-sailor, and an indentured servant girl fleeing a cruel master join forces to cross the Florida wilderness in search of buried treasure and a new life. (pb)

Wiregrass Country by Herb and Muncy Chapman. Set in 1835, this historical novel will transport you to a time when Florida settlers were few and laws were scarce. Meet the Dovers, a family of homesteaders determined to survive against all odds and triumph against the daily struggles that come with running a cattle ranch. (pb)

FLORIDA HISTORY
Old Florida Style: A Story of Cracker Cattle (DVD) by Steve Kidd and Alex Menendez, Delve Productions. Saddle up on a tough little cracker horse called a marsh tacky and explore old Florida—when cow hunters pulled the tough little Spanish cattle out of the palmettos and established this as a cattle state. This DVD showcases Florida's Cracker heritage.

Time Traveler's Guide to Florida by Jack Powell. A unique guidebook that offers 70 places and reenactments in Florida where you can experience the past, and a few where you can time travel into the future. (pb)

Florida's Past: People and Events that Shaped the State by Gene Burnett. The three volumes in this series are chock-full of carefully researched, eclectic essays written in Gene Burnett's easygoing style. Many of these essays on Florida history were originally published in *Florida Trend* magazine. **Volume 1** (pb) **Volume 2** (pb) **Volume 3** (pb)

Tropical Surge by Benjamin Reilly. This engaging historical narrative covers many significant events in the history of south Florida, including the major developments and setbacks in the early years of Miami and Key West, as well as an in-depth look at Henry Flagler's amazing Overseas Railway. (hb)

OTHER FICTION
Adventures in Nowhere by John Ames. A boy in 1950s Florida wrestles with adult problems and enjoys the last days of his boyhood in a place called Nowhere—sometimes fearing for his sanity as his family falls apart and he watches a house change shapes across the river. (hb)

Seven Mile Bridge by Michael Biehl. Florida Keys dive-shop owner Jonathan Bruckner returns home from Sheboygan, Wisconsin, after his mother's death. What he finds leads him to an understanding of the mystery that surrounded his father's death years before. (hb)

The Bucket Flower by Donald Robert Wilson. In 1893, 23-year-old Elizabeth Sprague goes into the Everglades to study the unique plant life even though warned that a pampered "bucket flower" like her cannot endure the rigors of the swamp. She encounters wild animals and even wilder men, but finds her own strength and a new future. (hb)

My Brother Michael by Janis Owens. Out of the shotgun houses and deep, shaded porches of a West Florida mill town comes this extraordinary novel of love and redemption. Gabriel Catts recounts his lifelong love for his brother's wife, Myra—whose own demons threaten to overwhelm all three of them. (pb)

Black Creek by Paul Varnes. Through the story of one family, we learn how white settlers moved into the Florida territory, taking it from the natives—who had only been there a few generations—with false treaties and finally all-out war. Thus, both sides were newcomers anxious to "take Florida." (hb)

Confederate Money by Paul Varnes. In 1861, as this novel opens, a Confederate dollar is worth 90 cents. We follow Henry Fern as he fights on both sides of the war. Through shrewd dealings he manages to amass $40,000 in Confederate paper money, and finally changes his paper fortune into silver and gold. (hb)

For God, Gold and Glory by E. H. Haines. The riveting account of the invasion of the American Southeast 1539–1543 by Hernando de Soto, as told by his private secretary, Rodrigo Ranjel. A meticulously researched tale of adventure and survival and the dark aspects of greed and power. (hb)

Nobody's Hero by Frank Laumer. Based on a true adventure of an American soldier who refused to die in spite of terrible wounds sustained during the battle often known as "Dade's Massacre" that started the Second Seminole War in Florida. (hb)

THE HONOR SERIES

"Sign on early and set sail with Peter Wake for both solid historical context and exciting sea stories."
—U.S. Naval Institute Proceedings

At the Edge of Honor by Robert N. Macomber. The first in a series of naval historical novels following the career of Captain Peter Wake, USN. The year is 1863 and Wake arrives in Florida for duty with the East Gulf Blockading Squadron, embarking on a series of voyages on his tiny armed sloop to seek and arrest Confederate blockade runners and sympathizers. (hb & pb)

Point of Honor by Robert N. Macomber. In this second book in the Honor series, it is 1864 and Lt. Peter Wake, United States Navy, assisted by his indomitable Irish bosun, Sean Rork, commands the naval schooner *St. James*. He searches for army deserters in the

Dry Tortugas, finds an old nemesis during a standoff with the French Navy on the coast of Mexico, and confronts incompetent Federal army officers during and invasion of upper Florida. (hb & pb)

Honorable Mention by Robert N. Macomber. This third book in the Honor series covers the tumultuous end of the Civil War in Florida and the Caribbean. Lt. Peter Wake is now in command of the steamer USS *Hunt*, and quickly plunges into action, chasing a strange vessel during a tropical storm off Cuba, confronting death to liberate an escaping slave ship, and coming face to face with the enemy's most powerful ocean warship in Havana's harbor. (hb)

A Dishonorable Few by Robert N. Macomber. In this fourth novel in the Honor series, the year is 1869, and the United States is painfully recovering from the Civil War. Lt. Peter Wake heads to turbulent Central America to deal with a former American naval officer turned renegade mercenary. (hb)

An Affair of Honor by Robert N. Macomber. The fifth novel in the Honor series. It's December 1873 and Lt. Peter Wake is the executive officer of the USS *Omaha* on patrol in the West Indies, eager to return home. Fate, however, has other plans. He runs afoul of the Royal Navy in Antigua and then is sent off to Europe, where he finds himself embroiled in a Spanish civil war. But his real test comes when he and Sean Rork are sent on a mission in northern Africa. (hb)

A Different Kind of Honor by Robert N. Macomber. The sixth novel in the Honor series. It's 1879 and Lt. Cmdr. Peter Wake, U.S.N., is on assignment as the American naval observer to the War of the Pacific along the west coast of South America. During this mission Wake will witness history's first battle between ocean-going ironclads, ride the world's first deep-diving submarine, face his first machine guns in combat, and run for his life in the Catacombs of the Dead in Lima. (hb)

The Honored Dead by Robert N. Macomber. Seventh in the award-winning Honor series. On what at first appears to be a simple mission for the U.S. president in French Indochina in 1883, naval intelligence officer Lt. Cmdr. Peter Wake encounters opium warlords, Chinese-Malay pirates, and French gangsters. (hb)

The Darkest Shade of Honor by Robert N. Macomber. In this eighth novel of the Honor Series, Commander Peter Wake meets Theodore Roosevelt and is assigned to uncover Cuban revolutionary activities in Florida and Cuba. There he meets José Martí, finds himself engulfed in the most catastrophic event in Key West history, and must make a decision involving the very darkest shade of honor. (hb)